NINETEENTH
STREET NW

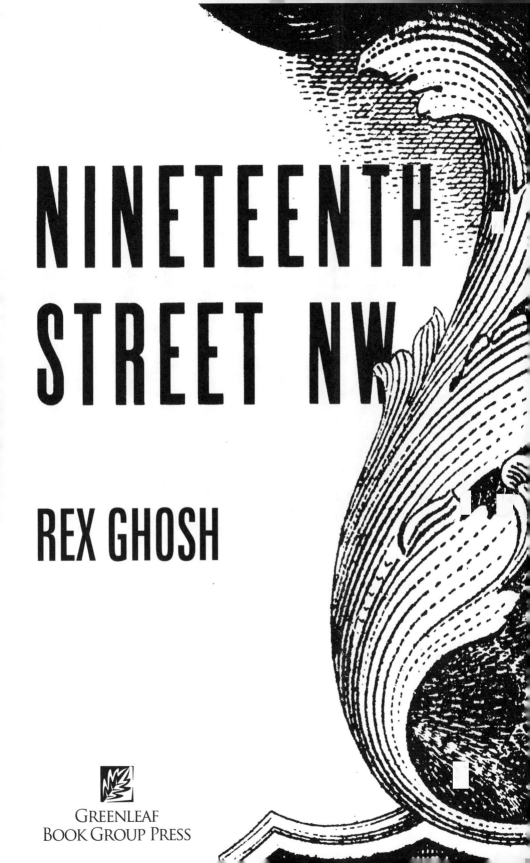

NINETEENTH
STREET NW

REX GHOSH

GREENLEAF
BOOK GROUP PRESS

Published by Greenleaf Book Group Press
Austin, Texas
www.gbgpress.com

First published by Vanguard Press in 2008 under author's pen name, Brett Wood.

Distributed by Greenleaf Book Group LLC

For ordering information or special discounts for bulk purchases, please contact Greenleaf Book Group LLC at PO Box 91869, Austin, TX 78709, 512.891.6100

Design and composition by Greenleaf Book Group LLC
Cover design by Greenleaf Book Group LLC
Cover photo based on The Solidarity of Peoples—View of the Ceiling Mural at the Palais des Nations, Geneva (Credit: UN/DPI Photo)

Publisher's Cataloging-In-Publication Data (Prepared by The Donohue Group, Inc.)

Ghosh, Rex.
  Nineteenth Street NW / Rex Ghosh. -- 2nd ed.

  p. ; cm.

  First ed.: Nineteenth Street NW / Brett Wood. Vanguard Press, 2008.
  ISBN: 978-1-60832-064-6

1. Women revolutionaries--Fiction. 2. Women political activists--Fiction. 3. Sabotage--Fiction.
I. Wood, Brett. Nineteenth Street NW. II. Title.

PS3607.H67 N56 2010
813.6   2010924701

Part of the Tree Neutral™ program, which offsets the number of trees consumed in the production and printing of this book by taking proactive steps, such as planting trees in direct proportion to the number of trees used: www.treeneutral.com

Printed in the United States of America on acid-free paper
10 11 12 13 14   10 9 8 7 6 5 4 3 2 1
Second Edition

TreeNeutral

To my parents

My long-suffering friends and family provided much moral support through the many drafts of this book. But it would never have been completed without the sharp pencil, straight ruler, and witty humor of my good friend and editor, Peter Winkler.

PREFACE

I N JULY 1944, THE ALLIED NATIONS met for the International Monetary and Financial Conference at Bretton Woods, New Hampshire. Determined that a Great Depression should never recur, the conference founded two new institutions. The World Bank was established to finance reconstruction and development. The International Monetary Fund was created to promote consultation and collaboration on international monetary and financial problems. More than half a century later, these institutions still stand—one on either side of Nineteenth Street, NW.

This book was written as a celebration of the lives and work of all who are dedicated to making the world better, safer, and more prosperous through international cooperation. But it is a work of fiction. Names, characters, places, institutions, and incidents are the products of the author's imagination or are used purely fictitiously. Any resemblance to actual events, locales, institutions, or persons, living or dead, is entirely coincidental.

CHAPTER ONE

S NOW COVERED NINETEENTH STREET. A dusting, no more, but already Washington was closing down. Thick rolling mist, punctured only by burning office lights, shrouded the buildings that lined the street. The snow swallowed the usual city sounds; for once, even the sirens were blessedly hushed.

But perched on the edge of her seat as the taxi nosed through the crawling traffic, Sophia Gemaye was insensible to the serenity. Her nerves felt ragged after spending an hour trying to get a cab willing to brave the trek to Dulles Airport. Frantic, she had called a dozen different companies. To scuttle the operation for want of a taxi would be beyond humiliating; it would be absurd. Each step had been planned meticulously: acquiring forged papers, concealing the explosives, priming detonators and timers, checking and cross-checking weather conditions and flight connections. Yet for all the obsessive plotting, it had occurred to no one, not even to Melamed, that Sophia might not make it to the airport in the first place. Then, just when she was close to sobbing with frustration, the first company she had called unexpectedly came through.

Sophia leaned back in her seat, forcing herself to relax. Checking her face in the mirror, she essayed a smile; it looked weak and unconvincing. Her eyes, normally so large and innocent, had sunk into their sockets. She rubbed her cheeks to draw some color, trying for a casual air, not this pale, pinched look that betrayed her fear.

The taxi stopped again, snarled in the traffic at the corner of Pennsylvania Avenue. The flight left at seven, and already it was ten past four. Sophia peered out the window. Ahead of her a forbidding cathedral of glass and steel disgorged office workers. They gathered in twos and threes, spilling into the street in anticipation of a green light, slowing the cars further. Through the swirling mist, she could just make out the words International Monetary and Financial Organization etched above the entrance. Sophia gazed at them in silence, as if seeking inspiration, until at last the cab jerked forward and Nineteenth Street faded from view.

It took nearly half an hour to reach the highway. She'd called the airline twice before leaving, and each time the clerk had been adamant that no delays for the London flight were expected. The clerk's English accent still rang in her ears, crisp as the falling snow, as though its owner would brook no nonsense, not even from the weather. How she yearned for the luxury of the same confidence.

At last the cab pulled into Dulles Airport, an oversized glass tent that seemed to sag in the center. The driver dumped her cases on the curb side, muttering some lie about extra charges for snow days. Too nervous now to argue, Sophia meekly handed over the money and entered the terminal, buffeted by a blast of overheated air.

She made her way to the water fountain, drank greedily, and removed her jacket. She was of medium height and honey complexion, with sculpted cheekbones and sharp delicate features. Her ensemble—black stirrup pants and white cashmere top, crimped by a purple belt to accentuate her slender waist—gave credence to her part as a well-to-do foreign student on her way home for the holidays. A final pat of her thick black hair, and she made for the check-in counter with a calmer, more confident gait.

The clerk, a balding man with steel-rimmed glasses, took her passport and ticket in one hand, deftly tapping the keyboard with the other. He stopped and looked at her—a cool appraising gaze. Sophia reached for her gold chain, twisting it around her finger. The clerk returned to the keyboard, and with a hostile flash of those spidery glasses said, "You'll change planes at Heathrow, but we can check your bags straight through to Geneva."

"One piece is it?"

Sophia nodded, then answered the usual litany of security questions. Had she packed her own case? Accepted any gifts? Packed any electronic equipment?

"Oh, just a laptop," she corrected herself, trying to sound nonchalant. "I really have to make a start on my dissertation these holidays," she added, remembering too late Melamed's warning to never volunteer information. But it sounded natural, and the clerk gave a knowing smile, as though he'd heard that one before.

"You'll just need to pass your case through security, ma'am. They'll give you your boarding pass after inspection."

"What? Oh, no. I want to check in my suitcase, not take it in the cabin with me."

"I understand. But you still need to pass it through security. Over here, on the right please."

Sophia turned. At the end of the row of counters was a makeshift table on which a team of security guards was searching through suitcases. A manual search! Sophia's face blanched. But surely, she thought, surely they just x-ray cases, they can't possibly go through each one by hand.

As if reading her thoughts, the clerk said, "All luggage that is taken on board is automatically screened. But at this moment in time, TSA is also requiring that we do spot checks manually. It's an additional security measure for the Christmas season. It'll only take a moment. Passengers are chosen at random," he added, consolingly.

Sophia stared at him blankly. For a moment, she thought of aborting the operation, but before she could protest, another clerk had seized her case and was marching toward the security station. Sophia followed meekly.

The guard who searched her case—a big, black man, crisp in his navy trousers and starched white shirt, the TSA emblem emblazoned proudly on the shoulder—was almost painfully polite and deferential. Melamed had warned her not to lock her case—it might invite attention, and they could force the locks anyway—but still the guard insisted on allowing Sophia to open the case herself. She wished he'd be rude or do something wrong—linger over her lingerie, crease her clothing, drop something on the floor—anything, as long as she could pretend to take umbrage, make a fuss, and distract attention. But the guard never gave her the chance, sifting through her belongings expertly, returning everything to its original place.

It took less than a minute, then the security guard was reaching for the lid of her case when suddenly he paused, and instead took out the laptop and placed it on the table. He flipped open the screen and ran his rubber-gloved finger around the edge, looking for the on switch.

Sophia stood mesmerized. She was conscious of the sounds around her—the child pleading for a box of crayons, the tinny voice on the PA system making unintelligible announcements, the Skycap porter rumbling by with his cart, whistling through his teeth—but she felt curiously detached from them. They were like characters in a film, engrossed in a world in which she did not belong.

Her breath was coming in short, sharp gasps, her fingernails digging deep into her palms. In a minute, in a second, the guard would push the button. And then? She could picture it all with horrible clarity: shouts, alarms, foot-steps, shots.

Just then a dog, escaped from its travel crate, scurried across the concourse, its harried owner in pursuit. The guard, momentarily distracted, closed the laptop absentmindedly and returned it to Sophia's suitcase. Another guard snapped shut the locks and slapped security stickers over them. Then he was handing Sophia her boarding pass. She was still too dazed even to feel relief. Finally she realized he was waiting for her to take the boarding pass and beginning to look at her oddly. She forced herself to unclench her fists to accept the boarding pass, muttered her thanks, and backed away, the next passenger already jostling into her place.

═══

There was no turning back now, no escape, Sophia thought, as she stumbled down the aisle, looking for her seat. She had never quite believed it would get this far, that she would have to confront this moment. Not even a week ago, as she'd watched Melamed assemble the device.

He had unscrewed the back of the laptop case, prying out the hard disk and most of the other components. In their place he had inserted a series of small silver packets, shaped like the pieces they replaced, containing densely packed explosives, hermetically sealed to prevent electronic sniffing. They looked like chocolate bars wrapped in silver paper. She had fingered one, marvelling at its innocence. Finally Melamed connected the detonator to a timer that ran off the computer's miniature battery and inserted it into an empty expansion slot.

Strangely enough, it was an experience that had reminded her of her father. When Sophia was a child, she and Daddy used to spend countless hours sprawled on the playroom floor, immersed in Meccano parts and happiness, assembling wondrous mechanical contraptions. For her seventh birthday Sophia was promised Meccano No. 10, the top-of-the-line model, with gears and girders and thousands of nuts and bolts, a hugely expensive extravagance for a favorite child. She and her stepmother—her own mother had died when Sophia was two—were in Geneva, sent there by her father when the troubles first began in her country. Daddy was supposed to join them a few weeks later, in time for her birthday. At last, the long-awaited day arrived, and with it a fabulous exciting package from Hamley's toy store. But no Daddy. For days, there were only vague rumors and frantic phone calls. Later, much later, Sophia learned the truth. But at the time all she knew was that Daddy had been plucked from her life, never to return. And she had never opened her magnificent Meccano set, always waiting, always hoping, for Daddy to magically appear and then they would open it together. Whatever happened to it, Sophia wondered, as she clicked her seat belt shut. It must still be up in the attic, virgin in its box, gathering dust and memories like some Victorian bride jilted at the altar.

At last the aircraft backed away from the gate and taxied into the white wonderland. It paused at the end of the runway as though taking a deep breath, then with a gentle rumble of the engines they were airborne, banking steeply to head out over the Atlantic. The captain's voice came over the speakers. It was going to be a short flight—six hours, perhaps less. Tailwinds across the Atlantic, he explained, always strong in December, were particularly fierce tonight.

Sophia reclined her seat, waiting for her dinner. She looked around the cabin, studying the other passengers, pondering their stories and wondering what fate had brought them on this flight. It was a solitary amusement, the sort of game she'd learned to play in the loneliness of childhood.

Beside her sat an American couple, off to their grand tour of Europe. The husband looked like a salesman. Used cars perhaps: he exuded the brash confidence that so often substitutes for quality merchandise. His wife, a teacher or a nurse, Sophia guessed, was working her way methodically through a stack of tourist brochures. Across the aisle, a businessman was trying to chat up the woman beside him with a bevy of pre-packaged phrases.

As Sophia returned to her magazine, immersing herself in the horoscope section, she felt a gentle tug at her sleeve. It was a little girl, perhaps eight or nine, with a face so angelic it made Sophia suspicious at once of the mischief it must conceal. Sophia reached into her bag and pulled out a roll of toffees. The girl smiled and took one, and after a moment's hesitation, took a second and popped it into her pocket. Then, like two grandees exchanging gifts, she proffered Sophia a scruffy pad of paper on which she'd drawn a noughts and crosses grid, but the child's mother spotted her and drew her back with an apologetic smile. Sophia wanted to protest, to say, *No, it's all right. I'd like to play*, but she was suddenly assailed by nausea, feeling at once hot and cold, her forehead clammy to the touch.

She was filled with revulsion at what was going to happen. People—real people—were going to die when the bomb exploded. People like the couple beside her, the businessman with his pathetic leering stares, the pert air hostess squeezing down the aisle, the little girl, now back in her own seat, playing happily with her mother.

Unbidden, unwanted, a memory hit Sophia with a jolt. It was the photo of an airline crash she'd once seen many years ago on the cover of *Paris Match*. Every detail of the image was carved into her mind: the carcass of the plane lying incongruously in a golden field, its belly ripped open as though savaged by some great beast, its metallic bones strewn indifferently across the countryside. There had been a fire, and the burnt bodies of the passengers lay around the wreckage. A doll had remained miraculously intact, its skin horribly pink against the seared flesh of its owner.

Glancing back at the little girl through the cracks between the seats, Sophia shuddered at the thought of this child being handled by the salvage crew with rubber gloves, stuffed into a body bag like some obscene biological specimen. *Oh, dear God, how did I get into this?*

But she knew.

It had all started innocently enough, some seven years ago, in the drafty drawing room of a Sussex country house. Sophia was dining with her boyfriend, Simon, and his parents. It was the first time she'd met them, and the last. As the evening progressed from bad to worse, Sophia couldn't decide which was more painful: the forced joviality of Simon's father or the frigid politeness of his mother. One thing was clear, though. Ten years of boarding school in England and an accent sculpted to perfection still hadn't made Sophia "English" enough to fit into their tidy little society. Simon had tried to shrug it off as Mother being her usual difficult self, but Sophia, deeply hurt, ended the relationship abruptly.

And yet, Sophia mused, peering at the inky sky through the cabin window, perhaps she should have known all along the futility of trying to fit in, for that night at Simon's had marked the end of her attempts at assimilation, not the beginning of her alienation. That had started earlier—much earlier. Twenty years ago? Twenty-five? Sophia couldn't have been more than eight or nine, packed off to boarding school in England, mistrusted because she was foreign, pitied because she was an orphan. Or close enough. Daddy had died a couple of years before, and her stepmother had been too busy in Paris or Geneva or Monte Carlo to claim Sophia for half-term breaks. How she dreaded those breaks—hanging about while the headmistress phoned up parents, trying to place Sophia with someone, anyone, even girls she detested. How she despised the other girls at school; how she longed to be one of them, too.

All through her school years, Sophia had struggled to fit in, to be one of the girls, to deny her alien roots and heritage. Then, in the pain of rejection by Simon's family, she became equally determined to know her native country, abandoned those many years ago. She went on a reading binge, plowing through everything she could find about her people, her history, her country, even digging up old United Nations reports from the 1980s that chronicled the human rights abuses already taking place.

The troubles in her country had started soon after Independence. At first, the government was too bristling with post-colonial pride to pay attention to anything a small ethnic minority in the northeast corner of the country said or did. But then they started discovering the ores and heavy metals in the region; there were lucrative foreign mining contracts to be awarded, fortunes to be made. Gradually, all this nonsense about autonomy and self-determination and—most egregious of all—separate statehood for the ethnic minority began to matter, and matter very much.

With sovereign brutality, the government clamped down. The Sedition Law (1977), the Proclamation of Territorial Integrity (1979), the Anti-terrorism Act (1984, amended 2002), and a dozen other laws and decrees mandated a single language, a single religion, a single country. Anyone daring to suggest otherwise or questioning the Republic or, God forbid, insulting the president, found himself thrown in jail for terms stretching two to twenty years.

In those days, the country was a front-line state in the War Against Communism, the president a stalwart ally of the West. In return, Western governments were willing to sell him the latest military toys and to overlook any oppression, any abuse, as long as they could operate their airbases and early warning stations from the northern territories. After the Cold War, the regime had fallen into disfavor with the West, and there was hope that international pressure might force it to mend its ways. The president had shown the good sense to keep a low profile, throwing the occasional bone to foreign journalists and human rights organizations—release of a long-time prisoner of conscience, promise of electoral reforms—while denying entry visas to the more meddlesome ones.

Now it was a different era. The president had handed day-to-day control of the country to his nephew—his own son he'd had murdered years ago for attempting an early power play—and the West's new cause was the War Against Terrorism. With canny prescience, the regime had signed on at once, eager to show it was willing to do its part. Not that there were any terrorists within the country—certainly none of global reach or with the remotest link to the Trade Center attacks—just a handful of freedom fighters calling for an end to the oppression and the beginning of a true democracy. But it gave the government the perfect pretext for renewing its clampdowns. Students, trade union leaders, political opponents—anyone could be rounded up in the name of security. And the Americans, good natured but simplistic, always viewing the world in black and white, good and evil, cowboys and Indians, "with us or against us," had swallowed the act, declaring the regime a force for freedom and a staunch ally in the global War on Terror.

Sophia was sickened to read of schoolteachers risking not just their livelihoods but their very lives for the sake of muttering a few words before class in the hope of keeping alive the culture, the history, the language of their proud and ancient people. At the time, Sophia was working on her doctorate at the London School of Economics. Before long she found herself embroiled in the debates and discussions of the various radical groups decrying the aborted birth of her nation, the president and "first family" pillaging the country's wealth, the silencing of any opposition, the complicity of the civilized world.

But her disillusion with them soon set in, as the Marxist-Leninists battled the Leninist-Marxists over the finer points of dialectical materialism. The radical students were all of a kind: unwashed and unkempt, with greasy skin and woolly sweaters, carrying about them the languor of late nights and the smell of stale smoke. Sophia soon came to realize she had nothing in common with them or their barren bombast.

It was only when she visited her homeland that she really understood. The little things, not the political mumbo-jumbo, struck her. Children playing with sticks and old tires in festering slums. Rotten heaps on which dogs foraged for food, their ribcages protruding, snouts pinched and vicious with hunger. The dusty shops selling smelly old clothes and broken hardware and all the assorted rubble that only the poor will buy. The mixture of reverence and resentment in peoples' eyes as the armored Mercedes sped by, shuttling the rich and powerful from one presidential palace to another. The grim-faced guards and dull-eyed women, and always and everywhere, the stench of refuse and corruption.

Sophia had returned to London filled with horror and disgust, ashamed of her relief at having escaped growing up under this oppression, and loathing the regime that had made it possible. Melamed, a veteran freedom fighter who'd been in the struggle for democracy ever since his own student days, spotted her at one of those meetings at the LSE. It was from Melamed that she finally learned the truth about her father—and what she could do about it.

Sophia's father had been a jurist of international renown, called to the Bar in London, and a prominent lawyer in his own country. Although students could be thrown in jail, dissidents made to disappear, a man of his standing could not be disposed of so readily. When he began defending dissidents and documenting disappearances, the regime resolved to silence him.

There was a small photograph in the newspapers the day he died—Sophia had gone to the British Library, finding it among the other obscure foreign newspapers of twenty years ago. She studied the picture through a magnifying glass, coveting every pixel, as if searching for some hidden truth. The body lay prostrate on the dusty road, distended in anguish. The car had broken his spine, his arms were flung forward, his head tilted back unnaturally. Sophia could almost hear the awful snap, the agonizing howl the instant before he died.

Anger had been her only solace, and taking refuge in it now, she glared at the couple beside her on the plane. Their faces were filled with plump complacency, their greatest worry whether to visit the Tower of London or Madame Tussauds. The wife was eating pretzels, stuffing her mouth a handful at a time. She drank her beer in great gulps, her double chin wobbling with the effort. The husband was picking at his nose with determined digs of his fingernail. Sophia looked at them with revulsion. Western governments were willing to support the regime, to tolerate any injustice and every misery in her country, so that people like these could continue their smug, inane existence.

Yet even that was an illusion, for the crackdowns in her country in no way impinged on them, in no way made them safer, in no way brought them justice for the attacks America had endured. And these people, Sophia thought, surveying the cabin—the couple beside her, the businessman with his bevy of pickup lines, the young woman studiously ignoring him—in whose name, and for whose sake, their governments had propped up the president and his cronies for thirty years or more, would never bother to learn the facts, study the history, discover the truths about her country or its suffering. To them it was an obscure and distant land of little import and less concern. What did they care if the regime used the War on Terror to promote its program of ethnic cleansing and political suppression with the connivance of their own governments? All they wanted was to feel safe, regardless of the price others might pay for their sense of security.

In their indifference lay their guilt, Sophia told herself, echoing Melamed's favorite refrain. Well, no longer. From tomorrow Western governments would learn that expediency exacted a price, that if they continued to prop up oppressive regimes so that they could buy their support and count on a few friendly votes at the UN for their latest crusade—be it against communism or against terrorism—then it would cost them dearly.

In just a few hours the computer's clock would generate a tiny electric current, disproportionate to its effect. The explosion would not be large, but enough to break the pressure seal of a cargo bay. Sophia wondered what would happen then. Would the plane plunge at once into the icy waters below? Would the oxygen masks pop down as promised in those announcements to which no one ever listens? Would the passengers be plucked out in tidy rows of three, helplessly clutching the arms of their seats? How many lives would be lost? A hundred, perhaps. But against them must be weighed thirty years of oppression against her people and the systematic murder, over the years, of thousands of men, women, and children. As Melamed liked to say, innocent people die all the time; they might as well die for a reason. And how can there be innocence when there is injustice?

The gin was doing its work, dulling her mind. Dinner came, followed by the movie. Here and there in the dimness of the cabin were little oases from the overhead lights. One was shining in the row behind Sophia. The little girl's mother was reading her a story. Sophia peered back at them again. The girl might easily have been Sophia twenty years ago, the woman her stepmother. Only her stepmother would not have been reading to her; she would have plonked a pile of comic books in front of Sophia and become engrossed in a cheap thriller.

The girl spotted Sophia watching them and smiled. And with that simple smile, she unravelled the cocoon of self-protection Sophia had woven herself, mocking her calculus of justice and justification.

Sophia turned away abruptly and closed her eyes, trying to shut out the kaleidoscope of images haunting her mind: the little girl beside her mother, the device nestling in the suitcase, her father's body prostrate on the ground, the doll buried in the rubble.

CHAPTER TWO

THE PHONE RANG, SHRILL AND DISCONSOLATE. Celine O'Rourke, ensconced in her office on the ninth floor of the International Monetary and Financial Organization in Washington, DC, stared at it in surprise. It was seven o'clock that same December evening, and IMFO had closed down hours ago, the staff fleeing the blizzard for the dubious sanctuary of their tidy homes and suburban wives. Snow blanketed the ground, mocking the efforts of plows, and across the street, the World Bank buildings had a forlorn air, with just the occasional mosaic of flickering office lights. Only the workaholics and lonely remain, Celine thought, counting herself among the ranks of both.

At the third ring she snatched up the receiver.

"Policy Review Department," she announced.

"Ms. O'Rourke? This is the office of the managing director. Mr. Kiyotaki was wondering whether you could come and see him."

"The MD wants to see *me?*"

"Right away, please."

In more than a dozen years at IMFO, Celine had never met the managing director in person, let alone been called to his office. She took the elevator, hastily checking herself in the mirror. She was a woman of slender build and medium height, with a clear complexion and smooth porcelain skin, but her greatest asset was the chestnut hair that cascaded carelessly onto her shoulders. She fiddled with the knot of her silk scarf, trying to guess what the call was about, unable to shake the feeling of a schoolgirl summoned to the headmistress. Celine stepped out, looking for the office of the managing director. A secretary waved her in.

The opulence of the place intimidated her at once. Luscious Persian rugs adorned the floor; wood panelling lined the walls, interrupted occasionally by muted lamps and Whistler etchings. Imperious behind his massive mahogany desk sat Toyoo Kiyotaki, managing director of IMFO.

Born in the late 1990s, IMFO had been established when the financial crises in emerging market countries threatened to overwhelm the World Bank and the International Monetary Fund, the twins that straddle Nineteenth Street. Watchdog of the world economy, IMFO's role was to provide stability to the international monetary system by enhancing surveillance and macroeconomic coordination. At least that's what's written, in five different languages, in glossy brochures littering the visitors' center. In truth, IMFO did little, and achieved less. It was routinely ignored by the governments it represented and the financial markets it did not. The *Economist* had dubbed Kiyotaki the "Toothless Tiger."

Kiyotaki glanced up as Celine entered and motioned her to a chair. She sat down, trying to look efficient and alert.

"Thank you for coming, Ms. O'Rourke." Kiyotaki switched on his table lamp, casting a sympathetic halo over his desk. "I'll try not to keep you long— I'm sure you're anxious to get home." He was leafing through a file. From its shocking pink cover, Celine could tell it was a personnel folder, and from the occasional furtive glance Kiyotaki gave her, she suspected it was her own.

"Tell me," he said, laying the folder down abruptly, "have you been following what's happening in Indonesia?"

The question took her by surprise, and Celine struggled to keep her face expressionless.

"I've had the Indonesian finance minister and the central bank governor on the line," Kiyotaki explained, "and I'm expecting a call from the president within the next hour or so. The Indonesian rupiah is taking a beating on the Far East markets, and they're worried it could turn into a full-blown run on the currency when their own money markets open. I'm sure I don't have to tell you what that could mean—not just for Indonesia, but for the entire region, and possibly other emerging markets as well."

Celine nodded. She'd been in Indonesia in 1997, during the worst of the great East Asian currency crisis, when financial panic had spread like tuberculosis, infecting every country in the region. Within weeks, the currency plummeted from 1,500 rupiah to the dollar to more than 15,000. Once the darling of Wall Street, Indonesia became a pariah overnight, with investors tripping over themselves to get their money out before it became worthless. The fat men in their fat Mercedes-Benzes, clogging the streets of downtown Jakarta, and the svelte women with their Prada bags and Hermès scarves, hopping from one glittering hotel to another, suddenly found themselves bankrupt.

But, as usual, the hardest hit were the poor. With the collapsing exchange rate came soaring inflation. The price of rice and the price of kerosene—the staple food and fuel of the working classes—rose several hundred percent, sparking riots throughout the country. The military was called out to restore law and order in Jakarta. For more than a week the threat of a coup d'état hung over the city like the pall of smoke over the burnt-out shops. It ended with hundreds killed and the Indonesian president ousted after thirty years in office.

"I've been on mission in New Delhi," Celine replied. "I just got back today. I'm afraid I haven't been following developments in East Asia very closely."

"But you *are* familiar with the country?" Kiyotaki pressed, picking up the file again and regarding her narrowly. His eyes were black and slightly protuberant; they seemed to sum her up in a single flicker and find her wanting.

"Yes," she admitted at last.

"Good. There's still a couple of hours until the Jakarta interbank market opens. If there's going to be a speculative attack on the currency, that's when it's going to happen. We've got to be ready to advise Bank Indonesia on how to handle it. What I need from you is an update of the current situation and an action plan for stabilizing the currency. Do you think you can get me something in the next hour or so?"

"Yes, sir." Celine stood up. "Is there anyone . . . ?"

"My assistant has been calling around," Kiyotaki added, anticipating her question. "The Asian Department staff are either on mission, or at home, or stuck in this wretched snowstorm. The roads are a nightmare; I doubt any-one's going to be able to get back here until tomorrow morning. I'm afraid you're on your own."

Celine hurried along the deserted corridors, her mind in turmoil, trying to think of someone, anyone, who could help her with the MD's assignment. Of course! Her friend Karin Wulf might still be around. Like many other singles, Karin lived in downtown DC, not out in the suburbs. Besides, with her extensive mission experience, she was just the person to cobble together a quick analysis of the Indonesia situation. Celine barged into Karin's office. It was dark.

Cursing Karin for leaving early, and herself for staying late, Celine raced back to her own office. As she approached, she noticed that one of the other doors in the division was underlined by a glimmer of light. It must be Harry Hoffinger's office. Hoffinger was a new arrival, having recently moved from the Research Department. Celine, who'd been away on mission, had yet to meet him. All she knew about him was that he had joined IMFO through the elite Young Economists Program—YEP in the parlance of Nineteenth Street—a couple of years after Celine and seemed to have spent much of his time ever since playing with weird and wonderful exchange rate forecasting models.

Hoffinger had a long list of prestigious publications, and though in prin-ciple Celine recognized the need for IMFO to stay on top of the academic literature, she was inclined to look on research types as impractical and naïve, and perhaps more than a tad parasitic, ensconced in the comfort of their ivory towers while others went out on mission, confronting real problems in real countries. They were stretched thin enough in Policy Review not to need an egghead taking up a slot. But Celine's division chief had recruited Hoffinger anyway, and now she was curious to see what he was like. Besides, she resolved grimly as she knocked on his door, regardless of his research cre-dentials, he could damn well get his hands dirty helping her put together the managing director's data.

Hoffinger was leaning back in his chair, his feet resting on the edge of the table, a keyboard in his lap. Seeing Celine, he swung his legs down and stood up.

"Hello," she nodded briskly, "I'm Celine O'Rourke. I'm afraid we haven't met because I've been away on mission, but I'm also in Policy Review. I'm the deputy division chief, in fact."

"Harry Hoffinger." A warm confident hand, and the suspicion of a Dutch accent.

"Look, I know you've just arrived in the division, and I hate to dump a lot of work on you, but it seems there could be a currency crisis brewing in Indonesia. The authorities have been on the phone to the MD, and he's asked me to provide him with a briefing right away. Do you think you could give me a hand putting together the data?"

"Sure." Harry's face creased into a smile. "Be happy to."

"Good. Listen, I'm going to need some basic macro indicators—all the usual suspects—monthly inflation rates, production indices, money supply figures, foreign exchange deposits in the banking system, overnight interbank interest rates, credit rollover rates . . ." She reeled them off like items on a grocery list. "Oh, and of course, hourly time series of how much foreign exchange reserves Bank Indonesia has left as well as their foreign exchange intervention figures for the past couple of days at least."

"Those won't be in the Global Economic Outlook database, will they?" Harry asked. "I'm sure they're restricted access. Who do I call? The desk economist?"

Celine shook her head. "The desk isn't here—apparently, no one from Asian is around. Shit, I hadn't thought of that. It's going to be a real problem if we can't get the latest intervention figures." She drummed her fingers along the back of the chair.

"Well," Harry said after a moment's thought, "maybe we don't need the desk. We should be able to get the reserves data directly from Statistics—their system must have all the FX intervention data. Anyway, let me see what I can dig up." He glanced down the list he'd been scribbling. "The rest of the stuff I ought to be able to pull off the GEO database myself. I'll start with that, and forward it to you the moment I'm done downloading."

"Okay, thanks. That'll be a great help." Celine checked her watch. "I'd better get cracking. I haven't much time. I'm meant to get back to the MD within an hour. If you need me I'm in my office—down the corridor, on the left."

But once there Celine sank into her chair, burying her face in her hands, rubbing her eyes tiredly. *Why Indonesia?* she thought. *Of all places, why did it have to be Indonesia?* Reluctantly she pulled away her hands, looking around with a faint feeling of distaste. Her office had the ephemeral, transient look of a motel room. Book boxes, never unpacked, lurked in the corner, blocking the air vents and tripping unsuspecting visitors. The battery in the wall clock had long ago expired, paralyzing the hands at ten past eight. A solitary calendar, two years out of date, dangled crookedly over the desk.

With a pang, Celine remembered her first IMFO office—her books proudly paraded across the shelves, sorted by subject and author; her prints, expensively framed and artistically arranged, bringing a touch of color to the blank IMFO walls; her rug, a handwoven Kashmiri, lying at a saucy angle.

The computer beeped, announcing the first batch of data from Harry, and Celine realized she'd wasted five of her precious minutes already. Clearing a patch amid the clutter of unread memos and unopened mail, she pulled a pad from the drawer and settled down to work.

Within a few minutes she had scratched out the basic calculations. Judged purely on the basis of economic fundamentals, the Indonesian rupiah had already depreciated enough, and no further depreciation was warranted. But it was an IMFO axiom, drilled into new recruits in the Young Economist Program from their first day on the job, that just because an exchange rate should be defended, didn't mean that it *could*. It all depended on the surety of having enough foreign exchange reserves and the vagary of market psychology.

Once the market believed that Bank Indonesia was running low on its foreign exchange reserves, there would be rush of capital flight, depleting the reserves and forcing a devaluation. In effect, a self-fulfilling run on the central bank of the country. But by the same token, if confidence were somehow restored, capital would come flooding back, replenishing reserves and sustaining the exchange rate.

Which begged the question of how much intervention Bank Indonesia had been forced to do over the past few days, thought Celine, and just how much foreign reserves it had left in its war chest. As if on cue, there was a tap on the door. Harry breezed into her office.

"The good news is that I was able to get hold of someone in Statistics," he announced, perching himself on the arm of her battered sofa. "The bad news is, the dragon down there won't give me the data."

"Why not?"

"Says it's absolutely confidential. Apparently, it can't be given out to anyone."

"If it can't be given to anyone, then why the hell do they bother to collect it?" Celine snatched the slip of paper from Harry's hand and began stabbing the buttons on the phone.

"Hello? Yes, this is Celine O'Rourke from Policy Review Department. We need some data on FX reserves and liabilities, and hourly data on central bank intervention for Indonesia," she said, all in one breath.

"That information is highly restricted." A fussy, officious voice. "It can only be made available to department directors—and even they only have access to the data for countries in their department. I've already explained all this to your colleague. I can't help you. And now, if you don't mind, I'd like to get home."

"Wait! You don't understand. This is an emergency. We *have* to have that data."

"Emergency or not, there are absolutely no exceptions to these rules," the woman announced with satisfaction.

"Now, you listen to me. The managing director has personally asked me to get this data for him. Immediately. And he will not be amused to hear that you (a) refused to provide it and (b) went home instead."

There was a long pause. Cupping her hand over the receiver, Celine rolled her eyes, while Harry grinned back, reaching over to the desk for her calculations.

"Yes. You do that. And once you've verified with the MD's office, I'd appreciate it if you would stop wasting any more of my time, and get me the goddamn data." Celine slammed down the phone. "Bloody bureaucrat."

Harry laughed. "So what do you think?" He pointed to her computations.

"Indonesia's inflation rate has been high, of course," Celine replied, "but on the other hand, the exchange rate has already depreciated pretty steeply to compensate. So in purchasing power parity terms, I don't think the exchange rate is overvalued—there's definitely no reason to let it depreciate further— they ought to take a stand."

"Right," nodded Harry. There was a pause. "But surely you're not basing your assessment just on some paltry PPP calculations?"

"No. No, of course not," she said hastily. "There's a whole lot more to consider: contingent capital outflows, short-term debt falling due, put options on medium- and long-term debt, interbank credit roll-over rates—"

"Precisely. And you've taken all that into account?"

"Well, I mean . . . it's largely judgmental, of course." Celine shifted uncomfortably. "Besides, in real world crises, theory isn't much use. It all depends on the psychology of the moment, and the commitment and credibility of the central bank," she added, feeling herself on safer ground.

"Yeah, well, all the commitment and credibility isn't going to do them a lot of good. If they've run out of foreign exchange reserves, they're screwed. The country has so much foreign currency exposure, they simply can't let the currency go into free fall. Their only option will be to jack up interest rates, and jack 'em up high to convince markets they're going to hang tough. But with Indonesian corporations so saddled with foreign debt, that could bankrupt half the economy, and probably bring down most of the banking system with it. God knows what will happen then." He gave a little laugh, "Riots, I suppose, when people realize they've lost their life savings."

"It's nothing to laugh at."

Harry stared at her in surprise. "I wasn't laughing, I was just pointing out . . . "

"I know, I know," Celine said hastily. "It's just that . . . well, sometimes it seems to me that we're a bit too glib at prescribing policies that other people pay the price for."

Harry shrugged. "You can shoot the messenger, but that doesn't alter the message."

"Quite. Look, thanks a lot for your help." She glanced pointedly at her watch. "I'd better write up something for the MD."

"Don't you want me to see whether we can factor some of the contingent capital flows and short-term debt into your calculations?"

"We haven't the time. Besides, I rather doubt the managing director wants fancy econometrics—he needs something rough and ready."

"Well, this is a damned sight more rough than ready," Harry retorted, tossing her pad back onto the desk.

Celine gave him a frigid glare and was just contemplating some acid reply in which she might include a jibe about armchair economists, when Harry impetuously pulled up to the computer—*her* computer, taking charge as men are wont to do.

"Tell you what," his fingers were already dancing across the keyboard. "It won't take me long to calculate the fundamental equilibrium exchange rate using the Research Department's methodology. You can't do the note for the MD until you get the intervention data from Statistics anyway, so just give me until then."

"Fine. Whatever." Celine shook her head. "If it makes you happy. But the moment I get the intervention data from Statistics, I'm going to need to send up a note to the MD."

Harry set to work and Celine, though impatient at first, found herself gradually drawn in as they hunched over the computer, dissecting data and discerning trends. Harry had a disciplined mind—she had to give him that—and he approached the problem with an analytical dispassion that Celine, who was more accustomed to relying on her instincts as an economist than on fancy econometrics, found challenging and refreshing but also oddly disconcerting. It was like being in the hands of a surgeon who you know is supremely competent, but who you also know is more concerned with the success of the operation than whether the patient actually lives.

Harry was standing very close to her—she could feel the texture of his suit tickling against her forearm as he indicated something on the monitor—and suddenly she became aware of him as a man. He was tall—a shade over six foot, guessed Celine—with fair hair and finely chiseled features. His jawline was firm, his muscles toned, and there was a sense of tamed power to his gestures.

"Sorry?" she said with a start, realizing that he'd stopped talking and must be expecting her to say something.

They were still debating the optimal exchange rate at which Bank Indonesia should try to take a stand when the door flew open. A dour woman with too much makeup marched in without knocking.

"Here's all we have on Indonesia." She waved the tables in the air as though to dry the ink.

"Thank you." Celine reached out to take them. But the woman had them clasped firmly within her claw. "The managing director's office instructed me to give these to you," she said in an aggrieved tone, "but you're to return them to me personally—not to anyone else, and not by interoffice mail—when you're done with them."

"Yes, yes."

"Also, making copies is strictly forbidden. If the security of this information is compromised, you will be held personally responsible." With an about turn, the woman left.

"Jesus!" Harry said. "You'd think they're giving us the combination to Fort Knox."

"I guess the intervention data is pretty sensitive stuff," Celine muttered, already perusing the tables. "What I can't figure out is how things could have deteriorated so rapidly."

She laid out the sheets on her desk, sorting them into chronological order. Harry leaned over her shoulder, his palm resting on the table, his arm stretched beside her, almost as if he were protecting her flank against some unknown attack. Celine could feel the warmth around her, and in that moment of insecurity, she found it oddly comforting. Instead of drawing away as usual, she allowed herself to edge closer.

Together they traced through the exchange market intervention operations of the past week. Bank Indonesia had started the week with almost seventy billion dollars of reserves—a respectable sum, albeit a tad on the low side—with some twenty billion dribbling out over Monday and Tuesday. But on Wednesday, reserves had plummeted to seventeen billion dollars, and another seven billion had been spent propping up the currency over the last twenty-four hours. It was now Friday morning in Indonesia, and the central bank was down to less than ten billion dollars in its war chest with which to defend the currency.

"Hang on." Harry turned back a page. "There's something weird here. Look."

According to the hourly intervention figures, Bank Indonesia had only intervened to the tune of five billion dollars on Wednesday. But somehow, official reserves had fallen by thirty-three billion dollars—it was as though twenty-eight billion dollars had simply evaporated into thin air.

Celine reached for the chair, lowering herself unsteadily.

"What's the matter? Are you okay?"

"You realize what they've done, don't you?" Her voice was hoarse. "The fools! Those bloody, bloody, bloody fools! We must've warned them a thousand times not to play this game. They've been using up their precious foreign exchange reserves to bail out their banks that are in distress. Now that Bank Indonesia needs those reserves to defend the currency, they can't get them back."

"But why would they be so stupid?"

"Politics, of course. Whoever owns the banks being bailed out must have plenty of political clout. Obviously, they don't want their banks to go belly up. What worries me is that if Bank Indonesia is recognizing it won't get back those twenty-eight billion of reserves, it probably means they've been doing a lot more of these bailouts than they're admitting to. I'm just wondering how much of the ten billion dollars they claim to have really exists."

"Well, Christ," Harry threw up his hands. "Then it's hopeless. They're going to have to devalue. We're just wasting our time. If they haven't even got ten billion bucks left, I don't see how they can afford to defend the currency against a speculative attack."

Celine shrugged. The jet lag had caught up with her, and she felt deflated. "I don't see how they can afford *not* to defend it," she replied. "You've seen the figures. There's a massive foreign currency debt exposure. If they can't stop the exchange rate from depreciating, half the country will go under."

"So what will you advise the MD?"

"I don't know." Celine rubbed her eyes. "I just don't know."

"Hey," Harry gestured at the clock. "Weren't you supposed to get back to him by eight o'clock?"

"That clock's wrong," she muttered mechanically.

"Well, anyway," Harry said, pushing back his chair, "I'd better leave you to it. Call me if you need anything else."

"Harry?"

"Yes?"

"No, never mind. Thanks for your help."

The minutes passed. Celine sifted listlessly through the charts and tables, a feeling of helplessness descending upon her. If only the Indonesians had called earlier, even yesterday, there might still have been time to cobble together a financial rescue package and avert a crisis. Now, confidence in the currency had been sapped—that much was clear from the sheer volume of intervention that Bank Indonesia was being forced to undertake just to hold the exchange rate steady—and the chances of avoiding a speculative attack were slim at best. Celine wondered what would happen when the inevitable devaluation was announced.

Memories, long suppressed, bobbed angrily to the surface as she thought back to the last time Indonesia's currency had come under attack, during the

East Asian currency crisis of a few years ago. Celine, freshly graduated from the Young Economists Program and brimming with enthusiasm, had been dispatched to Jakarta as part of the IMFO team.

Those had been heady days for Celine: flying in first class and being whisked through the VIP lounge flashing her LAISSEZ PASSER passport, dashing off a monetary program, a fiscal projection, a budget proposal; racing from her suite at the Mandarin Oriental to see the central bank governor, the finance minister, and even, once, for an audience with the president.

Her mission chief, Xavier Adanpur, a man in his mid-forties with expensive suits and beautiful bespoke shoes, had seemed to Celine to be the epitome of IMFO's voice and authority. She thrilled to listen to him lecture the governor or the finance minister about the need for restoring confidence and gaining credibility by hanging tough, closing down the defunct banks, and not succumbing to the political pressures to bail them out. Or to hear him tell the president that the days of crony capitalism were over, that if the government wanted international support it must clean up its act. Or to watch him handle the press that hounded the mission constantly, manipulating the media to elicit public support for the austerity program.

Later, she liked to think of it as nothing more than an infatuation, but at the time Celine felt giddy with love. Within days, she was having an affair with Adanpur, its intensity heightened by the stress of being on mission in the midst of a crisis, leaving her at once mentally intoxicated and physically drained. He rewarded Celine by choosing her, out of the whole mission team, to accompany him on some of the most sensitive, exclusive meetings with the authorities. It made Celine feel wonderfully grown up, the consummate IMFO insider, privy to special side letters and secret memoranda. Perhaps that was why she never questioned his judgment, despite her growing misgivings about the strategy for closing the banks and her deepening suspicion that Adanpur was more concerned about looking good in Washington than doing good in Jakarta. Even later, when blame for the disastrous decisions fell squarely on the government, Celine, a complicit lover, had kept her silence.

The problems had started when the government balked at closing the banks that were politically well-connected. Adanpur, eager to report progress back to Washington, had agreed to a more limited set of banks for closure, all the while insisting that there must be no promises of bailouts for the others. The Bank and Fund mission chiefs, more circumspect, had urged greater caution. But Adanpur, eager to make his mark, had been adamant, bullying them into agreement, and in the end he had prevailed.

Inevitably, all sorts of lists and rumors started circulating, with no one knowing which banks would close and which would not. Fearful for their meager life savings, the jostling crowds soon started pulling their money out of every bank—even those that were perfectly sound. By late December, what had started as a handful of problem banks had turned into a full-blown run on the entire banking system. Bank Indonesia was forced to use up the last of its foreign reserves salvaging the remaining banks. The exchange rate plummeted, food prices doubled and doubled again, and the country exploded into bloody riots.

At the time, there was a surreality to it all. Sheltered at the central bank or the sumptuous suite at the Mandarin Oriental, Celine had felt detached, divorced from what was going on in the dusty streets below, immersing herself instead in the technicalities of her job, seeking solace in her spreadsheets.

But when the riots started, Washington ordered the mission be evacuated to safe haven in Singapore at once. Amid the mad melee of the city, the car taking Celine to the airport took a wrong turn into a street that was being pillaged by a desperate mob. They were looting the shops of the minority ethnic Chinese who, like the Jews in interwar Germany, owned most of the businesses and were being blamed for the economic collapse. All around, bodies littered the street, their heads staved in, limbs hacked off.

Seeing the car with government plates, the crowd surged forward. Desperately, Celine tapped the driver's shoulder and ordered him to back out. But the mob had already closed around, cutting off their escape. Celine cowered on the floor as they rocked the car, trying to tip it over, their faces pressing against the windows. In that moment, she understood. She had been seduced by the glamor of her IMFO job, forgetting the hard lessons of her own childhood. All those fine phrases bandied about Nineteenth Street—confidence, commitment, credibility—and all Adanpur's smooth talk, were just that: empty words that carried no meaning for a mother scrounging to feed her potbellied child, or for an unemployed father watching his life's savings dissolve.

The owner of a grocery store, seeing the mob occupied, tried to dash down the street. But the crowd turned in an instant, like a shoal of predatory fish, and caught the storekeeper before his stubby legs could carry him ten paces. Celine watched in horror as men brandishing machetes split his skull neatly in two. The oddest details were the man's gold tooth and his inane grin the instant before his head was cracked open.

With a yell of triumph, the crowd abandoned Celine's car and poured into the store, slitting open the bags of rice, which spilled onto the ground, soaking up the blood like sand gulping water. A little boy rushed in between them and started shovelling the rice, sticky with blood, into his mouth like some primeval beast devouring its young. Just then, the driver saw his way through the crowd and the car jerked forward, mercifully leaving the scene behind.

Celine had never told anyone—not even Karin—of that day. She had buried the memory in the deepest recesses of her mind, until today, until an hour ago. She crumpled up the page she'd been writing on, crushing her determination into it.

She would not allow it to happen again. No matter what.

CHAPTER THREE

T HE LIGHTS FLICKERED. Sophia blinked awake. A moment later, heralded by a peremptory burst of static, the captain's voice filled the cabin. He apologized for the bumpy ride caused by the exceptional tailwinds, but by way of compensation promised an early arrival at Heathrow—perhaps as much as an hour ahead of schedule.

Sophia tugged for her watch. An hour would definitely be too early, she thought, shaking her head in frustration. Once the timer was set, there was no way to stop the explosion. They had discussed it for weeks, Melamed insisting that any radio-controlled device would look far too suspicious if spotted. They would do the calculations carefully, leave a small margin, and trust in God for the rest. But all along she had fretted that the operation relied too much on the capriciousness of the winds across the Atlantic. The whole operation depended on strong tailwinds getting them into London ahead of schedule, but too early would be as fatal as too late.

Sophia consulted the monitor showing their progress. She fingered her watch again. It should be all right. They were bound to run into air traffic congestion soon, which should delay them a bit. Sophia was amused by her own perversity. Now that the operation was in danger of failure, she no longer felt any qualms. The doubts and demons of the night before had disappeared, chased away by the rising sun. But she kept her eyes locked firmly ahead of her, ignoring the squeaky voice of the girl behind.

They circled Heathrow twice. London was overcast. The hostesses marched down the aisles, ordering seats back to the upright position and tray tables stowed away. Within minutes of touchdown the passengers were fidgeting, braving admonishments from the cabin crew and unfastening their seat belts.

Sophia nodded goodbye to the air hostess as she exited the aircraft. She walked through the jetway and entered the terminal, heading for the INTER-NATIONAL TRANSFERS sign. She needed to collect her thoughts. The time had come. She felt calm, almost indifferent to the outcome. She paused, hoping to be served by a man at the transfer desk. A woman might be more sympathetic, she decided, but in England much less likely to bend the rules. Sophia prided herself on her ability to manipulate men.

"Morning," she said in an upper-class drawl, handing over her ticket.

"I'm booked on your eleven o'clock flight, but we arrived rather early from the States. I see you have a nine thirty flight to Geneva." She pointed at the monitor. "Could you get me on that one instead?"

"One moment, miss," replied the clerk. Hunching over the computer terminal, he tapped away at the keyboard. Finally he looked up. "You have one piece of luggage booked through from Washington to Geneva?"

Not trusting her voice, Sophia nodded. The clerk glanced at his watch.

"There's plenty of room on the nine thirty flight, miss, but I doubt they'll be able to transfer your baggage in time. Your flight from Washington came in a tad too late."

Sophia pretended to think, her hand cupping her chin, drumming her lips with her fingers. "Well, it doesn't matter. Why not send my case on the next flight? There's nothing in it I especially need. I can even pick it up tomorrow."

"Can't, miss. Against regulations."

Sophia lowered her eyes. She had enhanced the puffiness around them with a smudge of eye shadow, giving her a decidedly vulnerable look. "Couldn't you possibly get me on the early flight?" she sighed, with just a slight flutter of her eyelashes. "The flight over was awfully bumpy, and I'm totally knackered. I'd really like to get home. You haven't a lounge for economy class passengers where I could rest and shower, do you?"

The clerk hesitated, then asked for her passport and flipped through it page by page. Every so often he would look back over his shoulder, as if hoping for his supervisor to arrive and unburden him of the decision. Sophia played with a pile of luggage tags on the counter, anxious not to appear anxious.

It was up to her to persuade the clerk, Melamed had told Sophia. She must get him to put her on the early flight, while her luggage—and the bomb—went on the later one. Ordinarily, he'd explained, passengers are never permitted to change flights if it means travelling apart from their luggage. The security risk is obvious. But if the airline thought the change of flight was for reasons beyond the passenger's control, lost luggage for instance, or an unexpectedly early or late arrival of a connecting flight, an exception might be made. The genius of Melamed's plan lay in knowing that strong tailwinds in December would bring in the flight from Washington early, apparently unexpectedly. Yet if she arrived in London too early, they would have enough time to transfer the luggage to the nine thirty a.m. flight as well.

The clerk hung up the phone and turned to Sophia. "I'm sorry, miss. They won't be able to get your luggage onto the earlier flight."

"I see."

The clerk shrugged. "Look, I'll put you on the nine thirty flight if you like, but your luggage won't get to Geneva until one p.m. It's up to you."

"Oh, yes. Yes," she agreed, almost too eagerly.

The clerk punched out a boarding pass and directed her to the departure lounge, saying the flight would be called shortly. Sophia made her way to the loneliest corner and collapsed onto the vinyl seat, drained of energy and emotion. She considered getting a cup of tea from the cafeteria, but could not be bothered. She felt no victory, no triumph, just hollowness. Above her on the wall, a digital clock flipped through the minutes. She yearned to be home and away from this place, for the operation to be over.

"I say. Excuse me."

She ignored the voice. "Excuse me," the voice repeated, this time more insistent.

With a sinking heart Sophia turned around and stood up. It was the woman from the plane with the girl. She strode up to Sophia, her daughter trailing shyly.

"Hello." The woman smiled pleasantly. "You were on the flight from Washington, weren't you? In the row in front of us."

Sophia nodded, loath to get into conversation.

"Go on, dear . . . show her," the woman told her daughter.

The girl delved into her bag, pulled out a roll of paper, and handed it to Sophia without a word. Sophia unrolled it, then sat down, staring at the picture. It was a sketch of Sophia, in black crayon, capturing the moment when she'd fallen asleep. The likeness was remarkable. The cascade of black hair, the high cheekbones, the pert nose, the large eyes with implausible lashes, the eyebrows that arched sharply—like Chinese hats, Simon used to tease. But there was something more, something vaguely disconcerting. The sketch had a quality, at once naïve and perceptive, that allowed a glimpse into the ravages of Sophia's soul.

"This is wonderful," she said at last. "It's really, really wonderful. Are you going to be a painter when you grow up?" She patted the seat beside her. The girl sat down, her shyness evaporating.

"I'm going to be a ballerina."

"Really? What's your favorite ballet?"

"*Sleeping Beauty.*"

"Mine too," Sophia lied. "Can you do pointes?"

The girl nodded. "Only with my ballet shoes on." But then she stood up anyway, making a pirouette, precarious yet precise. Sophia clapped softly. How wonderful it would be, she thought, to have a child like this.

Sophia's flight was announced. "I have to go," she said, unable to hide the reluctance in her voice.

"Are they calling your flight?" the mother asked. "Lucky you. We're stuck here until eleven."

A chill ran down Sophia's spine. The woman was holding their boarding passes. Sophia dared not look at the destination, knowing with horrid certainty what it would be. They were on the eleven o'clock flight to Geneva, the flight carrying Sophia's suitcase—and Melamed's bomb.

Sophia felt dizzy as the girl handed her the sketch to keep. They were announcing her flight again. She must leave now. She nodded her good-byes, clutching the sketch in her hand, and walked a half dozen paces before turning back. She reached for her gold chain, wrestled with the clasp, and placed it around the child's neck. Softly she kissed the girl's hair, then fled for her departure gate.

Much of the flight passed in a daze. They flew through puffy clouds and over quilts of ice carved into the ground as Sophia stared unseeing through the window. It wasn't too late. She could still demand to speak to the captain, have him send a radio message, alert the authorities. Call the bomb squad. Get the passengers off the plane.

She did nothing.

The bomb had been timed to explode shortly after the eleven a.m. flight took off, when the plane would be over the English Channel. She could picture the oil slick on the water, boats trawling for limbs and luggage.

A searing sensation rose in her throat. Sophia scrambled for the bathroom. She threw up once, twice. The rest of the flight she spent sitting on the toilet, her head in her hands, rocking back and forth, and returning to her seat only when the FASTEN SEAT BELT sign flashed. The air hostess asked whether she was all right and brought her a glass of water. They approached Geneva, swooping low—the Jet d'Eau had been switched off for the winter— and the lake looked gray and unfriendly, churning with small choppy waves.

Melamed was waiting for her at the arrivals hall, just past customs. A short man, he was standing on tiptoe, peering through his good eye over the crowd. He took one look at her and whispered, "Is everything all right?" Sophia didn't answer. "Did it go okay?" he pressed.

"Yes," she hissed back, then lapsed into silence.

The ride to central Geneva took only a few minutes. They didn't speak. It was twelve twenty local time, eleven twenty British time. The bomb would explode any moment now. Sophia was beyond caring; she had numbed her mind from thought.

Melamed had taken rooms at the Hotel des Bergues, taking cover in the spurious respectability of the rich. Once inside, he threw his arms around Sophia and hugged her closely, a paternal, comforting hug. Though yearning for the human contact, Sophia stiffened and pulled away as soon as she decently could. There was a dull pain behind her eyes, and the sour aftertaste of vomit still laced her mouth. Oblivious, Melamed picked up the remote control and calmly cruised through the channels, trying to find a twenty-four-hour news station. Sophia felt a flash of anger. She wanted to shout and scream at him, to hurl the foulest obscenities she could imagine.

Putting down the remote, Melamed glanced at his watch. "It'll be a while before it hits the news." He walked to the bar and plucked a bottle from the refrigerator.

"Champagne?" he smiled. "I picked up a bottle of your favorite, La Grande Dame."

"I just killed a hundred innocent people. *You* bloody well celebrate." She stormed out of the suite into her bedroom, and flung herself on the bed, too drained to cry. Nestling her head in her crossed arms, she tried to force tears from her eyes, as though they might cleanse her guilt. After a few minutes she got up and rummaged in her bag. Sophia pulled out the picture the girl had made, returning at once to the sanctuary of the bed, where she sat for twenty minutes, torturing herself. She wanted to grieve. For the little girl who would never be Sleeping Beauty. For her people, struggling for justice. For herself, reduced to murder. She kept tracing the sketch with her fingers until the lines were smudged beyond recognition.

A knock on the door. Melamed entered.

"Are you okay?"

Sophia said nothing, still rubbing the smudgy lines of the drawing, as if intent on obliterating herself. Melamed reached over and eased it from her hand. He stood staring at the picture, squinting at it through his good eye, as though trying to imagine a different face, another likeness, superimposed upon Sophia's. Finally, he let the page flutter back onto the bed and turned to look out the window.

"Have you ever seen the sunrise in our country?"

Sophia said nothing.

"Well, have you?

She shook her head.

"It's a different sun. It's not a harsh, burning light like here; it has a warmer, softer, deeper glow. When it rises in the morning, it starts as a tiny pinpoint that slowly seeps into the horizon. It looks so incredibly beautiful. I watched it rise, with both of my eyes, the day they blinded my eye."

Melamed spoke softly, without rancor, without regret, so softly that Sophia had to strain to hear him above the stillness of the room. His voice was low and mesmerizing. Soon, Sophia was no longer in that fancy hotel room overlooking Lake Geneva, with its king-sized bed and deluxe drapes. She was with Melamed, thirty years ago, in the dank cell as he watched the sun rise in all its glory, one last time.

With him as they dragged him down through the dark recesses of the prison to the interrogation room.

With him as he watched them remove a spoke from a rusty bicycle wheel, brandishing it in front of his face, before plunging it into the burning brazier.

With him as he saw the sharp, menacing tip approach and bury itself in his eyeball.

With him as he felt the searing pain pierce his eye and slam against the back of his head.

And with him as he heard his own screams and screams and screams bouncing off the blackened walls amid the raucous laughter of the guards.

"They were after our printing press." Melamed gave a brief, bitter laugh. "Crooked characters on cheap gritty paper, but we really believed we could prick the world's conscience with it. Instead, the Western countries flocked to curry favor with the regime and get their grubby hands on the mining rights."

"And the others? What happened to the others?"

"There were five of us in all . . . there was a girl." Melamed's mouth creased in a slow, embarrassed smile. "My fiancée."

Sophia stared in surprise, trying to imagine Melamed with a woman. It was like picturing your parents having sex. "What happened to her?"

Melamed shrugged. "Shot trying to escape. Killed resisting arrest. The usual sorts of things. I was the only one who made it. All because a prominent lawyer heard of my case and by God knows what means managed to persuade a judge to order my release. That lawyer," he added, "was your father."

Melamed turned to leave the room.

"Why didn't you tell me? About . . ." Sophia hesitated, too squeamish to mention his eye. "I always thought you'd had an accident handling explosives or something."

Melamed walked back to her, gently cupping his hand under her chin and lifting it so that she was looking up at him. "When you planted that bomb on the plane, you did it to bring justice for your people, not for the memory of your murdered father, and certainly not out of pity for an old man. Come, the news will be starting any minute."

By the time Sophia joined him in the living room he was already flipping through the channels. He beckoned her to the sofa beside him, but she remained standing. The news bulletin was just starting. They listened to the staccato sentences in growing disbelief.

"It is now confirmed that at eleven seventeen this morning an explosion occurred here at London's Heathrow Airport. Flights out of Heathrow were delayed following the receipt of a warning call, so the bomb, on board a flight bound for Geneva, exploded while the aircraft was still on the ground. One baggage handler received minor burns. There are no other reports of casualties at this time. The explosion appears to have ignited fumes in the fuel tank, and within minutes the aircraft was totally consumed by fire. Clearly, a major, major disaster had it happened while the aircraft was in the air. A splinter group of the Irish Republican Army is suspected of making a warning call about forty-five minutes prior to the explosion. According to police sources, the caller used the right code words for authentication, but spoke of a device in the terminal building and not on board an aircraft. We will bring you further information as it comes in."

They had failed.

Melamed hurled the remote against the wall.

Sophia burst into tears.

CHAPTER FOUR

G ELATINOUS WITH FATIGUE, Celine watched the thin white line slip toward the bottom of the monitor. She was in the Reuters Room, so called because of the array of trading screens giving up-to-the-minute information on dozens of different currencies, all flashing with self-importance. It was early morning in Washington, late afternoon in Jakarta, and from the moment of market opening the Indonesian rupiah had been in rout.

As Celine suspected, the Indonesian central bank had been using its foreign reserves to prop up the ailing banks—the governor had finally admitted as much in a mumbling conference call to the managing director—and they were now down to the last few billion in their coffers with which to defend the exchange rate. Kiyotaki was furious, using language seldom heard on the manicured playing fields of international finance. But there was no time for recriminations. If a complete collapse was to be avoided, decisive action was needed at once.

And so, at Kiyotaki's insistence, Bank Indonesia had raised its interest rates. Timidly at first, then with greater boldness, now with flat-out desperation. A second panel on the telerate screen showed the progress of BI's overnight interest rate, jerking upward in a series of uneven steps, like a staircase drawn on an Etch-A-Sketch: 12, 47, 63, 98, and now, less than an hour ago, to 140 percent—an unprecedented level for Indonesia and a staggering increase over the 10 to 15 percent it normally averaged.

He's playing it by the book, thought Celine, but he's playing it all wrong. Kiyotaki's plan was venomously orthodox: raise interest rates until they touch the face of God in the hope of attracting back speculative capital and replenishing reserves to stabilize the currency. And if half the country went bankrupt in the process, so be it. At least they wouldn't have blinked before the markets.

In Jakarta, two major banks had already closed their doors. The stock exchange had fallen 60 percent, with the reverberations in the financial markets echoing from Seoul to Singapore. Meanwhile, perhaps as a precursor of things to come, the military had issued a statement that it stood ready to maintain law and order, and there were preliminary reports of at least one bloody clash between riot police and students protesting against the incompetence of the government.

Viewing it through the dispassionate displays of the computer screens and the telegraphic sentences of the wire services, Celine grew increasingly convinced that Kiyotaki's strategy would never work. She'd tried voicing her concerns, but Kiyotaki had merely nodded impatiently and instructed the Indonesians to raise their rates even further. So horribly familiar.

Ever since that fateful day in Jakarta, when she saw the shopkeeper bludgeoned by the mob, Celine had asked herself the same question: Had she spoken up during one of those countless meetings at the ministry of finance, or in the black Mercedes, shuttling along Jalan Sudirman, or in bed with Adanpur, could it have been any different? Coming back from Indonesia, answering the unanswerable became an obsession. Celine had pored over memos and minutes and coded faxes in the files, wallowing in her guilt, until Karin, seeing her close to a breakdown, had forced her to change departments and move to Policy Review.

A patter of hurried footsteps interrupted her reverie. Celine spun around.

"Hi," Harry called from the door. "Thought I might find you here. The MD is waiting for those printouts."

"I was just getting them." From the puzzled look on Harry's face, she knew he was wondering what she'd been up to all this time. She punched the buttons and the printer coughed out the graphs. She snatched them up, still warm, then raced toward the elevators with Harry following closely behind.

"They told me to come up also."

"Oh." Celine tried to disguise her surprise. But Harry seemed to take the idea of meeting the managing director in his stride. Not for the first time, Celine marvelled at the ease with which men could assume authority.

Kiyotaki merely nodded as Harry introduced himself. "So, what do you have for me?"

"Not much, I'm afraid," Celine said. "The rupiah has lost close to 30 percent since this morning, and it's still on a downward spiral. The markets are jittery, and the other Asians look to be on the brink of following suit. The Japanese banks are vulnerable because of their loan exposure to the whole region, and of course, the contagion effects on other emerging markets could be catastrophic."

"Where's BI's interest rate now?" frowned Kiyotaki.

"Over 140 percent."

Kiyotaki stroked his chin. "Good. They're finally heeding our advice." He turned to Harry for the first time. "You've done work on currency crises," he said, almost accusingly. "I've seen some of your papers."

"Yes, sir. It's my main research area."

"So what do you think?"

"Well, 140 percent is pretty high. But historically, of course, it's nothing compared to what some other countries have done to defend their exchange rates. Sweden went to 500 percent during the European Exchange Rate Mechanism crisis . . ."

As he went on, though she could not fault him on the facts, Celine began to grow at first resentful, then concerned, and finally panicked. These men, she thought, they've no idea what they're talking about. They're just spewing words, without thought to what any of it really means.

It was a good performance, she had to give them that. The glib phrases, the macho militaristic talk of "standing tough," "warding off speculative attacks," and "deploying first and second lines of defence." Harry and Kiyotaki seemed oblivious to her presence, slipping effortlessly into the usual economists' euphemisms—from "fiscal retrenchment" to "labor market flexibility"—that disguise, even from the speaker, the unpleasantness of slashing budgets and throwing people out of work.

She interrupted, trying to tell them they were missing the big picture, that no economy could survive these punishingly high interest rates, but Kiyotaki was in no mood for such defeatist talk.

"Yes, yes. You've made that point already. Now I'd like to hear what Mr. Hoffinger has to say."

Celine fell silent again. To his credit, Harry did point out the devastating impact these skyrocketing interest rates might have on the economy. But he spoke without conviction, somehow making it sound all very remote and theoretical, like those warning labels on medicines, legally obligated to point out potential side-effects of a drug, but printed in the smallest type possible. And even then, Harry spoke only of the difficulties the large corporations and financial conglomerates would face. Of the corner grocery store, the local laundry, the newsstand man who'd invested his life savings in a kiosk, no one seemed to care.

Yet Celine knew how much worse it could be for the small businessman. Her father had been one, a manufacturer of highly specialized machine parts. Then, with the devaluation of the pound sterling, it all came abruptly to an end. The futile spike in interest rates had dealt his business a staggering blow. She could still picture him trudging home each night, bowed under by his hopeless struggle to save the company and his guilt at having let his family and his dozen or so employees down. He put on a brave face, but he went about with the look of a dumb animal caught in a trap as he searched fruitlessly for a new job—any job—each day a little more dejected, a little more dispirited, until that awful afternoon three months later, when Celine had come home to find her father dead. He'd had an accident, cleaning his hunting rifles.

"Credibility can't be bought, it must be earned," Kiyotaki was pontificating. "If the Indonesians are going to restore confidence to their currency markets, they've got to show they're willing to stomach tough policies and put the squeeze on speculators . . ."

Frustration welled up within Celine. She felt inarticulate, unable to counter his arguments or compete with his logic. Hot tears sprang to her eyes, adding to her humiliation.

"Bank Indonesia has been too timid in raising its rates," Kiyotaki continued, mercifully unaware. "They ought to have gone much higher, much more aggressively, instead of raising the interest rate in little dribs and drabs. This is a crisis of confidence. They need to do something dramatic to show the markets they mean business." He reached for the conference phone. "I'm going to recommend they raise rates to 500 percent. That's a good, round number, and it will have a big psychological impact on the market."

"No!" Celine cried.

Kiyotaki and Harry turned to her in surprise.

"What I mean," she said hastily, "is that I'm not at all sure that raising interest rates further is going to do any good."

"I see. And what would you suggest instead?" Kiyotaki asked.

"They've got to *lower* interest rates."

"Don't be ludicrous. It'll just prompt even more capital flight out of the country."

Harry was about to say something, but Celine ignored him, addressing herself exclusively to Kiyotaki. "We can't just keep raising interest rates. No business can survive paying 500 percent interest rates per year, even if it's only for a few days. We're just bankrupting the country."

Kiyotaki shook his head. "Nonsense." Like all weak men, he placed an undue emphasis on not changing his mind. Having recommended the interest rate increases to the Indonesians before, he wasn't going to reverse himself now, thought Celine.

"The only way to stabilize the currency is to offer such high interest rates that it's worth the risk for investors to hold Indonesian rupiah. What you're suggesting is tantamount to suicide. You're just back from mission. I'm sure you're suffering from jet lag. I suggest you call it a day."

"Don't bloody patronize me." Calm down, she commanded herself, or they'll just dismiss you as a shrill, hysterical woman. "I'm sorry," she said in as even a voice as she could muster. "I *am* tired. But don't you see, raising interest rates to these levels is a clear sign of desperation. And as long as investors see a desperate situation in Indonesia, capital isn't going to flow back, no matter what the interest rate is. We've *got* to bring rates back down."

Kiyotaki shook his head. "It'll cause an even greater depreciation of the rupiah. Can you imagine what effect that would have? Besides, BI is completely out of foreign exchange reserves. They've got no choice now but to keep raising the interest rate."

A long silence ensued.

"So why not give them financial support?"

"How? This will all be over in a couple of hours. If the rupiah is still depreciating when the Asian markets close, they're finished. They have to make a stand today and turn the tide. And we don't have any vehicle for getting them money at such short notice."

Celine nodded tiredly. The procedures for arranging an IMFO loan were endless: negotiating missions, letters of intent, staff reports, comments from reviewing departments, Executive Board discussion. Only then could there be a drawing. It normally took weeks, perhaps days in a dire emergency, but certainly not a few hours.

"But the market doesn't know that," Harry said suddenly.

"Of course they do. They know our procedures perfectly well."

"No, listen." Harry leaned forward, his boyish face flushed with excitement. "The main reason the Indonesians are in such straits is that they've been using their foreign exchange reserves to shore up their domestic banks, and they never told us about it, right? Well, suppose they'd told us back on Monday or Tuesday. What would we have done?"

"Rushed through an emergency drawing from the Enhanced Reserves Facility," Kiyotaki replied.

"Precisely. So why not pretend that we've already done that and announce to the markets that we've arranged for an immediate drawing by Bank Indonesia of, let's say, 1,000 percent of quota, which would be around thirty billion dollars. It could be just the trick that restores market confidence."

"We can't make false statements like that." Kiyotaki looked aghast.

"No," Celine said slowly. "But we could let the Indonesians make the press announcement and simply not deny it. After all, IMFO's officially closed today."

Kiyotaki scratched his head. "I suppose such an announcement could have a big confidence effect. But if the market doesn't believe it, Bank Indonesia still won't have the reserves to do the intervention."

"Doesn't matter. If they deal in the forward market, they'll only have to deliver the dollars several weeks from now—by which time they'll be able to make a drawing from us."

"They'd be gambling with reserves they don't have," Kiyotaki grumbled.

"They don't exactly have a choice," Celine replied. "You said it yourself. This is a crisis of confidence. If they manage to restore confidence, capital will come flooding back into the country, and they'll have more than enough to honor their contracts. If it doesn't work, they're dead anyway."

"And what will our illustrious Executive Board do when they hear I condoned making false statements about use of IMFO resources? They'll have my head."

"Not if we succeed," Celine countered, but she could see the concern in his eyes.

"I need to think about it." Kiyotaki stood up, walking slowly over to the window, and drew open the drapes.

Harry was trying to signal something to her, but Celine motioned him to be still. Kiyotaki was staring out the window. Studying his back, Celine wondered what was going through his mind. His second term would be up next year, and in his early sixties by now, perhaps he was thinking about his legacy. Little enough had been achieved during his tenure, and his time was running out.

By tradition, the World Bank is always headed by an American, the IMF by a European, while the Asians foot an ever increasing share of the bills. So after much wrangling, none the less fierce for its veneer of diplomatic urbanity, Kiyotaki had gotten the IMFO job. With his Oxford degree, yet credentials from the Japanese Ministry of Finance, he was the ideal compromise candidate—Asian enough to appease the developing countries and Western enough to reassure the Americans and Europeans. But in practice, it meant he could never be sure of support at the Board from the Western governments, while the Asians—not to mention the other developing countries— also viewed him with suspicion.

"All right." He turned toward them "Let's do it."

"And the interest rates?" Celine asked.

The slightest hesitation. Kiyotaki's eyes flickered toward Harry. Of course, she thought with a flash of anger, he doesn't trust my opinion. She was right about the interest rates. She knew it, and she didn't bloody well need to be backed up by an economist who'd probably never even been on a real mission.

But still she was grateful when Harry said, "Well, I suppose it is possible to get into a vicious cycle. You see, foreign investors want higher interest rates to cover the risk they are taking by lending to a country in a crisis. But the higher interest rates mean more bankruptcies, more loans going sour. Eventually, higher interest rates will mean lower—not higher—returns to investors, and they will want to get out even faster. Yes," he nodded pensively, "I guess it's at least theoretically possible that raising interest rates further could have a perverse effect, weakening the currency instead of strengthening it."

"I see," Kiyotaki nodded, though it was clear that he didn't. "Very well, then. Since you're both so convinced, I'll suggest when they announce that they're getting our money that they also start bringing interest rates down. In fact, it will give greater credibility to the story that we're providing resources. After all, if we weren't, it would be complete insanity to lower interest rates," he added, with a pointed look at Celine.

The announcement hit the wire services within the hour. At first, the market did not know how to react. It hesitated, like a dog cocking its ear at an unfamiliar sound. Celine spent a bad half hour glued to the Bloomberg screen that gave up-to-the-minute information on currency trades, hoping, praying for a nudge of the exchange rate in the right direction, painfully aware that they'd gambled everything on this single throw of the dice.

Then, around four a.m. Washington time, four p.m. Jakarta time, they saw the first uptick on the exchange rate. It might have been just an error, a glitch, an idiot who didn't know what he was doing. Celine forced herself not to pin her hopes on it. But five minutes later there was a second uptick, followed quickly by a third. It was gradually dawning on the traders that with the injection of funds from IMFO, the central bank would have more than enough reserves to defend the currency. With interest rates still in the high double digits, that meant dollar returns of 50, 60, even 75 percent! And interest rates were falling. How quickly now the herd turned, fearful of missing out on this opportunity.

Celine and Harry watched the rally on trading monitors, flipping incessantly from one broker's screen to another. Trading hours had come to a close in Asia, and Bank Indonesia was no longer in the market. But in the last half hour, they had actually *bought* a couple of billion dollars, and there was little doubt now that the rupiah was firming in the exchange markets. The Indonesians had at least gained enough time to launch a proper rescue package.

Harry switched off the screen. "Time to go home."

Celine nodded. It was morning, and the city seemed moribund in the snow. Kiyotaki had called down a few minutes ago to congratulate them. He'd said little more than, "Well done," but behind his words Celine could sense the relief. Though he still had a lot of explaining to do to the Executive Board, Kiyotaki could at least claim that a potential crisis had been averted. He had also asked Celine to go to Indonesia immediately, and she had accepted with alacrity. She realized she was no longer reluctant to return to Indonesia; she was eager for it. A full mission would join her just as soon as IMFO reopened and the team assembled.

"Want to grab a bite to eat?" Harry asked. "We could get some breakfast at the Mayflower."

"No." She shook her head. "I'd better get home and pack. Dulles is still closed, so I've got to take the flight from New York, and God knows how long it will take me to get there in this mess."

"Well then, promise you'll have lunch with me when you get back."

"Yes. Yes, I'd like that." For the first time in twenty-four hours, Celine smiled.

CHAPTER FIVE

OXFORD, OXFORD. THIS IS OXFORD. *Train arriving at platform two is the nine forty from London, Paddington.*

Sophia peered down the track with the anxious expectation of a passenger waiting for luggage to appear on the conveyor belt. She hadn't seen Melamed since the botched airline bombing four months ago. That same afternoon, Melamed had whisked her over the border into France, across the Channel to England, and dumped her in a safe house in Oxford. Then he'd promptly disappeared, distancing himself from her for security reasons, and going off on his usual round of mysterious trips and assignations for the cadre. Drained and distraught, Sophia was relieved to see him go.

But during those first few days, she had nearly gone into shock. Unable to sleep, she had only her own conscience for company. She would replay the events endlessly in her mind, sifting among the fragmentary images—the clerk staring through his spidery glasses, the bustling businessman trying to pick up the woman beside him, the little girl pirouetting without her ballet shoes—wondering if what she'd done could possibly be right. In the morning, she would wake up dull-eyed and exhausted, and spend the day wandering the winding banks of the Cherwell or meandering the market streets, where not even the bustling Christmas crowds could relieve her loneliness.

She received only the occasional terse, coded message from Melamed. He was using his contacts to learn how much the authorities had been able to figure out, assuring her that the risk of the bomb being traced to her suitcase was remote. Still, it added to her terrors. Sophia would go to bed at night half expecting the sharp rapping at the door, the blinding lights and blaring sirens, the snapping of cold steel around her slender wrists.

But presently, the ageless serenity of Oxford asserted itself, calming her nerves and soothing her soul. When Hilary term began and the students and tutors came pouring back, Sophia decided to remain in Oxford, arranging with her old college to use the library and dine in Hall in exchange for some vague tutoring duties.

The next two months were spent immersed in research, blissfully abstract and obscure, and of no conceivable value to her country, her people, or, indeed, to anyone at all. She would get up late, breakfasting on an obscenely frothy latte at the café on Turl Street before going to the Bodleian, working two, three hours, then lunching with an old tutor or a new friend.

The afternoons were spent visiting her old haunts, leaning on Magdalen Bridge, watching the Cherwell flow by, where Simon had taught her how to punt, and that all-important trick of giving the pole a sharp twist when it gets stuck in the mud, before punt moves ahead, and pole remains behind. Or traipsing across Christ Church meadows in green wellies and yellow mac. Or standing still in the deer park, gazing at the black-eyed does. Or peering at obscure artifacts at the Ashmolean Museum, and obscurer books at Black-well's. Or reliving the terrors of the Examination Schools and stodgy teas at the Randolph. The memories brought her no pain, but rather the vicarious pleasure of recollection, and she realized belatedly that she had been happy at Oxford after all. Even her breakup with Simon, so momentous at the time, now seemed little more than a footnote.

But of course it couldn't last. Sophia was on her way home from a college dance one evening—she'd gone with the Junior Tutor of Moral Philosophy, having finally succumbed to his pleadings principally as a pretext for ordering herself a new ball gown from Designing Women—when crossing a foot-bridge over the Cherwell she was assailed by a stench, at once nauseating and familiar. Some rotting refuse must have collected by the bank of the river, and the smell reminded her rudely of her native country. The dark images she had seen there still lurked within her mind—orphaned children crying in the dusty streets, mothers roaming morgues in search of missing sons, police swinging clubs and firing bullets into the crowd—and now in the instant of recollection they came flooding back.

She began to tremble, like an alcoholic with the DTs, feeling feverish and faint. She staggered back to her house on North Parade Road and swallowed as many sleeping pills as she could find the moment she got there.

The following day she saw no one and did nothing, taking refuge in her favorite alcove in Christ Church library, her legs curled up beneath her, hugging her arms for comfort, and rocking rhythmically back and forth.

She knew there was no escape. However much she had vowed not to, in the end she would pick up the phone and call Melamed, and volunteer for another operation. It was her destiny, her fate, and there was no point in fighting it. Yet, she was certain of one thing. The image of the little girl, who would have been blown to smithereens had the operation succeeded, would be with her always. Never again could she contemplate killing people. No matter what the plot, it could involve no bloodshed. Somehow, she must persuade Melamed of that. It was the essential dilemma, the cruel paradox: how to fight the regime without stooping to its level.

Oxford, Oxford. This is Oxford. Train now arriving at platform two is the nine forty from London, Paddington.

Sophia watched Melamed alight from the far end of the train. He was dressed to fit the part: tame sports jacket and knitted tie, with a small leather bag that could pass for an academic's briefcase clutched in his hand. He looked uncertainly up and down the platform, then seeing Sophia, broke into a smile.

"Hullo," he waved. "How've you been?"

"Fine." She was suddenly shy, unsure whether she should shake hands, kiss him on the cheek, or simply walk side by side with customary British reserve. "Where's your luggage?"

"I can only stay the day. I need to be in Zurich tomorrow morning."

"Oh."

"Never mind. It's a gorgeous day. I thought you might show me around Oxford and tell me what's on your mind."

They meandered up toward Carfax, past the prison and the forbidding fortress of Nuffield College, stopping for a coffee along the way.

"Before I forget, this arrived for you." Melamed fished in his pocket. "It was being held *poste restante* in Geneva." He handed Sophia a buff, official-looking envelope, addressed to her in the name she had used during the December trip. Sophia looked at it curiously, turning it over as though suspecting some kind of trick or trap, then tore it open with an impatient shrug. A small slip of paper tumbled out. Sophia picked it up off the floor, staring at in surprise, then burst out laughing.

"What is it?"

It was a check from the airline, compensating her for the loss of her luggage.

Melamed started laughing too, showing his discolored teeth. He had more good news. From what he'd been able to ascertain, the force of the explosion and subsequent fire had destroyed all hope of tracing which suitcase the bomb had been in. Sophia felt a warm admiration and gratitude toward Melamed as she listened to him explain how he had taken the precaution of designing the device to splatter chemical residues throughout the cargo bay, just to make it doubly difficult to trace back to her luggage. She also realized how absurd she'd been to think she might be able to design her own operation without his help. She *must* persuade him to go along with her plan.

In any case, Melamed was saying, the bomb scare at Heathrow had diverted attention to the IRA, and with breathtaking opportunism, two separate splinter groups had actually claimed responsibility for planting it. Sophia was safe. With a sigh of relief, she realized that chapter of her life was closed.

"So what have you been up to?" he asked.

"Nothing much," she said, but then couldn't resist adding, "I've been working on a book."

"Really? What about?"

It was about the economic origins of dystopia in Aldous Huxley's *Brave New World*, George Orwell's *Nineteen Eighty-Four*, and Yevgeny Zamyatin's *We*. In all three books, Sophia told him, warming to her subject, the economic structure of society is inextricably linked to the power of the ruling oligarchy to deny personal freedom and control individual thought.

Melamed listened, toying with his coffee spoon as she spoke. "Yes, of course," he nodded. "Economic interests *are* at the roots of political oppression." Then, reducing everything to the immediacy of the Cause as usual, he added, "You only have to look at our country to see that. If the minerals and metals weren't buried in our lands, I dare say our people would have gained independence long ago. But if you're going to write books," he said, looking at her quizzically, "why not write about our country's problems instead?"

"Oh, I don't know." Sophia played with her cup. She couldn't tell him that she had been tired of her country, sickened by the Cause, distraught over the bombing, and clutching at anything that might distract her mind. Then, as her book progressed, she'd found herself drawn in, loath to abandon a project once started. But it was true: working on the book had been nothing more than a personal indulgence, like a cream tea or new pair of evening shoes. Melamed's question carried a hint of reproach, and she was ashamed to have wasted time and effort on an undertaking of so little consequence.

Sophia glanced at Melamed guiltily, wondering how many secret trips home he'd made since they'd last met, how many comrades he'd found missing, how many friends arrested, how many children orphaned, how many women widowed while she'd been here wallowing in self-pity, or gallivanting around Oxford trying to forget.

He must have read her thoughts, for he took hold of her hand, stroking the back of it with his fingers. "I'm sorry I had to abandon you. I know it must have been hard on you. Very, very hard. But until I was sure you were in the clear it would have been just too risky for us to make contact."

"I know. Don't worry about it." She smiled bravely, remembering the nightmare of her first weeks alone. "It wasn't that bad. Besides," she added with a grin, "I met a most charming tutor of Moral Philosophy while writing my book."

"Oh, well." Melamed let go of her hand and looked down his nose in his best Victorian manner. "In that case, I trust he has good prospects and honorable intentions."

"Decidedly dishonorable, I'm afraid," Sophia laughed, then downed the rest of her coffee and tossed a couple of pounds on the table.

She took him around the sights of Oxford, trying to convey her love for the quads and cloisters, the ancient walls, the chilly chapels, the vaulted ceilings and sunken floors. Melamed, like a proud parent being shown the college precincts, seemed to enjoy the tour just as much.

Sophia was glad he had come to Oxford—he'd initially suggested they meet in London—and it occurred to her that she'd never seen him in so relaxed a setting before. Previously, she had found him cold and detached; not uncaring, but strangely aloof. Like the schoolteachers of her childhood, who Sophia used to imagine were put away into the closet at night, emerging fully clothed in the morning, with no existence outside the classroom, Melamed had seemed to be a single-minded freedom fighter, with no other life beyond or between. But today she detected in him a warm streak of humanity that she found attractive. She was used to thinking of him as master, mentor, teacher, leader; now she realized he might also be a friend. And though Sophia had originally proposed this meeting to discuss the plans of her new operation, as they circled the Radcliffe Camera, or tugged the bronze nose on the door of Brasenose College, or gazed up at the murals in the Sheldonian, she found herself reluctant to spoil the moment by bringing it up.

"Tell me something," Sophia asked, when Melamed insisted they rest a while on Magdalen Bridge. "When you were at university, what did you read? What were you going to be?"

"A surgeon. There are so few qualified doctors in our country. We need so many more."

"Why didn't you?"

"This, mainly." Melamed pointed to his blind eye. "You can't do surgery with one eye—no proper depth perception. You could be cutting too much and not even realize it. Of course, my good eye learned to compensate over time, but by then I'd been expelled from university. Anyway, I was too involved in the movement to have time for studies."

"Any regrets?"

"Plenty." He leaned over the parapet, watching the river wind lazily into the distance. "I wanted a simple life, to settle down with my wife, a small practice, a large family. You know, our hospitals and clinics don't have all the fancy equipment they have here in the West, especially not in those days. But so many patients die every year just because they can't get the most basic treatment. A qualified doctor can perform miracles by just being there." He laughed bitterly. "Sometimes I think I could've done a lot more good for our country if I'd completed my studies instead of doing all this."

"What was she like, your wife?"

"She was my fiancée. She was killed before we were married."

"I'm sorry."

Melamed shrugged. "I almost forget what she was like. I remember her young—your age, or thereabouts—full of passion and indignation that independence of our country from the colonial power had brought oppression to our own people. She was so beautiful . . . she had lovely, long black hair, and she had this way of tossing her head to clear it from her face.

"She was a literature student, very much into . . . what were they called— that French school that was so popular in the sixties?"

"Existentialists?"

"That's it. She was always going on about Jean-Paul Sartre and Simone de Someone . . . ," Melamed muttered, lost in recollection.

"She sounds . . . well, very different from you."

"She was. Maybe that's what attracted us to each other." He paused, his voice weary, as if the pain of his memories had whittled away his will to live.

Listening to Melamed, it struck Sophia that he was as much a victim as she. It made her feel almost ashamed of her own anger and pain at losing her father—a man she had barely known, and had admired only vicariously or in the hazy smudges of her childhood memories. She was not the only one to have lost a loved one—there were others, hundreds, probably thousands, whose fathers, mothers, brothers, sisters, sons, daughters, wives, husbands, lovers had disappeared into the dark prisons of the regime. For many, there was not even the consolation of finding the body—only years of uncertainty, denial, and finally acceptance. Melamed was as much a victim as any of them, but he was a victim who had not resigned himself to his fate, but had instead grasped and shaped his own destiny, a victim who refused to be victimized.

"I betrayed her, you know," Melamed was saying. "The day they blinded my eye, they wanted me to implicate the others. And in the end, I did. If they'd threatened to kill me, I wouldn't have talked. I could accept death, but not being left blind and useless. So I gave them the names they wanted. The bastards hunted them down until they were all dead, my fiancée included."

"How come you escaped?"

"I told you—your father managed to intervene with a judge and get me released. They could've trumped up some accident for me too, of course, but I guess I was more useful as an example to others. The police were worried the movement would spread on campus. People forget the dead very quickly, but see someone going around with his eye gouged out, and you'll think twice about joining any dissident groups. Besides," he added, his jaw line tightening, "those swine know perfectly well that people are like dumb animals—they respond to brute force and unbridled violence. It's what the world expects, what it respects. What was it your beloved George Orwell wrote in *Nineteen Eighty-Four*? 'If you want a picture of the future, imagine a boot stamping on a human face—forever.'"

"No!" Sophia cried. "That's horrid. That's absolutely horrid. And even if our enemies are like that, it's no justification for us to be the bloody same."

"Oh, so that's what this is all about." Melamed's face was taut, his knuckles clenched. Sophia fell silent. She had not intended to confront him about the morality of their acts, not now, at least. Perhaps later she would have no choice, but she'd wanted to lay the groundwork and build up to the idea of her new operation first.

"Listen to me." Melamed grabbed her roughly by the shoulders. "When an oil well bursts into flames, do you know how they put it out?"

Sophia looked at him blankly. "With a fire hose?"

"A fire hose," Melamed snorted. "There's millions of gallons of oil spewing out. It's a burning, raging fire—a thousand degrees hot. The hose would melt before you even got it near the fire. "No," he went on, "they put it out by exploding a bomb just over the well head, to starve the fire of oxygen. Sometimes that's the only way: fighting fire with fire."

"Is that the way the others feel?"

Melamed let go of her. "Others?"

"The others in the cadre."

"What have they got to do with anything?"

"You never tell me about them," she said, like a petulant child. "Who they are. What they do. What they think."

"It's for your own security that I don't tell you."

"But I know nothing about them. Absolutely nothing. Why don't you trust me even that much?"

"Of course I trust you."

"Well then, how many are there, for a start?"

"The whole movement? Hundreds, perhaps thousands. In our cell? Thirty, give or take."

"Men?"

"Mostly."

"Women?"

"Some." He smiled. "We're an equal-opportunity employer."

"How old?"

Melamed shrugged. "Some are even younger than you, others have been in the struggle longer than me."

"And they think it's okay to bomb airliners and blow up innocent women and children? It's justified as long as the Cause is advanced?"

"No," Melamed said gently. "No, they don't think it's okay, any more than you or I do. But I told you, violence is what gets the world's attention, it's what the world understands, what it respects. The others realize that, no matter how much they may dislike it."

"In other words, they're more committed to the Cause than I am."

"Not at all," Melamed replied. "But you must understand, it is easier for them. There are no ambiguities for them, no shades of gray—just black and white, good and evil, right and wrong. They've grown up under terror and torture. It's a part of their lives, a part of who they are, and what they have become. You're different. You haven't lived in our country, not since you were too small to remember. You grew up in places like . . . well, like this," Melamed swept his arm across the Oxford vista.

"And that's why I don't have the right to do something for my people? Because I didn't grow up there, because I haven't suffered, I don't belong?"

"Of course you belong."

"Oh, really. Well I bet you let the other members of the cell meet each other."

"Not always. It all depends," he replied quickly, and Sophia knew he was lying. "Besides," he added smiling again, "You *have* done something for your homeland—plenty, in fact."

"Oh, you don't understand." She felt deflated, her good mood punctured. Hearing Melamed talk about the others in the cell—picturing them huddled around a midnight lamp, discussing, debating, arguing, conspiring—made her feel very much an outsider, an outcast, like she used to be at boarding school. Turning away abruptly, she resumed walking across the bridge.

They lunched late, at a pub, sitting outside on a terrace that overlooked Christ Church Meadows. The publican, a jovial fellow with a scraggy moustache and a mousy wife, told them they could sit there as long as they liked. They spoke of everything, of Sophia's childhood and Melamed's mother, of art and literature, of politics and prose, of everything except the Cause. They were quite alone; the lunching crowd had fled long ago and the drinking crowd had yet to arrive. As the sun slipped behind some clouds, Sophia shivered inside her cardigan.

Melamed glanced at his watch. "I suppose I should get going at some point."

With a start, Sophia realized she hadn't even broached the subject of her operation. Cappuccinos arrived. Melamed dropped in three lumps of brown sugar and watched them sink into the foam.

As if continuing their earlier conversation, Sophia said casually, "I want to do another operation."

"No." Melamed didn't even bother to look up.

"Why not? You haven't even heard about it yet."

"I knew this is what you wanted to talk about. And the answer is 'no.' You've done your duty; you owe your country nothing more."

"I blew up a couple hundred suitcases. What bloody good did that do?"

"Nonetheless, you tried. That's a lot more than most people can say."

"Well, it's not enough."

Melamed shrugged and returned to sipping his coffee.

"You didn't answer my question. Why not? You think I can't pull it off? Is that it? You haven't even heard my plan yet."

"I don't doubt your abilities—I'm the one who chose you, remember? But you have your whole life ahead of you. I don't want you ending up like me. You'll be killed, or you'll get caught, and it's even worse if you aren't. Ours is a dirty, dreadful business. You think blowing up an airplane is the worst thing imaginable, but you have no idea. You haven't seen the ugly side of our work: the lies, the informants, the betrayals, the power plays. I've insulated you from all that.

"No," he repeated, softly, as if speaking to himself, "it was wrong of me to involve you in the first place. You said it yourself—you don't believe our ends justify our means."

"Ah," Sophia smiled, "now that's where my plan comes in. I've come up with a completely new operation that'll get us plenty of publicity for the Cause, without anyone getting hurt—no innocent victims, I mean."

"That's not the way it works," Melamed sighed. "Even the best planned operations go wrong, they have unintended consequences, and someone ends up getting hurt. This is war, and in war there are always casualties. Remember that."

She did remember. Before the airline bombing they'd been through the same routine a dozen times. Melamed would say that innocent people die all the time, they might as well die for a reason. Then he would say that there can be no innocence while there is injustice, and finally he would conclude that killing for a cause was its own justification.

"You must realize," Melamed was saying, "that an operation, once it begins, can't be stopped, can't be controlled. There's no turning back, no pulling out. You've got to be willing to see it through to the end, no matter what. You might not plan on violence, but if there's a threat the operation might be compromised, you must do whatever it takes to salvage it."

Sophia nodded.

"And you're sure you could do that?" he persisted.

Sophia closed her eyes, submitting to the familiar catechism. "Yes."

"Are you prepared to sacrifice your life?"

"Yes."

"To commit acts of sabotage and destruction?"

"Yes."

"To tell lies and falsehoods?"

"Yes."

"To prostitute your body?"

"Yes."

"To commit murder?"

"If there was absolutely no other way . . ."

"Yes or no?"

"Yes."

"To betray your friends, your comrades, your lovers?"

"Yes."

"To kill me?"

She opened her eyes in surprise. "Why would I want to kill you?"

"It's not a matter of wanting. If you had to. If I'd been captured and might betray your operation, and you had a split second to make the decision, would you be able to do it?"

"No."

Melamed nodded. "It's good you should tell me. All right, next question: why?"

"Why what?"

"Why do you want to do this? The operation."

"To teach Western governments," Sophia said, leaning forward earnestly, "that they can't go around pontificating about human rights and slapping embargoes and sanctions on regimes they don't like, but then turn a blind eye when there are abuses in countries where they happen to have their own strategic and economic interests. They're going to learn that it'll cost them one hell of a lot more to ignore the plight of our people—"

"No, no," Melamed interrupted impatiently. "I mean why do *you* want to do this? What's *your* motivation? What's in it for *you*?"

"What do you mean? I want to help our people."

"Rubbish."

Sophia was about to make some angry retort, when Melamed continued, "You want to do this because you're trying to make up for the failure in December. Or because of this absurd guilt of yours about not growing up in our country. Or because you still want revenge against the regime for robbing you of your father and your childhood. It's one of these, and I want to know which one."

Sophia glared at him. She banged her cup on the table, almost breaking off the handle. "Who the hell do you think you are, trying to analyze me with your pop psychology? *Why* I want to help our people is no one's goddamn business but my own. At least," she added viciously, "At least, *I'm* not trying to exorcise my own guilt for betraying my fiancée." Even as she spoke the words, she regretted saying them.

But Melamed seemed unperturbed. "All right," he nodded slowly. "Let's hear your plan."

CHAPTER SIX

IN THE DISTANCE, A CLOCK STRUCK SEVEN. Panic-stricken, Celine yanked open the oven door, burning herself in the process. "Damn!" She seized a fork off the counter and stabbed the chicken in the breast, as if in retribution for the stinging burn on the back of her hand. The cookbook said an hour to an hour and a half, but the sickly pink fluid oozing out of the breast could only mean it was nowhere near done. *I never asked him for the blasted ice cream,* Celine told herself as she slammed shut the oven door.

Harry, who must have pumped her secretary for information, had air-couriered a quart of Celine's favorite ice cream to Jakarta on her birthday. That was in late January, when the Indonesian banks were crashing like dominoes and the authorities seemed incapable of making any decisions, Washington was demanding results, and Celine, who had already spent Christmas away from family and friends, was facing the prospect of spending her birthday alone as well.

Upon hearing about the ice cream, Karin had immediately predicted a great romantic liaison. Celine told her not to be damned silly. She'd only met Harry once and hadn't particularly liked him, and besides, on principle she never dated men at the office. In the end, ignoring Karin's extravagantly absurd suggestions—such as inviting Harry to join her for a weekend in

Bali—she had sent him a staid thank-you note, three weeks late and one line long. Yet she could not quite get him out of her mind either. At odd moments she would remember with a smile that long December night, when Harry had come up with the idea of announcing the support package for Indonesia and Celine had persuaded the MD, against all odds and his every instinct, to lower the interest rates. The triumph of the occasion had formed, if not a bond, then at least a link between them—a link that, judging by the care and cost of shipping the ice cream, Harry might want to foster further.

Full of ambivalence, Celine had called him when she returned to Washington in mid-March, uncertain whether to be relieved or disappointed when she learned that Harry was away doing some research at Princeton University and not expected back until the fall. Then yesterday, quite out of the blue, he had phoned to say he was in town for a couple of days; Celine had invited him over to dinner.

She was just sneaking a peek at the chicken, wondering whether to admit defeat and call for take-out food, when the sing-song chime of the doorbell came floating through the house.

Harry was standing in the doorway, dressed casually in loafers and khaki slacks, with a crisp white shirt that wasn't quite loose enough to disguise the sculpted relief of his muscles. His hair was shorter than she remembered, and it gave him a more boyish, disarming look. Celine's eyes swept over his face, absorbing every feature—the faint laughter lines around his bright blue eyes, the symmetric spring of his nostrils, the fine scroll-work of his upper lip, the golden-tan sunburn of his cheeks that faded below the base of his throat and melted away under his open shirt-neck.

"I *have* got the right time, haven't I?"

"Yes, yes. Of course," Celine blushed. "Come on in."

"How've you been?" they both asked at once.

"You go first," Harry laughed. "Rumor has it, you single-handedly saved Indonesia."

"I'm not sure Indonesia's been saved—and I certainly didn't do it single-handedly," Celine replied. They fell into easy conversation; Celine regaling him with stories from her mission—the usual IMFO chit-chat of missions and memos and minutes, and what the central bank governor said to the deputy prime minister—while Harry told her about the research he was doing at Princeton, developing a new exchange rate forecasting model known as a neural net.

"What's it like there?"

"Princeton? Dull as dishwater. Luckily, it's only an hour away from New York, so I usually go to the city on the weekends to keep my social life from going totally rusty."

"Oh." Celine felt oddly deflated. The funny thing about being on mission is that you always assume that time back home has somehow come to a standstill. But it occurred to her that almost four months had passed since that December night and that while she had been away, Harry's life had carried on.

"What can I get you to drink?" she asked. "Glass of Chardonnay, maybe?"

When she returned from the kitchen, Harry was studying the art work on her walls.

"Now then," he said. "Having examined the evidence carefully, I'm ready to pronounce upon your IMFO career."

"Shoot."

"Well, you clearly worked on some former Soviet Union country." Harry pointed to a rather putrid orange-and-silver post-industrialist, neo-Socialist painting that Celine had bought because the authorities had taken the mission to visit an art gallery, and that was the least offensive piece she could find.

"Moldova, actually," she said.

"The icons look more Ukrainian than Russian, but I guess you could've gotten them anywhere in Eastern Europe."

"Hungary."

"Now this," he said, picking up a small gold ornament, "looks pre-Colombian, whereas the face masks could be from Nigeria or perhaps sub-Saharan African . . ."

Piece by piece, item by item, Harry cataloged her life. It's true, she thought, one always returned with some sort of token, be it an icon, a painting, a statue, a rug—something large or something small—by which to remember the late nights and early mornings, the enduring camaraderie and the eternal chaos of a mission. *Something to show the grandchildren*, they would say, descending upon the local merchants on the final day of the mission with the determination and desperation of last-minute Christmas shoppers.

"So," he went on, his eyes sweeping around the room, "have I missed anywhere?"

"Indonesia," she muttered.

=====

"Do you like it at IMFO?"

The question took Celine by surprise, and she took refuge in her wine. They were well into their second bottle by now, and the conversation, which had roamed uproariously over everything from Harry's childhood antics to Celine's mission anecdotes, was growing more serious and more philosophical by degrees.

"Yes," she replied at last. In halting, hesitant sentences she sought to explain how much the work meant to her, how it fulfilled her need for a sense of purpose and achievement.

Harry had a way of listening as she spoke—his head cocked to one side, his eyes following her every movement, as though intent on not missing a single syllable—that made her feel strangely wanted, and left her at once exhilarated and unnerved.

"I know I must sound like one of those silly propaganda pamphlets in the IMFO visitors center, but I really believe the only way to make a real dent in poverty is by getting countries to follow sound macroeconomic policies, and there we do make a difference—or at least, we can."

"You're right," Harry grinned. "You do sound like an IMFO pamphlet."

"Well, what about you?" Celine countered. "Why did you come to IMFO?"

"Oh, I'm different. I'm not out to save the world. I'd rather do my research quietly and leave the world alone. When you think about it, economics is about where medicine was in the Middle Ages, only our prescriptions are even more painful. Country's in crisis? Well then, tighten policies, raise interest rates, slash budgets, and while we're at it, bring out the leeches and bleed the patient as well."

Celine laughed. "I hardly think it's that bad. Besides, if we don't, who will? The government? It's the incompetent ministers and corrupt politicians who got the country in a mess in the first place. We may not always have the right answers, but at least we have the country's best interests at heart."

Yet even as she said it, Celine wondered if that was really true. Her mission chief, Adanpur, though he hadn't been motivated by the same crude corruption as the local politicians, was surely just as self-interested, pushing policies because he thought they'd make him look good back in Washington. And why hadn't she spoken up? Because she'd been blinded by love, or because she hadn't wanted to risk her cosy relationship with him by asking awkward questions?

"I dare say," Harry said dryly. "But the road to hell is often paved with good intentions. Our policies have real repercussions for real people—workers get thrown out of work, businesses go bankrupt, families lose their homes. So unless we know exactly what we're doing, we've no damn right to interfere."

His vehemence surprised her. It was almost as though Harry was afraid, afraid that someone, somewhere, might take his tidy theoretical models and fancy econometric estimates, and misuse them, doing harm instead of good. Yet surely the price of being a policymaker was the risk of making mistakes and having to live with the consequences. And it seemed to Celine that Harry's formula of confining oneself to pure research and refusing to take the tough decisions was too pat, too simple, too easy. Fundamentally, too cowardly.

Celine wished she hadn't had so much to drink, for she felt frustratingly inarticulate, and she wanted Harry to understand the doubts and demons she had endured. She wished she could magically transport him through time and space, back to her first Indonesia mission, and confront him with having to decide between trusting blindly in the judgment of her mission chief or going behind his back and warning Washington that they were headed for disaster. She was almost tempted to tell him the story of Adanpur, but she'd never told anyone before, and to tell Harry now would be giving away too much of herself too quickly—like going to bed on a first date.

"But don't you see, we can't just shirk our responsibility like that. We haven't that luxury. If we don't, others will end up making the policy choices—worse ones."

"As long as it's not me who's doing it," Harry replied, with a Sphinx-like aloofness that suddenly annoyed her.

"Well, you and Kiyotaki seemed pretty bloody cocksure when you were arguing for higher interest rates in Indonesia last December," she retorted.

"I did nothing of the sort," Harry said sharply. "I laid out the options, pointed out the risks, and summarized what had happened in other countries. I quite specifically did not argue in favor of raising rates."

"But we had to make a decision! Yes or no! Up or down! We couldn't duck the issue. And if you thought raising rates was a bad idea, why didn't you bloody well say so?"

"Because I didn't *know* it was wrong. After all, it's standard procedure for warding off a speculative attack. So, frankly, I don't see how my saying the opposite, with absolutely no evidence backing it up, would have helped in the slightest."

"Well, for one thing, if you hadn't been such a bloody coward, I wouldn't have felt quite so alone arguing with Kiyotaki."

An extraordinary silence fell between them. It went on and on, without respite. In the awful stillness of the room, Celine could hear the faint hissing of candles and the mournful barking of a dog outside. She wished they hadn't started talking about IMFO and Indonesia. She wished she could be free of it all, if only for a single day. The cosy atmosphere, so full of promise, had evaporated, and the sudden chill in the room was more than the April nightfall.

At last, Harry gave a shrug, a barely perceptible movement of his shoulders, and forced a smile. "Well, thanks for such a lovely dinner."

"Must you leave so soon?"

"I think I'd better."

"Look, I'm sorry—"

Harry cut her off hastily. "That's quite all right. But I really do need to get going—I'm driving up to New York early tomorrow morning."

Celine walked him out, racking her brain for something to say, and coming up only with banalities. "When are you back in DC?"

"Not until the fall. I'm off to Europe for the summer, then I wrap up in Princeton in September. Goodbye, and thanks again for dinner. I'll see you in September." He waved cheerfully and disappeared from view.

Closing the door behind him, Celine felt rather lonely, and strangely old.

CHAPTER SEVEN

S OPHIA DASHED FROM SHOP TO SHOP, trying in vain to dodge the fleeting rain. She made it at last to the lobby of the Hotel Intercontinental Geneva, where Melamed was pacing anxiously. After weeks of messages, back and forth, in the cumbersome code of innocuous phrases and inane chatter, he had finally secured a meeting with Huron, a rich exile from the old country and a potential sponsor of their new operation.

They rode the elevator to the penthouse suite, where the door was opened by Mathewsen, Huron's second-in-command. Sophia sauntered over to the window, peering out while they waited for Huron. On one side was the Palais des Nations, on the other the fleshy plume of the Jet d'Eau. Down below, the good Genevois scurried to and fro, lines of traffic gliding silently up and down the streets. Even the tourists marched toward the Palais entrance with ant-like discipline. Watching them, it seemed to Sophia that Geneva was not a real city at all; it was somehow too ordered, too tidy, too arranged, like some elaborate toy village in a giant's playroom.

Huron shuffled in a few minutes later. He was not at all what Sophia had expected. He was a small sunken man with a white stubble sprinkled on his chin and dressed rather shabbily in old corduroys and a sweater, flopping about in the free slippers supplied by the hotel. It was hard to imagine him being worth billions, and the contrast with Mathewsen—in his expensive business suit and his cream, monogrammed shirt with French cuffs—was strikingly incongruous.

Huron didn't bother with introductions. He greeted Melamed with a quick hug, formal but not without affection. Sophia, he flatly ignored. He sat down with an old man's fussiness in the vast leather sofa, then, with an imperious wave, bade Melamed begin.

"Brothers," Melamed started, then faltered. Sophia knew how he detested that term. It rang hollow, like the waitress's greeting at an American restaurant. He stopped pacing and turned to face his audience. "For twenty years we fought, and we have failed." And then he was off on the familiar refrain. Sophia had heard it all before—in different forms perhaps, but the substance was much the same—during student meetings at the London School of Economics. She had never quite realized, though, how compelling a speaker he was. He used his hands and arms to good effect, pulling the audience together and leading them on. Huron sat open-mouthed, drinking it all in. Of course he's good, thought Sophia. He captivated me, didn't he? Melamed had a way of making everything sound so reasonable—be it planning a protest or planting a bomb, and it crossed her mind that his insistence that she'd done enough might be nothing more than a device for heaping guilt on her for the December bombing—and for renewing her commitment to the Cause.

Sophia closed her eyes and leaned back as Melamed wove his argument. He had to tread with care. Huron, she knew, had once been part of the clique. As Minister of Industry and Mining, he had lined his pockets well when the mining concessions were first being given, until his falling out with the president. But by then he had amassed an ample fortune, carefully spirited out of the country, to comfort him in his exile. Nowadays he professed more democratic values and contributed frequently to the Cause. Still, it troubled Sophia to use his money. Any association with the regime, however tenuous, she felt, sullied the operation from the start. In his masterful way, Melamed had pointed out to her the irony of using Huron's money to help topple the regime, but Sophia remained uneasy. She knew that Melamed too, was suspicious of Huron's motives. Perhaps he was relying on Huron's hatred of the president to win his support.

Listening to Melamed catalog the regime's crimes against the people—arrests, detentions, disappearances—Sophia was struck by the sharpness of the contrast between the structured, ordered life in Geneva and the chaotic struggle for existence back in her homeland.

During the second week of her visit there, Sophia had passed by a primary school, a circle of dusty, shabby shacks, without even realizing the momentous event taking place. That morning, in flagrant defiance of the law, the teachers had turned up in gaily colored kaftans, the traditional garb of her people.

Funny that a yard or two of cloth could be so threatening to a regime replete with guns, bullets, and Black Marias. But within minutes, the security forces descended upon them. Anywhere else in the world, the children would have cheered at the prospect of missing a day or a week of school. But not here. Here, they huddled into a scared circle, eyes filled with fear and bewilderment.

The police were rushing the teachers to the wail of flying rubber bullets and the sickening crunch of swinging batons. Sophia watched as the teachers were dragged away, blood pouring off their faces, hurled like so many sacks of potatoes into the waiting police vans. When anxious mothers dashed into the melee, trying to retrieve their children, the police started arresting them too, bundling everyone indiscriminately into the Black Marias. Sophia's foreign passport was all that saved her from being rounded up with the rest.

Suddenly, Sophia realized that Mathewsen was watching not Melamed but her. She felt her face flush, and it was more than the vulnerability any woman might feel when a man stares. He had disconcertingly clear eyes that seemed to penetrate her thoughts, as though he knew that she had been relieved, not dismayed, when the bomb failed to kill the passengers. The slightest hint of a sneer creased his lips. Sophia pointedly returned her gaze to Melamed, as if rebuking Mathewsen for his wandering attention.

Melamed was telling them about the December attempt, extolling Sophia's skill in sneaking a bomb onto a major airliner despite all the security.

"But the attempt failed." Mathewsen pointed at Sophia. "She fucked up."

"That had nothing to do with her. It was just bad luck. It failed because of a freak IRA bomb scare," Melamed said hotly. "There wasn't even a real bomb at Heathrow—it was just a fake. Anyway," he continued, regaining his stride, "these high-profile acts—airlines, buildings, cruise ships—don't buy us much. They're bubbles that puff up with publicity and burst just as fast. Actions back home bring terrible reprisals and, as for international operations, they give the president the perfect excuse to tighten his grip further in the name of enhancing security. Atrocities can cost us as much in sympathy as we gain in awareness. No, if we are to make any real headway we must convince Western governments of our seriousness, that it will cost them more to ignore our cause than to support it. So tell me," he said, looking around the room with a professorial air, which indeed he might have been, in his gray flannel trousers and tweed sports jacket, "what drives the Western world? What blood flows through its veins?"

"Oh, God." Mathewsen rolled his eyes. "don't tell me you're going to try to disrupt the world oil supplies. Don't you get it? There's a dozen different sources, from Arabia to Venezuela. Even the Russians are getting their act together. You'll never disrupt oil supplies effectively. God knows how many times it has been tried before."

"Close, but no cigar," Melamed said, inordinately proud of his Americanisms. "Come now, gentlemen. What's the most important thing in the world?"

Bewildered silence. Huron sat stiffly, lips pursed, as though he didn't care for this pedagogical approach. Mathewsen was fiddling with his gold watchband, avoiding Melamed's eye. Outside, Sophia heard an ambulance braying, so different from the shrill piercing klaxon that fills the air in Washington. It seemed to be a cue.

"Money." The others turned to her in surprise, as though they had forgotten her presence.

"You mean to disrupt the flow of world money?" Mathewsen snorted.

"Precisely," Sophia replied agreeably. She stood up and walked to the window. Night had fallen and, bathed in the pale moonlight, the Palais des Nations building looked serene and ethereal. A monument to futility, she thought, as are we all. She licked her lower lip, a mite nervous after all.

Still gazing out the window, she said, "The global foreign exchange market handles more than three trillion dollars," she paused for effect, "a day."

She drew the drapes and turned to face them. "It's the world's largest and most important market. It never closes—it just follows the sun: Tokyo, London, New York . . ." She reeled off facts and figures. Huron played with the roll of flesh under his chin pensively as she spoke. But to her annoyance, Mathewsen merely nodded, plastic boredom molded on his face.

"So?" he spat out.

Unflustered, Sophia paused before answering. She and Melamed had debated how much to tell them. There was no commitment yet; better not to give too much away. Enough to entice, to lure, to snare, but nothing more. Like all good meals, it should leave them hungry for more.

"So the day the foreign exchange markets collapse, the whole world will take notice. Democracy, freedom, human rights—they're nothing but words when there's money to be made. And there's plenty in our country. The only problem is, it's the foreign multinationals and our illustrious president-for-life who are making it. They're ravishing our land and raking in the millions. Every year, whole villages are 'relocated' at whim, so the mining multinationals can make yet more money, and when the lode is finished the peasants are moved back to a scarred landscape pitted with dumps and despair. These corporations would never dare behave like that in their own countries—the environmental lobby wouldn't let them get away with it. But Western governments don't care when it happens in our country. All they care about is making sure that their precious supplies of metals and minerals aren't cut off—"

"Yes, yes. We know all that," Mathewsen interrupted. "But what's that got to do with the foreign exchange markets?"

"What nonsense this is," Huron said. "I thought you had a serious proposal—a plan to blow up the president, or at least his cabinet. You are growing old, my friend," he added, patting Melamed on the knee in a way that made him squirm. "You used to believe in action, not this cowardly talk of money and markets."

"It's a damned sight less cowardly than blowing up a plane load of women and children," Sophia retorted. "And probably a lot more effective."

"Are you calling me—" began Huron.

"Of course she isn't." Melamed threw Sophia a warning glance. "It's the Western multinationals that keep our beloved president in power. Without the hundreds of millions of royalty payments each year, he would never be able to buy the generals their latest toys. And to get at these multinationals, we must teach Western countries that if they ignore the plight of our people and continue to engage in trade and investments with our current regime, it will cost them dearly."

Mollified, Huron signaled Sophia to continue.

"You ask what's the foreign exchange market got to do with our country? Well, that's precisely what Western governments are about to find out. They're going to learn just how much their indifference can cost them. The world's financial system is a pyramid of credit, and the foreign exchange market its linchpin. Knock it out, and the whole structure comes crashing down. There'll be utter chaos: stock markets plunging, financial crashes, wholesale bankruptcies.

"Remember when the Dow lost a thousand points in a single day? Even the smug, middle-class Americans cared when they saw their precious pension plans and 401(k)s threatened. Do you remember the queues of panicked depositors trying to get their money out during the sub-prime crisis? When we attack, it's going to be worse. A lot worse. Major banks and corporations are going to lose hundreds of billions of dollars. And then, I promise you, Western governments will stop ignoring the plight of our people."

She paused to glance at her audience, pleased to see them rigidly upright. The ticktock of the clock had suddenly become very loud. Even Mathewsen had pulled himself momentarily out of his insolent slouch.

Huron glanced briefly at Mathewsen and asked, "But how will you do all this? You're just one person. A woman."

"With your help," Sophia replied, planting herself on the sofa next to Huron. "What I'm going to do is establish a hedge fund. And being offshore, it'll be virtually unregulated. With that hedge fund, we'll build up pressures in the foreign exchange markets in a matter of a few weeks." She leaned closer to Huron, so close she could smell the garlic on his breath.

"Then, when the time is ripe, we'll strike." Her elegant fingers darted forward, like a cobra striking for the kill.

Huron recoiled.

"We'll launch speculative attacks against all of the world's major currencies simultaneously," she explained, "until there's such pandemonium the market won't know which way to turn. At the same time, we'll create a little . . ." she paused, smiling tautly, then went on, "a little diversion. Just to distract the central banks of the major countries and make sure they can't get their act together and bring the situation under control." Sophia resumed her position by the window. "With the financial markets in rout, we'll get as much publicity as we could possibly want. That's when we'll announce to the world that we will tolerate the oppression of our people no longer. That if Western governments do not want to be taught a lesson like this again, they'd better stop supporting the regime and make sure there are reforms—real reforms—back home."

Mathewsen clapped, a slow sarcastic rhythm. "Very nice, my dear. But you haven't answered my question. How exactly do you intend to build up these pressures in the foreign exchange market? You talk so glibly about speculative attacks. You're only going to have a few hundred million dollars to play with. That's if . . ." he paused pregnantly, "*if* we decide to support you. It's peanuts in the global foreign exchange markets—you said so yourself."

"It's all I need," Sophia replied smoothly. "Pension funds and insurance companies may have the big bucks, but it's aggressive hedge fund managers who actually drive the market. Fund managers watch each other obsessively, trying to pick a winner. And because of that, once you have a couple of successes under your belt, you can generate huge pressures in the market."

She shifted her attention back to Huron. "Take your typical pension fund; it might be sitting on ten billion dollars of assets. If the exchange rate moves by so much as 1 percent, which can happen in seconds, the fund has lost one hundred million dollars just like that." She snapped her fingers.

"Obviously, the slightest inkling of a speculative attack, and they're going to dump the currency right away. And once the market starts dumping, the pressures on the currency become self-fulfilling."

"Brilliant," Mathewsen said. "But you're only going to get the market to jump on your bandwagon if you can show some pretty fucking spectacular successes first. Have you any idea what that would take? For starters, you'd have to be able to predict exchange rate movements to within a hair's breadth—and one hell of a lot better than anyone ever has before. And for that you'll need to know exactly what the central banks are going to do. Sometimes they intervene heavily and resist market pressures, sometimes they let the exchange rate depreciate. It's damn near impossible to find out exactly how much intervention they are doing, let alone predict it. That stuff's kept pretty bloody secret. In case you didn't realize, there's dozens of ways a central bank can intervene—different currencies, different markets, spot transactions, forward sales, non-deliverable forwards, swaps, puts, God knows what else—and every day they invent new ways of hiding their interventions. So maybe you could tell us," he concluded belligerently, "how exactly you intend to accomplish all this?"

Sophia reached into the minibar and took out a can of Coke, opening it with a startling pop. She took a few gulps then set it on the coffee table. Palms on her hips, she looked around the room and graced them with her most charming smile. "That will be the hard part."

CHAPTER EIGHT

"**Y**OU'RE MAKING A BIG MISTAKE. You realize that, don't you?" said Karin Wulf, a petite blonde, a good inch and a half shorter than Celine, with bold aquiline features and the air of a woman who knows what she wants. It was Friday, and with half the staff anticipating the weekend, they had no difficulty finding a quiet corner of the IMFO cafeteria where they could have a good old-fashioned girls' gossip.

Celine settled into her seat. "I don't see what the big deal is. All I did was send up my proposal for the Special Intervention Facility. What's wrong with that? If I say so myself, the SIF's a pretty damn good idea—it would've been a big help last December."

"Not that, silly. I'm talking about Harry."

Not content to just mastermind her own love life, Karin had taken it upon herself of late to manage Celine's as well. Ever since the ice cream incident, she had been determined to pair Celine off with Harry. Of course, she'd tried to worm out of Celine every last detail of their dinner together. The latest assault was prompted by Harry's having invited Celine to come up to New York for Labor Day weekend. Celine had declined.

"He's not *that* great." Celine grasped a salmon roll precariously between her chopsticks and dropped it into the soy sauce. Karin dipped hers delicately, all the while cataloging Harry's virtues. "He's good-looking, superintelligent, and head-over-heels in love with you. What more do you want? I think you're making a big mistake."

"It's not so simple." When Celine had returned from her first Indonesia mission, still traumatized by the events and her own complicity in Adanpur's cover-up, she'd instituted her golden rule to never date anyone at work again. Afterward, he'd left IMFO—technically, he was on leave, parked at some friendly central bank—and by rigidly avoiding any possibility of a romantic involvement, her resolve had never been put to the test.

But of late, Celine had found herself thinking all too often about Harry, arguing with herself that, even though they worked together, it didn't count— he was about the same age and position as herself—and surely there was no harm if they were to date. Gradually it dawned on her that her much-revered rule was less a shield to protect her from the likes of Adanpur than a shell into which she might scurry at the approach of any serious relationship. The truth was, she wasn't ready. Though the Indonesia scars were scabbing over at last, she had a sense that there was something she must do, some act she must accomplish, before the past could be erased and she could be redeemed. It was as though the confluence of events that had brought her into that mess was too absurd to be an accident: there had to have been some purpose to it all.

"You're not still worrying about dating someone at work, are you? That's ridiculous. Men do it all the time, especially with their secretaries."

As if on cue, a high-pitched laugh emanated from a couple a few tables away. Celine knew the man by sight, a mission chief in the Southern Hemisphere Department. The girl was much younger, and she might have been his secretary, but wasn't dressed well enough. Most likely a junior economist in his division. At any American corporation, Celine supposed, it might be considered harassment—probably grounds for a lawsuit. But at IMFO, such matters were handled along more gentlemanly lines, which meant keeping one's mouth shut—especially if the man was senior and the woman junior.

Whatever the man was saying, it was clearly intended to impress. The girl was lapping it up eagerly, nodding her head like a marionette with a broken neck, every so often saying, "I *do* so agree . . ." or breaking into her silly high-pitched giggle. Celine cringed. Had she been this impressionable, this credulous, this naïve with Adanpur, she wondered.

Karin finished eating, putting her chopsticks down with a clatter. Celine realized her mind had been wandering and Karin was regarding her reproachfully.

"Can I ask you something?"

Celine nodded slowly. She had divined at once what Karin was going to ask. Celine had never told anyone about her affair with Adanpur, and no one knew what she had seen during the riots. All Karin knew was that Celine had returned from Indonesia traumatized by the failure of the program and the collapse of the country.

"Hullo, girls!" It was Pettigrew.

Celine and Karin ducked down instantly, but it was already too late. Pettigrew had plonked himself down beside Celine, closer than she would have liked. He was an economist in the Research Department, who'd been in the same YEP class as Karin and Celine. Secretly, they thought he was still a virgin.

Pettigrew at once launched into a long, convoluted story about some triumph of his at a recent conference. Karin was almost physically willing him away with her eyes, but Pettigrew continued oblivious, pausing only to shovel his food in great hungry gulps.

"So, what have you two been up to?" he asked, turning to Celine when his story was finished at last. "Aren't you just back from mission?"

"Brazil."

"So I hear." Pettigrew gave a knowing smile and nodded at Karin. "You know, we're pretty privileged to be lunching with Ms. Celine O'Rourke. These days, she hobnobs with the likes of the managing director, not hoi polloi like us."

"What on Earth are you talking about?" Karin asked.

"She just sent a ten-page memo directly to His Eminence, the managing director."

"Who told you that?"

"I have friends in low places. A source right in the MD's office."

"He gets dozens of papers every day, and this source tells you about one little memo?"

"Sure he gets dozens of memos, but from department directors, not from lowly economists. One of the secretaries in the MD's office used to work in my division. I saw her this morning. She mentioned that she'd seen this memo, and said she hadn't realized you'd risen so far that you sent memos directly to the MD."

"You never told me about this," Karin said, turning to Celine.

"There's nothing to tell," Celine retorted. "And I did tell you. The idea for a Special Intervention Facility. I sent the memo up—I told you."

"But I thought you meant to your own department director, not the managing director."

"My director is useless. He sat on it for two months, said it was an interesting idea, and that was the last I heard of it. I waited weeks and weeks, and finally got fed up and sent it to Kiyotaki directly."

"Are you nuts? You can't just send memos to the managing director. They have to go up the food chain. You know what a stickler for hierarchy department directors are—they'll be furious. This could be a career-ending move."

"So what?" Celine said with a bravado she didn't feel. "Anyway, technically, I didn't send it to the MD; I attached it as an annex to the back-to-office report for my mission to Brazil, which goes up to Kiyotaki automatically."

Karin shook her head. "I still think it was a pretty stupid thing to do, especially as you're up for promotion in November."

It was, in fact, just the sort of bureaucratic trick that Adanpur might have pulled and Celine would have despised. She had dithered for days, trying to decide whether it was all right to bypass her own director and send Kiyotaki her proposal directly. Curiously enough, it was the invitation from Harry that had decided her. She kept thinking how hypocritical it was to accuse Harry of cowardice when he'd failed to challenge Kiyotaki on lowering interest rates in Indonesia, and then slink away from sending a simple memo just because it violated IMFO etiquette and would likely raise the hackles of her superiors.

"So you're thinking of some kind of pre-approved facility that countries could use in an emergency?" Pettigrew asked.

"Not exactly," Celine replied. "Basically, I'm thinking of a line of credit, say up to one hundred billion dollars, that IMFO could use to intervene directly in the foreign exchange markets. Back in December, we only managed to restore confidence in Indonesia by outright lying to the markets that immediate financial support was on its way. And we only got away with it because of the blizzard—IMFO was officially closed, so we didn't have to contradict the Indonesians' press statements. Next time we won't be so lucky." And maybe, she thought to herself, if we'd had this facility during the East Asian crisis, the banks would have been bailed out in time, and a thousand Indonesians wouldn't be dead today.

"Speaking of Indonesia, you know who's coming back?" Pettigrew said. "Old Whatshisname."

"No, actually, we don't know who Old Whatshisname is," Karin replied caustically.

"Yes you do. The guy who was mission chief in Indonesia."

Suddenly Celine realized he was talking about *her* mission chief, Adanpur. When he had left IMFO, she had thought it was all over, that she would never have to see him again. Never once had she imagined that he might come back one day. Karin and Pettigrew were still talking about Adanpur, but Celine's ears were buzzing, her head throbbing furiously. Her soup had gone stone cold, but she kept spooning it stolidly into her mouth.

"Coming back as what?" Karin asked.

"Rumor has it, something pretty senior—department director, or even special advisor to Kiyotaki."

"Why on earth are they promoting him? Didn't he screw up in Indonesia."

"Oh, come on," Pettigrew said. "That's not fair. Everyone knows it was the Indonesians who screwed up—you can hardly blame the poor mission chief. Isn't that so, Celine?"

But Celine had left.

CHAPTER NINE

IT WAS A SLEEPY SATURDAY IN GENEVA. Drained by her performance the day before, Sophia slept until noon. After she dressed she tapped on Melamed's door.

"I didn't want to wake you," he said. "I'm popping out for a few minutes, but you're just in time. I ordered you some lunch."

It was *filets des perches aux pommes frites*—very simple and very good. Sophia, sitting down to eat, realized she was ravenous. The meeting with Huron had lasted almost twelve hours, and it was dawn before she'd gone to bed.

She had just finished lunch and was wheeling the trolley into the corridor when Melamed returned. He flung his jacket carelessly onto a chair, kicked off his shoes, and eased himself down on the sofa, as if any sudden movement might snap his stiffened joints. Sophia sat on the edge of the bed and watched him.

"My back's killing me," Melamed said, pressing his hand against his lower back. "The meeting yesterday was torture. I tell you, Sophia, I'm growing too old for this game. Action I don't mind, but this fund-raising is bloody murder."

Sophia laughed, her cheeks flushed with success.

"When's your flight?" he asked.

"I'll leave for the airport in an hour." Sophia was returning to Oxford for a couple of months, where she would begin preliminary preparations before shifting her base to Washington in October. That end of it was already arranged; Sophia had been offered a position in the Young Economists Program of the International Monetary and Financial Organization.

"Good." Melamed gave a sly smile. "In that case, we've just enough time. There's something in the fridge. Be a dear and fetch it, would you?"

Sophia walked over to the kitchenette in stockinged feet and swung open the door of the tiny fridge. A bottle of champagne took up most of it. As she reached for the bottle, Sophia suffered a momentary pang, remembering how bitter and angry she'd been the last time Melamed had offered her champagne. But then she noticed the label—Moet & Chandon—and smiled at his astuteness. He would not have forgotten her penchant for La Grande Dame, but nor would he want to remind her of the guilt she had felt when she had thought she'd killed all those passengers on the airliner.

They toasted.

"You were magnificent. And I," he said, whipping out a small oblong box like a conjurer, "have a small present for you."

It gave her a curious sense of déjà vu. When Daddy would come home, he'd often stop by the shops—one of the fancy ones that stocked imported goods—and bring something for Sophia. Usually just a trifle, but he always remembered what she liked.

Sophia ripped off the distinctive CONFISERIE ROHR wrapper, knowing instinctively what it would contain. They were Vues de Genève, praline disks with famous Geneva views etched on the chocolate. They had been her childhood favorites, and during the lunch at Oxford Sophia had mentioned them to Melamed. She opened the box, at once pleased and vaguely disconcerted. It was somehow too perfect that he should remember and get them for her.

"Which one would you like?" she asked, offering him the box. His fingers hovered a moment, then delved in. "I think I'd better leave the Palais des Nations to you," he replied, and they both laughed. "Well, congratulations. You were absolutely magnificent. You had Huron eating out of your hand."

Sophia sipped her champagne. "I didn't like them, especially that Mathewsen. Huron is okay, but Mathewsen's a creep. Did you see the way his eyes lit up when he heard that the operation might net them a fortune? It was greed. I don't know about Huron, but Mathewsen's just in it for the money."

Melamed shrugged. "We are at war, and in war one cannot always choose one's allies. Their motives are not important; only their money is."

"What did you talk about after you dismissed me?"

After Sophia had made her presentation and answered Mathewsen's endless questions, Huron had curtly told her to leave the room. She had tried to convince them of the brilliance of her plan—how no one would be killed, no innocent lives lost, no principles compromised—but none of them seemed to care. Then, with a patronizing smile, Melamed had told her there were some details they still had to hammer out, and he'd see her back at their hotel.

Sophia was still angry about that.

"Just some details. I told you."

Sophia set her glass on the table. "What details?"

Melamed stood up and refilled their glasses. "You were angry with me that day," he finally said. "Very angry. The day of the airline bomb, when we were waiting for the news bulletin, and you thought you'd taken those innocent lives. You said you felt used, unclean—a whore." He put his hand out to ward off Sophia's interruption. "It is good you were angry. The humanity in you is not dead. But," he continued, and there was no mistaking the sternness of his tone, "we have declared war, and we must be willing to sacrifice, not just our lives but our qualms and petty prejudices. We are not merchants, weighing one life against another, we are patriots, fighting for a cause just and justified. Remember, in war there is no innocence, for how can there be innocence while there is injustice?"

Sophia was about to reply, to protest things were not so simple, but Melamed cut her off. "Do not concern yourself with these details—they are unimportant. What is important is that we shall triumph with your plan. We shall crush and annihilate our enemies like the vermin they are."

His face was exultant. He might have been drunk, but he'd only had one glass of champagne, and Sophia knew it must be on a more powerful intoxicant than alcohol. There was something chilling about it. She had heard him at student rallies before, whipping up the crowd. But this was different. He really believed what he was saying. As if the slogans, the shouts, the rallying cries filled his head, choking off any remorse, like globs of fat clogging up an artery.

"You didn't answer my question." She looked directly into his good eye. How unyielding it was, she thought, like a piece of coal, as merciless as a child.

"I told them that for security reasons, they're to have no more contact with you. I'll be the go-between. Mathewsen didn't like it, but Huron accepted in the end." Melamed drew near, then grasped her arms in a grip of surprising strength and pulled her close to his face. "The question is, can you deliver?"

"Yes." No quaver in her voice, no waver in her eyes.

He released her. "We haven't much time. After December, others are pressing for more direct action. I can protect you and the operation from them, but not for long."

"You promised me a year," she whispered, suddenly anxious.

"At most."

Sophia finished her drink in a gulp, gathered her shoes, and walked toward the door, where she stopped abruptly, as though she'd just remembered something. "When you spoke to Huron and Mathewsen—"

"Yes?"

"You did tell them, didn't you, that this time will be different, that there'll be no bloodshed, no killings?"

Melamed picked up the empty glasses and carried them to the kitchen. He didn't answer.

CHAPTER TEN

A MAN IS BETRAYED BY HIS SHOES, a bureaucrat by his desk. In the case of Xavier Adanpur, they were both equally flawless: his shoes polished to perfection, his desktop arranged with meticulous attention. The blotter was immaculate, the plump fountain pen aligned precisely, even the paper clips were gathered in a disciplined pile. Celine had never seen so tidy a desk before.

For weeks following her memo, she'd heard nothing from Kiyotaki. Then, this afternoon, she had suddenly been summoned to his office to give a briefing on her Special Intervention Facility. The grilling lasted the better part of an hour. Kiyotaki had finally nodded, telling her it was an interesting idea and that he wanted her to work with the "advisor" on developing the modalities further. Even then it hadn't sunk in, and it was only as the secretary led Celine down the corridor to the green baffled door that it dawned on her that the "advisor" was Adanpur, and that she was about to come face-to-face with him.

"Well, Celine. Long time no see." Adanpur fiddled with an oversized cuff link, flicking away an imaginary speck of dust from his sleeve. He was of medium build and indeterminate nationality, one of those people with too many passports and too few loyalties, whose only principles in life are self-promotion and self-preservation. He had gained weight, Celine noticed. The edges of his jawline were rounder, less distinct, and his eyes seemed to have shrunk and sunk into the puffiness of his cheeks.

"I should congratulate you on your promotion," Celine said evenly, surprised to find that she felt none of the emotions she had expected. She had so anticipated this moment—when she would tell him how he'd used her and hurt her, how his arrogance had cost a thousand Indonesians their lives, and herself her innocence—that now she felt nothing. It used to be a fantasy of hers that if she ever saw him again she would hurl the accusations in his face, and even if it achieved nothing, she could at least watch him stammer and squirm. But now it seemed utterly pointless, almost churlish to dredge up the past, and she realized that more than anything she felt bored at the prospect of a confrontation.

Adanpur nodded in a complacent condescending way, as though his appointment as advisor was merely his due rather than cause for celebration. Celine wondered what lay behind it. Somebody must be backing him, she thought, someone with clout—the Americans or the French perhaps. It occurred to her that, far from reeling from the Indonesia fiasco, he had been biding his time for the past few years, making the rounds of various finance ministries and central banks, quietly building his support base.

He indulged her with his smile. "And how have you been doing?"

"Fine."

"Fine? After all this time, that's all you have to say?"

No, she thought, that's not all I have to say. In as crisp a voice as she could manage, all she said was, "I believe the managing director spoke to you about this new Special Intervention Facility. He's hoping to get it to the Board ahead of the Annual Meetings, which makes for a rather tight schedule—"

"My word, Celine," Adanpur laughed. "How very serious and business-like you've become. Come," he added, moving over to the sofa and patting it. "I hardly think old warriors like us need be so formal with each other."

Celine hesitated, but she could hardly remain seated in front of the desk, and after a moment she joined him, careful to leave the full width of sofa between them. As she sat down, she got a whiff of a scent that she recognized at once, an eau de cologne that she herself had given him for his birthday when they were in Jakarta during the East Asia crisis. He hadn't particularly liked it, but it was all she had been able to find at the gift shop at the

Mandarin Oriental, and he wore it mainly to please her. There was something oddly disarming about him still using it, and remembering it gave Celine a peculiar pang.

"Can I offer you something? Tea, coffee, Coke?"

"Nothing."

"Are you quite sure? Well, maybe I'll have a cup." He stabbed the intercom line.

Suspecting that he was trying to impress on her that nowadays he was too important to fetch his own coffee, Celine couldn't resist saying, "Thanks, but the MD already offered me some."

He looked at her sharply, then chuckled. "So, tell me about this famous intervention facility of yours."

Celine repeated the rudiments of her scheme, warming to her subject as she spoke. By the end, she could hardly contain the enthusiasm and excitement permeating her voice.

Adanpur listened but seemed more interested in Kiyotaki's reaction than in the mechanics of the intervention facility. He kept plying her with questions: What had Kiyotaki said? What were his concerns? Whom had he consulted? Presently, he fell silent, stirring his coffee pensively, then drinking it in small sips.

"Well," she asked, "what do you think?"

He gave a short, mirthless laugh. "Honestly?"

"Sure."

"I think it's the last hope of a hopeless man."

"What does that mean?"

"Don't you get it?" he said, putting down his cup. "Kiyotaki's finished. His term's up next year. He's angling for another, but he's not going to get it. His only hope is for some dramatic success, and he thinks if there's a crisis he'll have this facility and save the world. That's his great plan, and you played right into it. No wonder he's so excited by your scheme. It's pathetic, really."

"I didn't play right into it. Far from it. I had a hard time selling him on the whole idea."

"I don't doubt it. Kiyotaki's the most indecisive man in DC. But don't kid yourself. Kiyotaki wants this intervention facility—and he wants it badly.

He hasn't even brought in his senior staff—department directors and the like. And why do you suppose that is?"

Sheepishly, Celine started explaining about her memo and how she'd gone behind her director's back to send it to the MD.

"Don't be silly, there's a lot more to it than that."

"So what is it?" she asked.

"Power politics. If the Executive Board thinks Kiyotaki's out to grab more power for himself, they'll reject the proposal out of hand. I heard what happened last December with the Indonesia loan, and I can assure you, the Board was none too pleased by that little stunt."

"But we succeeded in staving off a crisis."

"Precisely. The Board doesn't like having its power usurped. Anyway, coming back to your proposal, if it is rejected, it'll weaken Kiyotaki's position vis-à-vis the Executive Board. And by extension, it will weaken the staff as well. That may not matter much to Kiyotaki—he's practically a lame duck already. If he succeeds, great. If he fails, well, he's out next June anyway. But it's a different story for the senior staff. They don't care whether the intervention facility is a good idea or not. They worry that they'll pay the price if Kiyotaki's gamble fails. He knows they'll oppose the whole scheme—that's why he's keeping them in the dark."

"And you don't think it's a good idea, either?"

Adanpur shrugged. "The intervention facility? I didn't say that. For all I know, it's the greatest idea since floating exchange rates. But who cares? That's just mathematics—intellectual masturbation. The point is, it'll never get approved. Not by the member countries, not by the Executive Board. It's a dead duck before it even flies. It's like trying to block the gold sales—"

"What's that got to do with anything?"

"Well, you know how the Europeans have been pressing to use the IMFO gold for debt relief for the heavily indebted low-income countries?"

Celine nodded. Back in the old days, member countries had to pay one-quarter of their subscription to IMFO's predecessor organization in the form of gold bullion. Later, when IMFO was established, the gold—more than 147 million ounces of it—had been transferred to IMFO's Special Resources Account. On the books it was still valued at the 1971 official gold price of US$ 42 per ounce, but with the market price more than twenty times that, there was a mouth-watering capital gain of one hundred billion dollars or more to be made on the gold. The member governments were constantly bickering over its disposal, like relatives squabbling at a rich man's wake.

"Toyoo has always been adamantly opposed to the debt-relief proposal. But one of these days, the Europeans are going to outmaneuver him, and push through the gold sales, and Toyoo's going to end up looking like a damn fool."

"But why's he against it? Isn't it a good idea to use our gold stocks to help out the low-income countries?"

Adanpur smiled thinly. "Not necessarily. First, these countries aren't making debt payments anyway, so forgiving their debts makes very little difference to them. Second, most of the debt that would be forgiven just happens to be owed to the European governments—all the lousy loans they've made to Africa over the past fifty years. But the IMFO gold belongs to *all* our member countries. The Europeans are being bloody clever—they get the good publicity for pushing for debt forgiveness, while in effect, repaying themselves with the IMFO gold. That's why Kiyotaki is so opposed to it. On principle, he's quite right. What he doesn't understand is the need for compromise. The Europeans want the gold sales, and they want it badly. It's politically important to them, and by hook or by crook they're going to push it through. Toyoo should give them their silly gold sales, or at least part of it, and win their support for the things he really cares about—like your Special Intervention Facility." Adanpur shook his head. "Don't get me wrong. Toyoo's a good man, and I like him. But what have we achieved during his tenure? Nothing. The Toothless Tiger, they call him. Fact is, he doesn't know how to play the game, how to get what he wants."

But you do, thought Celine, you play it very well. In spite of herself, she couldn't help admiring him. Adanpur had an uncanny knack for seeing through the motivations and machinations of others, cutting incisively to the crux of the matter. Hearing him explain it all brought back her old feelings of inadequacy and inexperience.

All the time she had been talking to Kiyotaki, she had never once suspected what he'd been thinking. Yet Xavier Adanpur, who hadn't even been there, was able to piece together exactly what lay behind the various posturings. And it occurred to her that he had plenty of contacts and plenty of political savvy that might come in very handy if they were to press ahead with the Special Intervention Facility. She edged toward him on the sofa.

"Do you really think it's hopeless, then?" she asked, looking up at him.

"Nothing's hopeless. It just a question of how badly you want it, and what you're willing to do for it."

"I want it. Badly."

"Why?"

She started to tell him, explaining how useful such a facility might be in a crisis, but he cut her off.

"It's because you still harbor guilt about what happened in Indonesia—or at least, you think you should."

She stared at him in surprise. So, it's out in the open, she thought. "And shouldn't I?"

"Oh, Celine," he shook his head. "Of course you shouldn't. Whoever's fault it was, it certainly wasn't yours. Do you remember the last time we met, just before I left DC? You didn't say anything, but I could tell how upset you were, and I knew you blamed me for what happened.

"Don't think I don't blame myself. I do. These last few years have been hell for me at times. I wake up in the middle of the night wondering whether I was right or wrong. Should I have closed more of the banks or fewer? The small ones or the big ones? The Chinese-owned or the Bumiputras? I've wanted to call you countless times—I would actually lift the receiver and start dialing the digits—to ask you what you thought. Even to know I'd been wrong would've been better than this eternal pondering."

Celine could see his pain and anguish, all the more compelling for his male suppression of emotion, and something stirred within her. So he does care, she thought, he blames himself; he feels the guilt, he suffers the pain, he knows the anger. She felt an overwhelming sense of relief, as though a great burden had been lifted from her, and she realized that she had been right to fall for him after all.

"Then why *didn't* you call me?"

"Because I couldn't," he replied simply. "What right did I have to impose my doubts and worries. Good Lord, you were a freshly graduated YEP, and I was the mission chief. It was my responsibility, my fault."

"You still could have called."

"No." His jaw clenched. He turned away from her abruptly, gazing past the potted plants at some distant point on the horizon. "No," he repeated. "In our job, there are no easy answers. We try to do good, and sometimes we end up doing harm. We're the surgeon whose patient dies in the operating theater. Or worse, we don't even know if we did harm or whether things would've turned out even more disastrous without us. We have to make tough choices and difficult decisions, often without the benefit of any empirical data or theoretical models to guide us, and only our instincts as economists to rely on. Doctors think they have it tough, but when they screw up just one patient dies. When we screw up, we condemn entire countries.

"But the hardest part of our job is accepting that things don't always work out the way we planned, that economics is an inexact science, and the very best intentions are not enough to guarantee success . . . "

He spoke in low undulating tones, like waves lapping gently against the shore. Celine's eyes, half-hypnotized, were fixed on his. She'd forgotten how mesmerizing his voice could be, and she slowly allowed herself to be cast under his spell. She found herself drawing closer, at first simply to hear him better, then because she wanted to comfort him, and finally because she needed him.

It seemed to her that he was right. There were only two choices: one could duck responsibility and immerse oneself in pure research like Harry, or face the difficult decisions, right or wrong, and live with the consequences. And in the end, that was no choice at all.

Adanpur was still speaking, so softly now that Celine could barely hear him. But it didn't matter. In her mind's eye, she was nestling her head against his shoulder, tucking her face against his, feeling his arms protecting her, sheltering her, drawing her away from the difficult questions and impossible answers.

There was a knock at the door, bringing her back to reality with a bump. Celine drew away at once, regaining a respectable distance.

"Sorry to disturb," the secretary said. "But you asked me to remind you about the dinner at the Ukrainian Embassy at seven thirty p.m. And you wanted to stop in at the Turkish reception before that."

Adanpur glanced at his watch. "Thank you."

Celine stood up, grateful for the interruption, and hurriedly shoved her papers into the folder. "I've got to get going too," she said. "I'm going to be late."

━━━━━

But she wasn't, or at least only fashionably so. Harry was waiting for her in the foyer of his club on Massachusetts Avenue. Celine would have liked nothing better than to cancel her date, curl up at home and try to sort through her conflicting emotions, but she'd already had to cancel once, and she was afraid Harry would think she was avoiding him.

Afterward, Celine thanked him for the meal, which indeed had been delicious, but Harry suggested one of the private libraries for coffee and cognac. Celine wanted to go home, but even that seemed like too much bother, and she acquiesced mainly out of laziness.

They had the place to themselves. Celine sank gratefully into the massive leather chesterfield, kicking off her shoes and tucking her feet deftly beneath her.

"Do make yourself comfortable," Harry said dryly, handing her the cognac glass. He was in an expansive mood, regaling her with his boyhood antics and anecdotes, but Celine was past listening. She kept asking herself whether she'd made a ghastly mistake that afternoon. Her fine theories and principles about never dating men at work hadn't stood the test of seeing Xavier again, but she had wronged him cruelly in believing that he didn't care about the disaster in Indonesia. What had happened this afternoon seemed natural, even inevitable.

She suddenly realized that Harry had fallen silent and was waiting for her to say something. She had no idea what he'd been talking about.

"But didn't you hate being sent off to boarding school so young?" she ventured.

"No. Actually, it was my own idea. I imagined boarding school would be all about midnight feats and classroom pranks. Of course, I was in for a big shock when I got there, but by then it was too late. After the fuss I'd made about wanting to go, I simply couldn't back out. Anyway, I ended up having a great time, and I wouldn't hesitate to send my son there."

Yes, thought Celine, Harry was just the sort to enjoy boarding school—attractive, mischievous, good at games, popular with the masters and boys alike. It struck her that people like him never fully grew up.

Harry could immerse himself in his research because life was nothing more than a schoolboy prank to him. Even his sending her ice cream in Jakarta, though she'd thought it touching and romantic at the time, now seemed extravagant and immature.

"I could never send my children away like that."

"Oh dear," Harry chuckled. "I guess we shouldn't get married after all. On the other hand," he added, reaching forward and stroking her face gently, "perhaps we should cross that bridge when we get to it."

Celine sat very still, moving neither toward nor away from him. He pulled her closer, and suddenly she was snuggling against him, wallowing in the warmth of his body. She felt his lips graze her cheek, inching their way toward her own. They kissed, a slow satisfying kiss. Harry's hands moved down, caressing her breasts.

It broke the spell. Celine stiffened, pulling away like a frightened foal.

"What's the matter?"

"We can't do this. I'm sorry." She slipped into her shoes and stood up. "It isn't appropriate. It isn't right."

"But—"

"Thank you for dinner," she repeated, this time with chilling formality, then turned and stumbled out of the room.

CHAPTER ELEVEN

I T WAS RAINING. Not a sharp, spring shower as had flirted with Sophia in Geneva, but the dreary determination of an October downpour. The air in the Research Department conference room grew heavy, a comfortable lassitude settling upon the audience. Tucked behind a pillar at the back of the room, Sophia found herself becoming drowsy.

Four months had passed since her meeting in Geneva, and a couple of weeks since her arrival at IMFO, along with the rest of the fall intake of the Young Economists Program. Much of her time had been swallowed up in orientation programs and torturous lectures on everything from the arcane No. 1 and No. 2 accounts IMFO maintained with the central banks of its member countries, to the intricacies of the global network computer system that linked IMFO's various field offices.

Melamed had told her that he expected results, and quickly. Her first task was to get hold of central bank intervention data—how much were central banks intervening in the foreign exchange markets and when. But it wasn't enough to steal the data once; she needed continuous updates. That meant hacking into the computer systems of dozens of central banks, or getting the information from one central source.

Charged with macroeconomic surveillance of the world economy, IMFO was about the only place where she might hope to get all of the data. But even here it would hardly be easy, and so far she hadn't even found out whether IMFO got the data with the kind of detail and frequency she required.

Her more serious challenge was developing a computer model to forecast exchange rate dynamics. Without it, she would never get the rest of the market to join her speculative attacks, and they would simply fizzle out as central banks intervened to restore stability. Sophia had spent the last couple of months working on just such a model, but she had a long way to go before she achieved anything like the accuracy she required. It was turning out to be more difficult than she'd expected, and a lot more difficult than she'd admitted to Huron and Mathewsen. Then, last week, she had seen Hoffinger's seminar notice, 'Non-Algorithmic Methods of Exchange Rate Forecasting: A Neural Net-Based Approach', and decided to come along. She might pick up something useful.

Harry Hoffinger started the seminar. Its purpose, he explained, was to present some preliminary results from his latest exchange rate forecasting model—the neural network. The neural net, as he called it, provided an entirely new approach to forecasting exchange rates, based on the digital equivalent of a human brain.

Behind him was a schematic diagram of the neural net, drawn with a fading marker pen across a smudgy whiteboard on which previous erasures still made ghostly appearances. The figure consisted of a pyramid of dots held together by a web of connecting lines. He took them through it. The bottom row had twenty dots, labelled INPUT NODES in neat block capitals. Then two more rows, the first with six dots, the second with twelve, which he called the HIDDEN LAYERS. The upper rows were multi-colored, starting their lives in blue, ending them in red. And at the top, two great pregnant blobs, represented the output nodes.

Sophia watched the man, not the diagram, smiling at her own prejudice. Just because Hoffinger's work was deeply technical, she'd expected him to be bespectacled, gawky, and awkward—in short, the typical caricature of a research type. But he was quite the opposite: confident, not conscious of his looks. His face finely chiselled, his eyes blue—a blue so deep that she almost suspected contact lenses—his hair not quite blond, she decided, more a sandy brown. He wore a double-breasted suit that sat well on his broad shoulders and a striking tie of leaping leopards.

It occurred to her that persuading Hoffinger to work with her might prove more difficult than she'd imagined. She was familiar with his earlier work on exchange rate forecasting models from publications in professional journals, and if his claims about his new model were correct, it was vital she get her hands on it. Asking around, Sophia had already learned that Hoffinger was bit of a loner, seldom coauthoring papers. Well, she thought, her own research on exchange rate dynamics was nothing to be ashamed of, and she was willing to offer it to him. If that were not enough, she was willing to offer herself. And *that*, she thought with a defiant toss of her head, was nothing to be ashamed of either.

"Now," Hoffinger said, tapping the whiteboard sharply, "what I've put up is just a generic neural net architecture. The one I actually used to make the forecasts, of course, is much more complicated. The raw data—interest rates, GDP growth rates, jobless claims, monetary aggregates, and so forth—go into these input nodes. Then the connecting nodes, here and here," he went on, with two more sharp taps, "allow for various interactions between the input variables to produce the output nodes. Which, in this case, would be the one-day-ahead forecasts of the dollar-yen and dollar-euro exchange rates.

"The key to the neural net is these connecting nodes." He tried emphasizing some of the connecting lines, but by now the pen had died completely, and he threw it down in disgust. "Well, never mind. You can see that some of these connections will be strong, and others essentially nonexistent. You see, these nodes," he said, picking up the pen again and making a last desperate attempt, "are almost like muscles. The more a node gets used, the stronger the connections become. Every minute, the neural network gets another observation on the actual exchange rate. Then it checks what its forecast was and updates these connective nodes in light of its error. Basically, it learns from its own mistakes."

The discussion soon became technical. Hoffinger peppered his talk with jargon—sequential learning rates and back propagation, Jordan-Elman nets and vector autoregressions—but the gist was clear enough: the neural net could deliver what other models could not.

The rain fell relentlessly. Momentarily distracted by it, Sophia returned her attention to the room. She had met a few of them—Pettigrew, a pompous twerp in the Research Department who had already tried to pick her up, and Karin Wulf, the woman a couple of seats to the left of him. Karin had introduced herself to Sophia at a happy hour intended for new YEPs to meet the staff, and she claimed to have briefly met with Sophia at a conference at the London School of Economics.

"I understand the part about the neural net learning from its past mistakes, but I still don't get what's so special about it," Pettigrew complained. He had a plaintive, high-pitched voice that Sophia found especially grating.

"Well, for one thing," Hoffinger said, looking around the room a little anxiously, as though hoping to see someone who wasn't there, "it's a lot more flexible than standard models. Take an interest hike—any standard model will tell you that higher interest rates should stabilize the exchange rate."

"Obviously," Pettigrew responded. "Higher interest rates bring in more foreign capital and appreciate the exchange rate."

"Like it was obvious that the earth is flat and the sun goes around it? Actually, even though it's normally true that raising rates stabilizes the currency, when interest rates go too high, you're just bankrupting the country. And further increases just weaken the currency, as we found out in Indonesia last December. The neural net can capture those sorts of non-linearities admirably, but just try doing it with a standard model."

"But that's just a modelling detail," Pettigrew said. "What I want to know is what makes your neural network *fundamentally* different."

Hoffinger started to answer, then stopped. He tried again, pausing a second time as if seeking to capture some nebulous thought, then finally said, "Look, what does a model really do? Fundamentally, it's looking for patterns. In other words, let's say the rate of money expansion is slashed and the exchange rate appreciates. That's a pattern or correlation, right?"

"Or suppose US GDP contracts, and there's a dollar depreciation. That's another pattern. Figuring out exchange rate dynamics is basically a matter of discerning these types of patterns. But actually, computers are pretty lousy at recognizing patterns. Let me give you an example." He turned to the rest of the room. "Who can tell me what a chair is?"

They stared back.

"Come on," Hoffinger laughed. "What is a chair?"

"Something you sit on."

"Right. But how would you recognize one? More precisely, how would you program a computer to recognize one? It's not so easy. A chair can be a gilded Louis XIV armchair, or a Swedish leather executive chair, or even an upturned milk crate. It's pretty hard to tell the computer a precise set of rules—an algorithm, if you like—so that it recognizes a chair when it sees one. But ask any three-year-old kid, and he has no problem identifying a chair. The reason is that the human brain doesn't work by following a precise set of rules. Instead, it looks for patterns—and that's essentially what the neural network does."

Hoffinger stepped forward and leaned against the table. "So, to continue with the chair example, the neural net would first see whether the object has four legs. Now obviously, many things—say, a dog—have four legs. So that's just one input. Next, it will see whether there's a horizontal piece large enough to sit on. That's another input. Then it might check whether there's a back on it. That's yet another input node. Individually, none of these elements is enough to define a chair. Nor is any one of them essential for a chair—for instance, you could have a chair without a proper back to it. But when enough of these nodes are firing simultaneously," Hoffinger said, pointing to the diagram, "by which I mean that the answer to the various questions is yes, then the output node will decide probabilistically that the object is, in fact, a chair."

"Oh great," piped Pettigrew. "We can send Harry on technical assistance missions to any government finding an Unidentified Sitting Object."

There was a ripple of laughter. Harry joined in. "Okay, okay. Let me try to give you a more convincing example." He frowned, his brow knotted in concentration, then grinned impishly and scrawled the words NATURE LANE on the whiteboard. "Who can solve this anagram? I'll give you a couple of clues: its three words, and they're closely related to the subject of this seminar."

Sophia leaned forward, peering at the letters. She got it almost at once but held back until, finally, after a couple of minutes had passed and nobody else had guessed, she called out the answer.[1]

"Exactly," Hoffinger beamed at her, "but the real question is how did you figure it out? The algorithmic way would be to go through all possible combinations of the letters. But with ten characters and two spaces there are literally hundreds of millions of permutations. It would take forever.

"Obviously, that isn't the way to solve it. You just stare at the letters until the answer sort of pops into your head, right? Basically, you recognize a pattern. And that's exactly the way the neural net works."

But Pettigrew wouldn't let that pass. Elbows on the table, chin thrust forward, his whole body taut, he said, "That's precisely what's wrong with this whole approach. It's just a black box. You have your output, which is the predicted exchange rate, and you have everything you can think of plus the kitchen sink as input variables. And the relationship between them—what you rightly call the hidden layers—is just a black box. That's not an economic theory at all. There are no testable hypotheses, no scientific method. There isn't even any pretence of explaining *how* the various input variables affect the exchange rate. It's nothing but black magic."

Hoffinger nodded, a little wearily, like a man who must get through life without the comfort of his illusions. "As I said," he replied, trying to keep a note of impatience from creeping into his voice, "right at the beginning of the seminar, the whole purpose of this exercise is to get an operational forecasting tool. My neural net isn't supposed to be some tidy, theoretically derived model of exchange rate dynamics. I think we're all familiar with those types of models and their forecasting performance. Most of them can't beat a random walk: you'd be better off with a dartboard if you really wanted to make forecasts."

This was apostasy beyond hearing, since it was true, and Pettigrew interrupted angrily, "Well so far, we haven't seen any concrete proof that your precious neural net does any better."

Sophia edged forward; this was the part she'd been waiting for. In fact, she was surprised Hoffinger hadn't already shown them the model's mean squared forecast error. Admittedly, there was a lot of new ground to cover in explaining how the neural net worked, but the forecast error was the model's bottom line, the acid test of its performance. He would have to hurry; the seminar ended at four p.m.

"Well, this is just a preliminary version of the neural net," Hoffinger offered hastily.

"Oh, of course." Pettigrew looked around the room with a knowing smile.

But he had triumphed too soon.

"All right. All right." Hoffinger threw up his hands in resignation. "Since you insist. But I need a volunteer."

Karin Wulf raised her hand, but Hoffinger shook his head. "No, it has to be someone I don't know, otherwise I'll be accused of having an accomplice."

He glanced around the room. "How 'bout you?"

Sophia looked over her shoulder, but there was no one behind her.

"Yes, you," Hoffinger said. "Come on up."

Sophia threaded her way past the rows of chairs, wondering why on earth he needed a volunteer just to show a table with the model's forecast accuracy.

"Okay, first of all, you don't know me, right?"

Sophia shook her head. "No, I just arrived at IMFO."

"Good. Now then, this is a printout of the US dollar exchange rate against the yen and the euro, as of twelve noon GMT in London today." He placed the transparency on the overhead projector. "And here," he whipped out an envelope with the air of a conjurer, "is an envelope containing the neural net's forecasts of these exchange rates. Before you open it, I'd like you to verify that it's postmarked last week, and that there's an unbroken seal over the flap."

Sophia turned the envelope over, squinted at the postmark, then, feeling incredibly stupid, announced to the room, "Yes, it's postmarked last Friday, and the seal is unbroken."

"Ladies and gentlemen," Hoffinger said with a theatrical flourish, "the lovely lady has confirmed that these predictions were made more than a week ago. And now she will open the sealed envelope." He ceremoniously handed her a letter opener.

Sophia slit open the envelope and slid out another overhead transparency, which she laid next to the first one. The forecast error was less than one quarter of one percentage point—an extraordinary feat by any standard.

At the round of applause, Hoffinger took a small bow, then insisted that Sophia take one too. Smiling, Sophia returned to her seat. The seminar ended a few minutes later. The audience filed out, a few of them stopping to congratulate Hoffinger on his talk. He was standing in front of the whiteboard, cutting wide swaths through the ink when he spotted Sophia leaving.

"Hang on, don't run off. I'm sorry, I should've introduced myself." He held his hand out. "Harry Hoffinger."

"Pleased to meet you," she replied in her cultured English accent, the type a monied foreign student might acquire, along with the habit of afternoon tea and an account at Blackwell's. She grasped his hand with her slender fingers. "I'm Sophia. Sophia Gemaye."

CHAPTER TWELVE

THEY TROOPED IN, GRAY MEN IN GRAY SUITS. Even the sole woman among them somehow managed to blend in, having acquired along the way an instinct for colorlessness. Perched near the head of the horseshoe table in the seat normally reserved for the senior staff who had prepared the staff report, Celine watched the executive directors array themselves around the table. One or two of them glanced at her curiously, perhaps surprised to find so junior an economist seated there.

Celine flipped through the staff report, unable to suppress a thrill of pride. On the cover, listed as the staff "available to answer technical or factual questions" was her own name—the first time she'd been billed as the principal author of a staff report. No one else was listed, not even Xavier Adanpur, who was sitting at the back of the room, having insisted that Celine take the place of honor beside the managing director's chair, though he had shepherded her through the whole process.

Up until the last moment, Kiyotaki had fussed and fretted over every sentence and every comma. Even last week, he had gotten cold feet and wanted to limit the proposal for the Special Intervention Facility to a modest thirty billion dollars. It had taken all of Adanpur's powers of persuasion to convince him to stick to the one hundred billion dollars he'd originally planned, and the confident tone of the staff report gave no hint of the agonizing that had gone into it.

Even before they began, there was an air of subdued tension in the boardroom. Most meetings were a charade because the Board, which represented the member countries' governments, nearly always endorsed Management's proposal—be it a bailout of a country, or a paltry pay increase for the staff. Or, more precisely, the MD seldom put forward a proposal unless he expected unanimous support from the Board. Today's meeting was different. It was far from clear that a majority of the countries would support the intervention facility, and those that didn't would make every effort to kill it now, ahead of the Finance Ministers' Summit.

It was here that Adanpur had proved his worth. He had good contacts with the executive directors' offices, as well as many of the individual central banks and ministries of finance, and he had been able to tell Celine who would be likely to support the proposal and where more lobbying might be required. By his reckoning, they should just about squeak through. The French, ever interventionist, would certainly favor the facility. With them would come the Francophone Africans, always eager for their subsidies from the French Trésor. The Germans were reportedly more ambivalent, but out of European solidarity would support the French. The Italians, already in trouble in Europe on account of their budget deficit, wouldn't want to upset the Germans and would agree to whatever the Germans did. The Japanese, still worried about East Asia, would welcome it enthusiastically. The Indians and Chinese, always keen on flexing their muscles, would be pompous and tiresome but divided by their own squabbling, and ineffectual in opposition. As for the other developing countries, they were the most likely beneficiaries and could be counted on to vote in favor.

That left the United States and the United Kingdom. The Brits were being cagey, giving no indication of whether or not they would approve the facility. With the largest quota and biggest share of votes, the Americans would grumble but probably go along with the rest.

Toyoo Kiyotaki took his place at the head of the table, shot Celine an encouraging smile and the executive directors a more measured one, then called the meeting to order with a sharp tap on the microphone. They got through the first few executive directors, those who represented the minor countries, in reasonably rapid succession. Each director prefaced his remarks by saying he intended to confine himself to just a couple of points, and then proceeded to talk for the better part of ten minutes. But Celine had endured many Board sessions before, and she amused herself by examining the room from her new vantage point at the head of the table.

When Kiyotaki called on the UK executive director, Celine perked up. So far, the executive directors had all supported the Special Intervention Facility—the United Kingdom was the one she had the most doubts about.

"Thank you, Mr. Chairman," the UK director puffed pompously. "At the outset, let me commend staff on this well-written report . . . " His opening was ominous: whenever a director started by commending the staff, a "but" always followed. Sure enough, he droned on with a long string of questions and objections. Celine listened attentively, sifting through the verbiage, trying to gauge whether he would support the proposal or not.

She ran through the permutations in her mind. If the British opposed, the Scandinavians might also, just to show their independence from the Franco-German bloc. Then there were the Americans, always sympathetic to the British, especially if there was a split with France. Celine could sense Kiyotaki's nervousness as well; he kept tapping his fountain pen against the pad. Finally, the UK director concluded, "With these reservations, Mr. Chairman, my authorities would be pleased to support the proposed facility."

Celine breathed a sigh of relief; the rest of the meeting should be clear sailing. She leaned back in her chair, gently rocking it back and forth, wallowing in a sense of accomplishment—of redemption even. With this new facility, IMFO would have another instrument to help stave off currency crises, and in an odd way Celine felt as though she were finally making up for the disaster in Indonesia. Returning there last December, she had been appalled at how Jakarta, once a booming, bustling city, had sunken into poverty, its streets filled with bedraggled women peddling themselves and their wares, their faces pale with hunger, their eyes hollowed of hope.

Nothing could absolve Celine of her guilt over what had happened, but after today she would at least have made a recurrence less likely.

Bali, she decided. During that famous mission, she and Xavier had always talked of going to Bali when the crisis was over. Now they really could go. Over the past couple of months, they had resumed their relationship almost seamlessly, meeting discreetly after work to dine or dance, or simply spend a cosy evening together. A few artful questions had revealed that his wife had returned to Europe, so there was no longer an obstacle to his divorce.

There were times when Celine felt almost light-headed with happiness. Xavier had a special hold over her, an almost mystical power that made her putty in his hands. But far from resenting it, she relished the feeling. She wondered why. Objectively speaking, he wasn't that good looking, she thought, stealing a quick sidelong glance, though he always had a certain bearing. Part of his attractiveness, no doubt, was the confidence with which he comported himself. More than anything, he gave Celine a sense of security. When she was with him, it was as though all her cares and responsibilities could be relinquished onto his broad shoulders. She could be a child again, playing in the cosseting warmth of a protective parent—a luxury she hadn't known since the day her father's business had gone bankrupt.

Now she could picture the two of them running across the white beaches, frolicking in the sand, diving into the painfully blue waters. Yes, she thought, flashing him a smile, Bali it would be.

Thinking of Bali, Celine remembered Karin's suggestion that she invite Harry there, and she felt a momentary qualm of guilt. She had treated him abominably, leading him on, then behaving with cruel inconsistency. She must have hurt him deeply. Celine was still musing over the delicious complications of her love life, when, out of the corner of her eye, she noticed Kiyotaki stiffen. The executive director for France was speaking, and she could tell from the stillness in the room that trouble was brewing.

"My authorities fully share the views expressed in this admirable staff report about the vulnerabilities of the international monetary system to sudden speculative attacks," he cooed. "However," he went on, wagging a manicured finger in admonition, "this does not mean that this Executive Board should abrogate its own responsibilities. There have already been numerous concerns expressed at this table concerning the degree of discretion that Management has assumed in committing IMFO's resources . . . "

That was IMFO-speak for the little stunt Kiyotaki had pulled in announcing support for Indonesia last December. But the French director was exaggerating. The new facility was intended for use only in dire emergencies, when there was no time for the Board to approve a traditional IMFO loan. Yet the way the French made it sound, Kiyotaki would henceforth be making all the decisions, and the Board might as well go home.

"And therefore," the French director concluded, "my authorities are not in a position to support the proposed Special Intervention Facility."

Bastards! Celine looked around, unable to comprehend what was happening, when she caught sight of Adanpur. He was looking at the French executive director. Their eyes met, some unspoken message passing between them. And then Celine understood.

It had nothing to do with the intervention facility: the Europeans, long resentful of a Japanese managing director, were out to embarrass Kiyotaki, and today's session presented the perfect opportunity. If the intervention facility failed to go through, Kiyotaki would be a lame duck for the remainder of his term, and after today's fiasco, he could forget about getting another.

Celine didn't know quite what role Adanpur had played in the conspiracy, or what he hoped to gain. All she knew was that he'd deliberately misled Kiyotaki—and herself—into believing the Europeans would support the facility, lulling him into a false sense of security. She understood now why he'd been so helpful, so forthcoming, so insistent that her name be listed on the staff report and that she be seated at the head of the table next to Kiyotaki. And she had thought he was trying to advance her career! Celine glared at him with loathing, staggered by his perfidy, his betrayal hitting her like a blow to her solar plexus. He must have sensed her anger, for he turned slightly and saw her staring. He had the audacity to shrug his shoulders, as though disavowing any responsibility.

Kiyotaki remained remarkably inscrutable. He merely thanked the French executive director, then gave the floor to the German. The German director, a jovial fellow with a rubicund face and a portly belly, clearly ill at ease with this intrigue, gave a lengthy speech praising Kiyotaki, the staff, and the report. But in the end, he indicated that his government could not support the proposal. And now the tide turned quickly. Even some of the developing countries, mainly the larger ones who entertained absurd hopes that their own man might succeed Kiyotaki, scented blood. They started questioning whether the proposal was "premature," "required further consideration," with one director going so far as to call it "ill-advised."

This cannot be happening, Celine thought, watching the whole painstakingly constructed edifice crumble about her. Her ears were buzzing, and black dots were dancing before her eyes. In her mind, she was no longer in the staid boardroom at IMFO, she was back in Jakarta, hearing the sickening crunch as the mob staved in the shopkeeper's skull. She wanted to shout and scream at the executive directors that real people in real countries were dying while they played their parlor games.

Kiyotaki must have sensed her frustration, for he put a restraining hand gently on her arm. The only hope now was the Americans. If the United States endorsed the proposal, it could still go through. The executive director for the United States rocked his chair, creaking it as a sort of prelude to his speech. Then he drew himself nearer the table, placed his hands palms down on it, and launched into his text. He spoke at length, reviewing recent crises, praising the staff report, and expressing sympathy for the idea of the Intervention Facility.

But just as Celine was beginning to get her hopes up, he said, "Nonetheless, we share some of the concerns expressed by other directors today. In particular, the proposed facility would represent a significant commitment of resources—one hundred billion dollars." He paused, and looked directly at Kiyotaki. "My authorities would feel more comfortable supporting the proposal if the amounts involved were significantly smaller, perhaps in the range of ten to twenty billion dollars. At this juncture, therefore, my authorities would not be in a position to support the proposed decision."

That spelled the end of it. Kiyotaki could still insist on a formal vote, but it would only weaken his position further. Besides, he seemed resigned to the failure. His face had turned a tired, pasty gray. He was struggling to still his trembling hands, and he looked old and fragile. Celine felt a fresh anger welling up inside her.

"I would like to thank directors for expressing their views so frankly today," Kiyotaki said. "Clearly, much needs to be done before a consensus on this matter can be reached. But I firmly believe that the intervention facility would do much to enhance the stability of the international monetary system. The simple truth is, we lack the instruments to deal with systemic weaknesses, and in the event of a global crisis, it would take far too long to marshal the necessary resources and respond adequately.

"Therefore, in conclusion, let me urge directors to act, and to act quickly in this regard, lest we find that one day it will be said of us, 'They did too little, too late.' "

Kiyotaki stood up, and with as much dignity as he could muster, walked out of the room. Adanpur also stood, but instead of following Kiyotaki, started chatting with a small group of executive directors. As Celine walked up to him, he broke away.

"You lousy bastard," she hissed. "How could you?"

"Really, Ms. O'Rourke, I can't imagine what you're talking about." He glanced nervously at the US executive director, who was standing almost within earshot.

"You know perfectly well what I'm talking about."

"Lower your voice," he said sharply. "Look, I know you're upset, but there's more at stake here than you realize. A lot more." He smiled, his winning, million-dollar smile that he kept for special favors.

"Come up to my office in an hour or so, and we can talk about it."

"Thank you, but I'd rather see you in hell." Celine had a wonderful vision of taking careful aim with her pumps and kicking him as hard as she could on the shins. But Kiyotaki was fast disappearing from view, and Celine scrambled after him. She rounded the corner just as he was about to enter his office.

"Mr. Kiyotaki," she called out.

The managing director glanced back at her briefly, then turned away.

Celine watched helplessly. She'd had her shot. And she had missed.

CHAPTER THIRTEEN

S OPHIA TURNED THE PAGES OF THE NEWSPAPER IDLY. Harry was late. Rather ungraciously, his secretary had told Sophia she could wait in his office, all the time eyeing her warily, as though she couldn't be trusted not to steal the pencils. Not that there were any pencils to steal, thought Sophia, glancing around the room. Reams of computer printouts littered the desk, cables snaked to and fro, a dusty coffee mug stood guard by the monitor. It was chaos. Yet it was the sort of chaos where the owner—and only the owner—knows precisely where everything is to be found.

Sophia checked her watch again. Harry had said ten o'clock, and it was a quarter past already. She returned to the paper but after a moment put it down. Studying the results of Harry's model again over the weekend, she had realized how vital it was to get her hands on it. Building on his neural net model, rather than starting from scratch herself, was her only hope of meeting Melamed's insanely tight deadline. She'd made a good start last week after the seminar—piquing his interest in both her and her research—but she'd heard Harry was a loner who seldom worked with others.

She had spent the weekend mulling over how to persuade Harry to work with her. There was always chivalry, of course. But she could hardly do the damsel-in-distress act without revealing why she so desperately needed his help. No, she decided, somehow she had to turn the tables, make Harry grateful that she was willing to collaborate with *him*—not the other way around. She had to make the sale without cheapening the goods.

It wasn't quite hopeless. Harry had mentioned during the seminar that the neural net suffered from "overlearning," whereby it overadjusted its parameters in response to previous errors. It needed a more subtle, more sophisticated approach, and Sophia thought that a genetic algorithm might just do the trick. The use of genetic algorithms in economics was sufficiently novel that Harry was unlikely to know much about them. It could be her entrée to working with him. But was it enough? He might find her attractive, but she had to find some way of impressing him.

Abandoning the newspaper, Sophia turned her attention to the desk. With a backward glance to check that the door was closed, she began rummaging through the heaps of papers. Nothing she found was terribly remarkable: a pile of musty mathematics books, dog-eared from Harry's graduate school days, a yellow legal pad crawling with equations, a stack of graphs. Sophia pulled one out. It looked like a giant spider squashed between the pages, its legs flung out in mute protest.

She returned to the notepad and flipped through the pages. Harry had been struggling to solve a ferocious-looking partial differential equation. His various attempts were scrawled across the sheets. He would start out confidently enough, bold strokes that straddled the lines, dashing manfully from margin to margin, but then the writing would falter, trailing off as he realized he wasn't making any progress. By the end, it was a mere scratch, whimpering across the page. And then he would start again on the next sheet.

Something about it felt oddly familiar. With another glance behind her, Sophia moved closer to the desk and examined the equation more carefully. She stared at the pages, her brow knotted. She had solved a similar problem herself, she was sure of it. It was on the edge of her mind, infuriatingly out of reach. Then it popped into her mind—rather like the neural net, she thought with a laugh. All it needed was a transformation of variables, a rather unusual transformation that Sophia had discovered when she was working on her dissertation. She could still remember the hours spent in that beastly café on the corner of Houghton Street, wrestling with this very problem. Once the variables had been transformed, the equation could be reduced to a standard problem whose solution could be found in any textbook on partial differential equations.

Sophia heard someone coming and hastily thrust the papers back into the pile. By the time Harry's secretary entered, Sophia was seated innocently, engrossed in the newspaper.

"Mr. Hoffinger called to say he's sorry, but he's been detained. He didn't want to keep you waiting."

Sophia put down the newspaper, making an exaggerated show of consulting her watch, as though she hadn't even noticed the passage of time. Then she stood up, brushing her dress. "Yes, I've got to take care of a few things. Would you let Mr. Hoffinger know I'll be in my office?"

She was still hunting for a copy of her dissertation—inevitably it was in one of the boxes she hadn't unpacked—when Harry called. She told him she'd be over in a minute and hung up. Finally she found what she was looking for—Harry's partial differential equation was indeed equivalent to hers. A last check in the mirror, and she hurried to his office.

"Hullo," he grinned, standing up. "Sorry to have kept you waiting, but I got stuck in a meeting."

He dumped a pile of folders from the armchair onto the floor and bade her sit down. He drew his own chair closer and leaned forward, lips slightly parted, palms resting upon his knees. And when he spoke, she noticed his eyes straying over her, lingering just a tad longer than was strictly necessary. They got through the usual platitudes and pleasantries and were soon discussing various exchange rate models. Harry was certainly knowledgeable and full of enthusiasm for his work, but he spoke with the implicit assumption that he was there to impart information, she to listen. Sophia found it irritating. Worse, he seemed to be steering the conversation, and Sophia was unable to establish either ascendancy or rapport.

"That was quite a performance you gave on Friday," she said.

"Thanks to you."

"Oh, well, I didn't do much," she said, then added with a smile, "I suppose that you'd mailed yourself a dozen different forecasts, with some kind of mark on the envelope, and chose the one that was closest."

Harry looked startled, then grinned like a schoolboy who's been caught. "Not a dozen—only three. And the predictions *were* the model's central forecast. It's just that . . ." He drew closer, as though to include her in the conspiracy. "Well, there are still some wrinkles to be sorted out with the neural net—especially its tendency to 'overlearn' that I talked about at the seminar. But the main problem isn't with the neural net, it's with the central banks. They're forever intervening in the foreign exchange markets, especially the Asians, and of course that messes up the neural net's predictions."

"I meant to ask you about that at your seminar. How come you didn't include central bank intervention as one of your input variables?"

Harry nodded. "I was surprised no one asked. The trouble is getting hold of the data. Most of it isn't published or released. At best, you might get data on holdings of foreign exchange reserves. But that's pretty much useless because the central bank will often sell foreign exchange one day and buy it back the next, so monthly or even weekly data don't really tell you anything. Then, of course, there are all sorts of valuation effects and forward market transactions—"

"But IMFO gets the intervention data."

"Sure we do," Harry agreed. "Under the Special Data Disclosure Standards, we get minute-by-minute data on intervention in all of the major currencies—spot markets, forward markets, derivative liabilities—the whole caboodle. But that doesn't mean you can access it. The data are kept by Statistics, and they only release them with special permission, normally with a three-year lag if it's just for research purposes."

"Three years! That's useless."

"Precisely. And that's why I don't include intervention as one of the input variables."

"I see," Sophia muttered. Best not to draw too much attention to her interest in the intervention data, she told herself. Not yet, at any rate.

"About that overlearning problem you mentioned," she said, changing the subject. "That's when the neural net adjusts itself too quickly to the inputs, right?"

"Yes, exactly. It's like the child who falls down the stairs, then never dares climb a ladder when he grows up. In the same way, the neural network can become too sensitive when it's learning from its errors. God knows how many permutations of the parameters I've tried, but the stupid thing either adjusts too fast or too slowly."

"I was just wondering whether a genetic algorithm for the learning part might help."

"Well, it might," Harry said cautiously. "Rather esoteric, though, aren't they?"

"Not really. Have you tried using them? Genetic algorithms can be incredibly powerful, and they're ideally suited for this type of task."

"Why's that?"

"Because there isn't a right or wrong answer in the learning process—it's a question of gradual adjustment to its past errors. And that's precisely what genetic algorithms are good at solving."

"Actually, I don't know too much about them. How exactly they work, I mean."

"Oh, the basic idea's quite simple," Sophia said. It was her turn to show off her knowledge and for Harry to listen. Just as nature follows certain principles—such as mutation, cross-breeding, and natural selection—for evolving species, she explained, the same ideas can be used for solving mathematical problems. A genetic algorithm takes a set of potential solutions to a problem, selects the best solutions, then breeds and mutates them until a better solution evolves. Each "generation" of solutions represents an incremental improvement.

"But how do you implement all this?" Harry asked.

"Well, of course, that's not so easy. I spent ages getting mine to work when I was doing my PhD."

Harry regarded her closely.

Sophia smiled to herself, knowing exactly what was going through his mind. He was thinking that his name was Hoffinger, and hers Gemaye, and in any joint paper her name would be listed first.

"Perhaps you wouldn't mind giving me a hand with some of this genetic algorithm stuff," he said. "It might be worth a shot."

Yes, I bloody well would mind. Sophia's eyes narrowed. Helping Harry Hoffinger was the last thing she had in mind. She needed to get her hands on his model, and that meant being a full coauthor. "Well, I don't know. I mean, of course I'd be happy to give you whatever help I can, but seeing as I'm new here, I'm not sure how it's going to fit into my schedule."

"Oh."

"I tell you what, though," Sophia said, with a hollow brightness in her voice. "Why don't I jot down some of the references for you." Grabbing the pad off the table, she wrote down a half-dozen titles, racking her brains to remember the ones that were the most abstruse and technically demanding. If Harry did read them, she certainly didn't want him thinking he could manage without her.

As she handed back the pad, she stopped. "Wow, that looks nasty," she said, pointing to the differential equation.

Harry laughed. "I've been struggling with that for the last couple of weeks. I don't think an analytical solution exists."

"Sure it does."

"That's what I thought, initially. But now I'm pretty sure that it doesn't."

"It must." Sophia ripped off the top sheet and started working on it.

"Let's see." She sucked on her pen, wrote furiously for a few lines, then tore up the sheet and started on another while Harry looked on, smiling complacently.

The phone rang; Harry picked it up. "What? I'm not sure. Hang on, let me check my calendar." Harry cupped his hand over the receiver. "Have you got lunch plans?" he whispered to Sophia.

"No, actually I don't," she replied, looking up.

"Great." He turned back to the phone. "Sorry. I've already got a lunch appointment today. How 'bout sometime next week? Okay, I'll send you an e-mail. Pettigrew," he explained to Sophia as he hung up.

Sophia smiled. "Here, recognize this?" She handed the pad to Harry, looking over his shoulder as he read what she'd written.

He shook his head. "No, I still don't —"

"Hang on." She took back the pad, wrote a couple more lines, crossed out various terms on either side of the equation, and then rewrote the answer more succinctly.

"Oh, of course," Harry said, slapping the table. "How bloody blind of me. It's amazing how neatly it comes out." He flipped through the pages, following her derivation. "No, this can't be right . . ." he began. "I see what you've done. Hey, that's really clever." He pulled a pencil from the drawer and started checking Sophia's work. It was her turn to grin complacently. "The trick is the change of variable you did back here."

Harry tapped the page with his pencil. "But how on earth did you guess that was the right transformation to do?"

Sophia smiled enigmatically. "Feminine intuition."

"Quite an intuition." He placed his pencil on the desk, where it promptly rolled out of sight. "Look," he said. "I know you're busy with your own research, but I could really use your help. If you like, I'll have my division chief speak to yours and square things with him so we can work together. I reckon you might be right, that your genetic algorithm stuff really might improve the neural net's learning routines. If it does, that should improve its forecasting capabilities pretty dramatically. It would be very well received here, and a shoo-in for publication in any top-rated journal. And," he added bravely, "I think it would only be fair if you were lead author."

Sophia's lip curled into a smile. She had made the sale.

Just then, there was a knock at the door.

———

Taking a deep breath, Celine rapped on the door, the sound echoing the hollowness of her defeat. All weekend long, she had hungered for human company—a shoulder to cry on, a friend to commiserate with—and all weekend long, pride had prevented her calling. Of course she'd tried Karin, phoning twenty or thirty times, and of course Karin was away, probably gone to New York with some new boyfriend, and as usual switching off her cell phone when she was on one of her escapades. What Celine wanted was sympathy; she didn't just want it, she craved it. Remembering the night they had dined together at her place, it seemed to her that Harry had a quality, so rare in men, of listening—not offering pat answers or simple solutions—but just listening. She decided to tell him all: her own hopes, the MD's disappointment, the cruelty of the Board, the perfidy of Adanpur. She would unburden herself to him.

Celine knocked again. She could almost feel the texture of his jacket caressing her cheek as she nestled on his shoulder, and the heavy warmth of his arm around her, holding her, comforting her, protecting her.

"Come in," Harry barked from within, but before Celine could turn the handle he'd cracked open the door.

"Oh, hi." He seemed surprised to see her. "Can I help you?"

"May I come in?" she asked, somewhat deflated by the coolness of his reception. The slightest hesitation. "Sure." He opened the door fully, stepping back to let her into the room.

"I have to speak to you—" Celine stopped short, surprised to find someone with him. A woman in her late twenties or early thirties, Celine thought, though one never could tell with these exotic women. She had a honey complexion and high cheekbones, and was dressed with the simplicity that only money can buy. Her black linen dress and cream jacket fitted her perfectly, so much so that Celine guessed they must be tailor-made. Lounging on the floor beside her was a pert Gold Pfeil briefcase, so stylish it could not possibly hold anything useful. The woman was ensconced in Harry's armchair, looking very much at home, curled up like a contented cat. She didn't stand up when Celine entered.

"Have you two met?" Harry was asking. "This is Celine. Celine O'Rourke. And this," he added, turning back to Celine, "is Sophia Gemaye."

"I don't believe I've had the pleasure," the woman said smoothly. She held out her hand. Celine scanned the fingers automatically; the woman sported neither engagement nor wedding ring.

"How do you do?"

"Sophia's just joined the Young Economists Program," Harry said.

"Oh really? Where are you from?"

"All over," the woman shrugged. "Right now, I'm coming from Geneva. I did my PhD at the LSE, and before that I was at Oxford."

Of course, Celine thought, I should have guessed from the accent. She turned to Harry. "Well, I'm sorry, I didn't mean to interrupt . . ." she paused expectantly.

"Sophia and I are going to be working on the neural net together. We were just discussing it."

"Well, it's good of you to show the ropes to a newcomer," Celine said, recovering quickly.

"What did you want to talk to me about?"

"What? Oh, nothing important. It can wait."

"How did your Board meeting go?"

Celine looked at him sharply, wondering what he had heard. "It went fine. A number of executive directors commended the staff report . . . of course, they didn't come to any firm decision regarding the Special Intervention Facility, but at least we've laid the groundwork."

"Good." Harry's eyes flicked over his watch.

"Well, I just stopped by to say I'm going off on leave for a few weeks."

"Oh, I hadn't realized." Harry looked at her curiously. "When did you decide to go?"

She had, in fact, decided at just that instant, feeling suddenly that she must get away from IMFO, with all its politics and intrigues. She yearned to be back in England, locked away in some tumbledown country cottage, stalking through the wet woods with only her camera and a sandwich for company.

"Some time ago," she lied, not caring that Harry would have seen the divisional-leave roster and would know that she hadn't put down for any leave. "I promised myself some leave once the Board meeting was over."

"Well, enjoy your vacation then." Harry stood up. "Let's do lunch when you're back."

"Thanks," she said, then paused. "Don't suppose you're free today, are you?"

She could sense his hesitation. "No. No, I'm afraid not." He stole a guilty glance at the woman, who was watching Celine, an undefinable look in her eyes. Celine had met her type before: spoilt, developing-country dilettante—Nineteenth Street pullulated with them. Their fathers were usually big shots in their governments back home, and they spent their two years at IMFO strutting about in fancy clothes and going to posh Georgetown parties. They were cliquish and clannish, and could appear ever so innocent and helpless whenever they wanted something. Men fell for it every time.

"Perhaps when I get back, then?" Celine tried to keep a note of appeal from creeping into her voice.

"Absolutely." Harry escorted her to the door. "Let's definitely have lunch when you're back."

Celine reached the door and turned back. The woman was still watching her. And now Celine recognized the look in those black, feline eyes.

Triumph.

CHAPTER FOURTEEN

T HEY STARTED THE FOLLOWING MORNING. Harry's office became their
headquarters. Five new computers were brought in, wangled from the
department's formidable Administrative Officer, and connected together to
allow parallel processing. They hummed day and night, belching out heat and
a dizzying array of numbers, and within Policy Review, colleagues would stop
by just to admire this latest tourist attraction.

As far as Harry was concerned, the project was nothing more than pure
research, an effort to improve the performance of his exchange rate forecasting
model. When the time came, Sophia would have to co-opt it to her own purpose—quite how, she hadn't yet figured out. Meanwhile, the work absorbed
them, swallowing their lives whole, like whales gulping down shrimp. Soon
they were at it ten, twelve hours a day, oblivious to the world around them.

They formed the perfect team, each feeding off the other's obsession.
Harry might be analytically more adept, but Sophia brought ingenious short-
cuts to finesse the myriad technical problems, and gradually each had earned
the other's respect.

Over the coming weeks and months, Sophia found herself growing closer
to Harry. She put it down to their working together—there was no doubt he
was brilliant, and Sophia congratulated herself on her prescience at having

spotted him—but beyond this, and the simple physical desire accentuated by the stress and tension of her double life, she began to suspect there might be something more.

One evening sometime after Thanksgiving, watching Harry hunched over his desk in the upstairs study of his modest townhouse on the fashionable edge of Georgetown, Sophia was reminded of her father, with almost painful vividness. Both men could be so utterly focused on their objectives: Daddy on battling the injustices of the regime, Harry in perfecting the neural net. When Sophia was a child, sometimes late at night she would sneak down the spiral staircase in her father's library and watch Daddy through the banisters as he sat at his desk, absorbed in his writing. Suddenly, he would look up and spot her and smile, as Harry did now. Much to her disconcertment, Sophia realized how easily she might fall in love.

Guilt and emotion were not what she'd bargained for, and work was the only palliative, taken constantly like aspirins to numb her feelings. There were times when she was tempted to come clean, to explain about her people and their cause, to tell him about her operation and admit the real reason she so desperately needed the model to work. More than once, she very nearly did. But she doubted she could make Harry understand. He lived in a world where theory was more real than reality, and reality more theoretical than theory. Sometimes, his lack of interest in what was happening in the real world astounded her. Besides, Melamed would never countenance such a breach of security.

At first, they made little headway. They spliced Sophia's genetic learning algorithm to Harry's neural net, but it required hundreds of hours of computing time before the learning routines showed any signs of convergence at all. Then gradually, as they tweaked the parameters and twiddled the nodes, the model's forecasting performance began to improve.

By mid-December, it had become truly impressive; even Pettigrew admitted as much. It was doing about as well as could be hoped without the intervention data. They had applied for access to the central bank intervention database a couple of weeks ago, only to be summarily turned down, and Sophia had already broached the idea, only half-jokingly, of somehow stealing the data. Harry had simply laughed.

Meanwhile, they decided to celebrate the model's success. They left work early that day and bought all their favorite Lebanese foods: hummus, kibbeh, grape leaves, tabouleh—Sophia insisted on at least one healthy item—and those funny little sausages whose name she could never remember. Harry made his specialty for dessert, an assortment of berries warmed in a soup of raspberry coulis and topped by a ball of vanilla ice cream.

Afterward, they moved to the living room and lingered over the second half of a Châteauneuf du Pape.

"God, I ate too much," Sophia sighed. She stretched out luxuriously on the sofa, burying her face in a cushion. The fire gave off a contented glow.

Harry was fiddling with the stereo. "Shall I put some music on?"

"Yes. Hang on." She reached for her bag. "I've got a surprise."

It was a music CD she had picked up when she'd visited her home country; beautiful, haunting music, the strained tones of a pained people. Harry sat on the sofa beside her, trying valiantly not to fidget, and finally admitted he preferred something classical. By which he meant Western.

"Don't you ever read these?" Sophia asked, spotting the week's supply of the *New York Times*, still unopened, stacked neatly beside Harry's collection of CDs.

"Eventually," Harry replied cheerfully. "But I prefer my news once it's matured a bit, like a good wine. That way, you know what's going to turn out important, and you don't waste a lot of time with stories that don't go anywhere."

Sophia laughed. "But don't you want to know what's happening in the world?"

"We get summaries of the major economic events on the 'Morning Press' blue sheet every day in the office."

"But what about the rest? Politics, for instance."

"It's the policies, not the politics that matter," Harry announced, echoing a popular IMFO refrain.

"I meant more broadly. East-West, North-South, wars, famines, political persecutions, human rights, and all that. Don't you care about any of them?"

"Oh, sure I do. But I'm a firm believer in comparative advantage. Rather than trying to figure out which dictator is doing what abuse, it's much more efficient and effective for me to write a check to Amnesty International. In fact, I send them money every year." He frowned. "At least, I normally do. Though, come to think of it, I can't seem to remember doing so this year . . ."

"The trouble with you, is that you're an intellectual without a cause."

Far from taking offense, Harry found this brilliantly witty, flinging his arms around her in delight. And in that instant, Sophia knew he would never understand her commitment to the Cause. She knew it, and in her heart she forgave him for it. Her body softened against his. Harry squeezed her a little tighter, then they slowly pulled apart.

A log crashed in the fireplace with a spray of sparks. They watched it in silence a moment, then Harry looked at her. "Would you like a back rub, Sophia?" he ventured.

Yes. Very much. She knew it was folly to continue, that it would cause no end of complications later, but she suddenly didn't give a damn. She wanted him. For once, she told herself, she would indulge her desires.

She looked at Harry, a hungry spark in her eyes. "What sort of back rub?" she asked him. "Don't be coy. If you mean a massage, then say so." She paused provocatively. "And yes, as a matter of fact, I'd love one."

"Actually," Harry said, grinning sheepishly, "I think I've got some massage oil somewhere around here. Sandalwood, I think. Don't move, I'll be right back." He returned a moment later, laden with freshly laundered towels and clutching a bottle of oil.

Sophia took the bottle from him and examined the label. "Curious the things you just happen to have lying around."

Harry grinned. "Just lie down, relax, and place yourself in my singularly competent hands."

She did.

———

I'm a whore, a whore, a whore. Sophia scrubbed herself viciously, hot with shame. How could she have done it? A wave of nausea hit her, and she had to turn the water completely to cold to stop herself from gagging. Sleeping with Harry meant nothing. She would do it again, making love a thousand times to a hundred men if necessary. It was her duty; Melamed expected nothing less. But to have enjoyed it like that, to have derived pleasure from it, to have exulted in the sensuousness of the experience . . . Betrayed by her base appetites, she had sullied the mission, devalued the Cause.

Sophia stopped herself, amazed at her own emotions. She was being ludicrously melodramatic. They *were* making progress, the operation *was* advancing; surely she had earned the right to indulge her appetites and emotions this once. Then what was troubling her? she wondered. That she might succumb to the cosy warmth of Harry's love? That, in the end, she would realize Melamed's worst fears and fail to see the operation through? Or was it simply that her carefully sculpted relationship with Harry had slipped, if only for a moment, perilously out of her control?

And suddenly, Sophia remembered Melamed's warning during their lunch at Oxford.

There was a light tap on the door. "Sophia? Are you okay?"

"Yes, yes. I'm fine," she called out. "Sorry. I'll be right out."

In atonement, she resolved that she would get Harry to agree to steal the intervention data this very day. Even if they didn't succeed in actually getting the data, Sophia wanted him as an accomplice so that he would at least be used to the idea of using the stolen data for the neural net.

It might be better to wait a little longer, to lay the groundwork of their relationship, but time was running out. Besides, Harry would be in a confident mood right now, pleased with his conquest. Yes, she decided, as though settling a matter of principle, they would try for the intervention data today.

She brought it up after brunch, when half the day had been frittered away—sipping coffee, reading comics and horoscopes, swapping stories, and laughing at each other's jokes—mentioning the matter casually.

"You know, I meant to tell you. I was speaking to this guy from Information Services, and he told me that all the data at IMFO physically resides on the same computer server system."

Bent over to load the dishwasher, Harry grunted, "So?"

Sophia gave a little laugh. "Nothing," she said. "But it did occur to me that the intervention data must be on there somewhere."

"Doesn't mean we can access it."

"I'm not so sure. You see, my division chief must have privileged access to the system—and I've got his login name and password."

"How come?"

"Oh, he's completely computer illiterate, and now that I've become the desk economist, I have to handle all sorts of stuff for him, so he gave me his password."

"I'm not sure I like where this is heading," Harry said, looking up.

Sophia crouched down beside him, nestling her head against his shoulder as she passed him the last of the plates. "You know how activist central banks have been in the forex markets over the past couple of years. The neural net is never going to perform optimally unless it can learn the central bank intervention patterns. And for that we need to feed in the actual minute-by-minute intervention data. Otherwise, it'll never give the accuracy that I know your model is capable of delivering. Couldn't we try it, just this once?" she cooed. "Wouldn't you like to see how well your model can do when we feed in the intervention data? I bet it blows any other model right out of the water."

"Our model."

"*Your* model," Sophia insisted, passing her fingers idly through his hair and tousling it. But Harry shook his head clear.

"Have you any idea of the kind of trouble we could get into if we're caught?" He let the door of the dishwasher slam with an air of finality.

"We're not just talking about getting fired—we could face criminal prosecution."

Sophia stood up, shrugging. "If we're able to access the data, we could just claim we didn't realize it was so secret. And if we can't, we'll simply pretend that we were looking for something else and came across it by mistake. Of course, if you're worried . . ." she let her voice trail off, knowing he would be piqued by the implication.

"It's not that I'm afraid," Harry said quickly, "but I don't see any point in taking useless risks. I mean, even if we somehow managed to access the intervention data, it wouldn't help because we couldn't publish the results of the neural net without admitting we'd stolen the data in the first place."

"So what? *We* would know how well it can do. Come on, Harry," Sophia said, slipping her arm around him. "Where's your intellectual curiosity? You've spent more than a year working on this model, and you know how much better it'll do with the intervention data. Surely you owe it a shot?"

Owe to whom, she could see him thinking. To himself? To Sophia? To the neural net, their virtual child, conceived not in the frenzied lovemaking of the night before but in months of painful labor?

"All right," Harry nodded at last. "We'll try. But we'd better not get caught."

CHAPTER FIFTEEN

WITH GROWING APPREHENSION, Sophia watched the weeks glide by, fretful that her timetable was slipping out of reach. She had managed to fob off a threatened visit by Melamed and Huron back in December, but January, blustery and lachrymose, was already drawing to a close.

Harry was away, skiing in Europe with his parents. He had tried to persuade Sophia to join them, even getting his mother to write her a special invitation. The irony was not lost on Sophia: if Simon's parents had been half as forthcoming, she might never have ended up here. But she couldn't go. Melamed would never allow it. Besides, she was hopelessly behind schedule; so far, she hadn't even been able to get hold of the intervention data, let alone incorporate it into the neural net.

Her attempt to access the data with Harry in December had come tantalizingly close. They had actually reached the menu that specified which intervention data they wanted, when suddenly the screen went blank, then spat out, INVALID LOGON ID FOR REQUESTED SERIES. ACCESS DENIED, and bumped them off the system. Worse, they'd very nearly been caught by Pettigrew, who apparently had nothing better to do than prowl about the office on the weekend. After that, Harry had flatly refused to try again.

Since then, Sophia had found out that only certain members of the Statistics Department staff had unrestricted access to the intervention data. Once she managed to infiltrate one of their accounts, it would be a simple matter to reconfigure the protection attribute on the file server and gain access to the data from any terminal on the network. The difficulty was breaking in. Melamed had sent her a hacker program, a piece of Russian junk, that so far had succeeded only in locking up her own account.

Sophia was just wondering whether she dared to call Information Services, when there was a knock on the door, a menacing sound that echoed through the room. A rather overweight man filled the doorway.

"Hi," he grunted dourly. "You're having mainframe access problems?"

"No. I mean, yes," she laughed. "What I mean is, I think I forgot my password—I can't get into my account."

The man gave an exaggerated sigh. "Oh, is that it? They could've done a reset downstairs. I don't know why they sent me up here."

"I'm sorry."

"Well, I might as well check your connection." He waddled to the back of the computer.

Sophia realized the hacker program was on her desk, the skull and crossbones logo on the label foolishly proclaiming its nefarious purpose.

"Nah, there's nothing wrong here," the man said, abruptly turning around.

Sophia tore her eyes away. "Oh," she said, edging toward the desk to hide the disk.

"I'll just call them downstairs and have them do a password reset for you." He dialed, magically bypassing the voice mail system. "Okay," he said, after a few moments. "They've set your password to your logon ID. You can change it once you're into the system."

"Oh, thanks." Sophia graced him with a smile. "I'm so sorry to have dragged you up here for nothing."

It wasn't just that she smiled, it was that he knew she didn't have to waste a smile on him. "Look," he said, with a quick glance around the room, as though suspecting someone might overhear. "We don't normally encourage users to do this, but I'll show you an easy trick to keep you from forgetting your password. You see how these keyboards have a PROGRAM key? Here, on the upper right-hand corner?"

Sophia nodded.

"Yeah, well you can assign any sequence of keystrokes to a particular key or combination of keys. So look, hit the program key, then the key that you want to assign the script to—let's say, CTRL-ALT-F1—and then you can store your logon ID and password. Just remember to separate them with a back-slash. When you're done, you just hit program again.

He typed rapidly, pecking at the keyboard with two fingers. "*Et voila!*" he said in a grotesque attempt at French. "Now, when the network prompts you for ID and password, all you have to do is hit CTRL-ALT-F1. Of course, it's not very secure, but heck, everyone does it, and it's probably no worse than using your birthday as your password. You didn't learn this from me, though," he added with a grin, then wished her a good evening and left.

Sophia hurled the wretched hacker software into the trash the instant he was gone. She would call Melamed tomorrow to see whether he couldn't get hold of a better program and, she decided defiantly, to demand to know what had happened to the money she was promised. For all Huron's griping about her lack of progress, he had been curiously quiet about coming up with the funds she needed for the operation.

Sophia left the office, walking up Nineteenth Street. Outside, it was bitterly cold; not the bright, crisp cold so characteristic of Washington winters, but an insidious damp chill that seeped through her coat and poured into her bones. It reminded Sophia of her first year at school in England. That winter—Michaelmas, as it was officially known—was the worst; tepid baths in two inches of water, foul food, freezing hockey games, and the desperate loneliness of an eight-year-old foreign girl trying to fit in at a British boarding school. The only good part about Michaelmas term was that on weekend evenings the girls would get to see a film, played on the wheezing projector in Great Hall instead of being expected to play outdoors.

One December night it was *Escape from Colditz*, standard British fare: prisoners of war tunneling their way out of a German camp. It was their inspiration to escape from boarding school.

The five other girls in Sophia's dormitory set to work stealing provisions from the pantry, sneaking copies of railway timetables from the headmistress's study, and, most important of all, tunneling their way through an old sewer-age pipe that led from the scrubby vegetable patches into the surrounding woods. Why they bothered when they could have simply walked through the gates was beyond explanation—it was all part of the fun, the excitement, the adventure. Through much of this, Sophia was excluded, admitted to the group only grudgingly because she was willing to do the grunt work of dig-ging out the accumulated mud.

The tunnel was ready at last; an engineering marvel, they were sure, on par with the Channel Tunnel being bruited at that time, and the girls drew straws for the honor of breaking through to the other side. Sophia won. Cyn-thia, the dormitory captain, wanted her excluded, but for once, the others stood up for her. It was Sophia's proudest moment.

Halfway through, the tunnel collapsed.

There was a long, shocked silence. Finally, a muffled sound reached her. One of the girls was calling frantically, "Sophia, are you all right?" Then again, louder. "Sophia? What happened? Can you hear?"

Then Cynthia's desperate command. "Shut up, you fool! We'll be caught."

The first girl, once more. "Sophia's in trouble!"

But Sophia could still breathe, and after a few minutes' struggle she man-aged to poke a small hole through to the others and tell them she was all right, but firmly stuck. A heated debate followed. Some of the girls were for staying and digging her out. But Cynthia, asserting her authority as dormitory cap-tain and afraid of getting caught, was for clearing out at once, even if it meant leaving Sophia trapped in the tunnel.

Horrified, Sophia wanted to cry, *No! Don't leave me, I'm scared! It's dark and cold and frightening!*

But then she heard Cynthia saying, "Wogs are all the same—little yellow-bellied cowards. She'll get us all caught and expelled."

Fierce, foolish pride made Sophia reply before she could stop herself. "Go. I'll be okay. Get out of here before you're caught. I won't give you away." She had no watch, and wouldn't have been able to read it anyway. It was cold and dark and lonely. Sophia spent the time crying and praying that somehow, through some miracle, Daddy would come back to life and rescue her. And perhaps at some point, when she thought she could bear it no longer, that the soil would suffocate her and the earth crush her, his ghost really did come back, holding her and hugging her, imbuing her with the strength and resolve to see the night through.

They found her the next morning after she'd missed roll call, numb with cold and exposure. Sophia was sent home, both as punishment and as convalescence. She remembered her stepmother's resentment at having her home, unspoken yet revealed in a hundred little ways. Through it all, Sophia refused to give the names of the other girls. But far from earning her friendship, her defiance gained her only the jealous hatred of Cynthia, who mocked her looks, her accent, her everything, with the cruelty that only children can know. And never, ever, did Cynthia allow Sophia back into the group.

———

There was a parcel awaiting Sophia when she reached home that evening. She scooped it up, a thin, oblong package, its shape oddly familiar. Once indoors, Sophia turned it over in her hands and ripped off the brown paper wrapping. It was a box with four Vues de Genève chocolates. Sophia stared at them, puzzled. They were from Melamed, of course, but why send them now? A belated Christmas gift?

She rummaged in the packaging, looking for a note or a letter but found none. Then she laughed and dashed into the kitchen, returning with a knife. She pried off the white chocolate tops of the Vues. *Yes!* Melamed had buried the miniature digital disk in the Vue of the Palais des Nations.

Sophia slipped the disk into her computer, where it whirred and hummed a moment before loading. Mathewsen and Huron had come through. They had sent the money.

Seeing it all there gave the operation a frightening sense of reality. There were lists and lists: monies deposited, accounts opened, portfolios created. A history of relations with established financial firms in the United States, Europe, and Asia had been conjured out of thin air—dozens of accounts invested in various currencies and assets, running into hundreds of millions of dollars. Sophia scrolled through them anxiously. She had warned Mathewsen that to bypass Securities and Exchange Commission disclosure rules, each fictitious investor would have to be accredited as a high-net-worth individual, meaning each had a million dollars at least. For once, Mathewsen had listened, and with a sigh of relief Sophia found that the smallest investment was for two and a half million dollars. When the time came, these accounts would be used to generate capital flows, propagate rumors, launch speculative attacks, and spread panic in the international financial system. Meanwhile, she intended to move the money out of the accounts, away from the prying eyes of Mathewsen and Huron.

She locked away the disk and returned to the kitchen, munching the remnants of the chocolates. Yes, she conceded mentally, Huron had come through, better than she'd ever expected. The sum they had given her was staggering. Buying on margin and leveraging herself to the hilt, she could easily have ten times that amount at her disposal. But it also meant that Huron would be more impatient than ever, pressing her for progress with the rest of the operation. Besides, an even more compelling deadline was looming: the Finance Ministers' Summit had been scheduled for late April.

She *must* find some way of getting hold of the intervention data, Sophia told herself for the umpteenth time. And a gun. Melamed had been nagging her for weeks about it. She needed a weapon, as a last resort, in case things went badly wrong. Next week she would go to some shady corner of Virginia and arrange to buy one. It was plausible enough; although buying a gun was difficult in Washington, DC, many women got one from Virginia for protection.

The kettle started whistling, and she was just pouring herself a cup of tea, when she had an inspiration. It was so remarkably simple, she could scarcely believe it might work.

Sophia took a taxi back to the office. With an enquiring glance, the guard signed her in. Sophia muttered something about a damn deadline, and he nodded sympathetically. She went up to the seventh floor, then stopped, cursing her stupidity. She should have checked whether anyone from Statistics had signed in. Peering up and down the corridor, she slipped into the first office and pulled the door closed behind her. There was just about enough ambient light to work with, but she decided it would be more suspicious to be caught fiddling about in the dark. The neon lights flickered, trying to catch hold.

The computer booted up with a horribly loud beep, then went through an interminable login sequence. Finally, the prompt appeared. Stretching her fingers, she typed CTRL-ALT-F1, all at the same time.

Nothing happened.

In desperation, she tried CTRL-ALT-F2. And then she was going through all the combinations. Nothing worked. She knew she should get out. She had been there too long already. Somebody was going to catch her. The thoughts tripped through her mind in rapid succession, but still she kept trying, wiping her sticky palms on her skirt. No good; she'd have to try the next office.

She was working her way down the corridor, when the lights suddenly went out. For a moment, Sophia was close to panic. Then she remembered that in the evening, the lights went out automatically periodically, which meant she had been at it at least half an hour. Her luck wouldn't last forever; at some point, the guard would be coming around. There were twelve more offices, so she must choose judiciously.

Sophia settled on the department director. He was probably the most computer illiterate and the most likely to store his password in a key sequence. She marched into his office, carelessly flicking on the lights. If she got caught now, there would be no bluffing her way out. She might find some excuse for being in another economist's office, but she would never be able to explain her presence here. She switched on the machine, waiting for it to boot up.

And then it caught her eye. A beautiful journal, bound in calfskin and held closed by a brass clasp. Sophia slipped off the clasp and flipped through the pages. There were entries for almost every day. It brought to mind the diaries Daddy used to keep . . .

The computer beeped impatiently, interrupting her thoughts. She leaned over the chair and reached for the keys without much enthusiasm. She was in. It all happened so fast, she barely had time to realize she had succeeded. The magic CTRL-ALT-F1 had been the key. She loaded a virus routine that invisibly changed the server drive attribute from "protect" to "read only." Now, with the right commands, the data could be accessed anytime, anywhere, from any computer on the system.

At the sound of a footfall in the corridor, Sophia switched off the computer and the lights, then cracked open the door. The security guard was passing on his rounds. She waited until he was around the corner, then edged out. She had just reached the elevator when she remembered she'd left the diary out of place. She hesitated, torn between the desire to get away and the risk of arousing suspicion. She finally went back, slipping in and out of the office in an instant, but bumped smack into someone just as she turned to leave the room.

Karin Wulf.

"Hullo!" Karin said, startled.

"Christ, you frightened the hell out of me," Sophia said, clutching her hand to her chest.

"What are you up to?"

"Me? Nothing. The lifts were taking forever, so I thought I'd walk down to the K Street exit, but I got totally lost in the building."

"It's a terrible maze," nodded Karin, "especially when you're new."

But that hardly explains what you were doing in the director's office. Sophia could see the thought flitting through Karin's mind. There was an awkward pause while the two women stood face-to-face, Sophia trying to conjure up some excuse, Karin eyeing the door suspiciously.

Then Sophia gave a conciliatory little laugh. "Truth to tell," she said, "as I was walking past, I saw the director's door had been left a bit ajar, so I thought I'd sneak a peek at how the other half lives."

"Oh, yes." Karin brightened, as though relieved. "They've got pretty fancy offices, haven't they?"

"I guess it'll be a while before I get one like that."

"'Fraid so," Karin laughed, "Are you headed home?"

"Well, I was trying to."

"Come along, then. Follow me. I'll show you the way out."

Once outside, Sophia walked away quickly, huddled against the bitter, gritty wind that assailed her from the north, thinking not of her close call with Karin but of the diaries Daddy used to keep. She had found them one day by chance, almost ten years ago, while hunting in the attic for an old doll's house. At first she couldn't figure out what they were. Whenever she'd asked for her father's papers before, her mother would tell her none had survived. But there they were, dozens of black leather-bound notebooks, tossed into a trunk and forgotten these twenty years.

It was all there, in meticulous lawyerly script, covering page after page of the quarto notebooks: the love for his daughter and young wife, his fears for their safety as he started defending the politicals, his agony over the decision to send them abroad.

As a sort of homage to her father, Sophia had read and reread the diaries, memorizing whole chunks of them. The last entry, written in blotchy blue ink, she could still picture precisely in her mind:

I know I shall not succeed in saving these brave men and women, but if I can at least expose the lies and propaganda, and preserve the truth for posterity, then one day surely it shall rise up and strike terror in the hearts of tyrants. I am sad only that I shall not see my darling Sophia again. I know that now. They have made clear that I must desist or face the consequences. I do not know how or when, but they will find some way of silencing me. I only hope, dear God, I shall at least have done my duty and can face my Creator with clear conscience.

Then, scribbled hastily below in pencil:

Call Hamley's Toy Shop, re: Meccano No. 10

Sophia wiped the tears from her eyes, assailed not by the wind now, but by self-doubt. What would Daddy have thought of what she was doing? The airline bombing would have horrified him. He was a decent, kindly, gentle man, he would never have countenanced such an act. She must have been mad to have agreed to it. Somehow, though, it hadn't seemed real until it was too late. But it was as though Daddy's spirit had intervened, saving her from becoming a murderer. Sophia coddled herself in the comfort of that thought, hugging her jacket close against the biting wind and the insecurity of the moment.

She crossed the road, sheltering in the doorway of a church, but praying to some more ancient god for some hint, some sign, some omen, that what she was doing was right. At that instant, the moon pierced the dark clouds, revealing the Washington Monument, breathtaking in its simplicity.

And she knew, she just knew, that Daddy was telling her it was all right, that she should go ahead, that he would be there if she needed him.

CHAPTER SIXTEEN

F LUSHED WITH ENTHUSIASM, Sophia and Harry started the day he returned from Europe. But almost at once they ran into problems, individually of no account, but together adding up to long, frustrating delays.

First, the special software they ordered took two weeks instead of two days to arrive. Then they found that the genetic algorithms were unable to digest the mass of intervention data they were pouring into the model and had to be reprogrammed from scratch. To top it all, Sophia was dispatched on her first mission—a fruitless, frustrating trip to New Delhi, entirely spent arguing with the impossible Indian officials—which cost her another fortnight. So it wasn't until mid-March, long after Sophia's original schedule demanded, that they finally succeeded in incorporating the intervention data into the neural net.

But now Sophia got greedy. It occurred to her that there was plenty of other intelligence at IMFO, much of it highly confidential, on what was happening in various member countries. Getting it would improve the model's forecasting power, along with Sophia's chances of success. There were useful nuggets to be found in everything from briefing papers to back-to-office reports, and Sophia was soon foraging through stacks of folders, in search of any titbit to feed the ever voracious neural net.

As a first-year YEP, she didn't have access to the highly sensitive cases. She needed Harry for those. But of late, relations with him had come increasingly under strain. He made no secret that he was wearying of the project and of Sophia's near-obsession to perfect the neural net. Worse, Harry was getting nervous about the sheer volume of confidential reports they were pilfering to feed into it. He told her repeatedly that there was really no point in continuing, since they wouldn't be able to publish the results of the model without revealing the source of their data anyway. They had already satisfied themselves on how much better the neural net performed once it had the intervention data, and they ought to be content with that. His obsession was that they publish the results from the basic version of the neural net before somebody scooped them with a similar model.

News on the home front was no better. Huron and Mathewsen were carping about her lack of progress, and Melamed had sent her a disturbing message about the December bombing a couple of days ago. The authorities had figured out that the bomb was in a suitcase that had been transferred from another flight at Heathrow, not one that had originated there. Though this did not entirely rule out IRA involvement, it certainly made it more implausible. The police were still a long way from tracing the suitcase to Sophia, and Melamed told her not to panic. But reading between the lines she could sense his worry, and it added to her own.

One morning, toward the end of March, Sophia was rummaging in Harry's file cabinet, looking for the Turkish staff report, when she came across a stack of Country Strategy Briefs secreted in the bottom drawer. CSBs detailed each central bank's contingency plans in case of a speculative attack against its currency. They were a gold mine for planning Sophia's own speculative attacks, and for weeks she'd been pestering Harry to get her copies. But he always fobbed her off, saying they weren't of any use for improving the neural net, and that he didn't have access to them anyway. Now, she realized he must have had them all along.

Harry normally arrived around nine thirty a.m.; she had ten minutes. Sophia pulled out a pad and set to work at once, jotting down some notes for the most crucial countries. Suddenly, she became aware of a presence behind her. She whipped around.

Celine stood in the doorway. "Hello," she nodded, looking around the office. "Where's Harry?"

"He hasn't come in yet. I was just waiting for him; he should be here any minute."

"Well, in that case, perhaps I'll just wait here." Celine entered the room and planted herself in Harry's armchair.

A long silence fell between them, punctuated by the whir of the printer. Sophia smiled, a taut, nervous smile as she edged away from the desk and the stack of gray folders with RESTRICTED SUBSCRIPTION emblazoned across them in giant, scarlet letters.

"So, how's your research with Harry coming along?" Celine asked.

"Pretty well. Of course, we still have some bugs to work out of the neural net, but with luck, we should be done some time next month. We're sending out an academic version for publication, and Research wants to adopt our model for their Exchange Rate Early Warning System."

"That's good."

They lapsed into silence again.

Sophia glanced at the clock nervously. Harry would be arriving any moment and would wonder why the Country Strategy Briefs were lying on the table.

"Was there something in particular you wanted to talk to Harry about?" she blurted out. She knew immediately it was the wrong thing to say; it sounded condescending and possessive. She could see the flicker of resentment in Celine's eyes. "What I mean is, Harry might be a while. If you like I could give him a message, or just tell him you stopped by."

"It's okay. I'll wait."

They lapsed into silence again. Finally, Sophia could bear it no longer.

"What do you think of the gold sales?" she essayed, pointing to the pile of "Morning Press" blue sheets that littered Harry's desk. It was the latest buzz on Nineteenth Street—the Europeans had gone public with their proposal to use the IMFO gold for debt relief.

Celine shrugged. "It's sheer hypocrisy."

"But surely it's a good idea—I mean, if we can use our gold to forgive the debts of the poorest countries, then why not?"

"I don't know what you mean by 'our' gold," Celine replied coldly. "It belongs to our member countries—all of them. The Europeans are being very smart. They get the good publicity for proposing debt relief, and in effect pay themselves back with the IMFO gold. And it doesn't even help the poor countries since they aren't making debt payments anyway. That's why Kiyotaki is so opposed to the whole scheme."

"Well, I suppose Kiyotaki doesn't always get his way with the Board," Sophia said, realizing too late her *faux pas*.

Celine's face flushed, a dull, angry red. Abruptly, she stood up. "Perhaps I will just leave Harry a note, after all."

"Oh, of course." Sophia reached across the desk for a pad and a pencil hurriedly, before Celine could get too close. But Celine had already spotted the stack of CSBs. Her eyes strayed from the files, to Sophia, to her notebook, as if connecting the dots.

"Those aren't CSBs, are they?"

"What?"

"Country Strategy Briefs," Celine frowned. "They're restricted to Policy Review. Did Harry ask you to make those notes?"

"Well, yes. He had a whole pile of CSBs to plow through, and he asked me to help him by jotting down some notes."

"Indeed. I'll have to have a word with him about this."

"About what?" Harry asked from the doorway.

The two women spun around.

"Oh, hullo, Harry. Sophia tells me you asked her to summarize some CSBs. I don't like to be all bureaucratic and officious, but they are strictly restricted to Policy Review."

"I didn't . . . ," began Harry.

For God's sake, back me up. Sophia shot him a desperate, pleading glance.

"Oh, right. I'm sorry," Harry went on, coming into the room. "My fault. I know they're restricted. It's just that since Sophia and I work together so much, I guess I consider her a *de facto* if not *de jure* member of the department."

"And I'm sure we'd love to have her as an honorary member," Celine laughed in a more conciliatory tone. "But that's not the point. These are numbered copies that really do have to be restricted to members of the department.

Otherwise, you could both get into one hell of a lot of trouble. An economist was fired from IMFO last year for inadvertently leaking a Restricted Subscription file."

"Okay," Harry nodded.

"And when you leave your office you should return them to the file room, or at least lock them away in your desk."

"Yes, yes. I will."

"All right, enough lecturing. I actually came by to tell you I'm having a dinner party next Friday, before I head off to the wilds of Ukraine. Just a small gathering for a few friends. Can you make it? And Sophia too, of course. Around eight?"

"Sure, sounds good to me. That okay with you, Sophia?"

"Oh, yes. Yes. Very much. Thank you."

"Good. It's settled then. Next Friday at eight. Don't forget what I told you about the files," Celine reminded Harry, then gave Sophia a sidelong glance and left.

Sophia closed the door, heaving a silent sigh of relief. But Harry was looking at her pensively. Before he had a chance to ask any questions she delved into her briefcase and handed him a wad of printouts—the latest run from the neural net. He flipped through them perfunctorily.

"It's just like I thought," he said, tossing the pile onto the desk. "All this tinkering about isn't getting us anywhere. We should write up the paper and send it off before someone scoops us."

Sophia picked up the pages, instantly annoyed. She remembered Harry's initial excitement at getting the intervention data. At one time, they used to joke that the neural net was their virtual child and would lavish every attention on it like doting parents, celebrating its successes, commiserating its failures, willingly giving up every waking moment of their time to its existence. Now Harry didn't seem to give a damn. Just like a man's attitude toward sex, Sophia decided. Full of passion to the moment of climax, boredom the instant after.

"You didn't look at the simulations."

"What's to see?"

"Here." Sophia handed the stack back to Harry. "I tried reparametrizing the back-propagation routines, and that seems to help."

"Only marginally."

"Precisely. And that's why we need to be more systematic about cleaning up the back-propagation routines. You know, we've patched them and repatched them dozens of times. Don't you think you should rewrite them from scratch now?"

"You've got to be kidding. Those routines took weeks to write."

"True, but now you know how to do them. It won't take you nearly so long."

"It won't take me any time at all, because I'm not going to do it."

"Then I'll do it myself," Sophia said, tossing her hair.

"You? You don't even know the programming language."

"I'll learn."

"Well, you haven't much time because come hell or high water, I'm wrapping up this project next week."

"Then I'll just have to learn quickly, won't I?"

"Suit yourself. But I still think it's a total waste of time. Speaking of which, I've got a meeting in an hour that I have to prepare for."

"Right."

Sophia paused at the door, and turned around. Harry was at his desk, gathering up the CSBs, putting them into a tidy pile. He never said a word.

———

Celine walked back toward her office, pondering her encounter with Sophia. Previously, she wouldn't have given the matter a second thought, but time hung heavy on her hands these days. She supposed she should be preparing for her Ukraine mission, but somehow it seemed such a hopeless, futile assignment that she simply couldn't be bothered. Besides, she had a morbid fascination with finding out more about Sophia.

From the guilty look on Sophia's face and the startled look on Harry's, it was obvious he had never asked her to redact those files. That Sophia should be curious and take a quick peek was nothing very remarkable. But to be taking notes suggested a deliberateness that couldn't be explained away as mere idle curiosity. Sophia must have some reason for wanting those Country Strategy Briefs.

The odd thing was that Sophia didn't strike Celine as the prying sort. The chief complaint the other YEPs had about Sophia was that she was a snob, seldom joining in their social activities. Above all, Celine decided, Sophia was an enigma. True, she had all the right credentials, from her expensive schooling in Switzerland and England to her degrees from Oxford and the LSE, but beyond that, no one seemed to know much about her. She seemed to defy categorization. At first, Celine had been inclined to dismiss her as one of the spoiled, rich international jet-setters who hang about New York and London and Paris, with the occasional exile to Geneva or Washington. But from what Celine had seen of her these past three months, Sophia was no dilettante dabbling in the world of international finance for the glamour or the fun. Unlike Harry, she wasn't motivated by purely intellectual interest either. Rather, she seemed driven to a particular purpose as though on some quest or crusade. But what?

On a sudden inspiration, Celine remembered that the division should have all the YEP's personnel files since they were circulating across departments for the YEPs to be chosen for their second-year assignments. After some argument with the secretary, she managed to get hold of Sophia's.

Back in her office, Celine opened the file gingerly. But there was nothing remarkable: a flattering photo, Sophia's original application form listing her various qualifications, two application essays, and a glowing Interim Performance Assessment from her current division chief. Celine leafed through them, realizing how absurd she'd been to think she would find some great revelation about the woman here.

Still, she plowed through the file, taking an occasional note on the back of an old envelope. Finally, she put the file down and stared out the window. Only two things struck her as strange. First, a small discrepancy in dates, a missing period of perhaps six to nine months between the time Sophia had finished her doctorate at the LSE and her joining IMFO. Of course, it might be nothing more than an extended vacation, but Sophia also seemed to have taken inordinately long doing her PhD, as though she might have taken a break in the middle. But if so, she hadn't listed any work experience.

The other thing was Sophia's response to why she wanted to join IMFO. She had written: "I want to help my people." *My people*, not my country. It seemed to be a strange way of putting it. Surely, Celine thought, it would have been more natural to have written, "I want to help my country," or "I want to help the world," or "I want to help developing countries," or whatever corny crap one writes in application essays. But "I want to help my *people*," struck her as decidedly odd. It made Sophia sound like some Che Guevara freedom fighter.

It wasn't much to go on. But then why was it that the moment she had spotted Sophia taking notes on the Country Strategy Briefs, she'd instantly been suspicious of her? Then it came to her. It was something Karin had mentioned quite casually, weeks, perhaps months ago. Something about catching Sophia snooping in the statistics department director's office late one night. Karin hadn't thought much of it, and at the time, neither had Celine. But now she wondered.

There had been instances in the past of staff being involved in illegal insider trading. With so much confidential information being bandied about Nineteenth Street—everything from news of impending devaluations to the imminent fall of governments—and with the potential profits running into the millions, the temptation was just too great for it never to happen.

Celine had never heard of a case of someone joining IMFO just to steal such information, but why not? A single, well-planned trade could earn you enough to retire on. And with money fungible across countries and continents, virtually impossible to detect.

Perhaps she was just being fanciful. Her run-in with Adanpur and the perfidy of the Executive Board had made Celine unduly sensitive, bordering on paranoid. She was seeing ghosts and conspiracies at every turn, she told herself. There were probably quite innocent explanations for Sophia's behavior. Next week, when Sophia came over for dinner, would be the perfect opportunity to find out more about her.

Meanwhile, Celine could do some snooping of her own. She reached for the computer keyboard and called up the DOCUMENT MANAGEMENT FACILITY, which gave staff on-line access to the archives and various IMFO documents—briefing papers, BTOs, staff reports, and Board papers. But more important, the system kept a record of previous requests so they could be updated automatically whenever a new paper on a particular country or topic was issued.

The standard was the person's surname as the user name and first name as the password. Celine tried Sophia's, but that didn't seem to work. Celine stared at the screen a moment, then laughed and typed GEMAYE for the user name, and HARRY rather than SOPHIA for the password. The cursor blinked a moment, then the screen filled with the listing of Sophia's document requests. Celine scrolled through the pages in growing astonishment. Most IMFO documents carried the standard confidentiality strictures against public dissemination, but were otherwise unrestricted to the staff. In a typical year, Celine might consult thirty or forty documents, covering perhaps a couple of dozen countries. Yet in the space of six short months, Sophia had ordered well over three hundred. Celine switched off the machine and leaned back in her chair. Ms. Gemaye, she decided, most definitely warranted watching more closely.

CHAPTER SEVENTEEN

H ARRY POPPED HIS HEAD INTO SOPHIA'S OFFICE. "Don't forget, eight o'clock. We mustn't be late. Shall I pick you up from home?"

"What?" Sophia looked up from the computer manual she'd been perusing. The muscles at the back of her neck felt as tightly wound as a spring, and her eyes ached dully from staring at the screen so long.

"Celine's dinner party. Don't tell me you'd forgotten?"

She had, of course.

It was Friday, and they had not seen each other all week. Sophia had been avoiding him ever since the incident with the Country Strategy Briefs. The weeks and months of deception were taking their toll, and she was tired of the lie. Harry would suggest a summer vacation in San Francisco, and Sophia would accept, only to remember she'd be long gone by then. Or he'd innocently ask where she'd been, and Sophia, who'd been traipsing the wilds of Virginia in search of a gun, would have to invent some mumbling story. Or, worst of all, he would talk of their future together, and Sophia would fall silent, knowing they had none.

They were small lies of no special importance but carved deeply into their relationship, and their pettiness made Sophia feel shabby. Yesterday, she and Harry were supposed to go to the Kennedy Center for a concert, but she had to beg off, pleading a headache and a touch of cold. She had finally found someone willing to sell her a gun with a silencer. She returned late at night, walking through the drizzling rain, which she hoped would somehow clear her mind and cleanse her soul.

The problem wasn't Harry, it was herself, and her growing temptation to abandon the operation and settle down in Washington instead. Perhaps that was why she'd put off reporting to Melamed for the past three weeks. Sick of his urgent appeals for information, she had simply stopped decoding his messages.

But this morning brought a rude shock. On her voice mail was a message, announcing the arrival of Melamed and Huron on the afternoon flight from Zurich and ordering her to meet them this evening.

"No, no. Of course I didn't forget." Sophia paused. "Could you come and take a look at these Laplace algorithms? There's a bug in here somewhere, but I can't figure out where."

"Oh, Christ. Don't tell me you're still struggling with those wretched back-propagation routines." Harry plonked himself in Sophia's chair, making no effort to take the proffered printout.

"Yes, I am."

"What for?"

"Well, since you obviously can't be bothered—"

"No, I damn well can't. First of all, I've just come from an idiotic five-hour meeting arguing about the Global Economic Outlook forecasts, and I'm in no mood for debugging computer programs. Second, reprogramming the back-propagation routines is going to make damn little difference to the neural net. And third, I think you're becoming dangerously obsessed with this stupid project."

"You don't understand," Sophia snatched back the printout.

The threatened arrival of Melamed and Huron had given her an added sense of urgency, and she had spent the day in a frantic effort to at least get the back-propagation routines done.

"Understand what?"

Sophia bit her lower lip. "Nothing," she muttered, turning back to the computer. In the reflection on the screen, she could see Harry shrug.

"Well, do you want me to pick you up or not? I don't mind coming by, or you can go straight to Celine's."

"Oh, Harry, I can't go," she said, her eyes big and pleading. "Tell Celine I'm sorry, but I really don't feel up to it."

"If you didn't want to go, you should've said so earlier. We can't cancel now. It would be terribly rude—her party is in less than three hours. Besides, Celine has been going through a hard time for the last couple of months, and she was kind enough to invite us to dinner. I'm certainly not going to let her down."

Sophia closed her eyes and let her shoulders sag, hoping her tiredness might magically drain away. "Well, I can't go," she repeated more firmly, then returned to the computer manual, thumbing through the pages in search of the index.

"Hang on," Harry said sharply. "You can't go because you're not feeling well, or because you want to continue work?"

"I told you, I'm not well."

"Like last night?"

"*Yes.*"

"Oh, I see. I was just curious, because when I came to your place last night I found you'd made a miraculous recovery and gone out for the evening."

Sophia whipped around. "How dare you! Who the hell do you think you are, checking up on me like that? For your information, you don't own me, and I most certainly don't have to justify where and how I spend my evenings."

"I wasn't checking up on you. I came by with some Thai shrimp lemon grass soup for your cold, and to make sure you were okay since I hadn't seen you all week."

"I went for a walk."

"Of course," Harry nodded. "You refuse to go to a concert because you say you've got a bad cold, so you go out in the pouring rain for a couple of hours instead."

"Yes," Sophia snapped. "If you must know, I needed some fresh air."

"Oh, really."

"Don't you trust me?"

"Should I?" Harry shrugged. "You don't even want to move in with me," he added, dredging up a long-standing aggrievement.

"What's that got to do with anything?"

"Well, for starters, it gives a pretty clear indication of your commitment, or lack thereof, to our relationship."

"No, it doesn't," Sophia protested. "I've told you a million times, it's not that I don't want to be with you. It's just that I have to have a place of my own."

"Sometimes I wonder what you do want from our relationship. All you really seem to care about is getting your hands on the neural net. If it weren't for that, I wonder whether you'd bother with me at all."

"That's not true! You mean a lot to me. You know that."

Harry shrugged again. "Look, if you don't want to go to Celine's, that's fine. I'll go and tell her some fib or other about why you couldn't make it.

"God knows," he added under his breath, "I have to lie for you often enough these days."

"Harry," she said, her voice breaking. She wished she could admit it all. She wanted to tell him about her people, their struggle, her own meager attempts at justice. She would tell him the truth and revel in the luxury of telling no more lies.

But by now Harry was on the other side of the room, and the stained regulation IMFO-beige carpet stretched forlorn between them. She knew she could never make him understand; she said nothing. After a moment, Harry turned and left the room, quintessentially out of reach.

═══════

How absurdly amateurish, Sophia thought as she left the office an hour later and headed down Pennsylvania Avenue. Melamed and Huron had landed at Dulles airport a short while ago and were demanding a meeting right away. But Huron was afraid that Sophia might be seen at his hotel, and Sophia was damned if she was going to bring him to her apartment, so she was told to come up with a place that was public yet secluded enough to allow them to talk in private. She thought of all the usual tourist spots, smiling at the image of them standing about the Lincoln Memorial, conspiring under the steely eye of Abe. A shopping mall? Too crowded, too noisy. And then she remembered Lauinger Library at Georgetown University. Perfect. The place was open to the public, and the university provided the ideal cover. As Sophia remembered, there were sound-proof study rooms on the third floor—relics of the days when students hammered out papers on typewriters—secluded at the back.

Still, the whole business of crash meetings and secret rendezvous struck her as being not merely childish but senselessly risky. Huron and Mathewsen knew nothing about running an operation, that much was clear. All they did was hang about their five-star hotels, dreaming of toppling the president and dipping into their stolen millions occasionally to bankroll one hopeless scheme after another. Their silly jitters and amateur theatricals might jeopardize the whole operation one day. But that was the price of their money; she and Melamed just had to make the best of it.

Sophia was still muttering to herself about Huron's stupidity, when some sixth sense made her turn around.

She was being followed.

The man was thickset, completely hairless, with an ugly bulbous nose, a pockmarked face, and no apparent neck. But his eyes frightened her most. They were the most remorseless eyes she had ever seen, shuttered windows into a soulless man. Even Melamed's blind eye, staring milkily heavenward, seemed less desolate. There was something horribly systematic about the way the man was scanning her every movement, and she felt like a gazelle caught in the sights of a cheetah. She shuddered, turned away quickly, and hurried on.

At first, she couldn't be sure he was really following her. He was walking along the parallel sidewalk, sometimes ahead of her, sometimes behind, always keeping a decent distance. She cast her mind back, trying to remember if he'd been following her since she left the office. Hadn't she first seen him lurking at the corner of Nineteenth Street, half-hidden behind a newspaper?

She tried weaving in and out of the various M Street shops, from the overpriced art galleries to the understocked bookshops, but to no avail. The man would either go in behind her or loiter somewhere outside. She thought of stopping a policeman, but she had no proof that the man was following her. Besides, she had a sudden clutch of fear that he *was* a policeman, or with the FBI, the CIA, or whatever other agency might be involved with counter-terrorism.

Sophia had assumed that the purpose of Melamed's summons was to give her a dressing down about her lack of progress, but now it occurred to her it might be something more sinister. Perhaps the authorities had traced the bomb to her baggage. They wouldn't necessarily arrest her right away; they might watch her for weeks, even months, hoping she would lead them to her co-conspirators. Maybe Melamed and Huron were coming to warn her to keep a low profile, or help her escape.

But then she thought, surely not. If Huron knew of any danger, the last thing he'd do would be to risk his own skin warning Sophia. And if she were in any imminent danger, Melamed would have ordered her to get away at once, then link up with him later. Besides, if they suspected Sophia, would the FBI have assigned only one person to follow her? That thought was even more chilling, and she soon found herself suspecting everyone, from the dapper clerk emerging from the sex shop with his fishily hopeful eyes, to the homeless man panhandling on the corner, to the Pakistani cab driver parked illegally by the curb.

Or this man might be an accomplice of Mathewsen and Huron, who were fed up with waiting for her report and intent on keeping tabs on her. But why now? They would be meeting her in half an hour anyway, and though she couldn't be sure, Sophia didn't think the man had been following her before.

Then she hit on another explanation. Celine O'Rourke had been suspicious last week when she caught Sophia taking notes on the Country Strategy Briefs. And a couple of days ago, when Sophia logged on to the Document Management Facility, the system claimed her previous login had been last Friday, while she was quite sure that it wasn't. At the time, she hadn't given the matter much thought, but it occurred to her now that Celine was a deputy division chief, and if she were genuinely suspicious she could probably use her position to find out what other documents Sophia had been pilfering.

Sophia's mind raced ahead. Maybe Karin had told Celine about the time she spotted Sophia coming out of the Statistics Department. And perhaps Pettigrew *had* noticed something that day he'd barged in on them downloading the data, then later mentioned it to Celine. She cursed Celine roundly. *That bloody busybody*, poking her nose in other people's affairs. Celine brought to mind the English girls of her childhood who were always conspiring against Sophia and managing to make her school days such a misery. This man was likely some friend or colleague of Celine's, and she'd asked to keep an eye on Sophia.

Of course, Celine was not the only one getting suspicious. That story Harry had told about bringing her soup for her fever was absurdly lame. He knew she could've ordered food delivered if she'd been hungry. This man could just as likely have been sent by Harry, wanting to know what she was up to tonight.

But then again, would Harry, or Celine for that matter, actually know such a person? Sophia wondered. With his brooding scowl and expressionless eyes, there was something deeply unsettling about him. Though it was still daylight, and there were plenty of people about, Sophia felt the primeval feminine fear of the male.

She finally came up with a plan for evading him. Ducking into one of the chic women's clothing boutiques, she grabbed a dress and made straight for the changing rooms, where the man couldn't follow. She waited a moment to lull his suspicions, then dumped the dress and walked to the back of the shop, exiting through the employee door.

Once outside, she heaved a sigh of relief. Making her way along Thirty-third Street, she started looking around for a cab. Then her blood froze. The man was back, standing with his arms crossed in front of a tobacco shop, watching her. If she jumped in a cab now, he would simply follow her.

Sophia felt faint and had to force herself to breathe deeply to keep from passing out. She looked around for someone, anyone, to help. But then she remembered the operation. Whoever he was, she couldn't risk compromising Melamed and Huron. And time was running out; she was supposed to meet them in twenty minutes.

Though she was outdoors, Sophia felt claustrophobic, as though they were all—Celine, Karin, Harry, Huron, Mathewsen, Melamed, and the scores of nameless, faceless FBI agents—crowding in on her. She found herself breathing in sharp, painful gasps, almost hyperventilating, like the time she was trapped in that tunnel at school. If she didn't manage to get away from this man at once, she was going to have a full-blown anxiety attack.

She hurried into a large chain bookstore with a coffee shop, the neighborhood public library for yuppies. She rode the escalator to the second floor, heading for the coffee bar, picking up an expensive-looking art book along the way. Sure enough, as she rounded the escalator at the top, Sophia saw the man entering the store and looking around hesitantly.

Sophia settled into the far corner and searched through the book, running her nail along the spine of each page. About two-thirds of the way in, she found the thin, white magnetic inventory-control strip and slid it out. The man had found her now; he was across the aisle, browsing through books for expectant mothers.

Sophia walked toward him. The man turned his face away as she passed by, and she slipped the inventory-control tag deftly into his jacket pocket, then headed down the escalators to the checkout counter. When he was just a few yards behind her, Sophia dropped the book on the counter, quickly made for the exit, and dove into a passing taxi. Just as she slammed the cab door closed, she heard the shop's anti-theft alarm go off and the security guard, politely but insistently, detaining the man who had been following her.

By the time she reached the university and was scurrying up the steps to Lauinger Library, her nerves had calmed a bit. She went from room to room, peeping through the glass slits in the doors, until at last she found Melamed. Seeing him, she felt the sudden relief of a lost child in a shopping mall who finally finds its parent. She wanted to fling her arms around Melamed, tell him about the man who'd been following her, let him comfort and hold her, and snuggle in the warmth of his protection. But Huron was there, seated stiffly against the wall by the blackboard, and she had to content herself with a quick peck on the cheek.

Noticing her anxious look, Melamed drew her aside. "Everything okay?"

She nodded distractedly.

"You look pale," he said plaintively. "You've lost weight."

"I'm fine," she said, mindful of Huron. "What's this meeting about?"

"We haven't heard from you in weeks and were getting worried. You should've responded."

"I was busy."

Melamed was about to say more, when Mathewsen came into the room, looking too debonair in his Yves Saint Laurent blazer and Salvatore Ferragamo tie to be a student. Again, he stood in sharp contrast to Huron, who was swathed ridiculously in sweater and scarves, determined to resist any hint of draft. Only Melamed had dressed the part, a respectable retiree out to broaden his mind and slim his wallet in some continuing education course.

"We want to know what you've been doing," Mathewsen began without any preamble.

Why he should be the one to speak instead of Melamed or Huron, Sophia didn't know. She knew only that she resented it. Her nerves were still on edge, and she was in no mood for any nonsense.

"Plenty. I hadn't realized I was supposed to report to you. I thought it had been made quite clear to you that there was to be no contact between us."

"That's before the money went missing." Mathewsen approached her, nodding. "Oh, yes, we're not that stupid. We checked the accounts; they've been completely cleaned out. So, my dear," he said, grabbing her by the wrist and twisting her close, "we want some answers, and we want them now."

"Who the hell do you think you are, interrogating me like this?" Sophia tugged sharply, breaking free of his grip.

"The people who're bankrolling your little jaunt, that's who. And we'd like to know what you've been doing with our money."

She was about to come back with an angry retort when Huron intervened.

"Nobody is interrogating you, nor are we suggesting any impropriety," he said smoothly, with a warning glance at Mathewsen. "But we're naturally anxious to know what was holding up your operation—and whether we might be of any help."

"Nothing is holding it up." For a moment, Sophia toyed with the idea of telling them about her difficulties with the model, but she rejected it right away. They would never understand, and she didn't want to admit to having problems. "The operation is going perfectly. The launch date is late April, and I intend to be on time."

"Then why is the money missing?" Mathewsen asked.

"For God's sake, it's not 'missing'! I simply transferred the funds from the individual accounts to the hedge fund, as if those individuals had invested their money in an offshore hedge fund based in the Caymans."

"So, where is the money?"

"Physically? Well, the hedge fund's own accounts are on deposit in a Geneva bank."

"But we don't have access to those accounts. We don't control them; we don't even know how much money they have in them. Have you at least been making profits?"

"Some. Nothing too conspicuous. But yes, the money has grown."

"I see," Mathewsen said. "And other than making these profits, which I'm surprised you didn't report, what else have you been doing?"

"I'm sorry," she said frostily. "I hadn't realized you wanted financial reports. But I'll be more than happy to provide them."

"You didn't answer my question."

"What I've been doing is none of your goddamn business," Sophia snapped. "And I'm not going to answer questions put to me like that. It may be your money, but you don't own me." She turned angrily to Melamed, wondering why he didn't intervene. Didn't he trust her either?

"I think," Melamed said, staring at Mathewsen, "an apology would be in order."

Even then, Mathewsen said nothing, until Huron nodded his head. "I'm sorry I got excited," he muttered. "There's a lot at stake here."

A lot of money. That's all he really cares about. But Sophia nodded, somewhat mollified. "Well, briefly, I've been able to get hold of the central bank intervention data, and I'm just about done developing the computer model I need to predict exchange rates when I launch my speculative attacks."

"You mean you've really succeeded in making this model?"

Sophia nodded. "I'm down to a forecast error of less than one-tenth of one percentage point—depending on the currency and the exact circumstances, of course."

"Have you any proof?"

"Proof of what?"

"That you can really predict exchange rate movements so precisely."

"No, of course not." Her anger returned at once. "I could show you reams of computer printouts, but you wouldn't know whether they're real or completely made up. So let's stop playing these silly games, shall we?" she said, in an unreasonably reasonable voice. "And maybe you can tell me what's really bothering you."

"Good idea." Mathewsen came around the table and planted himself squarely in front of her. "I'll tell you what's bothering us. You take a few hundred million dollars from us, and that's the last we hear from you. Yes, perhaps the hedge fund's been established, but you moved the money out of the accounts without our authorization, without even informing us. Melamed is your controller, and we're told that for security reasons there should be no direct contact between us, and that you can only confide in him. Fine. But you haven't, have you? He admits he hasn't heard from you in weeks. So I'll tell you what's bothering us, it's that one of these days, you and the money are going to conveniently disappear."

"Don't be stupid," Sophia replied. "I'm not an airline running on a schedule. I've got to lead a normal life here. How do you suppose I have access to the intervention data? Through my job, obviously. And it's not just a one-time thing. I need continuous updates. If I get fired, it's over. I also need someone's help with the neural net. I'm living with this man, using him, making love to him, all to get him to work for me. Don't you realize I can't just pick up the phone and give reports? It all has to be done in code. And the code has to be changed for each message—there are computers constantly monitoring international phone calls looking for code words that can lead to a tip-off. All this takes time, lots of time. I'm already working fifteen, twenty hours a day, and I'm not going to waste my time on reports when I've got nothing to report. Didn't he tell you all this?" she concluded, gesturing at Melamed.

"Of course I told them. But they needed to hear it for themselves."

"Nonetheless, we shall need some additional safeguards from now on." Mathewsen snapped open his briefcase—a leather case, with too much shiny brass—and pulled out a thick sheaf of papers. He held them out to her. "These are instruments of power of attorney. We need you to sign them under the names you've used to establish the hedge fund accounts, and any other deposits as well."

"No." Hands on hips, tightened lips.

"Why not?"

Sheer perversity, she might have told them. But it was more than that. She simply didn't trust Mathewsen and Huron. Once she handed over control of the hedge fund's assets, she would be at their mercy. Right up to the last minute of the operation, the hedge fund's assets would be completely legitimate. With the power of attorney, Mathewsen or Huron could pull out of the operation, or at least siphon off some cash, whenever they wanted.

"Security," she replied. "Mine and yours. The less connection between us, the better. You certainly wouldn't want my activities traced back to you, would you?"

Huron nodded slowly. "This man, the one who is helping you, Hoffinger, does he have the computer model, the neural net or whatever it is you call it?"

"What do you mean?"

"Physically. The disks, memory sticks, and what not. Who has them—you or him?"

"He does. But don't worry, I always keep the latest version backed up in my apartment. And once the model has been fully developed, I can run the neural net on a portable platform by connecting four laptops in parallel. I won't need the network anymore—except for updates of the intervention data, of course."

"I see," Mathewsen nodded. "And you're sure, quite sure, that you don't have to rely on him—you've got everything you need to run the neural net in your own apartment?"

"Yes."

"Where?"

Sophia hesitated. "Hidden among my collection of music discs," she said at last, unable to come up with a convincing lie. "I've got dozens of them. No one's going to know which ones are genuine and which ones have data recorded on them."

Mathewsen and Huron exchanged quick glances, then nodded.

"Good," Huron said. "And afterward, you will eliminate him."

"No!"

It was Melamed who spoke before Sophia could even absorb what Huron was saying. "We are not killers, murdering without rhyme or reason," he said, inches from Huron's face. "We are patriots fighting for our freedom. This man has done nothing to deserve death, and I see no purpose in eliminating him."

The two men stared at each other, Huron's eyes shifting uneasily, Melamed's single eye resolute and unwavering. Then Huron gave a little laugh, his lip curling into a sneer. "This woman," he said, without even deigning to point at Sophia, "has made you soft, my friend."

Melamed said nothing.

"Very well," Huron went on, "It's your show. But be warned, I'm not taking risks just because you've become squeamish. If I find you've left any loose ends, I'll tie them up myself."

"There'll be no loose ends."

"Precisely," Mathewsen interjected smoothly. "That's why we want these PA forms signed."

Sophia stared at him, a cold clutch in the pit of her stomach. The bastard! Mathewsen had divined her weak spot—the threat was clear enough: either she toe the line and sign the power of attorney forms, or Harry's life was in danger.

Mathewsen was still holding out the forms to her. He had her, and he knew it. She reached forward wearily, slipped the pages from Mathewsen's hand, and flipped through them rapidly.

"By all means, read them through."

"Thank you, I shall," Sophia said, grateful for even this little show of defiance. She pulled up a chair and began reading leisurely. She was about to sign the first of the documents, then paused. "What does this clause mean?"

Mathewsen looked over her shoulder. "Oh that . . . nothing. Most power of attorneys expire with the death of the principal. Of course, we don't expect anything to happen to you, but if it did we'd hardly want to go to probate to get our money back. It's a standard clause," he added.

Sophia forbore from saying that if most PAs expired when the principal died, then it could hardly be a standard clause. "Very well. Do you want me to sign the ones for the hedge fund now, or do you trust me enough to wait for the whole lot tomorrow?"

"Tomorrow will be fine." Huron seemed embarrassed, eager to get away. He clasped Sophia's hand. "Good luck. And God bless you for what you're doing for our people."

The moment they were gone, Melamed put his arms around Sophia and kissed her hair. "I'm sorry you were subjected to all that nonsense," he said, "but I had no choice. They turned up a couple of days ago, demanding to know what was going on, and what had happened to the money. When they found out I hadn't heard from you, they insisted on knowing the whole plan, every detail. It was hard to refuse them. Frankly, your not responding to my messages didn't help."

"You didn't tell them, did you?"

"What do you take me for? But bringing them here and having you sign those wretched papers was the only way to appease them. I'm sorry, but I had no option. You're not too upset, I hope."

Sophia shook her head.

"Good. I have to go to New York with these clowns on Sunday, probably spend the better part of the week there. But I can stop for a few days in Washington on my way back to Geneva." He paused. "If you want me to, that is."

"Yes." Sophia threaded her arm through Melamed's, resting her head against his shoulder. "Meanwhile," she sighed, "I'd better get back to Harry. We had a row yesterday."

"You're in love with him, aren't you?"

"No." She pulled away to retrieve her jacket.

"Look at me." When she turned, Melamed gently swept aside a wisp of hair from her face. "Now tell me the truth."

Sophia looked up at him defiantly, saying nothing.

Melamed shook his head. "I should have guessed this would happen. Was that why you didn't answer my messages, because you're having second thoughts about going through with the operation?"

"Of course not. I told you before, I've been busy, and I wanted to wait until I had something more concrete to report."

Melamed sighed. "And how close are you? The truth, mind you. Not the bullshit you fed Mathewsen."

Sophia shrugged. "I'm close, I really am. But I can't finish without Harry's help. And he's getting sick of the whole project. I'm not sure I can persuade him to continue."

"Is he essential?"

"If I'm to be done in time."

"And what will you do afterward?"

"I don't know," she whispered. "I don't know."

"Well, don't say I didn't warn you about this before you started," Melamed said as they left the room. "Operations always end up like this, with unanticipated, unintended consequences."

"They're not really thinking of killing Harry, are they?"

"No, that's just cowboy talk. As long as your friend doesn't know who Huron and Mathewsen are, he poses no danger to them. Anyway, don't worry, I won't let them do anything to him. But we must watch Huron and Mathewsen closely. They're nervous, and nervous men are dangerous."

"What are they afraid of—that I'm going to run off with their precious money?"

"Partly, but it's more than that. They're afraid you might fail and get caught. If there's any link traced back to Huron, he could have all his assets—not just the money he lent us—frozen, sequestered by the authorities. I'm sure he's got plenty stashed away around the world, but even so, he stands to lose hundreds of millions. Still, God forbid you should fail, Mathewsen and Huron will be the least of our problems. It's the others in the cadre back home I worry about. They're getting impatient. So far I've been able to hold them back and protect you and your operation. But they want action, and they want it fast. They don't believe in all this fancy stuff about speculative attacks and collapsing currencies. Quite frankly, they don't understand much of it. They're pressing for something more traditional, more spectacular—a hijacking, a bombing, maybe even a full-blown civil war back home. You'd better make sure nothing goes wrong with your operation, or there could be a bloodbath in our country."

"Well, nothing will," Sophia replied. Melamed smiled his agreement.

But when they passed through the exit, as the work-study guard was making a perfunctory search of Sophia's bag for stolen books, she remembered the man who had been following her. Her confidence evaporated.

"Let's take a cab," she suggested.

"Oh, no. The hotel's not far, and it's such a lovely night. Besides, I like walking through Georgetown. It's the nicest part of Washington."

Sophia scanned the streets. The man was nowhere to be seen. Still, she hesitated, but Melamed was already walking down O Street. She hurried to catch up with him, her heels clicking along the cobblestones.

Melamed was in fine form, enjoying the evening stroll, telling her of the various preparations he was making in Geneva. He'd already made a complete reconnaissance of the site. The Semtex had been smuggled from Bucharest to Berlin, and should arrive in Geneva early next week. The key, he told her, relishing the details, would be to use a shaped charge and place it just right at the base of the pillars. Otherwise, they'd either end up with a dud bang or an uncontrollable inferno.

Sophia nodded, her mind elsewhere. Something was worrying her about tonight's meeting, something that had been said that didn't ring true, but she couldn't figure out what. As she walked with Melamed, she kept sensing that they were being watched, though each time she tried looking around—adjusting her shoe, bending over to pick up a coin, or pausing to gaze at a shop window—there was no one in sight.

Finally, Melamed stopped abruptly at the corner of Wisconsin Avenue. "All right," he said. "What's the matter?"

"Nothing." But there was no fooling Melamed, and she finally told him about the man who had been following her that afternoon.

Melamed discounted the possibility that it was the police. Even if they knew what connecting flight the bomb had come from, it would still require an extraordinary feat of detective work to trace it back to Sophia. Besides, he added, the tail sounded improbably amateurish, unless it was a decoy and someone else had been watching for her reaction to being tailed.

"Do you think Huron and Mathewsen might have someone watching me?"

"Possibly. In fact, from your description, that's much more likely. It would make sense, since they've been worried you might disappear with their money. But if they've got someone, they certainly haven't told me. How long have you been followed?"

"I can't be sure."

"I shouldn't worry. It was probably just some weirdo who took a fancy to you," Melamed told her, as though it were a comfort. "After all," he added with a smile, "you *are* an attractive woman."

She left him at his hotel and continued toward Dupont Circle. She was just about to cross the street, about a block away from the hotel that Huron and Melamed were staying at, when a yellow sports car rounded the corner and roared down the road. Even before seeing the vanity plates, she knew it was Karin Wulf's MGB. As the car shot past, Sophia could see Karin at the wheel, and a tall, fair-haired man beside her who looked awfully like Mathewsen for an instant. Sophia shook her head. You're becoming paranoid, she told herself.

But as she trotted up the stairs to her apartment, she realized what had been troubling her. She had never mentioned Harry's name to Huron and Mathewsen, yet they seemed to know all about him. No doubt they'd found out from Melamed. But then again, she couldn't remember telling Melamed Harry's last name either.

═══

Harry helped Celine with the dishes. The others had left, and she felt the evening had been a success. She had first come to IMFO with the vision of entertaining regularly—select soirées, where there would be fine wit and fine wine, with the fate of nations being decided twixt dinner and dessert. Though it had never been quite like that, she and Karin had been known for their festive parties and frequent receptions during the halcyon months, before her disastrous mission to Indonesia. But Celine preferred quieter, more intimate gatherings these days. She was either getting too old for those boisterous parties, or she was beyond trying to prove her popularity.

Harry walked into the kitchen, laden with dishes. "Shall I put them in the dishwasher?"

"No, no. They need to be washed by hand. Just put them down by the sink. I'll deal with them tomorrow." They were gold-rimmed and pedigreed Villeroy & Boch dinner plates that had originally belonged to Celine's grandmother. That they had survived her father's bankruptcy proceedings was testament to her mother's determination to cling to the vestiges of gentility.

"Nonsense. We can do them together in no time. Besides, you're off tomorrow, and you're bound to be busy."

"Actually, I'm not leaving until Sunday. But if you're sure you don't mind . . ."

They worked in silence, comfortable enough not to have to make small talk. From time to time, Celine would glance at Harry, wondering when to bring up the subject of Sophia. During dinner, of course, there had been no opportunity, and now Celine was reluctant to break their rhythm of work. When Harry announced, "Well, that's the lot," she realized she'd missed her chance.

But afterward, lingering over a decaf espresso and some brandy, she said, "It's a shame Sophia couldn't make it. I was looking forward to meeting her—socially, I mean. I hope she feels better soon."

Harry said nothing.

"Nothing serious, is it?"

"Oh, no." Harry stared into his cup. "Just a touch of cold. She was worried she might give it to you before you went off to Ukraine."

"Well, it's a pity nonetheless. She seems a very nice girl . . ."

"Oh yes," Harry agreed quickly.

Celine fell silent again, struggling to find some way of sounding her suspicions without appearing paranoid or absurd. The candles flickered, as though caught by a breeze, and it occurred to Celine that she hadn't been this close to Harry since that night at his club. They were both leaning back on the sofa, barely a foot apart, and Celine had only to stretch out her fingertips to caress the sculpted contours of his face.

But she had the oddest sensation that she wouldn't be able to touch him if she actually tried. It was as though Sophia, invisible but corporeal, was lying in that narrow space between them. The feeling was so real that Celine was almost tempted to try. She wondered how Harry would react, whether he still felt anything for her. All she could think of was what a fool she'd been to miss her chance at happiness. And for what? For a middle-aged, married man who wasn't a man at all—just an excuse for a hole in the air—who'd betrayed her trust and used her not once, but twice.

Perhaps Harry sensed what was going through her mind, for he edged away slightly, avoiding her eyes, as though he didn't trust himself not to succumb to temptation.

"Harry?" she asked tentatively.

"Yes?"

She gave a nervous little laugh. "It's none of my business, of course, but . . . do you and Sophia have plans for the future?"

Harry nodded slowly. "I know I have. Sophia's still a YEP, and I think she needs to feel more settled before she makes any decisions. I can't imagine what she's worrying about—her division chief in Research thinks the world of her. They're bound to offer her a regular staff appointment when she finishes as a YEP. Still, I suppose it's hard for her to focus on her personal life for the next few months, but I'm very hopeful."

Celine felt a curious pang at his words. She had long known about their relationship, of course, but deep down she had harbored the hope it would prove just a fleeting fancy. Harry and Sophia weren't actually living together—that much she'd found out from Karin—and with Celine finally free of Adanpur, there seemed at least a chance of resuming her relationship with Harry. Even this evening, when Harry had turned up alone, at least for an instant, part of her was hoping they'd had a fight and broken up. But looking at him now, Celine realized it was no mere flirtation. He was committed, his jawline drawn with hungry determination, as if to say he would do anything and everything for Sophia.

"What do you know about her?" she asked.

"What's there to know? Her parents are dead, she was brought up in England and Switzerland, and she got her degrees from Oxford and the LSE."

"Christ, men are useless! I mean, what's she *like*? As a person? What are her passions and prejudices?"

"Oh, I don't know. She's very serious about work. She likes the ballet and dislikes the opera. She hates novels written in the present tense, and has a passion for the old 60s TV series—especially *The Avengers*."

"*The Avengers*? Oh, then, she can't be all bad," Celine laughed.

She went over to the drinks trolley, retrieved the bottle of cognac, and poured them each a generous portion. She took a deep breath and said, "Harry? Can I ask you something?"

"Sure."

"Those Country Strategy Briefs . . . you never really asked Sophia to summarize them, did you?"

"I don't know what you mean," he said stiffly.

"Last Friday, when I found Sophia rifling through the CSBs, she claimed you'd asked her to make notes for you. But you had done nothing of the sort, had you? And another thing," she continued quickly, before Harry could respond, "why has Sophia checked out more than three hundred staff reports and BTOs in the last couple of months? What's she up to?"

"What exactly are you getting at?"

"I don't know. But she's—"

"Well, I do," Harry interrupted angrily. "I know exactly what you're trying to do, and I think it's utterly unworthy of you."

"Harry, it's not what you think. I'm not trying to break up the two of you. It's just that . . . I'm afraid she's using you for her own purposes."

"Please stop!" Harry stood up. "I really don't want to discuss this matter further. Anyway, it's getting late. I should be going."

Celine looked up into his eyes. What she saw wasn't anger, but resignation. He knows, she thought, he knows she's using him, but he loves her nonetheless. "I'm sorry," she said. "Honestly, I didn't mean any harm."

"It's okay. Don't worry about it." Harry bent down and kissed her on the cheek to show there was no ill-feeling. "Have a good mission to Ukraine," he added. "Tell you what, when you get back from mission, Sophia and I will have you over for dinner."

CHAPTER EIGHTEEN

THEY CAME SUNDAY MORNING, a man and a woman, special agents of the Federal Bureau of Investigation. *What makes them special* wondered Sophia, *and are there ordinary agents as well?* But thinking it impolitic to ask, she simply smiled and invited them in. The man was dressed formally, in a gray suit that matched his graying hair. The woman, young enough to be his daughter, was dressed more casually. She was wearing jeans, a T-shirt, and a sports jacket with the sleeves rolled up. They flashed their IDs, but Sophia never caught their names. In her mind, she dubbed them Tweedledum and Tweedledee.

Just some routine questions, they assured her. Sophia nodded. She'd thought she had her cover story down pat, but now she was filled with doubt, anxious of being tripped up by some innocuous inconsistency and wishing she'd rehearsed it more.

Should she flatly deny being in Washington last December? What if they knew she'd taken the flight? Admit as much, and play innocent about losing her luggage on the London-Geneva leg? They may suspect, she told herself, leading them into the living room, but they don't yet have any definite proof.

"I guess you know what we're here about, ma'am," began Tweedledum.

"We'd be interested in any information you can provide," continued Tweedledee.

"Well, of course." Never volunteer information, she admonished herself, remembering Melamed's mantra. "Actually," she said, looking at him steadily, "I'm not quite sure I do know what this is all about. Perhaps you could fill me in."

They stared at her in surprise. "It's about the stabbing that took place on R Street last Friday night," said Tweedledee.

"The victim just died in the hospital from the wounds he sustained, which makes it a murder case now," added Tweedledum.

"Oh, *that.*" Sophia felt the relief flooding through her. "I heard about it on TV, but I'm afraid I really know nothing about it."

"Oh." Tweedledee looked so crestfallen that Sophia couldn't help feeling sorry for her.

"Won't you sit down?" she asked, gesturing toward the sofa. "Can I offer you some coffee? I was just having some myself."

"That would be great," Tweedledee replied.

Sophia plunged the coffee press and poured out two cups, topping them with some frothy milk.

"When exactly did you say it happened?"

"Friday night, sometime between eight thirty and eight forty-five p.m. Just on the corner of R Street," Tweedledum said. "We were wondering whether you might have seen something. Anything at all."

Sophia frowned. "Friday night . . . ," she began. She had been in Georgetown, meeting Melamed and Huron. She swallowed, shaking her head, "No, Friday night I left the office late, then went to Georgetown to do some shopping. I didn't get back home until past ten p.m."

"Oh, where do you work?" Tweedledee asked casually, adding sugar to her coffee and settling more comfortably into the sofa.

"IMFO. The International Monetary and Financial Organization."

"Oh, how *interesting,*" Tweedledee gushed. "Must be *such* an interesting job."

"Well, yes," Sophia admitted. "It has its up and downs, but on the whole I'm enjoying it. Of course, I haven't been there long . . . "

How long? And before that? Wow! Oxford *and* the LSE! So, it was really *Dr.* Gemaye. And how was she enjoying Washington? Yes, *great* city isn't it? First time here, or had Sophia been in the States before? Oh, New York, naturally. And why Dupont Circle and not Georgetown? Oh, absolutely, *much* more fun, but more crime as well.

No, a condo's pretty safe. Did Sophia travel much? Oh, of course she would, wouldn't she, working at IMFO? Must be great, going off to those exciting, exotic locales—and at the taxpayers' expense!

"No, no," protested Sophia, "IMFO isn't funded by taxpayers—at least, not beyond the initial capital subscription."

"Really? So who pays for the billions in bailouts?"

"They're not bailouts, they're loans. IMFO's a bank, with member countries owning shares according to their quota, and getting proportionate profits annually in return."

Tweedledum was getting bored. His eyes kept shifting from side to side, scanning the room. Finally, with a vague "Do you mind?" he shuffled off toward the bathroom. But Tweedledee continued, undaunted, and soon they were discussing all manner of things, from where to go shopping to the best Ethiopian restaurants.

Sure, there's a great place for petite-sized shoes, Tweedledee told her—designer stuff, half price, too! No, afraid not, the big malls are out in the 'burbs. But the new mayor's much better, not like the last one. Yeah, well, it's not an easy place to run, especially when it snows.

"Were you here during the big blizzard last December?" Tweedledee continued, refilling her cup.

Sophia was about to nod when she remembered that she had already claimed to have only been to New York before. This woman's dangerous, Sophia thought, suddenly very much alert. Even her pretext of questioning Sophia was thin. There *had* been some sort of mugging reported on the news, she remembered, but now she thought that had been Thursday night, not Friday. And anyway, would the FBI get involved in a simple stabbing? Besides, why the interest in Sophia? It required some stretch of the imagination, or at least a stretch of the neck, to see R Street from her window.

They had been chatting away merrily for the better part of ten minutes, and Sophia was appalled at just how much information she had inadvertently let slip. And where the hell was Tweedledum? The bathroom was through her bedroom; he'd been gone most of the time they'd been talking. Desperately, she tried cataloging in her mind whether he might find anything compromising, all the while trying to continue the inane conversation with Tweedledee.

There were stacks of printouts from the neural net, of course, but there was nothing particularly incriminating about those. And he might come across some of the intervention data, but she doubted he would realize the significance. The disk with Huron's accounts, thank God, were hidden among her music discs. She must remove it, she reminded herself. Then she remembered. The gun! The goddamn gun! It was hidden in the tower case of the large, defunct computer. The back of the machine was fastened with a couple of butterfly nuts, readily removed, and allowing easy access to the gun. But would he think to look there? Would they arrest her right away? And on what charge? Weapons possession, or something more serious?

Just then, Tweedledum reappeared, pointedly adjusting his belt as if he'd just come out of the bathroom. Sophia forced a smile and stood up.

"Tell me something," she said. "Of course, my only source is the movies, but I thought the FBI doesn't normally get involved in simple stabbing cases."

Tweedledum looked at Tweedledee. And Tweedledee looked at Tweedledum.

"It's a gay man."

"A homosexual," Tweedledum nodded solemnly.

"I don't quite—"

"Could be a hate crime, see?" Tweedledee explained, suddenly very businesslike. "The victim was stabbed repeatedly, but nothing was stolen from him. That's why it's being treated as a hate crime, and the Bureau's involved."

"Oh, I see." It was a masterful explanation, and though Sophia didn't believe it, she couldn't fault it either. "Well, I'm sorry I wasn't able to be of any help."

"That's not your fault, ma'am. We'll just have to keep going door to door and asking around. Someone must have seen something. Anyway, many thanks for your cooperation."

"And for your coffee," Tweedledee smiled sweetly.

Sophia saw them to the door. As soon as they left, she rushed into the bedroom to check the bolts on the back of the computer. As far as she could tell, they hadn't been disturbed. They might have been suspicious of her, but replaying the conversation anxiously in her mind, she couldn't find anywhere she had slipped up.

Sophia returned to the living room, pouring herself some more coffee, when she caught sight of Tweedledum and Tweedledee leaving the building and getting into their car.

They hadn't questioned anyone else.

———

"Poor old Harry," Karin laughed. "I think he's pretty smitten by that woman."

It was Sunday afternoon, and Karin had dropped around for a cup of coffee before Celine left for the airport. Karin had missed Celine's dinner, and though she hadn't specified why, Celine rather suspected it had something to do with her new boyfriend.

"Did I tell you," she went on, biting into a remnant of the white-chocolate cake, "that I spotted Harry at the library the other day? You know all the ethnic-political problems they've had for donkey's years in Sophia's country? As far as I know, nobody even remembers what the conflict is all about. Well, Harry was reading up on it. He'd checked out a whole pile of books, even musty old UN Human Rights reports going back to the bloody eighties. Of course, he was very embarrassed to be caught out like that. He tried to pass it off as just a casual interest, but I guess he's serious about her. He wants to be culturally attuned, so to speak."

"I wouldn't be surprised if he pops the question one of these fine days."

"Jealous?"

"Yes," Celine replied without hesitation. "Yes, I am. No, don't tell me 'I told you so.' You did, I admit it. But it wouldn't have worked between Harry and me. Not then. I still hadn't got that bastard Adanpur out of my system. You know, after Indonesia, I developed this elaborate set of rules about never dating anyone at the office, and it even extended to men at the IMF and the World Bank. But in the end, I realized it was really just a defense mechanism to make sure I wouldn't meet anyone and still be available for him."

"Just because you didn't date men at work didn't mean you wouldn't meet anyone."

"No, but it certainly narrowed the possibilities. After all," she added dryly, "not all of us are so prolific as to pick up men in passing airplanes."

Karin grinned. "But I don't get it. If you really hated him so much, why did you want to keep yourself available?"

"I didn't. That's to say, not consciously. But I guess I never accepted that he'd been using me. Subconsciously, I didn't want to believe it, and that's why I wanted to keep myself available. And that's why, like a little idiot, I fell for him again."

Karin nodded. "And now?"

"Now I'd like to sue the bastard for sexual harassment."

"Don't. This isn't the US." Karin gave a little laugh. "I mean, of course, it *is* the US, but we're considered extraterritorial—US laws don't apply in the hallowed halls of IMFO. At best, it would go to the Administrative Tribunal, and those guys know which side their bread is buttered on. They're not going to find against Adanpur—he's an advisor, for Christ's sake! He might even become the next MD. There's no way the Tribunal is ever going to rule against him. You're the one who'll end up losing her career."

"Don't worry, I was just kidding. I'm not that stupid. I've learned my lesson. I'm not going to rock the boat. Besides . . . ," her voice trailed off.

During the weeks that Celine had been seeing him again and they had been working together on the Special Intervention Facility, she'd felt a singular vigor, a sort of vehemence of mind and soul that she hadn't known since her Indonesia days. She'd felt alive again, filled with hope and self-assurance, able to take on anything. The truth was, even now, she still wasn't sure she wouldn't succumb to him again. "How 'bout you?" she asked, eager to change the subject. "How's your love life? You're being very secretive about this one."

Karin laughed, a complacent, self-satisfied laugh. "I'm off to London with him on Wednesday."

"How long are you going for?"

"Just a couple of days. We're going to see *Giselle* at Covent Garden. I told him it's my favorite, and he went out and got us tickets and arranged for the flights and all."

"You're going all the way to London just to see a ballet?"

"Sure, why not? It's not very far—especially by private jet," Karin replied airily.

"He has a private jet?" Celine asked, her eyes wide.

"Yup. Well, technically I suppose it belongs to his company, but he gets to use it. Besides, we're not only going to see the show. He's got some work to do, and I'll get my London shopping done."

"Well, I suppose it's all right for some," Celine laughed. "Meanwhile, I'm off to Ukraine. And all I can say is it's one helluva long way to Kiev—and there's not much shopping at the end of it!"

═══

Sophia sighed. Seeing Harry this evening was the last thing she wanted. Unnerved by the morning's events, and tired from traipsing out to the airport to see Melamed and Huron off, all she really wanted to do was order some take-out food and curl up with an *Avengers* episode Harry had given her at Christmas. But on her voice mail, sandwiched between a solicitation for a new credit card and an offer to switch phone companies, was a message from Harry apologizing for losing his temper on Friday and inviting her to dinner. Though she knew it was the perfect opportunity to patch things up—and get Harry back working on the neural net—her heart sank at the prospect of prostituting herself.

All of the doubts and fears that had been percolating these past months seemed ready to bubble over. She was sick of the constant prevarications. She was lying to Mathewsen and Huron about the readiness of the operation, to Melamed about the extent of her feelings for Harry. And most of all, to Harry, about their future together.

The meeting with Huron and Mathewsen had suddenly brought the end of the operation into sharp relief. She had always known that she must disappear afterward. Yet it was only now that the full implication was sinking in. There would be money for her, of course, but little else. Her friends, her comrades, her work—she would have to renounce them all. A new identity, a new life; her soul a palimpsest on which each new lie must be written.

She would abandon the operation and marry Harry instead, she thought, indulging in the daydream. They would settle down to the not uncomfortable life of international civil servants—a flat in London, a New York pad, a Georgetown house big enough for children. How she yearned for a child!

With a start, Sophia realized twenty minutes had passed. She called Harry, took a hot shower to wash away her reluctance, then dressed in a summer frock, at once elegant and enticing.

She noticed the refreshing smell of pinewood as she entered the house. The place looked unusually tidy; Harry's maid came on Saturday afternoons, and not even Harry was capable of making a complete mess within a day.

"Harry?" she called out.

"Back here."

She walked past the dining room, where supper was already laid out on the table, to the covered patio at the rear of the house, which looked out on the garden beyond and the darkened skies above. Harry was lounging in one of the wicker chairs, trying to ease the recalcitrant cork from a dusty vintage. The lights were off, but a dozen or so candles flickered constantly, casting deep, mysterious shadows.

He smiled as she came over, motioning her to sit while he poured the wine into two large glasses that stood perched at the edge of the table, like two red-blooded lovers ready to leap off a cliff together.

"Cheers." He handed her a glass.

"Cheers," Sophia replied, pleased that she had come. She eased back into her chair contentedly, slipping into the serenity of the moment and watching Harry in shadowy silhouette.

"So what do you think of the wine?"

"Deliciously contradictory," she teased, holding the glass up to the candlelight and turning it slowly. "Robust but supple, rambunctious yet restrained, structured but spirited . . . "

Harry laughed. "Well," he said after a decent interval had passed, "I suppose I should apologize."

"No." Sophia placed her hand gently on his arm. "I'm the one who should be sorry. I lost sight of what's important in life."

It was true; she was no longer playing a part. Until now, she hadn't known. She had suspected as much. Yes, she had surely feared it, but she hadn't *known* she was in love with him. Whenever she was with him, she felt a giddiness of mind and soul, and she recognized it now for what it was. It came not as a blinding revelation, but with the immutable logic of mathematical proof. She had made up her mind. She loved him, and she was going to marry him. They would have children and spend their lives together.

I love you. She pictured those words written all over the skies in a thousand fancy fonts. Funny how she had never told him that, as though afraid to put the very thought into words. It occurred to her that they'd had sex, but had never made love before.

"Anyway," Harry was saying, "I felt a bit bad when I got home from Celine's. I realized what a complete jerk I've been toward you." He paused, reached under his chair for a thin manila folder, and handed it to Sophia.

There were just a few sheets inside, a couple of tables and some graphs. Sophia strained to read them in the fickle candlelight.

"How on earth . . .?" she asked, incredulous. They were the forecast errors from the latest run of the neural net, and well within the accuracy bounds she needed.

Harry grinned complacently. "I reprogrammed the back-propagation routines."

"But it must've taken you hours!"

"Midnight Friday until midday today, to be exact."

"But how come? I thought you said you weren't going to."

"Well," he shrugged, "I guess I was wrong, and you were right. Cleaning up those back-propagation routines made all the difference. Frankly, I still don't see why you're so obsessed with getting pinpoint accuracy from the model, but if it's important to you, then I guess it's important to me."

"Oh, Harry," Sophia said, her voice breaking. She closed her eyes and clenched her teeth, afraid she might start crying. "You can't imagine how much this means to me," she managed to say at last, struck by the irony.

She had come this evening ready to relinquish her cause, her people, her operation for Harry. And as a token of love, Harry had worked thirty-six hours straight, ensuring that she would go ahead.

"Glad you're glad," he said, with a man's awkwardness. "It'll take us a couple of days to clean up the rest of the programs and get it fully functioning. And then, of course, we have to extend it for the other currencies. But I reckon we should be done by the end of the week—if that's okay with you."

Sophia nodded, too overwhelmed to speak.

"Meanwhile," Harry went on, reaching again under his chair, "I've got a little something for you."

He handed her a thin oblong box, red and faded with age. Sophia pried it open, the spring creaking in protest, and held them sparkling to the candlelight.

"Are these . . .?"

Harry nodded. "They belonged to my grandmother. Mum said I should give them to you, when the time was ripe. Which I guess is now," he laughed nervously.

Sophia said nothing but nestled against him, and then his arm was around her—for love, for protection, for truth, for innocence. He pulled her closer, her hair folding softly against his cheek as emotion engulfed her, convulsing her with sobs. She felt his lips graze against her cheeks, caressing her salty tears. And then they were kissing.

Sophia pulled away at last, wiping her eyes. "I'm ruining my makeup," she laughed. "And now you'll find me all ugly and leave me."

"Never!" Harry scooped her into his arms and carried her up the stairs.

Dinner lay forgotten on the table.

CHAPTER NINETEEN

I T WAS A BOLD MOVE, by all accounts, when Türkiye Cumhuriyet Merkez Bankasi, the central bank of the Republic of Turkey, announced on Friday morning that it was raising its discount rate to 60 percent. But whether it was a wise move was quite another matter.

Speculators took it as a sure sign of desperation that the exchange rate could no longer be sustained and moved in for the kill. Short-selling lira assets became all the vogue as nervous investors dumped their remaining holdings of Turkish treasury bills in a frantic effort to get out. Within hours, Merkez Bankasi had exhausted its foreign reserves, losing a record eighteen billion dollars in the space of a single day.

At six p.m. Ankara time, ashen-faced and exhausted, the governor went on national television denouncing the foreign speculators and admitting defeat; the currency was in collapse. Ten minutes later, the undersecretary of the Treasury declared an immediate moratorium on all debt payments. The country was in default.

A small group had gathered in the Reuters Room on the third floor of IMFO to watch the final demise.

"Well, that's that." Pettigrew switched off the screen. But still they hung about, like spectators at a traffic accident.

Karin, who covered Turkey for Policy Review, was still shaking her head. "I can't believe it happened so bloody fast," she said, recounting the week's events in an aggrieved voice, as though the currency's collapse were somehow a personal affront.

The first inkling that something was afoot had come late Tuesday morning, when the trading desk at Merkez Bankasi learned that a certain Liberty Fund—a hedge fund based in the Cayman Islands—was short-selling liras in the forward market. What caught their attention was the scale of the operation—close to a billion bucks—and the surprising lack of anonymity.

Far from being secretive, as hedge funds usually are, this Liberty Fund seemed to go out of its way to advertise its strategy, which was simple enough. It was betting against the Turkish currency.

Wednesday, Merkez Bankasi mounted its first defensive operations. But each time they eased the rate and tried to make a stand, the market simply took its profit—and then started selling the lira anew, forcing the bank to intervene with more of its precious reserves, until the new parity had to be abandoned and a fresh defense attempted. And so, a trickle at first, and then a torrent, by close of business, half the foreign reserves were gone.

Thursday, the salmon pages of the Financial Times picked up the story. The monthly treasury bill auction was an utter disaster, with the Treasury not only failing to raise fresh funds but unable to roll over existing debts. Collapsing prices and soaring yields wiped out the boutique banks in the repo market, and within hours the Istanbul Stock Exchange had suffered a 40 percent loss. By now the exodus was no longer limited to a few foreign investors pulling out their pension money; it was a stampede as Turkish banks and conglomerates rushed to close credit lines ahead of impending devaluation, and the central bank was forced to make massive liquidity injections just to keep the financial system afloat.

Friday, Merkez Bankasi reversed tactics in an abortive bear squeeze, spiking interest rates, first to 70 percent, then to well over 100. But no interest rate would lure investors back now; they were simply bankrupting the government and ruining the economy. By market close, it was over.

Standing at the edge of the group, listening to Karin's recital, Sophia felt at once exhilarated by her success and daunted by the power of the forces she had unleashed.

The last few days had been schizophrenic. Running the neural net secretly in her flat each night, plotting her moves and planning her trades. Getting up by two a.m. to catch the European markets and fire the first salvos of her speculative attacks. Arriving at the office by eight a.m., helping Harry produce briefing papers and staff appraisals of the currency crises cascading across the developing countries. Rushing home at midday to carry out the very speculative attacks she and Harry had spent the morning warning about. Returning to the office early afternoon to download the most recent intervention figures and learn the latest policy moves. Then home again in the evening, preparing the neural net for the following day.

The whole ritual had an air of surreality to it, so much so that Sophia felt it couldn't have been her doing all these things. She almost had to hear the others discussing the week's events to believe they were really true.

"Who *are* these Liberty Finance Fund guys?" Pettigrew was asking.

"There's a smart-ass article in this week's *Economist* called "Life, Liberty, and the Pursuit of Money," Karin replied. "But of course, as a private hedge fund based in the Caymans or somewhere equally dubious, they're completely unregulated and can't be made to disclose anything. No one knows much about them except that they're pretty new on the scene, aggressive as hell, and leveraged to the hilt. Apparently, they also masterminded the speculative attacks on Colombia and Venezuela last week, and for all we know, they're the ones behind Ukraine and the others as well. But you can't pin all the blame on one hedge fund. The currencies themselves must have been vulnerable. These guys are just smart enough to predict when and where the next crisis will occur."

"So how come we're not?"

"I don't know. Perhaps we should ask Sophia." Karin turned toward her.

"How would I know?" Sophia asked sharply.

"Well you're the one with the fancy forecasting model."

"Yes, how 'bout that?" Pettigrew called out as Harry entered the room.

"How come your famous neural net didn't predict the currency collapse in Turkey?"

"So it's true?" Harry came up to them. "The Turks have thrown in the towel?" For once, he looked worried. His hair was tousled, his eyes pale and weary, and even his famous leaping-leopards tie was askew.

"Five minutes ago. They let the rate go—and it's depreciated by 30 percent."

"Jesus! That's going to put the cat among the pigeons for the other emerging markets. Thank God it's Friday, and they'll get some breathing space over the weekend."

"But how about the neural net?" Pettigrew persisted. "Isn't it supposed to predict these sorts of crises?"

"As a matter of fact, it did." Harry nodded at Sophia. "And for Colombia and Venezuela. We've been sending warnings since the middle of last week. But what are we supposed to do? Currencies collapse so fast these days, there isn't even time for a mission to get out there, let alone negotiate a loan. Besides, at least in Turkey's case, it's pretty obvious that someone at the central bank or Treasury has been doing some insider trading. The markets are just too well informed for it to be a coincidence. And of course, in that part of the world, it's hopeless to try and track down the culprit—the whole place leaks like a sieve."

"So who's next?"

"God knows. Could be anywhere. Russia, India, Hungary, Hong Kong, Brazil—they're all vulnerable to contagion effects. We're reviewing the Country Strategy Briefs with each of the central banks to make sure they're fully prepared, though a fat lot of good those CSBs are going to do if markets continue to behave like this."

Harry turned toward Sophia. "That's what I wanted to tell you. I'm sorry, but I can't make lunch today; we're having conference calls straight through. Come hell or high water, we're still on for tonight, though." He gave her a discreet peck on her cheek, nodded quickly to the rest of them, and left.

Sophia left right behind him. The idea of lunching alone in the cafeteria was just too depressing. Besides, there was always the risk that Pettigrew might invite himself to join her. Instead she went to the Hotel Washington, where Harry had taken her that first day they had lunched together. It was a rooftop terrace, a few blocks from IMFO, and afforded the most magnificent view of the city.

Sipping a Chardonnay, she had a wonderful end-of-term feeling about her. It brought to mind the beginning of the summer holidays at boarding school, when the bad food and cruel taunts were at last behind her and only the prospect of long lazy picnics by the lakeside with Nanny stretched blissfully ahead.

It's going well, Sophia thought, plunging into her crab cakes. Much better, indeed, than any of them had the right to expect. Melamed, calling from New York last night, had been effusive in his congratulations; even Huron and Mathewsen were said to be pleased with her progress. Melamed had told her he would stop briefly in DC on his way back to Geneva for the final phase of the operation.

Meanwhile, the speculative attacks were paying off handsomely, more than doubling Sophia's initial capital. Equally important, she was beginning to establish the Liberty Fund's reputation in the markets, which would be crucial when it came time to tackle the currencies of the major countries.

She'd heard nothing more from the FBI. She was now inclined to believe that it had indeed been a perfectly innocent investigation of the gay man's murder.

And no one, she was sure, was following her around these days. But what gave her the greatest satisfaction was the knowledge that this was *her* operation, conceived, planned, and executed by her alone, and that this time there would be no bombs, no bodies, no ballet shoes. No victims, no violence, no guilt.

Sophia was happy.

═══

Which is more than could be said for Celine, as she sat shivering in the governor's office at the National Bank of Ukraine. She was bored, tired, hungry; but most of all she was cold. A sudden snap had brought heavy snowfall and frigid temperatures. Heating season ended in March, though, and in any case, with the huge payment arrears on energy imports, all gas supplies from Russia and Turkmenistan had been cut off weeks ago.

Oblivious, the governor was berating the international capital markets for attacking Ukraine's fragile exchange rate regime. Since he couldn't very well rebuke the markets themselves, he seemed intent on venting his frustration on Celine instead.

What the hell does he expect? she thought. With a half-dozen currencies succumbing to speculative attacks this past week, how could a country that couldn't even afford to pay its heating bills hope to emerge unscathed? Of course, she said nothing of the kind. She merely clucked sympathetically at the governor's tirade and, smiling at her own hypocrisy, assured him that with resolute policies and far-reaching reforms the country would ultimately prevail.

The governor seemed unconvinced. He started reeling off long lists of statistics, too fast for the interpreter to keep up and too fast for Celine to follow anyway. She caught only the occasional useless fact about pig iron production—down 17 percent, year-on-year—or the average old age pension, but she nodded anyway, astonished at her own indifference.

I've lost my faith, she told herself. There had been a time when she would've been appalled at such economic devastation, but now it required a definite mental effort even to care. Like raindrops bouncing off the windowpane, the figures and statistics still pouring from the governor's mouth made no impression on her. Somehow, she couldn't visualize the misery they indicated, and even if she could, she had grave doubts these days about being of any help.

And why *should* she care? Just yesterday, when she finally read her emails, Celine had seen the announcement: Xavier Adanpur had gotten his promotion to deputy managing director, putting him firmly in line to succeed Kiyotaki. Meanwhile, those who *do* care find their careers going nowhere, assigned to hopeless countries that can't even pay their bloody bills on time.

The Ukraine assignment might have been exciting five years ago. It would have been the pioneering, missionary sort of work that Celine would have relished. Now, the country was going nowhere, the government had no intention of undertaking reforms, and the economy was in a state of shambles. It was a dead-end assignment for a dead-end career, and she was sure she had Adanpur to thank for it.

There was, she decided, something wonderfully liberating about not caring. She wanted to say to the governor, *Frankly, my dear, I don't give a damn*, but she withdrew her mind instead, admiring the design of the National Bank, a vaguely Art Deco building constructed in the late 1920s, with plenty of intricate, marble inlay work, now sadly in disrepair. She'd be home in a week, filing her back-to-office report—no special annexes to the MD this time!—and planning her summer vacation. She wondered idly what Harry and Sophia were up to.

But at the same time, some part of her regretted losing her faith. It seemed to make her work utterly meaningless. She realized how depressing it was to be stuck in a job she no longer believed in. The only thing to do was to give it up, and she resolved then and there to hand in her resignation the moment she returned to Washington.

A couple of hours later, Celine emerged from Restaurant Studio—the latest hangout of the monied, young mafiosi—her temper much improved, having spent, she reflected ruefully, almost twice the average monthly old age pension. The snow had stopped, though a bitter wind swept across the street carrying eddying flurries with it. She looked up and down the street, but there were no taxis. She would have to walk back to the hotel.

Just as she was setting out, Celine spotted an old babushka begging by Studio's entrance. The woman was kneeling on that frozen ground, her hands forward in supplication, her head bowed down, her whole body creaking back and forth. Celine was reaching instinctively for her purse when a big, black BMW pulled up.

One of the darkened windows hummed down. A hand dangled a hundred-dollar bill in front of the woman's nose. For a moment, the woman sat staring in disbelief, then struggled to her feet with a strange ripping sound. But before her bony claw could close around the note, there was a burst of raucous laughter and the car revved away, soaking them both with freezing slush.

Celine ran after the car, shouting obscenities, but they were long gone. Turning back, Celine could see a dark patch on the ground where the woman had been kneeling, the remnants of her swathing. They must have stuck to the ground in the cold, tearing as she had stood up. The woman stood paralysed, her face pink with shame, her gray, flaccid legs horribly exposed, until some last instinct of respectability made her cross her arms over her body in a futile attempt to cover her nakedness.

Celine slipped off her own coat and wrapped it around the woman's slouching shoulders. Then, thrusting a fistful of cash into that bony hand, she hurried away before the poor woman was humiliated further.

The climb up the hill back to the Hotel Kiev was vilely cold, the wind cutting her from every side. The sensible thing would have been to retrace her steps, gone the long way round, but Celine, already shivering without her coat, decided to continue along Ulitsa Hruschevsky despite its steep ascent. The distance was perhaps half a mile, but she kept sinking into the snow, which made it seem twice as far. Then, just outside the Cabinet of Ministers building, at the steepest part of the hill, she slipped on a hidden patch of ice and went tumbling down twenty yards.

The monolithic Cabinet building loomed above her. Its heavy history—built as NKVD headquarters, serving the Gestapo during the War, reverting to the KGB afterward, and now housing the main ministerial offices—seemed to press down on her. Celine felt a primeval fear, as though the cries of the building's victims were echoing about her. She hobbled to her feet, anxious to get away from this place. She slipped twice more—for part of the way, she actually had to crawl—until frozen and exhausted, she finally made it back to the Hotel Kiev.

They looked up expectantly as Celine entered, the four girls lined up against the radiator for some imaginary warmth. They were prostitutes, blond, leggy Ukrainian girls, all dolled up in their why-bother skirts and cheap fur coats, and all terribly young. But behind those powdered, rouged faces, with makeup so gauchely applied it was almost touching, their eyes were tired and haggard.

With the economic depression and collapsing currency, a trick with a foreigner is nothing to be sneezed at, and Celine could sense their disappointment—resentment almost—that she was a woman. They stared at each other; Celine distressed to see them so young, they surprised to see her so dishevelled.

Celine would have liked giving them each one hundred dollars and sending them home, so that at least one night they wouldn't need to debase themselves, but then she remembered she had given away all her cash. It would have been a useless gesture anyway. She limped up to her room, threw herself on the lumpy mattress, and buried her head in the pillow.

Celine wept.

CHAPTER TWENTY

L OUNGING LAZILY ON THE SOFA, Sophia brought Melamed up to date.
"But how did you choose which currencies to attack?"

"They had to be ripe for the plucking," she said. "Big deficits, overvalued exchange rates, dicey politics—the usual culprits. I used the neural net in reverse, getting it to tell me which currencies were most susceptible to a speculative attack by the market, and then choosing those very currencies."

"So it really works, this neural net business? It was worth all that time and trouble?"

"Oh, yes. I could never have pulled it off without it. You should've seen poor Harry last week," she laughed, "dashing off memos to management about which currencies the neural net thought were vulnerable and where the next crisis might erupt. Little did he realize I was the one on the other side of half the transactions! Of course, it's not just a question of choosing vulnerable currencies. Size matters also. I needed countries big enough to matter but small enough that I could have an impact. Don't forget, I only had a couple of hundred million to play with."

"I thought you said you bet close to a billion."

"That's just leveraging—buying on margin: I had less than a quarter of that in cash. When you enter into foreign currency contracts, you don't have to have cash on hand—you can buy on margin. Because you're not likely to lose all your money, you can basically borrow by using your seed money as collateral. Then, when the exchange rate moves the way you were betting, you pay off the margins with your profit."

"And if you're wrong?"

Sophia shrugged. "You're screwed."

"Well," Melamed said doubtfully, "I hope you know what you're doing. It sounds very risky to me, betting all the money Huron lent us. I can't say I understand how all this high-finance stuff works."

Sophia put her cup down. "Let me take you through it again."

"No, no," Melamed said hastily. "It's not important. I trust you—I'm sure you know what you're doing."

Despite his protestations, Sophia knew Melamed harbored doubts about the operation. He would have preferred a more frontal attack—a bombing, a hijacking, an assassination. Melamed had been in the movement since its earliest days, and violence and struggle had been his life for so long that he knew no other. Sophia neither judged nor blamed him for this. But Daddy, faced by the same dilemma, had chosen to further the same cause through different means. And if only out respect for her dead father, Sophia set about explaining the dynamics of a speculative attack with all the zeal of a missionary. She was just getting into multiple equilibria and self-fulfilling runs, when the telephone rang.

"Saved by the bell," Melamed grinned, as she reached for the phone.

"Sophia? It's Harry. I need to speak to you."

"Sure, go ahead."

"No, not on the phone. Come over right away."

"I can't right now." She glanced at Melamed. "I'm busy."

"Then make yourself unbusy," he snapped. "This is serious."

"What's it about?"

"I'll tell you when you get here."

"All right. I'll be over in half an hour." She hung up the receiver, too puzzled to be annoyed.

"What is it? Something the matter?" asked Melamed.

"No, nothing." Sophia regained her seat. "I need to go and see Harry in a little while, that's all."

Something was wrong, but she couldn't collect her thoughts. Mechanically, she began pouring a fresh cup of coffee for Melamed and was just adding his customary three spoonfuls of sugar, when the spoon dropped from her hand, landing with a clatter on the glass table.

"Shit!" She ran into the bedroom. By the time Melamed joined her, Sophia had tipped her handbag on the floor, and was sifting desperately through its contents.

"What are you looking for?"

Sophia flung open the closet door without answering, and thrust her hand into her jacket pockets. "The disk," she whispered, her face blanching. "I've lost the disk!"

"What disk?" Melamed grabbed her by the shoulders.

"*The* disk. The one with all the account numbers and portfolios. I've lost it."

"Where did you see it last? Think!"

"It was in my handbag," Sophia cried. "I kept it there in case this place got searched. Harry had to borrow my keys last night . . . he must have seen it in my bag and borrowed it, thinking it was a music disk."

"But it doesn't play music, does it?"

"Of course not. And when it didn't, he probably popped into his computer to see what it was."

"Will he recognize it?"

"Well, it's hardly likely that I'd have hundreds of millions of dollars, is it? He's bound to wonder what's going on. That's why he told me to come over right away."

"All right, don't panic." Melamed paced the small bedroom. "How strong is your hold on him? Does he love you? Would he be sympathetic to our Cause? Can you at least persuade him to keep his mouth shut?"

Sophia shrugged. "I don't know. Yes, maybe. I just don't know. Harry can be very obstinate. He'll be furious about the deception. But maybe it'll be okay. He's . . ." How could she possibly explain to Melamed, who had devoted his life to the Cause, Harry's aloof, apolitical, academic attitude. And besides, she couldn't get into the complexities of her relationship with Harry now.

In any case, Melamed wasn't listening. He was pacing up and down, deep in thought, rubbing his hand over his chin constantly; Sophia could hear the rasping of his unshaven stubble. Finally, he said, "All right, let's not panic." He stooped down, shovelling the contents back into Sophia's bag.

"You're going there right now. Calm him down. Tell him anything you like. The truth, if it helps, but ask for some time, and make sure he promises to keep his mouth shut for the moment. He'd be an accomplice before the fact, so he can't go to the authorities without getting into trouble himself."

Sophia shook her head. "Harry's not like that. You're not going to be able to blackmail him into silence."

"Doesn't matter. We'll think of something. The important thing now is to make sure he doesn't tell anyone before you've spoken to him. Here," he added, swinging Sophia's handbag toward her. "Now go."

Sophia stumbled into a taxi, dully resentful that Melamed had left her to deal with the problem. Could Harry be trusted with the truth, she wondered, unsure of how to begin explaining. He knew nothing about her family, her background, her people. She remembered the night she'd tried playing some of their music, and Harry had asked her to play something Western instead.

And yet he loved her. She was certain of that. Somehow, she would make him understand. He would be furious, of course, but she would let him have his say, vent his anger, then tell him all and throw herself at his mercy. She could do it, Sophia kept telling herself. All too soon, the taxi deposited her in front of Harry's house.

As she stood outside the house fishing for her keys, the door opened. Harry must have been waiting by the entrance ever since the taxi drew up.

"Hullo, Sophia." He closed the door, locking it behind her. "Thank you for coming."

"Sure. What's so urgent?"

Harry didn't reply but led her into the living room, stopping by the banisters. Sophia looked around uncertainly, then sat on the sofa.

"By the way, Sophia," he said, his voice deliberately casual. "I came across this, and I'm just wondering what it is." In his hand was the disk.

"Oh, that's mine," she replied. "I've been looking for it."

"Really?" His hand closed tighter around the disk. "May I ask what it is?"

"A computer disk."

"I can see that. What I'd like to know is what's on it."

"What's on it is none of your business. And in the future," she added quietly, "I'd appreciate it if you didn't go snooping around my things."

"For your information, I wasn't 'snooping around.' I found it on the floor—it must've fallen out of your bag yesterday. And I would say it is very much my business, especially since I appear to be unwittingly involved in some scheme of yours. I think you owe me an explanation."

"I've already explained. It's my disk, and I'd like it back."

"Now you listen to me," he said, waving the disk angrily. "You've bloody well been trading in the forex markets, haven't you? Who are these guys? There's hundreds of accounts. They can't all be yours—there are millions and millions of dollars in them. You took my model and my software and stole the intervention data from IMFO to make yourself a tidy little bundle. Do you get a percentage of these, or what? No, don't interrupt," he said fiercely. "Just listen." He paced the room, too angry to sit down.

Sophia watched in silence, with a vaguely uninterested air that seemed to infuriate him further.

"Do you think this is some sort of joke?" he shouted. "Well, it bloody well isn't. You could end up in jail for this, not to mention getting us both fired."

Sophia shrugged, refusing to catch his eye.

"Well, fuck you then." Harry flung the disk on the floor. "I'm not losing my career just so you can make money on insider trading. I'm going to report this right away." He'd turned toward the phone, when another thought struck him. He gave a mirthless laugh. "That's all you wanted from me, wasn't it? God, what an idiot I've been! You never loved me in the least. All you wanted was to get your sticky little hands on my neural net programs so you could make your grubby little money."

"No, Harry," she protested at last. "It's not like that at all. You don't understand."

"Oh, I understand all right. 'I'll always be happy to be your friend. I really appreciate your friendship,'" he mimicked cruelly. "What you really meant to say was, 'I really appreciate your model and the chance to make some money in my pathetic, shabby life.' Do you think that's what my research is for? To be prostituted for your fucking money? You've been clever, all right. Getting hold of that intervention data. 'Don't you want to see how well *your* neural net really works?' How bloody stupid of me not to suspect you might have some other motive. Do you know what you are, Sophia? A whore. Nothing but a dirty, little whore. But don't worry, my dear, if the information on that disk is accurate, you've prostituted yourself for the highest price any whore has commanded in all of history."

By now, he had worked himself into a paroxysm of rage, spittle forming on his lips as he heaped on the abuse. Sophia suffered through it meekly, allowing him to vent his rage. After going on for a good five minutes, Harry finally exhausted himself and lapsed into silence.

"When you've quite finished," she said, "perhaps you'd like to hear what I've got to say. After all, you're the one who asked me here to give you an explanation." She paused, returning her gaze to the garden. When she spoke again, it was very slowly and very quietly.

"You're right," she nodded, "I *am* a whore. But not for the reasons you think. I'm a whore because I fell in love with you. Do you think this is about money? Well, it isn't. I don't give a damn about making money for myself."

"Then why have you been trading in the forex markets?"

Sophia shook her head. "You've completely missed the point. You're supposed to be intelligent. You've been to the best schools, the best universities in the world, yet have you ever once bothered to find out about what's going on in my country? Can you imagine students—boys and girls younger than you and me—rotting their whole lives away in jail just because they attended some perfectly peaceful protest against the oppression and corruption? Mothers roam the morgues for sons who've disappeared, teachers have their faces smashed in for trying to keep our language alive, and mysterious hit-and-run accidents just happen to befall anyone who opposes the regime?

"We're a tiny, forgotten minority, and the world doesn't give a damn, as long as they can keep getting their grubby hands on our mines and minerals. And if someone like you, with Harrow and Harvard, and all the other advantages in life behind you doesn't care, who will? Who will grieve for my people? Well, *I* will. And if that makes me a whore, so be it. You're no better. You prostitute your brains and your talents just as much. No, not for money. For a few publications in academic journals. Talk about pathetic!

"With all your education and intelligence you could actually do something for the world. But no, that would be beneath you, wouldn't it? You prefer to hide behind your intellectual purity and sneer at those who do want to make a difference. You're too damn superior, and too damn cowardly to ever confront the right and wrong of what *you* do. You'd rather solve an equation than save a life. In all the years you've been at IMFO, you've never done anything but your own selfish research, building up your publications record. You're as much a whore as I am, my dear, only our prices are different."

Harry looked bewildered. Sophia could see the words 'I thought you loved me' crystallizing in his mouth, when two red blossoms suddenly appeared on his shirt in rapid succession, spreading like ink blotches on blotting paper.

Sophia hadn't even heard the shots. She whirled around. Melamed was standing by the door holding a silenced gun.

Time seemed to dilate. First she was staring at Melamed in horror, then hearing Harry's body hit the floor with a thud, and then screaming and screaming and screaming. Melamed reached her in two bounds and slapped her face. She started pounding his chest with her fists. "You killed him, you bastard," she sobbed. "You killed him."

Melamed held her tightly, letting her emotion exhaust itself, then lowered her onto the sofa. She looked up at him with the same confounded expression she'd had the day her stepmother had told that she would never see Daddy again.

"Why did you kill him? He trusted me, he loved me. Why did you kill him?" she kept repeating uselessly.

Melamed shook his head. "Because I had to," he said. "We can't afford the risk."

Sophia stared at him, no longer bewildered, but enraged at the casualness of his justification. She sprang up to hit him, but he shoved her back down on the sofa, banging her head against the wall.

"Pull yourself together," he ordered. "And touch nothing." He left the room, returning a moment later with a large, black trash bag from which he drew a pair of gloves, throwing them to Sophia.

"Does Hoffinger usually have visitors?"

Sophia stared ahead blankly.

"Cleaning lady, repair men, anyone?"

"His maid," Sophia muttered. "She normally comes around two o'clock."

"We haven't much time then." Donning his gloves, Melamed unlocked the door to the garden, then locked it again from the outside using the key, *her* key, which he must have stolen when she tipped out her handbag.

Watching him, it occurred to her that Melamed had planned Harry's murder the instant she told him about the disk, now lying so harmlessly on the floor. Without even thinking, Sophia plucked it up and popped it into her bag, regaining the sofa at once.

A crash of breaking glass, then Melamed's brown hand snaked through the hole and unlocked the garden door. "Come up with me," he commanded.

In spite of herself, Sophia obeyed. To reach the staircase, she had to pass Harry's body, lying prostrate in a pool of coagulating blood. Sophia stared, scarcely believing that a minute ago this thing had been Harry. She gagged, holding her hand to her mouth. Melamed grabbed her by the arm and dragged her up the stairs.

They went to the master bedroom first. "Find any small valuables—watches, cuff links, anything else you can find, and put them into the bag," he told her.

On the bedside table were Harry's wallet and his Patek Philippe watch—a graduation present from his parents—and an assortment of cuff links. Sophia stood staring at them, not moving. With an impatient cluck, Melamed pushed past her and swept the various items into the black plastic bag. Then he moved to the study. In a glass cabinet was a collection of antique toy cars—Geschas, Mettoys, Tippcos and the like, some of them worth a couple of hundred dollars apiece—that had been Harry's pride and joy. It sickened Sophia to see Melamed scatter them to the floor. Even the Schuco Mercedes Sportster that Harry had always pined for, and Sophia had finally managed to track down in a New York antique shop and given him for Christmas, went sailing into Melamed's bag.

Melamed stopped in front of the computer screen. "Come here," he ordered. "What is this? Do you need it for the neural net?"

Her mind still on autopilot, Sophia walked across the room and squinted at the screen; the monitor glared back, mute and accusing. "No," she said at last. "I've got everything I need. Harry must've logged on to the network. He was probably checking what files I'd downloaded."

Melamed nodded and was about to switch off the machine, when he paused. "This is a listing of computer files, right?"

"Yes."

He stabbed the screen with a gloved hand. "Here's one that Hoffinger must've opened this morning. It's got today's date, but the time's all wrong. Is there some way of altering the time on this thing?"

"I guess so. The network actually runs on London time, which is why the time stamp looks funny."

"Okay." Melamed glanced at his watch. "That's perfect. It's almost one p.m. now, which would make it . . ." He frowned. "Is it five hours or six hours' difference to Britain?" He looked around anxiously. "Phone."

Sophia reached for the telephone.

"No!"

She looked at him, confused.

"Your cell phone. Give it to me."

He dialed the operator and asked her the current time in London, England. After a pause, he said, "five forty-eight p.m.? Okay, thanks." He beckoned Sophia. "Alter the file's time stamp to eighteen fifty-three. That'll give you plenty of time to establish an alibi. Here, use the tip of this pencil so you don't disturb his fingerprints on the keyboard."

"No." She was surprised by the firmness of her own voice. "I'm not going to do it."

"Don't be a damn fool. You could end up in prison."

"I don't care. I will have nothing more to do with your bloody, murderous schemes."

Melamed reached in his pocket for the gun. "Oh, yes you will."

"Go ahead. How many more people are you going to kill? I already told you I'd never work with you again if it meant killing innocent people."

"Yes, you did," he conceded, lowering the gun. "But do you honestly think, after all this struggle, that I'm going to let your squeamishness get in the way of the operation? Even if I wanted to, there are others who are pressing for more direct action. I warned you long ago that once an operation has started, there's no going back and no giving up. So you're going to go through with this, and here's why." He drew close to her, staring into her eyes. "Not because of any threats against you—I know you well enough to know that wouldn't work. But because if you don't, we'll go back to bombing airliners and buildings and playgrounds. And all those innocent people you're so worried about are going to pay the price for your misguided morality. And I know what you're thinking," he added quickly.

"You want revenge for Harry's death, and you're wondering whether betraying me will solve your problems. I promise you, it won't. The others will carry on, and with much more devastating consequences. You know perfectly well I've barely managed these past months to restrain them. Without me, who knows? Perhaps they'll decide to blow up your friends at IMFO."

Sophia felt her knees weaken; her head was swimming, and she was close to fainting. Dancing before her eyes was the image of the little girl on the airplane, not in the safety of the terminal building but trapped in the burning hulk of the aircraft, making an obscene pirouette as flames danced around her body. Sophia started hyperventilating.

Melamed guided her to a chair, but she pulled away abruptly. "Don't touch me," she hissed. She couldn't think clearly, she only knew that she was trapped. There was no debating Melamed, no arguing with his twisted logic. For now, she would go through with his plan, then figure a way out later.

Without thinking, without feeling, she made her way to the computer. She sat down at Harry's desk and started altering the time stamp, taking solace in the mechanics of the task.

"Good," Melamed said, watching her. "Now we need to find you an alibi." He thought a moment, drumming his fingers on the edge of the table. "Do you have some friend, preferably a woman, whom you could be with? Go shopping, have coffee, anything?"

"I suppose," Sophia murmured, still intent on changing the time stamp.

"Call her and arrange to meet as soon as possible. Make sure you're with her for the next couple of hours at least—until the evening, if possible."

Sophia nodded.

"All right, you'd better get going. I'll finish up here and get rid of this stuff." He jerked the plastic bag. "I'll see you in Geneva."

Sophia glared at him, furious that he should be so sure of her that he was willing to leave her alone in Washington while he went ahead to Geneva. But looking at Melamed, who was methodically securing the last of Harry's valuables into the bag, she realized he was right. She was committed to seeing the operation through. Not for the suffering masses back home, or for her own sense of guilt, or for revenge of her wronged father. But for the innocent victims if she failed.

CHAPTER TWENTY-ONE

THREE HUNDRED KILLINGS A YEAR IN WASHINGTON is a statistic; one murder in Georgetown, a tragedy. Or so it seemed to Celine, when returning from Ukraine she learned of Harry's death. Today was Friday, almost a week since the murder, and so far it appeared that the police had progressed not one iota in apprehending the killer. Not that they were giving out any details, but Celine had gotten the story from Karin.

Harry was last seen alive on Saturday morning by Sophia, who had been having coffee with him before heading out to meet Karin for lunch around one fifteen p.m. at Bistro Français. They had spent the afternoon shopping at Georgetown Park and the M Street boutiques before returning to Harry's around three o'clock, only to find the cleaning lady in hysterics and the police combing the place for clues.

At first, Sophia had completely broken down, not shouting or screaming but going into a state of nervous shock, a kind of waking coma in which she neither heard nor said anything, and which, according to Karin, was much more disturbing than the maid's hysteria. But afterward, once the police had photographed the scene and taken away Harry's body, Sophia pulled herself together and agreed to help determine what was missing.

Accompanied by Karin and a couple of police officers, Sophia had gone from room to room, making an inventory of what had been stolen: some silver candlesticks, a pair of onyx-and-gold cuff links, a Patek Philippe watch. For these few trinkets, Harry had lost his life. But when they got to his study, seeing Harry's prized collection of toy cars smashed and scattered all over the floor, Sophia had burst into tears, sobbing inconsolably and saying over and over again, "Why did he have to do that? Why did he have to take those?" It seemed, indeed, a wantonly cruel act, for it was doubtful the thief would have even known their value.

The police were willing to resume later, and Karin also thought it best to get Sophia home. But wiping her tears and biting her lip bravely, Sophia insisted they carry on. It was lucky that she had, for it was Sophia who found the vital clue that enabled the police to pin down precisely the time of Harry's death.

It had something to do with a computer file Harry had been working on. With the permission of the police, Sophia logged on to Harry's network account and listed the time stamps on all his files. She explained to the police that the IMFO computer, in order to coordinate with IMFO's Resident Representative offices around the world, was set to British time. From that, they had established that Harry must have started working after Sophia had left and been alive at least until one fifty-three p.m., Washington time, which was within the bounds of the medical examiner's estimate. The maid had discovered the body at around two thirty p.m. The police set about interviewing the neighbors at once, but no one admitted hearing anything unusual between those hours. And though the police had not said anything explicitly, according to Karin, they had taken note that she and Sophia had each other as alibis for the time that Harry must have been killed.

And that was the extent of Celine's information. Harry was the first person of her own generation she'd known to die, and the only one—save her father—to have suffered a violent death. A rude reminder of her own mortality, Harry's murder left Celine curiously empty, devoid of energy and purpose. She was numb—unable to grieve, unwilling to come to terms with the loss. With the same instinct that makes a child wag a loose tooth, she kept wondering what might have been had Harry not died. True, he had been practically engaged to Sophia, but Sophia was safely out of sight and out of mind—she had removed her things from Harry's office the day after he died and taken administrative leave immediately following the memorial service. In the luxury of Celine's fantasy, she could imagine that her relationship with Harry would have blossomed well beyond friendship.

At work, Celine was distracted. The Summit Meeting of Central Bank Governors and Finance Ministers was coming up next week, and the recent turmoil in the currency markets—Brazil, Argentina, and India were the latest victims—had lent it special urgency. But flipping through the draft communiqué, Celine saw that it was just a rehash of the usual stuff—exhortations for greater international cooperation and coordination, admonitions for prudent monetary and fiscal policies—and the idea of trudging through the same trite, tired phrases trotted out each year like forgotten medals at a Veterans Day parade filled her with revulsion. The only remotely interesting part of the report concerned the recent decision on the gold sales. About 10 percent of the IMFO gold, some fifteen million ounces, was to be sold over the next couple of years and used for debt forgiveness—with the promise of more to come in the future. The fiasco with the Special Intervention Facility had clearly weakened Kiyotaki's position at the Board, and now, at long last, the Europeans had managed to push through their proposal. So that was their payoff for supporting Adanpur, she thought. As for Adanpur, the rumors were already flying that he was in line to be the next managing director.

Celine threw down the communiqué in disgust. Surveying the mess on her desk—the yellow sticky notes, plastered indiscriminately; the half-filled coffee cups, each a different vintage; the tottering stacks of memos, all unread—she was filled with a loathing for it all, convinced she was throwing away her life one spreadsheet at a time. She came early and left late every day, traipsing home to a loveless house and a sexless bed, with microwaved pizza or instant noodles for dinner. And for what? Her views were ignored, her career was in the doldrums, and she no longer believed in what she was doing. Harry's death only served to underscore the futility of it all.

It was high time she left this job, she decided, remembering her resolve back in Ukraine to resign the moment she returned to Washington. She reached inside her drawer for the box of stationery buried at the bottom. Positioning her pen precisely in the center of the page, she wrote, *Effective immediately, I am resigning my position as Deputy Division Chief, Policy Review*

Department, International Monetary and Financial Organization, then signed it with a little flourish and dated it on top.

It looked rather neat, the single stark sentence standing there all by itself like a declaration of undying love. Celine folded the page carefully into its matching envelope and glanced at her watch. It was past six o'clock; there were no more interoffice mail collections that day.

Never mind. Monday will be good enough. Without so much as a second thought, she tossed the letter into her outbox.

But later that night she wept, sobbing unashamedly into her pillow, allowing herself at last to grieve the friend she had lost. She slept fitfully, interrupted by complex, troubled dreams. She woke suddenly in the darkest hour of the night, conscious that something was bothering her, something that had struck her as not quite right about Karin's story that day. But the harder she tried to pin it down the more obstinately the thought remained out of reach. Eventually she fell asleep again, with the nagging doubt lingering insidiously at the back of her mind that she was missing something—something important.

When she awoke again, it was seven a.m., sunlight streaming through the window. And she knew now what was troubling her. According to Karin, the time stamp on the computer file read eighteen fifty-three, which was how the police had determined that Harry was alive at one fifty-three, Washington time. But Celine had called London just before going on mission to Ukraine, and she was sure that the time difference between Britain and the United States had been four hours, not five.

She pondered the matter, still groggy with sleep, wondering whether the police had made a mistake or if Karin had somehow misunderstood. The answer finally came to her. The normal time difference *is* five hours, but when she had called, Britain had not moved to Summer Time while the United States was already on Daylight Saving Time. Now that Britain had moved to Summer Time, the difference was back to five hours.

Celine smiled with satisfaction; the discrepancy had been troubling her. But in the same train of thought it occurred to her that if Britain had already moved to Summer Time, then what Sophia had told the police was not strictly correct. IMFO's network did not run on "British Time" as such; it ran on Greenwich Mean Time, the idea being to have an international standard so that files sent from IMFO's far-flung Resident Representative offices could be synchronized.

But that made all the difference.

If the time stamp of eighteen fifty-three referred to GMT, wouldn't it mean Harry was alive at two fifty-three p.m. Washington time, not one fifty-three p.m. as the police believed? But that made no sense. How could Harry have been working on the computer at that time? And, more important, thought Celine sitting up very much awake, it meant Sophia had no alibi for Harry's murder.

The thoughts clicked into place, like the teeth of a zipper. No, Celine thought, she was being absurdly fanciful. The first thing to do was to check the facts. She glanced at the bedside clock: barely eight a.m. and a Saturday morning. Karin wouldn't be up for at least another couple of hours.

Celine grabbed the phone and started dialing regardless.

CHAPTER TWENTY-TWO

H ARRY WASN'T DEAD. He couldn't be. It was nothing but a silly nightmare, a sick joke Sophia's mind was playing on her. Any moment now the
phone would ring, and Harry's cheerful voice would come booming down
the line. He would call Sophia a lazybones, tell her that if she didn't get out of
bed and come over at once there would be no scrambled eggs left for her.

She tossed restlessly, willing the phone to ring and wake her from this
horrible dream. The funny thing was, she knew perfectly well it was only a
dream, a remarkably unconvincing one at that, riddled with absurd inconsis-
tencies that made it seem wholly implausible. She almost wanted to laugh at
her mind's sorry attempt to frighten her.

First, she dreamed that Melamed was in Harry's living room. He and
Harry were fighting over something, trying to wrest it away from each other.
Sophia could not see what it was, but it seemed fragile, like a sheet of paper
that might rip apart. In her mind, she knew it was her soul they were struggling over. Then magically, she appeared on the scene, trying to intervene and
make peace, but they ignored her, and continued their insane tug-of-war.
Out of nowhere, Melamed produced a gun and was waving it about while
Sophia tried to run between them and prevent him from firing. But something kept holding her back. The harder she pulled, the tighter this invisible

force seemed to grip her. And then, though she never even heard the shots, Harry was dead, his body lying crumpled on the ground, his face staring up at her, gaunt and glassy-eyed.

The alarm clock by Sophia's bed exploded into a vile, reverberating clamor, wrenching her violently from her dreams. She sat up in her bed, trying to blink away the nightmare.

It was Sunday. Sunlight was peeping through the blinds; in the distance, church bells had started their long, melancholy peal. What a silly dream, Sophia told herself, peeling back the blanket. And for perhaps half a minute, in her somnolent state, she really believed it had only been a nightmare. She stumbled into the kitchen to get herself a glass of orange juice. But as she opened the refrigerator door something caught her eye, a jar of her favorite marmalade from Fortnum's that Harry had brought for her in January.

A deadly pang cut through her viscera. It had really happened. Harry was dead. Melamed had shot him, and Sophia was responsible. With a small cry, she slammed the refrigerator door shut. She staggered to the living room, and slumped onto the sofa. She remained there for the better part of an hour, her legs drawn up, arms clasped around them defensively, chin buried between her knees, not moving, not thinking, just gazing unseeing at the world beyond the bay window.

How can I? How can I possibly go through with the operation?

She knew now that it wasn't about fighting for freedom and justice and democracy and all the other fine ideas and ideals she'd spouted to Melamed and Huron. It never had been. Perhaps she'd known that all along, but Harry's death had forced her at last to admit it—if only to herself. The Cause was just an excuse, a chance to exorcise her demons and exact revenge on the regime that had robbed her of father and her childhood. The realization made her feel shabby and unworthy, but she could not decide whether that meant she should give up because her motives weren't sufficiently pure or carry on, lest Harry's death be in vain.

Ironically, the operation was proceeding brilliantly. The Liberty Fund's reputation and capital were growing by the day. The markets, ever more jittery, were looking with increasing desperation to the upcoming summit meeting to restore stability. And one-by-one, currencies were succumbing to Sophia's speculative attacks. Only the Brazilians had put up a decent fight.

Ministers meeting in smoky emergency sessions had cobbled together a fiscal package totalling a whopping five percentage points of GDP, and the Bank of Brazil unblinkingly had jacked up interest rates, 30, 50, finally 70 percent. The worst moment had come late Wednesday afternoon, when IMFO managed to arrange another emergency loan, with even the US Exchange Stabilization Fund chipping in, valiantly supporting the Brazilians. Learning about the rescue package just in time, Sophia had been forced to gamble almost every penny of the Liberty Fund's capital. But in the end, it had paid off handsomely; the currency was in complete rout devaluing 17 percent—just shy of the 17.2 percent the neural net had predicted—and netting Sophia a cool 40 percent rate of return.

But now she was trapped, caught by her own cleverness and conceit. She laughed at herself mirthlessly, remembering how proud and excited she'd been when she had first conceived the operation and told Melamed about it. She had led him on all these months with the promise of a brilliant blow for the Cause. Now, there was no going back, no escape; she had seen as much in the unyielding glint of his unblinking eye. Even if she somehow managed to pull out, the cadre would simply return to its old ways, bombing planes and playgrounds indiscriminately. The blood of its victims would be on her hands. Sophia clenched her fists, her fingernails digging into her palms a sharp reminder of her guilt and responsibility.

How could I not? How could I possibly not go through with the operation?

It was past ten o'clock before Sophia stirred from the sofa. Tonight she was leaving for Geneva. Melamed had told her to join him last week, but wanting to delay the inevitable, Sophia had argued that Monday was soon enough. After much debate, they had finally settled on Sunday, which still left two full days before the summit opening Wednesday morning.

With a supreme effort, Sophia got up and fetched her suitcases from the basement storage. Most of the stuff in the apartment would be abandoned, but a few personal belongings—and, of course, all the disks and equipment she needed to drive the neural net—had to go with her. Opening the cases on the living room floor, she made a desultory attempt at packing, meandering about the place with a distracted air, picking up odds and ends, then forgetting at once where she had put them down.

By midday, she could bear it no longer. Donning a light jacket—it was a warm but windy day—she left her apartment with no particular destination in mind, but feeling that if she remained cooped up inside any longer she'd go mad.

At Dupont Circle, the farmers' market straddled the streets: it met every Sunday, rain or shine, March to October. Sophia stopped at one of the stalls and picked up a bagful of plums and peaches before venturing up Massachusetts Avenue. She and Harry had once taken a bike ride down it, and Harry had hilariously started mocking the various foreign embassies. There was the British Embassy, its statue of Winston Churchill positioned with one foot on British soil, the other on American, so that he looked less like a great statesman striding out to save the world than a harried clerk trying to hail a taxicab; the Brazilian, a bizarre black box balanced on a base too small and looking as ready to teeter as the country's currency; the Finnish glasshouse, its only saving grace the ivy that hid it; and the various African embassies, their entrances adorned with ghastly green Astroturf that Third World dignitaries are so curiously fond of.

It gave Sophia a pang of remorse to remember Harry's laughter. She hurried on to the intersection of Wisconsin Avenue, eager to distance herself from her memories. To her left stretched the streets of Georgetown, but it was brunch time, and they would be filled with boisterous cheerful crowds. Above all, she wanted to get away from everyone and everything, from the teenyboppers with their cellular phones and celluloid lives, from Melamed and his all-consuming Cause, and from herself, if she could possibly figure out how. Then she remembered that the sprawling woods of Glover Park were nearby. Turning north, she headed toward them.

═══

Ever since that early morning call to Karin, suspicion had festered in Celine's mind like some consumptive disease breeding in a slum. At first, she kept telling herself she was being absurd, that this sort of thing happens in novels, not in real life, and that people like Sophia simply do not go around bumping off their lovers. And it wasn't even as though Sophia and Harry were married. If they'd had a fight, Sophia could've just left him. Celine doubted that Sophia inherited anything under Harry's will, or that he even had one.

But then she remembered the neural net, and Harry's secretary recounting how Sophia had marched into his office the day after his death, demanding that all the computers and ancillary disks and papers related to the neural net be handed over to her at once. That Sophia should want to carry on Harry's work was natural, even commendable, but to grab all his disks the very next day suggested a loyalty that bordered on the ruthless.

She also remembered the long list of confidential staff reports Sophia had ordered through the Document Management Facility. In a leap of logic that Celine herself could not explain, it seemed obvious that the speculative attacks on the world's currencies, Sophia stealing the neural net, and Harry's death were all somehow connected. Harry must have caught Sophia doing insider trading, and she had murdered him in cold blood.

Proving all this was quite another matter. Celine had only one piece of hard evidence: the discrepancy in Sophia's alibi. Karin, none too pleased about being awakened at that hour, had nevertheless confirmed the details about the computer time stamp. Celine had not pressed the matter, but Karin must have started having suspicions of her own later, for she'd left several messages Saturday afternoon asking Celine to call her immediately. But when Celine called back that evening, Karin was not at home and didn't answer her cell phone either. It was now Sunday, and though Karin's disappearance was probably nothing more sinister than a trip to New York to see her boyfriend, Celine could not help feeling a twinge of anxiety.

Finally, she decided to sneak into Sophia's office and take a look around. At IMFO, she was in luck. The security guard in Research, a friendly Filipino who'd known her for years, accepted without question her tale about needing some files from Sophia's office, and promptly unlocked the door with his master key.

Once inside, though, Celine was at a loss. Sophia's office looked no different from the hundreds of others at IMFO, a drab room that looked onto the inner courtyard. The very ordinariness of the place brought home to her how fantastic a theory she had spun. Celine sat down at the desk, poking and peeking at the various piles of paper. They were mostly computer printouts—all sorts of stuff about back-propagation coefficients and regression values—that were utterly unintelligible to her.

But buried near the bottom of one stack was a set of tables that she recognized at once. They were hourly updates on the central bank's exchange-market interventions during the Turkish currency crisis. How Sophia had managed to get hold of them, Celine could not imagine, for they were highly confidential. The most disconcerting part was that the notes scribbled in the margin were unmistakably in Harry's handwriting. Celine shook her head, refusing to believe that Harry might have been guilty of insider trading also. She thrust the sheets back into the pile.

She quickly searched the rest of the room. Though she found nothing directly incriminating, there was much that was suggestive, from the confidential staff reports stashed in the filing cabinet to the mysterious notes scribbled on a pad.

As she turned to leave, Celine noticed the pile of mail waiting patiently in the in-tray. There were some administrative circulars, a few memos and seminar notices, and Sophia's IMFO phone bill, the listing produced each month so staff members could pay for personal calls. Idly, she picked up the bill. There were dozens of international calls to London, Geneva, Zurich, and the Caymans. Celine jotted down the numbers and carefully replaced the bill in Sophia's in-tray. Then she spotted the memo from Administration approving a security pass for Sophia to the summit meeting in Geneva.

====

Glover Park was desolate, matching her mood. No one seemed to be around, the only sound an occasional shout in the distance for a dog that had wandered off. Sophia plunged into the woods, grateful for the solitude.

She scampered down the first descent, then picked her way more gingerly through the mud, fearful for her new shoes. She navigated past the muddiest patches along the footpath, thinking it curious that she hadn't heard from the FBI again, even after Harry's death. Indeed, beyond that initial interview at Harry's house, they seemed supremely uninterested in her. But it did occur to her that for the past few days—ever since Harry's death, in fact—she'd been careless about checking for tails, and it was just possible that the police were quietly keeping tabs on her. This was a decidedly disquieting thought, and she suddenly began to wonder whether one of the cars passing along Massachusetts Avenue hadn't been driving inordinately slowly, as if trying to keep pace with her.

Sophia frowned, trying to remember whether it had been deliberately hanging back and how long it had been following her. Anyway, she thought as she resumed her ascent, going for a walk was scarcely a crime. But she must be more vigilant from now on.

She made her way to the top of one of the hillocks and perched herself on the broad beam of a fallen tree trunk. Down below, winding its way through the woods, was a small stream, swollen by the recent rains. Sophia watched it a while, then bit into one of her plums, which was moist and plump and succulent. She attacked the rest of them with gusto, letting the juice dribble unabashedly down her chin and making a game of trying to reach the stream with the stones. She was just wondering whether one day there would be a cluster of plum trees growing there—the stones always fell short of the river—when she heard, or rather sensed someone coming up from behind.

She turned, then gasped.

It was Mathewsen.

Sophia was too astounded at first to saying anything. As far as she had known, Mathewsen and Huron had left the States weeks ago—she'd seen them off at Dulles herself—and were now back in Zurich or Beirut or London or wherever else they hung out.

"What on earth are *you* doing here?" she finally managed.

Mathewsen didn't answer at once, his pale gray eyes surveying their surroundings, as if sizing up the situation. Sophia felt a clutch of fear in the pit of her stomach. She kept telling herself that her fear was irrational and absurd, that Mathewsen was an ally; but she had never liked him, never trusted him. The woods had grown horribly quiet, and what had seemed a comforting solitude before felt now like a chilling loneliness. The sunlight barely penetrated the leaves. Sophia shuddered, unable to shake her foreboding.

"What are you doing here?" she repeated, more harshly.

"You made a mistake, you know," Mathewsen eased closer.

"A mistake?"

"When you killed Hoffinger," he said, explaining in a few short sentences the discrepancy about the time stamp on the computer file.

Sophia picked up the last plum stone and flung it into the air. For once, it reached the stream; she fancied she could her the faint "plop" as it landed in the water. Then she nodded briskly. "Funny how the little things trip you up. You're quite right. I assumed London time meant GMT, and that's what we used to reset the time stamp on the file. I forgot that Britain had moved to Summer Time."

"It's not just Britain. It's the whole of the European Union. They've harmonized it across Europe."

"Well, that's a comfort," Sophia retorted. They lapsed into silence for a moment. "How come you know all this?" she asked suddenly.

"From Melamed, of course. He made a full report of what happened."

Sophia's eyes narrowed. Mathewsen was lying, that much was obvious. Melamed was too security conscious to have confided in Huron and Mathewsen. Besides, Melamed wouldn't know about the peculiarities of the IMFO computer network. But in that case, how *had* Mathewsen found out? She searched his face, and then she found the answer.

"It *was* you I saw in Karin Wulf's car that night as she drove by!"

Mathewsen seemed to stiffen at the mention of Karin, but then his face broke into a slow, feral smile. "Very clever. Yes, she's been my source all along. She was puzzled by the discrepancy in your alibi, but she wasn't sure what it all really meant, so she asked me. Of course, it didn't take me long to put two and two together and realize what had happened."

"But I don't understand. Where does Karin Wulf fit into all this? How do you even know her?"

Mathewsen laughed. "I've been fucking her the past five months, that's how. Did you really think we were going to let you go off with a couple of hundred million dollars and not keep tabs on our investment? I've been using her to keep abreast of what you've been up to—completely unwittingly, of course. She knows nothing about the operation. We "met" on a flight from New York, and a charming lady she was, too."

"*Was?*"

"I shouldn't worry about Ms. Karin Wulf anymore," Mathewsen replied softly. "She's been taken care of."

You bloodless bastard. Sophia glared at him, filled with loathing for this man, with his manicured nails and the faint smell of cologne that always hung about him like an air of disrespectability. She hadn't know Karin well, and it would be a stretch to describe her as a friend, but it still sickened Sophia to think that the happy, carefree girl was dead.

"And now," she said wearily, "I suppose you've come to escort me to Geneva."

"I'm afraid it's not that simple." Mathewsen reached into his pocket.

In his hand was a gun.

Sophia nodded slowly. She should be shocked but wasn't. From the moment she had seen him, she'd had a premonition of evil. She could guess what had happened. Paranoid that Sophia might be caught, and his assets sequestered by the authorities, Huron had been persuaded to dump her and the operation. And as for Mathewsen, he had never believed in the operation. From the beginning, his only interest was in making more money. There was only one question in her mind, but Sophia hesitated to ask, afraid of this last betrayal.

Mathewsen shook his head as if reading her thoughts. "Melamed's a sentimental old fool, dreaming of liberty and justice and all that crap for a bunch of bloody peasants that nobody gives a damn about anyway. But if it's any consolation, the answer is 'no.' This is my own little operation. Melamed knows nothing about it."

"You mercenary little bastard. You never gave a damn about the Cause at all, did you? All along, it was just about making more money for yourselves. That's what you wanted the neural net for."

Mathewsen shrugged. "We put up the capital; it's only reasonable that we should get the reward. Which reminds me, would you please give me the master disk for the neural net?"

"I don't know what you're talking about."

Mathewsen laughed. "Come now, surely you can do better than that. Please don't insult my intelligence. I've already been to your apartment and found your laptop computers all neatly packed away. But I know there's a master disk missing. Either you've got it on you or it's in your bag. I doubt you want me to strip-search you, so why not be a good little girl and give it to me." He held out his hand.

"What about Huron?" she asked, playing for time. "Is he part of this, too?"

"Huron's a sentimental fool also, but he dreams of being president of our glorious dump of a country. God knows how much money he's sunk into one harebrained scheme after another to topple our illustrious president. But this time, fortunately, I managed to talk him out of it. Now that disk, please."

Sophia silently cursed herself. Mathewsen would not be able to get updates of the intervention data from IMFO, but the neural net and data she had collected already would be enough to earn him millions. And thanks to the power-of-attorney forms she'd been forced to sign, he would have no difficulty cleaning out the Liberty Fund's accounts. She wondered whether he'd been planning this all along, with Harry's death just a convenient pretext.

"Come on, we haven't got all day."

Sophia reached into the bag.

"Hold it," Mathewsen said sharply.

She paused, her hand in mid-air.

"On second thought, just hand me the bag."

Sophia shrugged and handed it to him. He tipped the contents at the base of the tree trunk, rummaging through them with one hand, keeping the gun trained on her with the other. He smiled wolfishly as he spotted the minidisk, still snug in its plastic container.

"Okay," he said, backing away from the tree, "go on, put everything back. After all, we mustn't litter."

Sophia hesitated, feeling extraordinarily helpless. In a minute, she would be dead. It seemed so fantastical that her mind refused to accept it, but she could see no way out of this predicament. She wondered whether Harry had felt the same when he saw Melamed's gun pointing at him, whether he had thought it unreal and absurd even as he felt the bullets puncturing his body.

"Hurry up!" Mathewsen barked.

Sophia started tossing her things back into her bag: keys, wallet, credit cards, perfume bottle . . . her perfume bottle! In a single, smooth motion she flicked off the lid and jammed her thumb down hard on the plunger, spraying the perfume into Mathewsen's eyes.

Mathewsen raised his hands to cover his eyes, howling in pain. At that instant, Sophia lunged at him. Catching him off guard, she managed to trip him over. They went tumbling down the hill, fighting and clawing each other, until Mathewsen's head struck an outcropped rock. There was a sickening crunch, then his body rolled to a halt a few yards farther down. Sophia caught up with him a moment later. Panting, she felt for a pulse. Nothing.

As she stared at him with morbid fascination, it slowly dawned on her that she must dispose of the body. But how? Then she remembered the stream. She eyed the distance—fifty yards—it shouldn't take more than a couple of minutes. But she hadn't reckoned on the unwieldiness of a dead body, it was worse than lugging a futon. She tried lifting it, but it was hopelessly heavy, so she began rolling it down the hill instead.

The body wedged in a rut and wouldn't budge. Sophia tugged frantically, a prickly heat breaking about her. She paused to wipe her forehead, then realized with horror that her hands were sticky with blood. Gripping Mathewsen's jacket more tightly, she yanked again, at last managing to pull him free.

She heard a rustling in the undergrowth and froze. Finally, she lowered herself quietly to the ground and looked around. Nothing. Just the wind. She stood up. But no! There it was again, someone poking about the bushes. Sophia's heart was pounding now, her breath coming in harsh, painful gasps.

A black snout appeared out from among the leaves. A dog! Sophia almost laughed in relief. Grasping Mathewsen's body again, staggering under the burden, she resumed her course, sliding toward the stream below. Presently, she realized that the dog was following, watching her through his glassy, protuberant eyes.

"Go away!" she hissed, unnerved. "Go on, shoo!"

But the dog continued following her faithfully. In desperation, Sophia grabbed a stick and threw it as far up the incline as she could; the dog scampered off. Half carrying, half dragging, Sophia managed to get Mathewsen's body to the stream, where she spotted a wide waste pipe with a metal grille that ran into the stream. Sophia waded in, oblivious to the cold water, then heard a splash behind her and whirled around. The dog was back, the stick clutched firmly in his teeth, his tail wagging energetically.

"Rex! Rex! Here boy! Where are you? Come here, boy!" the voice floated through the trees.

Sophia looked around in panic. The voice was growing louder, closer.

"Rex! Here boy, let's go!"

"Go, damn you!" Sophia told the dog. She crouched down and tried to hold Mathewsen's body underwater, but it kept bobbing up under its own buoyancy. From the corner of her eye, Sophia saw a man appear at the top of the hillock. Instinctively, she crouched lower, knowing it was futile. He would spot her any moment now.

Sophia could hear him thrashing through the undergrowth, less than thirty yards away. Too late, she remembered Mathewsen's gun, which must have fallen somewhere in the struggle. Not daring to budge, Sophia remained locked in her crouch, faint with fear.

"Come on, Rex! Let's go. Good boy!"

The dog gave Sophia one last reproachful glance, dropped the stick, and tore off up the slippery bank.

Sophia waited several minutes more, until the seeping cold made it unbearable, before daring to stir. Peering up, she scanned the horizon. She was alone again. But there was still the matter of disposing of Mathewsen's body. She tugged at the grille but to no avail, it seemed determined not to budge. Groping under the water, she realized that silt had jammed it in place. Sophia searched in vain for something to dig with, then finally reached for her shoes and used them to dredge away the mud.

It seemed an eternity, but it was probably no more than five minutes before she could swing the grille up on its hinge. A pile of accumulated refuse gushed out, flowing over her naked feet. Sophia grasped Mathewsen's body and pushed it up the waste pipe, letting the grille slam back into place. With any luck, the body wouldn't be discovered for days, maybe weeks.

Sodden and exhausted, Sophia clambered up the bank. As she slithered in the squidgy mud, she happened to glance down at her new shoes. They were quite ruined.

CHAPTER TWENTY-THREE

WITH THE UNEASY FEELING that she was making a prize fool of herself, Celine entered the managing director's anteroom. Clutched in her hand were three paltry pieces of evidence: the printout with the Turkish intervention figures, the memo from Administration approving Sophia's security pass to the summit, and the copy of Sophia's phone bill. Checking out the phone numbers, Celine had learned that they belonged to various banks and financial institutions in London, Zurich, Geneva, and the Caymans.

It was enough to convince, if not convict, and first thing Monday morning Celine had requested an urgent meeting with Kiyotaki. She refused to give his assistant any explanation, merely insisting it was vital that she see the managing director right away. To her relief, his assistant called back within the hour to tell her that an interview had been granted for that afternoon. But now, as Celine paced the floor, she feared she was making a ghastly mistake, and that Kiyotaki would simply scoff at her suspicions.

"This way, please." The secretary led her a short distance down the corridor. Celine didn't remember going to Kiyotaki's office this way before, and she seemed to vaguely recall the leather soundproof baffling on the door being green, not burgundy. But before she had time to really register the thought, the secretary was pulling open the outer door and pushing in the inner one.

Celine stepped forward, then froze.

Seated behind the desk was not Kiyotaki, but Adanpur.

"There's been some mistake." Celine turned to the secretary. "I was supposed to meet Mr. Kiyotaki."

"No mistake." Adanpur stood up and came around the desk. "Toyoo's terribly busy at present. He asked me to meet with you and find out what this is all about. If need be, he can see you later."

"Oh." She felt strangely trapped as the secretary closed the double doors behind her.

"Won't you have a seat? Can I offer you anything?"

"No. No, thank you." Celine sat stiffly. "I'm fine."

Adanpur reached over the desk, and stabbed the intercom button. "No interruptions, please." He planted himself next to her on the sofa. Celine edged away, remembering the last time she had come to his office. This was a different office, of course, much larger and grander, befitting his promotion to deputy managing director, and she felt slightly intimidated by it.

"Why didn't you come and see me before?"

She said nothing.

He cocked an eyebrow and gave a wry smile. "Don't I even merit a response?"

"You know perfectly well why," she replied.

"You're not still sore about the Special Intervention Facility, are you?" he laughed. "That's very foolish of you, Celine, very foolish indeed. You're a clever girl, you should know better."

"All I know is that it was a damn good idea, and you sabotaged it."

"I did nothing of the sort. The Board decided against it."

"With your connivance."

He shook his head. "I warned you from the start that the proposal wasn't going to fly. It was a simple question of *realpolitik*. Poor Toyoo never understands that; he doesn't know which battles should be lost so the war may be won. The man's an idealist, but a fool. As for me, I saw an opportunity and I took it."

"Even if it meant using me and humiliating him?"

He shrugged. "Did you come here to quarrel?"

"No," Celine said. "No, I came about something else. Something quite different."

She took a deep breath and launched into her story, starting with her initial suspicions about Sophia, then the discrepancy in Sophia's alibi and her mysterious request for a security pass to the summit. Celine spoke for the better part of twenty minutes, all the while aware how painfully lame and unpersuasive it sounded.

Adanpur sat silently as she spoke, his face inscrutable, a thin smile—or was it a sneer—stretched across his lips, a curious, faraway look in his eyes. Celine began to have the feeling that he wasn't listening at all. As she finished, he leaned over and began running his fingers lightly through her hair, as though humoring a child. Celine shook free, annoyed less by being touched than by not being taken seriously.

"Please don't do that."

"Why not?" he asked, sounding genuinely surprised.

"Because I don't like it."

"But I do," he persisted. "I love your hair, the way it falls across your face, framing it like a great masterpiece."

"Please stop that. This is a very serious matter."

"Poor old Celine," he laughed. "You try so hard, don't you? Saving the Indonesians one day, the world economy the next, always trying to undo that which cannot be undone. You do realize, of course, you've completely lost your sense of perspective, your sense of reality?"

"So you think I'm lying?"

"Oh, I believe *you* believe it, all right. But frankly, I think your frustrated femininity is making you neurotic. You're jealous of this girl, Sophia Gemaye, and of course you're upset about the death of your friend Harry. Between them, you've managed to concoct this wildly implausible tale about murder and mayhem in the international capital markets. I mean, just listen to yourself. Have you any idea how utterly ludicrous you sound?"

"Go to hell," Celine stood up. "Go to bloody hell. For your information, my love life isn't in the least bit 'frustrated,' and I don't have to put up with your psychobabble. If you're too stupid to believe me, that's fine. I'll go to Kiyotaki."

"Don't leave." He pulled her down again. "Look, I want to believe you. Honestly, I do. But you've got to admit it's a pretty wild tale. Give me some time to check things out. We don't want to make fools of ourselves by rushing into anything. Besides," he added with his winning smile, "I haven't seen you in ages. What's your hurry? Stay a while."

"No, I should be going."

"Nonsense."

Celine tried to wriggle free, but he was gripping her wrist tightly. With an abrupt movement he pulled her closer, until her face was buried in his chest, and his arms were clasped around her. She struggled for a moment, but then forced her body to relax, submitting to his caresses. His hands were slipping under her blouse, loosening the clasp of her brassiere expertly.

She could feel his hot breath against her cheek, and it brought to mind some furry beast, all too friendly and cuddly but liable to turn wild and dangerous at any instant.

"No!" she cried. "Stop!"

"Don't be silly. It's me. We've done this dozens of times before."

"I don't want it. I don't. Stop!"

"Hush," he said. "You'll enjoy this. You need it."

He had pushed her down on the sofa, one hand tugging at her brassiere, the other clamped across her mouth. The smell of sweat on his palm filled Celine with revulsion. She struggled to break free once more, but he slammed her down again, bumping her head violently against the arm of the sofa. Mustering all her strength, Celine sank her teeth into his hand.

With a yell of pain, Adanpur let go, then slapped her across the face. "You lousy bitch! Jesus, look what you've done to my hand. What the hell did you do that for?"

Celine sat up, still groggy from the blow to her head.

"After all I've done for you," he went on. "You were nothing, a nobody, a goddamn YEP. I showed you the ropes, gave you every opportunity, and that's the way you repay me—"

The intercom buzzed, interrupting him in mid-sentence. "What?" he barked. "I told you no damn interruptions!"

"Mr. Kiyotaki is free now, sir," the voice floated back. "He'd like to see you and Ms. O'Rourke in his office."

"Oh. Very well, then. Tell him we'll be there in a moment."

Hot tears of shame and humiliation trickled down Celine's face.

"Go on," he said, "Get out of here. I'll join you in a couple of minutes. Here," he added, throwing Celine his starched handkerchief, "you'd better freshen up first."

Celine let the handkerchief fall to the floor, untouched, and stumbled out of the room.

It was her own fault, her own fault entirely. She should never have gone to his office, never have resumed her affair with him. She should never have had an affair with him in the first place. The thoughts tumbled through Celine's mind, and even before the meeting began, she knew she was in no state for it. Five minutes had passed since she escaped Adanpur's office, and though she'd tidied herself hurriedly in the restroom, she still felt dishevelled and dirty.

Kiyotaki looked up briefly as she entered, greeting her with a chilly, "Good afternoon, Ms. O'Rourke," and directed her to one of the stiff, uncomfortable chairs facing his desk. As she sat down, he picked up his fountain pen and resumed working through a pile of papers on his desk.

Reading, signing, reading, signing, reading, signing. He seemed to have aged since Celine had seen him last. He had an impatient distracted air that did not bode well for her endeavor.

Adanpur, thank God, had not showed up yet. She was just beginning to hope that he would shirk the meeting, when he sailed in flashing one of his perfect toothy smiles, looking as calm and unconcerned as ever. His sense of shame, if he'd ever had one, must have atrophied long ago from lack of use.

But there was no time to think of that now, nor to dissect her own emotions about what had just happened, for with a preemptory nod Kiyotaki bade her begin.

Celine started all over again. But this time she could feel Adanpur's ominous presence—his chair was positioned to her left and slightly behind her, just beyond her peripheral vision—and it unnerved her. She knew she sounded rambling and incoherent but couldn't focus on what she was saying.

In her mind's eye, he was creeping up on her, ready to seize her from behind. Absurdly, she kept looking around to make sure he had not moved.

When she finished, Kiyotaki did not respond at once. He removed his glasses and polished them with slow deliberate swipes of his handkerchief before perching them on his nose again. He turned to Adanpur. "What do you make of all this?"

"I'm sure Ms. O'Rourke must be very upset about the tragic death of young Hoffinger—indeed it's been a terrible shock to us all—but frankly, I think it has made her overwrought. Of course, Ms. O'Rourke enjoys our full confidence. Nonetheless . . ."

He spoke as though Celine were not in the room, or a child whose views could safely be ignored. She wondered whether he genuinely did not believe her or whether he was just trying to punish her. No that it mattered much. The battle lines were drawn, and she knew he was going to fight her every inch of the way.

He can't touch me, she kept telling herself. I'm safe here. If I tell what he tried to do to me, he'll be ruined. Then she remembered Karin's admonition. It was true; IMFO was mostly men, and mostly from developing countries. It was the culture of the place. It would be his word against hers, and no one would believe her. For that matter, seeing Adanpur as suave and collected as ever, she could hardly believe it herself.

Besides, it *was* her fault. She had started the affair with him in the first place, and she was the one who had resumed it later. She should never, ever have gone to his office again. In the end, she knew she could never tell anyone what had happened. And he knew it also.

"What about the computer file?" she said instead.

"What about it?"

"Well, at the very least, it means Sophia has no alibi for Harry's murder."

"Nonsense," he replied crisply. "Why should she be a suspect in his murder anyway? You've taken a few unconnected facts—if they are facts— and spun them into a ludicrous tale of murder and mayhem in the global financial markets."

"Have you spoken to the police about this matter?" Kiyotaki asked quietly.

Celine shifted uncomfortably. "No sir. I thought . . . well, it could be embarrassing. I wanted to investigate the matter more carefully first." The truth was, she had called the police that morning, but the detective in charge was out on another case. The man she'd spoken to had said he knew nothing about any computer files and was disinclined to discuss any details of a case under investigation.

"Quite right," Kiyotaki said at once. "Quite right. But to your knowledge the police do not have any concerns about this time-stamping business?"

"No, sir."

"I see. And what about Ms. Wulf? Should we call her up here and see whether she can help shed light on this matter?"

"We can't. She's disappeared."

"What do you mean 'disappeared'?"

"I last spoke to her Saturday morning, and I've been trying to get hold of her ever since. Apparently she sent an email over the weekend, saying she was taking a couple of weeks' leave."

"And I suppose," Adanpur interrupted acidly, "that Ms. Wulf's 'disappearance' is also part of this global conspiracy?"

Celine fell silent.

After a moment, Adanpur continued in his cynical, contemptuous tone. "Let me get this straight. You are accusing Ms. Gemaye not only of murder but also of using insider information to launch speculative attacks against dozens of currencies. Meanwhile, you haven't even checked with the police about this computer file business. And conveniently enough, Ms. Wulf, who put you on to all this in the first place, can't be found?"

"I would hardly call it 'convenient,'" Celine retorted.

"What about Ms. Gemaye?" Kiyotaki asked. "Has she gone away also?"

"I believe so. She hasn't been coming to the office for the past few days, and I tried her flat this morning, but there's no answer. She's probably left for Geneva already. She has family there, or at least she used to live there."

"She was Harry Hoffinger's partner?" Adanpur asked.

"That's right. They were working on the neural net together, though I think most of the original work was actually done by Harry. She teamed up with him later to take advantage of it."

"No, no. I mean, were they romantically involved?"

"Yes."

"And what about you?" he continued. "What were your relations with Mr. Hoffinger?"

"We were friends," Celine said, furious at the blush seeping into her cheeks.

"Is that all?"

"*Yes.*"

From then on, Celine knew she had lost. Each time she tried to answer back, Adanpur would manage to twist what she said, pouncing on her admission that she had illegally accessed Sophia's Document Management Facility and, worse still, had peeked at her personnel file without permission or authority. The meeting soon became more a trial of Celine than an investigation into Sophia. He even managed to cast suspicion on Harry, pointing out that the printout of the Turkish intervention figures Celine had found in Sophia's office must have belonged to Harry originally, and was only transferred to Sophia when she'd inherited the project.

Why are you doing this to me, thought Celine miserably. Haven't you hurt me enough already?

But he hadn't. Systematically, and with malicious precision, he dissected her arguments, trapping Celine into making wilder and wilder allegations about Sophia, accusations that she could not possibly hope to substantiate. Of course, every time she did so, he pressed home his advantage. By the end of it, Celine was feeling ragged and worn, almost beyond caring whether Kiyotaki believed her or not. All she wanted to do was get out of there. Get out and go home, take a long, burning hot shower and wash away every last vestige of the day.

"Even if you're right . . . which, frankly, I have grave doubts about," Kiyotaki said at last, "I don't see what you would have me do. Offshore hedge funds aren't subject to regulation, neither by us nor by their national authorities. They can do pretty much as they please."

"Couldn't you at least get Sophia's security pass to the summit meeting canceled?"

"Why? What do you think she's going to do there?"

"I don't know. But the very fact that she wanted to get into the summit makes me suspicious. Maybe she intends to do some insider trading ahead of the official publication of the summit communiqué. In any case, it surely doesn't hurt to cancel her pass."

"No," Kiyotaki said, stroking his chin slowly, "I suppose not."

But Adanpur was shaking his head. "Are you sure that's wise, Toyoo? Canceling her pass now would mean having to inform the United Nations in Geneva. They're prickly enough as it is about offering the use of the Palais des Nations for these summits. It would hardly be seemly to go cap in hand to them now and tell them one of our staff members could be involved in insider trading or some other form of illegal activity."

That argument clinched it, of course. A look of wariness instantly came across Kiyotaki's face. "No. No, you're quite right. I hadn't thought of that. Our relations with the UN are tenuous enough already. I don't want any further embarrassments."

"Besides," Adanpur said, his voice richer now, more confident of victory, "despite all the to-do the press and the markets make about these summits, very little gets done at them, and I doubt Ms. Gemaye would gain much insider-trading advantage. As for her wanting to attend, I see nothing wrong in that at all. Since we act as the secretariat for the summit, we're always assigned a number of free seats for the Visitors' Gallery. They're up for grabs for any staff member who's interested. Ms. Gemaye was perfectly within her rights to request a seat, and Administration was quite correct to give her one. Obviously, we wouldn't pay for a YEP to fly to Geneva on official travel, but if she's there on vacation, I see nothing wrong in her wanting to attend. On the contrary, it shows quite the right spirit. Wouldn't you agree, Toyoo?"

Celine felt a rising panic of frustration, an inarticulate anger suffusing her face. She was no match for Adanpur; he was too adept at this game, too smooth, too practiced. She remembered how cleverly he had dealt with the Indonesian ministers, never coming out with specific recommendations, never quite committing himself, manipulating and exploiting their individual foibles and vanities behind the scenes so that later, when things went wrong, he was able to disassociate himself with ease from the disastrous decisions that had been made. He had even managed to parlay the Indonesia defeat into an appointment as advisor and, now, deputy managing director. How could she possibly compete?

For a moment, Celine toyed with the thought of telling Kiyotaki all that had happened. But she knew that even if she did, this posturing sycophantic bastard, with his Italian-cut suits and handmade shirts, would somehow twist the facts to his advantage. She would be branded a neurotic frustrated woman, who had preyed upon a married man and was trying to get revenge for being jilted. Tears of hurt and anger appeared in the corners of her eyes. She tried to blink them away, but they rolled down, hot and plump, tracing the contours of her cheeks.

Adanpur was still deriding Celine's suspicions, when Kiyotaki noticed the state to which she had been reduced, and abruptly told him he would like to speak to Celine alone.

"Yes, of course." Adanpur gave Celine a quick glance, in which there was perhaps just a twinge of anxiety, and it occurred to her that he might be worried she'd been pushed too far. Encouraged by this tiny triumph, Celine reached into her bag for a handkerchief and dabbed her eyes.

Kiyotaki, sat silently, poking holes in his blotter with a small, dagger-like Moroccan letter opener. He finally put it back in its holder and gave Celine a sad little smile.

"Mr. Hoffinger was a close friend of yours, wasn't he?" he asked, not unkindly.

"Yes."

"Yes. You must be very upset and distraught over his death. Perhaps you should think of taking some leave—get away from Washington and get a complete rest."

"I'm all right," she protested.

"Nonetheless, I think it would be best." Kiyotaki reached for a small notepad—it had *Office of the Managing Director* embossed along the top, Celine noticed inconsequentially—and uncapped his fountain pen. "I am suggesting to your department director that you be given some time off. You can take your annual leave or, if that's run out, be put on administrative leave instead."

Celine stared at him. She knew he was giving her a way out, a face-saving exit from the absurd accusations she had made. It made her angry that he should think she needed it.

"And if I refuse?"

Kiyotaki paused, his pen frozen in mid-sentence. He put it down, shrugging slightly. "Well naturally, that's your prerogative. But I cannot have you going around making these outrageous accusations, and we should be very sorry to lose you." He smiled, a bland, diplomatic smile. "I'm sure you'll be sensible about this matter."

Celine stood up. There was nothing more to be said. She remembered her letter of resignation. It must be winding its way through Administration— she had clean forgotten about it. She wished she had it with her now, so she could slap it down on Kiyotaki's desk and tell him to go to hell. She strode purposely from her chair and had just reached the door, when she heard Kiyotaki call her name.

"Yes?" She turned, her jaw clenched in anger.

"If you *are* thinking of taking some vacation, you might consider Geneva. I understand it's very pleasant at this time of year."

CHAPTER TWENTY-FOUR

L ATE SUNDAY NIGHT, Sophia caught the Swiss flight through New York. Morally responsible for Harry and Karin's deaths, she felt a suffocating sense of guilt. The Cause had seemed so simple at one time, so noble, so undeniably *right*. But there had been too many lies, too many betrayals, too many deaths. Now it filled her only with disgust. But if Harry and Karin's deaths were to have any meaning at all, she must continue. And in a strange way, the encounter with Mathewsen had doubled her determination to see the operation through to the end.

Sophia began to shiver on board the airplane, reminded of the bombing attempt last December, when she had very nearly taken a hundred innocent lives. She felt the same fever and torment she had suffered as a child, when, in punishment for some act of defiance, Sophia's stepmother would lock her in the large chest of drawers in the bedroom. She would lie there for an hour, sometimes two, shivering in the dark as she fantasized that by some miracle Daddy would return and rescue her. Later, but only after Sophia repented and promised not to make a nuisance of herself again, she would be allowed out, and Nanny would put her to bed and comfort her.

Seeing Sophia's condition, the ever-solicitous air hostess rushed to bring her a glass of warm milk, then tucked her in with a duvet. Slowly, Sophia brought her emotions back under control. For the remainder of the flight Sophia sat stiffly, clutching the duvet until her knuckles hurt, wanting to stoke her anger at Melamed for murdering Harry and at herself for letting it happen, but all she felt was emptiness and pain. And by the time she landed in Geneva and saw Melamed peering anxiously for her at the arrivals hall, she couldn't even feel any resentment, only stabbing remorse. There was no sense blaming Melamed for Harry's death, or even Mathewsen and Huron for Karin's. The operation was hers and hers alone. She was responsible, she was to blame.

Perhaps it would have been different had it not been for Mathewsen's betrayal, but as it was, Melamed was the only person now to whom she could turn. He stepped forward as she emerged from the customs area, and she allowed herself to be hugged and held, softening to his touch. Then, before she knew it, she was sobbing on his shoulder, like a prodigal daughter returned to her father.

Thankfully, there was much to be done. The first order of business was annulling the power-of-attorney forms before Huron raided the accounts, stealing not only his original seed money but also the profits Sophia had made in her speculative attacks. Luckily, it was still early Monday morning. Huron wouldn't have had a chance yet, but Sophia was nervous and they went straight from the airport to the bank.

Melamed took her home afterward, a rented villa on the outskirts of Geneva near Mies, where she set up the phalanx of computers and trading systems for the neural net. The system was fully automated now. She need only decide which currencies to attack and when, and the computers would generate the relevant buy and sell orders based on the neural net's predictions.

They lunched at one of the overpriced restaurants by the lake. Sophia had no appetite, picking at her food while she worked on drafting their statement. The text would be sent immediately following the explosion at the summit meeting—while the markets were still reeling from the news—to the governments of all the major industrialized countries and to more than a dozen national and international newspapers. Sophia was confident of one thing: the billions lost in the market turmoil would be a blow not soon forgotten, and their modest demands—immediate sanctions against the regime, with no trade or investment by any Western country until the release of all political prisoners and the promise of free and fair elections—were likely to be met. There was probably little hope of things changing overnight, but without the latest toys to amuse the army and suppress the people—and more important, the money to pay for them—the regime would lose its power base and eventually be toppled, and in the ensuing power vacuum, democracy might just get some breathing space.

Late afternoon, they headed back into town, driving to the Palais des Nations in a black Mercedes with stolen diplomatic number-plates for added respectability. Security had already been tightened ahead of the summit meeting. The tourist entrances were closed, and the guards were scurrying about with a self-important air. Sophia presented her pass to the policeman at the main gate, who studied it a moment, then gave Melamed an enquiring glance.

"He's with me."

The guard hesitated, looked back toward his supervisor, then nodded slowly, his eyes lingering on the two pregnant briefcases lying on the back seat. Sophia couldn't resist following his eyes. The cases contained the explosives. Suddenly, she realized what was wrong. The briefcases were identical. Two people, two cases. But identical ones were patently implausible. How could they have made so elementary a mistake, she thought angrily.

But the guard didn't seem to notice. With a jerk of his head, he let them pass. Sophia steered the car through quickly, before he could change his mind. She switched off the engine in the parking lot, a comforting silence descending upon them.

"Security will be much tighter on Thursday," she said. "We'll need a pass for you as well—I won't be able to get you in on mine."

Melamed took the pass out of her hand and held it up to the light. "It's a holographic photo. Don't worry, I should be able to make a passable forgery." He tossed it back to her. "Well, shall we?"

The guard at the entrance regarded them suspiciously. Melamed, stiff in his unfamiliar suit and hugging his bulging briefcase, simply didn't look the part. Sophia edged forward, flashing her pass as she gently shepherded Melamed with her free arm. She nodded condescendingly to the loitering guards and walked on confidently, afraid that any hesitation would invite suspicion.

The summit meeting would be held in the Council Chamber of the Palais des Nations, which should not be far, but they soon found themselves thoroughly lost in the labyrinth of corridors—some dark and dimly lit, others bright and airy, looking out on breathtaking vistas of the Palais gardens, Lake Geneva, and Mont Blanc beyond. The passageways twisted and turned, up one staircase, down another, past offices identified only by cryptic acronyms, with mousy bureaucrats whose heads were bent over reports, or pompous diplomats dressed in three-piece suits, at once dashing and fifty years out of date. The whole effect was vaguely Kafkaesque.

Sophia said little as they walked, her mind occupied elsewhere. The yen had come under heavy pressure in the Far East markets this morning, depreciating further when New York opened. Fund managers, already skittish from the beating they had taken in the emerging market countries over the past weeks, were fleeing out of exotics to quality, good old US Treasury bills. Sophia would start on the euro tomorrow. The European Central Bank, its reputation tarnished by constant political bickering, should be easy prey; one good nudge should start an avalanche of short-selling. By Thursday, she hoped, the markets would be in a frenzy, worrying what would come out of the Finance Ministers' Summit and whether the turbulence was finally over or just beginning. Yes, Sophia decided, by Thursday they should be just ripe for the little surprise she and Melamed had planned.

"Damn," Melamed said. "We've come around in a circle. How the hell did we manage that?"

Noticing their lost look, one of the guards broke from the group and started toward them. But Sophia, still self-conscious about the identical briefcases, started talking loudly to Melamed about the urgency of finishing the Interim Committee Report. They walked past the guards with feigned nonchalance and, once out of sight, hurriedly retraced their steps. This time, they managed to find the way, emerging at last at the entrance to the Visitors' Gallery that overlooked the Council Chamber.

Sophia had not been here in twenty years. Nanny used to bring her as a child, when there was none of this nonsense about security. Anyone could wander freely about the Palais des Nations to admire the murals of José Marià Sert—the Giants' Room, Sophia used to call it. Now she hesitated, afraid the place had changed, afraid the giants were gone. But Melamed did not want to start setting the explosives until at least seven o'clock, when there would be fewer people about the Palais, so they had half an hour to kill. In the meantime, they found a convenient cubby hole to conceal a gun, then Sophia nudged open the door to the Visitors' Gallery.

They paused, transfixed by the murals. Sepia, sienna, ochre, black, smatterings of gold. Sophia and Melamed stood in silence, staring at the colossal, apocalyptic scenes. Memories flooded back to Sophia: her mother shooing them out of the house, long walks along the lakeside with one hand clutching Nanny's coat, the other a sticky vue de Genève, the obligatory stop at the *Presse Bar* with a *café renversé* for Nanny and a *chocolat chaud* for Sophia, and afterward, if the Council Chamber wasn't in use and Sophia had been well-behaved, a visit to the Giants' Room.

The murals, Sophia explained, remembering what Nanny used to tell her, depict all that separates man from fellow man—war, hatred, cruelty, vengeance, exploitation, injustice—and all that brings him together—peace, liberty, freedom from drudgery and enslavement. There was Hope, a mother and child standing astride defunct cannons, revelling in peace while crowds hurled away their guns, drunk with joy that wars have ended; Scientific Progress, doctors liberating mankind from the scourge of disease; Social Progress, slaves shattering their chains; and Technical Progress in the far corner, the cogs of civilization relieving mankind from the burden of physical toil.

But most magnificent of all were the figures overhead, which spanned the expanse of the ceiling. They were Sophia's childhood favorite, five great, sinewy giants reaching across the room with clasped hands, drawing, coaxing, pulling the world together.

"Why five?" asked Melamed.

"The five continents."

"And that?" Melamed pointed at a small figure in the corner of the mural. "Who's he supposed to be—the man standing by the church spire?"

"It's the cathedral of Salamanca. The man is Francisco de Vitoria, a famous sixteenth-century jurist who argued for human rights, using the law to protest cruelty and abuse of native Indians by the Spanish conquistadors in South America." Rather like Daddy, she might have added.

"What are those paintings behind us?" Melamed turned to the murals behind them, one with a long funeral procession, the other an anguished mother clutching her dead child and shaking her fists toward the sky.

"The Conquerors and the Conquered. The moral of the mural is that even the Conquerors are burdened by the loss of their dead. As for the Conquered, they seek revenge even in defeat, wishing ardently for the fight to begin anew."

"Like us," Melamed muttered.

"Oh no," Sophia said. "Oh no." She placed her hand on Melamed's shoulder and leaned against him, burying her face in the soft wool of his jacket. "We're not out for death and destruction—only for justice."

Melamed looked at her oddly, almost as if he was surprised. Then, very gently, he kissed her on the forehead. "Come," he said at last. "Let's get to work."

═══

The balcony in the Visitors' Gallery ended in a bronze railing that curved like a horseshoe, overlooking the Council Chamber below though not affording direct access to it. To reach the Council Chamber they had to leave the Visitors' Gallery again and descend by the grand marble staircase to the atrium, a sunny, cheerful space with light streaming in through huge skylights. Ahead of them was the main entrance to the Council Chamber, flanked on either side by doors that led to the two smaller side chambers.

Melamed reached into his jacket pocket and pulled out a slim box, perhaps a quarter of an inch thick and made of some metallic-looking material.

"What is it?"

"Sandwich wedge," Melamed grinned. "You just press hard here, near the middle, until you hear a snapping sound then shove it under the door immediately. It uses a chemical trigger. There's some kind of weird composite material sandwiched between the two plates that expands and hardens almost instantly. Because it fits under the door, once the wedge expands, the doors are virtually impossible to unjam—and with these bronze doors, they'll need an acetylene torch to open them."

Sophia nodded. After the screw-up with the airliner bombing, Melamed had sworn never to trust a pre-timed detonator again. They would come as far as the entrance to the Council Chamber on Thursday, make certain the summit was in session, and detonate the charges manually. But they still needed a few minutes' delay to make their getaway, so they needed to jam the doors and keep the delegates from escaping in the interim.

"Neat." Sophia handed it back to Melamed. "Where did you get it?"

"London. Counter Intelligence Contraptions on Bond Street."

"Bond Street, of course," she laughed as they entered the Council Chamber, "where else would the well-tailored terrorist shop?"

Once inside, they grew serious. Melamed set to work preparing the explosives, while Sophia checked around the Council Chamber. At the far end of the room, near the front, were connecting doors to the two side chambers. These doors were also made of bronze. Sophia ran her fingers along them, feeling the cold touch of the metal and the raised relief of the inscriptions. She twisted the large silver ring that served as a handle until it yielded with a stiff creak. Sophia pushed hard against the door, but it would not budge—they must be blocked off. The only other exit was through the windows, but they were up at the Visitors' Gallery level and impossible to reach from below.

Melamed had the explosives laid out in a row, like bricks in a wall. There were a lot of them, much more than Sophia had imagined. They'd had a huge fight early on in the planning of the operation, Melamed favoring a massive explosion that would kill the delegates in a single swoop, Sophia adamantly opposed. Eventually, though, he had accepted her logic; trapping the finance ministers and central bank governors would be a lot more effective in creating panic than killing them. No one would know who had survived and who was in charge, causing paralysis of governments and chaos in the markets. Besides, Melamed knew full well that Sophia would never countenance a massacre. She had made him promise solemnly that he would lay the explosives in such a way as to minimize the risk of injury.

But seeing all those explosives now made Sophia nervous. She had no idea whether it was too little or too much, which made her realize how much she detested having to rely on others for expertise.

Melamed smiled as if reading her thoughts, "I leave the economics to you, you leave the explosives to me. Come give me a hand getting these grilles off. I need to position the shaped charges very precisely so they bring the pillars down and block the exits without crashing down on top of the delegates."

Melamed had finished priming the explosives. He connected the spidery wires to the radio-controlled detonator, dropping a tiny snippet of wire.

Meanwhile, Sophia was struggling with the heating grilles. Finally, with Melamed clucking impatiently, she managed to get the first one off. In an instant, he'd dropped the explosives in place and was replacing the cover.

They worked around the room, absorbed by the work at hand. But now that there was a real risk of getting caught, Sophia could hear all sorts of sounds: footsteps echoing in the atrium, a peal of laughter bouncing off the walls somewhere, a door slamming in the distance. But it was nothing, nothing but the imagination of a guilty mind. It took three minutes to lay the first set of explosives. Sophia kept wiping her hands on her skirt. She could not stop them from trembling and, to Melamed's annoyance, kept fumbling with the screws.

"Wait here," he told her curtly. "I'll deal with the others myself."

Sophia nodded, her mouth too parched to answer. Melamed grabbed the second briefcase and set to work on the other side of the room. Sophia looked around nervously, sure she was being watched, then realized it was the giants on the ceiling gazing down on her. When she was a child, they had always seemed friendly and protective, but now they looked fearsome and unforgiving, as if they knew Sophia was up to no good. It's just nerves, she told herself, unable to shake the feeling that the giants really were watching her. Finally, she could bear it no longer. "I'll wait for you outside," she called out to Melamed.

She felt calmer in the atrium, and not a little foolish over her panic attack. She slumped on to one of the marble benches, burying her face in her hands and rubbing her eyes. Melamed was taking an awfully long time, she thought, checking her watch. It would be early afternoon in Washington now. She wondered what was happening at IMFO at that moment, and what that busybody Celine was up to.

"May I help you?" A pompous, officious voice.

Sophia turned sharply.

It wasn't a guard, rather some sort of administrator, the very caricature of a bureaucrat: a squat dumpy man, with a fat inscrutable face and small, shifty, pig-like eyes.

"Oh, no. I was . . . I was just taking a rest."

"The Palais des Nations is closed to tourists today."

"I'm not a tourist." Sophia pulled out her ID card indignantly.

"Well, you're still not supposed to be here. The place is off-limits. The *hussiers* need to make preparations for the summit meeting."

"Yes, of course. I'm sorry." Sophia stood up, praying that Melamed would not suddenly appear. She started walking away, but the man was not following her. He turned to enter the Council Chamber.

Sophia looked around desperately. She had to distract him somehow—anyhow. The man was turning the handle; any second now he would discover Melamed and the explosives. She wanted to shout, to warn Melamed, but there was nothing she could do. It was like the awful feeling of helplessness when one drops a glass and watches it falling toward the ground, about to shatter. As the bureaucrat cracked open the door, Sophia threw herself on the floor and cried out as though she'd tripped.

"Are you all right?" the man called out, scuttling over.

Sophia nodded, clutching her ankle. "I'll be all right. But I'm feeling a bit faint."

"I'll call for the medical services."

"No, no," Sophia said quickly. "I'm fine, really. I just hurt my ankle a bit."

Torn between gallantry and indolence, the man stooped to help her up. From the corner of her eye, Sophia saw Melamed appear, clutching the now empty briefcases. He slipped away down the other staircase.

"Thank you." Sophia stood up, dusting off her skirt.

But the man wasn't watching her. His eyes were on the heavy doors of the Council Chamber as they slowly swung shut, kissing each other once again.

CHAPTER TWENTY-FIVE

H IGH ABOVE THE COUNCIL CHAMBER, sunshine streamed through the windows, bringing warmth but not hope. The markets had fallen frighteningly since Monday, and what had started as a handful of speculative attacks against the doubtful currencies of a few dubious countries was fast becoming a crisis of global proportions. No longer confined to the emerging markets and developing countries, the turmoil had reached the major currencies as well. On Monday, the yen had taken a severe beating, and yesterday was the euro's turn. Full of bravado, the European Central Bank had issued a statement, ten a.m. Frankfurt time, announcing its "steadfast and unequivocal commitment to maintaining the parity at a level consistent with economic fundamentals," only to see the euro dumped unceremoniously by the markets, and the parity slipping 3 percent in the first hour of trading.

Nervousness pervaded the trading rooms across the globe. But the City Boys—young, brash, and self-confident—were gung-ho to get into this speculative orgy. The hedge fund attacks on the Turkish lira, the Brazilian real, the Korean won, and a dozen different currencies had whetted their appetites and fuelled their fears. But no one knew which way the market was heading. Momentum traders, chartists, technical gurus, and assorted charlatans—all were equally in the dark. At the flick of a switch, a flutter of a chart, hundreds of billions of dollars flowed from one continent to another, riding only on gossamer wings of rumor and gossip. The market, having devoured a dozen currencies, was now devouring itself.

Perched in the Visitors' Gallery, Celine watched the large telerate screen—installed expressly for the summit and looking absurdly anachronistic amidst the regal splendor of the Palais des Nations—as it scrolled tirelessly through the major exchanges and equity markets of the world. Inevitably, the nervousness of the currency markets was spilling on to stocks and bonds. Yesterday, the Dow had closed with its single largest daily loss ever. Market opening today in Europe had been nothing short of disaster. The German DAX, the French CAC, and the London FTSE had all slipped more than 10 percent at once, the minor bourses even more so, before automatic circuit-breakers had suspended trading. Something had to be done, and fast, or the deflationary shock would knock the world economy into depression.

Not that there was much hope of anything coming out of this lot, Celine thought, surveying the ministers and governors and their surrounding entourage of eunuchs. She had arrived yesterday morning, full of nervous anticipation, just in time to catch Kiyotaki's presentation of the Global Economic Outlook.

To the condescending nods of the ministers, Kiyotaki had warned of the increasing vulnerabilities and volatilities of the world capital markets, and the urgent need for decisive measures. The managing director of IMFO is not invited to participate in the summit with ministers and governors, and both protocol and pride dictate that he leave immediately following the GEO presentation. But once he'd left to return to Washington, DC, the ministers proceeded to ignore the current turmoil and spend the rest of the day pontificating about their grandiose schemes for reforming "the international monetary architecture," apparently oblivious to the markets tumbling about them.

But the overnight plunges in the Far East seemed to have shocked markets and ministers alike. Today the mood was more sober, more subdued. There was even talk of ending the summit early, so ministers and governors could return to their own capitals and deal with the impending crises. But in the end they decided against it, for fear of spooking the markets further.

This morning's session had started inauspiciously enough, with the German *Bundesfinanzminister* insisting on a coordinated interest rate cut by the major central banks—thereby sabotaging any hope of such a move, since the central banks, ever jealous of their independence, would scarcely want to be seen pandering to a finance minister's demands. The ministers, for their part, had no intention of funding a "war chest" for the central banks to squander on futile interventions in the foreign exchange markets. And so it went, minute by minute, hour by hour, until half the day had been whittled away in fruitless discussion.

Forgoing the dubious pleasure of lunch with her senior colleagues attending the summit, Celine spent the break catching up on the news. In Turkey, the Islamist parties were calling for the immediate imposition of capital controls and the nationalization of foreign investments. In Moscow, there was a threat of a clamp-down on foreign investors and all engaged in "speculation against the interests of the State," while in Kiev, the Donbass miners were staging a massive strike to protest against their wage arrears. There were reports of riots in Caracas as the government raised domestic oil prices 20 percent in a desperate bid to stanch the deficit and defend the currency. The Indian rupee had been devalued, the Philippine peso was in free fall, and even the long-cherished Hong Kong currency peg was under attack. Most frightening of all, the Chinese were rumored to be dumping dollars, having lost confidence in the reserve currency status of the once-mighty greenback.

Celine watched the facts and figures scrolling on the screen. Trillions of dollars were being wiped off the valuations of global stock markets. Millions would see their pensions and savings and 401(k)s melt before their eyes. Millions more would be thrown out of work. But the magnitude of the impending disaster was too big to comprehend in these statistics. Celine kept thinking back to that poor woman in Kiev, stripped of her dignity and her clothes, somehow flattened by economic events beyond her control. Or of those four wretched prostitutes waiting in the hotel, hopeful for a trick that might make them a few bucks. Or her father trudging home each evening, hopeless of saving his business or finding a job.

And when she thought of them, or the crowds jostling in Jakarta trying to retrieve their meager savings before the banks collapsed, it brought home to her what all this turmoil in the markets might really mean—real people in real countries were going to suffer, tossed about by forces they could not hope to comprehend, like sailing ships caught in a storm. She remembered a horrifying story a colleague had told her about the Argentine devaluation, when a woman who had lost all her savings walked into the bank, doused herself with alcohol and, in full view of the bank clerks and clamoring customers, immolated herself in a great fiery torch. Celine shuddered, recalling too the famished mob hacking the poor shopkeeper to pieces during the Indonesian riots.

Even in advanced economies, she knew, when the crisis struck, there would be pandemonium. During the "sub-prime" lending crisis, panicked customers had lined the pavements for days, desperate to get their money out before their mortgage bank collapsed. And if that could happen in England, with the Treasury and Bank of England standing fully behind the handful of problem banks, then how much worse would it be when whole banking systems were at risk, and in countries where governments and central banks are much less trusted? Once those collapsed, crisis contagion and domino effects would bring global banks—too big to fail, too large to save—tumbling down, and with them the whole international economy. It was going to be a disaster on an epic scale—a Great Depression of truly global proportions.

There were still some fifteen minutes before the conference resumed. Celine slipped out of the Palais building in search of some fresh air. The gardens were laid out formally, with pleasing symmetry, sloping gently toward Lake Geneva. A blue flag with the UN symbol fluttered in the wind, while in the distance, Mont Blanc looked down in frosty disdain. A peacock roaming the Palais gardens took a particular liking to Celine and started following her about on her walk.

Meanwhile, there was no sign of Sophia. Her request for a pass to the summit must have been quite innocent. At any rate, she had not appeared yesterday, and the meeting would be ending later this evening. Celine also found it hard to understand how Sophia was profiting from all this turmoil—unless, perhaps, she had started the ball rolling with the Liberty Fund's speculative attacks, only to see it spin out of control. Celine was even beginning to have doubts about Sophia's involvement in Harry's death.

Celine wished she wasn't here at all, wasting her time on this wild-goose chase, but back home, back in the thick of things at IMFO, helping to cope with the currency crises. What she had told Karin was true: working at IMFO is like catching malaria—once it's in your bloodstream there's no getting it out. She reached into her bag and pulled out her phone, toying with the idea of calling someone, anyone—Pettigrew, even—to find out what was going on. But she stopped herself. She suddenly realized that her IMFO days were over. Even if Kiyotaki forgave her, his term was up in July. There was no hope now of another term for Kiyotaki, and, in all likelihood Adanpur would succeed him. Having to work for *him* didn't even bear thinking about.

Celine trudged back to the Council Chamber. At the conference, ministers were at last cobbling together some sort of emergency package. By midafternoon, consensus was at last emerging—simultaneous interest rate cuts by the central banks of the major industrialized nations, some meager lines of credit for the developing and emerging market countries, some modest fiscal expansion by the Group of Twenty, and a small war chest for coordinated intervention to bring sanity back to the foreign exchange markets. The package would be announced in the summit's final communiqué, scheduled for eight p.m. Geneva time—and timed so that the all-important New York market could close on positive news.

Well, it was something. Whether it was enough remained to be seen, thought Celine, finding herself ravenous. Lunch had ended long ago—it was past three o'clock—but there must be a cafeteria somewhere in the sprawling Palais des Nations where she could get a coffee and a pastry. She had just left the Visitors' Gallery and was descending the staircase to the atrium outside the main entrance to the Council Chamber, when she saw an all too familiar figure dash around the corner and disappear from view.

━━━

At the gate, they were made to wait. Sophia clutched her handbag guiltily. Inside was the remote control to trigger the explosives. Mostly made of plastic, it should escape detection by the metal detectors, but nonetheless Melamed had given it to Sophia just before they got to the Palais, as she was less likely to be searched. The guard studied their passes suspiciously, holding them up to compare the photos with the real thing. He finally motioned the other guard—the older one, who had been lounging in his chair, a copy of the *Tribune de Genève* spread across his knees—to watch them as he disappeared into the small security office.

"Is something the matter?" Sophia's voice was dry and cracking, and she coughed to disguise her nervousness. "What the devil's the matter?" she asked, drumming up all the arrogance and impatience she could muster. They were supposed to be delegates to a summit meeting of finance ministers and central bank governors, the guard would expect them to be pompous and impatient, the sort of people who are used to being spared formalities.

The guard stared stonily ahead, pretending he hadn't heard.

"Really!" Sophia said. "This is unacceptable. If we are late for the plenary session, I shall most certainly report this incompetence to administration."

"Well," Melamed said soothingly, "we mustn't be impatient. They're only doing their jobs. After all, ensuring our security is their only concern. Isn't that so, officer?"

"Yes. Of course, Monsieur," the guard replied gratefully. He had a benign face and a cheerful smile, and probably the last thing he wanted was to make any trouble. "I am very sorry for this delay. My colleague is just . . . ah, here he is."

The first guard returned, clutching a clipboard and shaking his head. "I do not see his name on the admittance list."

An admittance list! It had never occurred to Sophia that the security pass would not suffice to enter the building. Her own name would be on the admittance list, of course: IMFO would have arranged it when she was given her pass. But Melamed's pass was forged.

"Well, find it," she said.

But Melamed held up his hand and gave the elderly guard a knowing smile, as if to say that the impatience of youth must not be indulged. "Perhaps you would be kind enough to check again. It would be a shame if we missed the plenary session."

The older guard took the clipboard. He quickly flipped through the pages, painfully mouthing the multinational names. "Is this you?" He pointed at a name vaguely like Melamed's.

Melamed squinted at the page. "Ah, yes," he smiled. "That must be it. They misspelled my name, that's all."

"Good." Sophia pushed forward.

"One moment," the younger guard said sharply. "Open your briefcase, please."

Sophia fumbled with the locks, wondering how she was going to explain away the remote control in her handbag. The younger guard was rummaging through the papers, delving into the various compartments of her briefcase. As he withdrew his hand, Sophia tipped the case forward so that the pages fell out, fluttering to the ground.

Both guards rushed to pick them up, comically bumping into one another in the process. They hurriedly stacked the papers into an untidy pile and handed them to Sophia, who shoved them back into her case.

"Perhaps you would like to check my lipstick also?" she said coldly, proffering her handbag under the older guard's nose.

"No, no," the guard said, embarrassed. "Please pass through."

"Thank you," Melamed nodded with unfailing courtesy. "*Bonne journée* to you both."

"*Bonne journée*, Monsieur. Madame."

Sophia's legs felt weak. She would have liked a moment's pause, though not because she was tired or afraid. Now that the moment of truth was upon them, she was filled with doubt. She turned to speak to Melamed, hoping to gain some reassurance, some comfort, but he had lost his gentle paternal look. His face was flushed with excitement, making the cold, hard impassivity of his dead eye all the more disconcerting. Somehow, she divined he was thinking of his fiancée's murder, and his own maiming those many years ago, and she faltered from saying anything.

They crossed two more checkpoints without incident, arriving at the atrium outside the Council Chamber right on schedule. There were no guards here—guards were not allowed in the vicinity of the summit itself, lest they overhear market sensitive information—and the place was eerily quiet. Sophia retrieved the gun from the cubby hole and put it in her bag.

Melamed tiptoed to the heavy doors and cracked them open to check that the summit was still in session, then, in a single rapid movement, snapped the sandwich wedges, shoving them under the doors and jamming them in place.

"Remote," he hissed.

Sophia pulled out the small electronic box from her bag. Melamed's hand was outstretched, but still she hung on to it, curiously afraid. It wasn't just excitement she saw on Melamed's face; it was a terrible ecstasy, a fanaticism born of anger and revenge.

"Give it to me."

Slowly, reluctantly, Sophia edged forward under his spell. Melamed took the remote out of her hand and punched the digits for the arming code.

A small green light flashed alive.

Melamed's lip curled into a cruel smile. "For years I have waited for this moment," he breathed. "For years, our pleas have been ignored. Well, it's time Western governments learn a lesson they won't forget—and a roomful of dead ministers will teach it to them."

It took several seconds for his words to sink in, crucial seconds during which Melamed pressed the button. The indicator light on the remote turned from shy green to promiscuous red. The charges were armed. The explosives would go off in ten minutes.

"You bastard!" Sophia cried with the rage of a woman too long deceived. "You lousy bastard! You've killed them, haven't you? You set the charges to kill them all!" She grabbed the door handle and pulled with all her might, but it wouldn't budge. She pulled again, this time pressing her legs against the wall for leverage, but it was no use. "You promised me," she sobbed, giving up. "You promised me no one would get hurt."

Melamed was trying to explain, telling Sophia her plan had been too subtle, too complex, too clever. Besides, all the world ever really understood, ever really respected, was violence. He was telling her, but she wasn't listening. There was a buzzing in her ears, a fury bursting from within her.

The remote! Melamed still had the remote that controlled the explosives. Sophia lunged for it, but he must have read her mind, for he dashed down one of the unlit corridors. Sophia stood, unsure whether to wait and warn the delegates or pursue Melamed. But the doors were solid metal and jammed in place. By the time she summoned help it would be far too late. The only hope was to get hold of the remote. She pulled the gun from her bag and tore after him.

Melamed had reached the other end of the corridor, then turned left. Sophia was running, oblivious to time and space, her only touch with reality the rhythmic thumping of her heart. Her foot slipped; she struggled to regain her balance. Now where? Up or down? Sophia listened; she could hear the footsteps—no longer confident, a nervous jittery trot. Up or down? Up.

She couldn't be certain; those damned marble floors echoed mysteriously, the sounds bouncing off odd angles of the walls.

She looked around for a guard, a security detail, anyone. But this side of the Palais was dark and empty. The rooms had a closed, forgotten air; the entire wing must have been closed off for the summit meeting. Sophia was breathing in great, burning gasps now, climbing round the staircase, pausing to see which way Melamed had gone, then racing up the next flight of stairs. All around, dark shadows played tricks on her eyes. She started down one corridor, then hurried back. She started off again, more assured now. The chase was over. There was nowhere else to go.

They had reached the rooftop terrace, the end of the road.

———

Recovering from her first astonishment, Celine began chasing after Sophia, wondering what the hell was going on. She was about to call out, to challenge and confront her, but Sophia was already too far away. Soon, all Celine had were the clicks of Sophia's heels to guide her. They passed through a maze of somber corridors and darkened stairwells, emerging at last into the light at the terrace on the top of the Palais des Nations. Celine turned the corner and gasped. Sophia and a thin, wiry-looking man were by the railings, at the far end of the terrace. Celine could see a small black box in the man's hand, rather like a TV remote, which Sophia was trying to wrest away from him. Celine watched as they struggled, their bodies locked together, leaning precariously over the rusty railings. Sophia was shouting something, but Celine couldn't hear what she was saying. And then there was a single shot.

The man's body seemed to go limp, but not before he had broken free of Sophia's grip and hurled the black box over the edge of the terrace into the gardens below.

Sophia dropped the gun, which fell to the ground with a loud clatter. Celine dashed forward to retrieve it, while Sophia, face buried in her hands, seemed mesmerized by the body.

"You flaming bitch!" Celine screamed. "How many more people are you going to murder?"

Sophia spun around. "Celine! I haven't time to explain, but you've got to help me. There's a bomb in the conference room, and it's set to go off in less than eight minutes. We've got to get everyone out."

"What the hell are you talking about? Were you behind this Liberty Fund business and all these speculative attacks? And Harry's death? Were you responsible for that too?"

"Yes," Sophia said simply. "But we haven't time for all that now. I told you—there's a bomb, and we've got less than eight minutes left. You've *got* to believe me."

"Believe you? I ought to damn well shoot you in cold blood, the way you did Harry," Celine snapped. This woman, who had enjoyed every privilege and every advantage in life, had betrayed everyone and everything. She had seduced Harry, used him for her nefarious schemes, then disposed of him with as much compunction as one might a spent sponge. Quite possibly, she was responsible for Karin's disappearance as well, and she had certainly been behind all the havoc wreaked on the world's currencies. Yet strangely, Celine felt not so much anger as burning curiosity. She could not believe that Sophia had been motivated by greed alone. There must be something more to it.

"I didn't mean to hurt anyone," Sophia was saying. "You *have* to believe me," she pleaded, "or we'll be too late, and dozens more will die in that conference hall."

Celine stared uncomprehending, the gun still pointed at Sophia.

"For Christ's sake! We're losing time. If you don't believe me, you're going to have to shoot me in the back. But I'm going back to the Council Chamber to get those delegates out." Sophia started running across the terrace and down the stairs.

"Damn!" Celine lowered the gun, watching her go. "Damn!" she repeated, then started after Sophia.

They made it down two flights of stairs, and were racing toward the Council Chamber, when Sophia tripped and crashed to the floor. "Go!" she shouted to Celine, who had slowed down to help her. "You'll have to enter through the Visitors' Gallery—the doors to the Council Chamber are blocked off."

Celine ran as fast as she could, knowing it wasn't fast enough. A precious minute passed before she reached the Visitors' Gallery. She burst in shouting, but the Italian finance minister, who had the floor, continued speaking with arrogant dignity, ignoring the commotion.

Celine paused to take a deep breath, then tried again, her voice surprisingly calm and steady. "I want your attention, and I want it now. There is an explosive device in this meeting hall. You are to evacuate immediately. I repeat, there is an explosive device in this room. You must evacuate at once."

They stared at her in disbelief, unmoving.

She shouted again, this time with greater desperation. "Everybody out now! There's a bomb in the room."

The word "bomb" goaded them into action. They all clamored toward the exits; no panic, no screaming, no running—yet. Those in the upstairs Visitors' Gallery were streaming out, but the ministers and governors down in the Council Chamber found the doors jammed. They started beating on them, their blows hollow and ineffective as they shouted vainly for help.

Sophia appeared, blood streaming from a gash in her forehead. She ran to the front of the Visitors' Gallery, clambered over the railing, and leapt into the Council Chamber below. Celine jumped after her, looking around desperately for some means of escape. The main exits were jammed, the delegates still beating upon them futilely.

Celine looked around again. The bronze doors! They were the only hope. She pushed her way back through the crowd toward the front of the room, where the huge ornamental doors to the side chambers stood forgotten. "Never mind the exits," she shouted. "Try the bronze doors."

The delegates stood petrified, watching her. Celine hurried to the right hand door, twisted the large silver ring, and battered the door with her shoulder. It wouldn't budge.

From the corner of her eye, she could see Sophia trying to tear out the heating grilles that ran the length of the floor. Her fingertips looked raw and bloody already, but she kept on, oblivious to the pain.

Celine returned to the door. *Pull, don't push*, a voice screamed within her mind, *the doors must open* into *the chamber*. She yanked the handle. The crowd had abandoned the main exits and was pressing against her. Slowly, painfully slowly, one of the doors creaked open. Celine peered in. Of course! It was one of the small side rooms. Its exits would probably be blocked off too, but the heavy bronze doors should afford at least some protection from the explosion.

She looked back at the frightened faces behind her. "In here," she shouted, moving aside to let the delegates lumber past. She glanced back at Sophia, who was still struggling to loosen the covers. It was hopeless, she would never make it in time. And God knows what would happen when news of the ministers' and governors' deaths hit the market, Celine thought as she fought her way through the crowd to reach Sophia. There was one more screw holding the grate in place, which Sophia had been unable to loosen. Celine poked her fingers through the holes in the grate. They pulled together, until the screw gave way with a violent snap, and the grate lifted upward, sending the two women tumbling to the floor.

"Now go!" Sophia said. "I'll deal with the explosives."

Celine hesitated.

"Get out of here! They're booby-trapped, and you don't know how to disarm them. Go!"

Celine pulled away reluctantly. The crowd in front of her had broken into panic, shoving their way into the side chamber. But there could not be much more than a minute left, and unless Sophia succeeded in defusing the bombs, at least on this side of the room, Celine doubted that anyone would live. Her ankle was throbbing from the jump off the Visitors' Gallery, and the delegates kept trampling her as they elbowed their way past. The room reeked of sweat and fear, and the pressing crowd was suffocating her, making her feel faint. Images started dancing before her eyes. She was back in Indonesia, seeing the man with the gold tooth, his face being staved in by the angry mob.

Gold! Suddenly, Celine had the solution. Praying the battery in her phone was still charged, she punched the digits.

"Office of the managing director," came the prim voice, distorted by the static.

"This is Celine O'Rourke, Policy Review Department calling. This is an emergency. I must speak to the managing director immediately."

"I'm sorry, he's at the Board."

"Patch me through to him."

"I can't do that," replied the voice, scandalized. "The Executive Board is in session."

"Goddamn it! This is an emergency. Patch me through *now*."

An interminable pause, a series of clicks, the beeping of the satellite connection.

"Kiyotaki," the growl came at last.

"Sir? It's Celine. Celine O'Rourke. There's no time to explain, but there's going to be an explosion at the summit meeting. We're trying to get the delegates out, but there may not be enough time."

"What?"

"An explosion. A bomb. There's been a plot to cause a global currency crisis. You're going to need to stabilize the markets when the news hits."

"With what, damn it! We're facing total meltdown here. Investors are fleeing every currency—they're even dumping dollars now. The major stock exchanges have suspended trading, and the forex markets are in free fall—"

She could picture them around the boardroom, pompous yet impotent, engaged in endless debate as the markets collapsed about them. "Yes, yes, I know that," she began, then heard the dreaded beeps that told her the phone battery was dying. "Use the gold!" she shouted, not knowing whether Kiyotaki could hear her or not. "Use the IMFO gold to stabilize the currencies!"

But a deep rumbling sound drowned out her voice, and a shock wave knocked her to the floor. Celine heard the explosions—two of them—followed by the sound, quite distinct, of her ribs cracking as she hit the floor.

Then, mercifully, she passed out.

═══

The first explosion flung Sophia across the room, the second buried her under a mass of rubble. One of the marble pillars teetered, then came crashing down, breaking her back. The dust clogged her mouth, choking the breath from her. Sophia gasped, a searing pain wracking her body and tearing through her lungs.

She was in school, trapped in the collapsed tunnel, the mocking voices of the girls ringing in her ears.

She was at home, locked in the chest of drawers, pounding feebly against the sides.

She was at Harry's, watching his body crumple to the floor.

The room advanced and receded from view, taking her from past to present to future. Pinned by the pillar, staring at the ceiling mural, it seemed to Sophia that the giants were beginning to stir. Through the swirling dust, she could see them turn toward her. They smiled beatifically, love and sympathy etched on their faces as they clambered from their lofty perch. With powerful scoops of those sinewy arms, they were clearing away the rubble, gently wiping the dirt from her face. Then, with infinite care, they were lifting her broken, battered body toward the ceiling.

Sophia felt free at last, free from fear, from pain, from guilt, from hate. She was floating, gliding, soaring, effortless and carefree, high above the Council Chamber. And it was only now that she realized she had been mistaken all these years. The figure at the corner of the ceiling, standing at the foot of the Cathedral of Salamanca and waiting anxiously to welcome her, was not Francisco de Vitoria, the ancient Spanish jurist. She could see that plainly now.

It was Daddy.

CHAPTER TWENTY-SIX

The Executive Board of the International Monetary and Financial Organization, meeting today in emergency session and acting under the authority of Article VII, paragraph 6, of the *Articles of Agreement*, stands ready to purchase United States dollars against delivery of gold, at this morning's London price-fix for delivery in that market; at that price plus ½ percent *loco* Paris; at that price plus 1 percent *loco* New York.

The International Monetary and Financial Organization is further prepared to purchase all and any of the currencies of its member countries against delivery of gold at these prices, *loco* London, Paris, and New York respectively, and at the dollar cross-rates for these currencies prevailing yesterday at 12:00 Noon Greenwich Mean Time, London.

"It went out just before midday, Washington time," Kiyotaki explained as he handed Celine a copy of the statement. She reached for it cautiously, her ribs still smarting under the tautness of the bandages. A week had passed since the summit, much of it spent at the Hôpital Cantonal de Genève, but she had finally been discharged and had arrived back in DC this afternoon.

"News of the explosion had just hit the wire services, and there was utter turmoil—literally hundreds of billions of dollars swishing around the global financial markets searching for safe haven. Trouble was that no currency, not even dollars or yen or euros, looked safe at that point, so when we offered to sell gold against any major currency it was a godsend to the markets."

"Did we end up selling a lot?"

"Actually, no—only about one hundred billion dollars' worth. Just our being in the market, guaranteeing exchange rates at a time of total chaos, was enough to help calm things down. By then the news services were reporting that the ministers and governors had in fact survived and were being rescued, so confidence was restored quite rapidly. Of course, many individual banks and financial houses have been badly burned, especially those with derivatives exposure, but at least we were able to avoid a systemic crisis and prevent a full-blown global meltdown."

Celine smiled wanly. They were still giving her painkillers, and she was jet-lagged from the flight. She should, she supposed, feel exhilarated.

Instead, she felt despondent. It was more than the sharp anticlimax after the action and excitement at the summit; she was suffering from an acute sense of loss. They were gone—Harry, Karin, Sophia. Celine wished now that she'd taken the time to get to know Sophia better, to understand what had motivated her, what had driven her. She was a brave girl, thought Celine, remembering those last instants before the explosion. "A very brave girl," she muttered out loud.

"Sorry?" Kiyotaki had been regaling Celine with his exploits of how he'd bullied the Board into approving the gold sales to stabilize the markets.

"Nothing. I was just thinking of Sophia."

"Oh, yes," Kiyotaki frowned. "Naturally, we have emphasized in our press communications that Ms. Gemaye was not one of our regular staff members. In fact, she joined IMFO under patently false pretense. If you should have any contact with the press, kindly remember that."

"She never meant any harm."

"She certainly caused plenty."

"All she wanted was to draw world attention to the injustices in her country."

"Ah, well, there she may well have succeeded." Kiyotaki pointed at the pile of newspapers stacked on the coffee table. "The press have been having a field-day with all this. It looks as if there may be some changes in that part of the world. At any rate, there's pressure for full economic sanctions to be imposed until the human rights record improves."

Kiyotaki paused, as though this would have to be Sophia's epitaph, then said, "Anyway, you must be tired. Take a few days off, then I want you back at work. There's a lot to be done. Our member countries," he added, trying to hide his pleasure but not succeeding, "have asked me to stay on for another term, to provide some continuity after this crisis."

"Have you decided to accept?"

He liked that.

"Yes," he nodded. "I felt it was an obligation I could not refuse."

"Well, congratulations."

"Incidentally, there was a Board meeting yesterday to reconsider the idea of the Special Intervention Facility in light of the crisis."

"Oh?"

"Yes, indeed. If it hadn't been for our gold intervention, the global economy might have been in very serious trouble. There's now growing recognition in the international community that IMFO must have some sort of rapid response facility to deal with currency crises. Unfortunately, the Board resoundingly rejected the proposal. I suppose it would've been just too embarrassing for them to approve the Special Intervention Facility now, so soon after rejecting it before. They would've looked like fools."

"Yes, I suppose so."

"However, this might interest you." Kiyotaki plucked a sheet of paper from his desk and handed it to Celine. "After consulting their respective governments, the Board unanimously approved the Systemic Intervention Facility yesterday—a five hundred-billion-dollar facility that we can use to intervene in the markets immediately in the event of a crisis."

Celine stared at the paper, puzzled. "So what's the difference?"

"The name."

It took a moment to sink in, then Celine burst out laughing.

Afterward, she went downstairs and slipped quietly into her office. Her heart sank. A heap of mail and messages awaited her, the indicator lamp on her telephone was flashing furiously, and she hadn't even started checking her emails. With a heavy sigh, Celine pulled up to the desk. She was rummaging in the drawer for something to write with, when she came across a small card. It was the note Harry had written when he'd shipped her the ice cream to Jakarta. All it said was, *When the going gets tough, the tough go for ice cream. Keep cool. All the best, Harry.*

Celine clasped the card tightly in her hand, forcing back her tears. She pushed aside the piles of messages and mail, scattering them to the floor, and fled the room.

But standing outside, as though he'd been waiting for her, was Xavier Adanpur. "Hullo," he said, "I heard you were back."

Celine stared at him blankly.

When she said nothing, he added, "I came to say goodbye."

"You're leaving?" she asked, finding her voice again.

"Yes. I'm joining the private sector." He forced a laugh. "Make a bit of money."

"Oh." Celine thought of all the things she might say, all the anger and abuse she might heap on him, but somehow she simply couldn't be bothered. He isn't even worth despising, she decided. She turned and walked away without a word.

But as she reached Pennsylvania Avenue, she slowed her pace, realizing she had nothing to do, nowhere to go. She retraced her steps hesitantly, eventually walking to the café at the corner of I Street and taking an outside table.

Celine ordered an espresso, then remembered the sheet of paper Kiyotaki had given her. She fished it out of her bag and started reading. But ten lines in, she stopped, her soul rebelling at the thought of wading through the bureaucratese. She crumpled up the sheet and tossed it back into her bag. A bird swooped down, thinking it was food.

All around her people were streaming out of offices eager for the weekend. And in the cloudless sky, the sun smiled unblemished upon Nineteenth Street.

THE ECONOMICS OF NINETEENTH STREET NW

"**C** OULD IT REALLY HAPPEN?"

When I wrote the first edition of *Nineteenth Street NW* in late 2006 (published in the United Kingdom by Pegasus Elliot MacKenzie in 2008), I added an afterword on whether a financial crisis as depicted in the novel could really happen. My purpose was both to explain some of the economics behind the story and to convince any sceptical readers of its plausibility.

Since then, of course, the global financial crisis of 2008–09, which has racked up over US$ 2.8 trillion of bank losses, unemployment rates virtually unseen since the Great Depression, and global output losses estimated to be at least US$ 60 trillion (the equivalent of 100 percent of annual world GDP), will surely have convinced any sceptics that devastating financial crises are a very real possibility.

It turns out that we did not need nefarious terrorists plotting the downfall of the global financial system—greed, hubris, stupidity, and a lack of financial regulation were enough. How much worse could it have been if it were the result of enemy action? Hopefully, we shall never find out.

Prior to the crisis, there was also talk of "decoupling"—that is, the economic fates of advanced economies and those of developing and emerging market economies may not be so intertwined.[2] The crisis soon put that hypothesis to rest. The fact is, through trade and capital flows, the global

economy has become ever more integrated, and while that brings many ben-
efits, it also means that if one sneezes, they all catch a cold. The epicenter
of the 2008–09 crisis happened to be in the advanced economies (particularly, the United States and the United Kingdom).[3] With globalization,
however, a crisis anywhere—even in very small economies (especially if in
several simultaneously)—could have disastrous consequences worldwide. For
example, bursting housing bubbles in the tiny Baltic states and other eastern
European countries in early 2009 threatened the integrity of major western
European banks—and hence the global banking system.

In the novel, Sophia Gemaye triggers a global financial crisis by first
attacking the currencies of the more vulnerable emerging market economies.
If one were interested in deliberately causing a global economic crisis, this
would be the most plausible strategy, both because crises in emerging market
economies are more common, and because the financial resources required
to launch speculative attacks would be more manageable (although, in 1992,
George Soros successfully attacked the pound sterling). The essential point
about globalization is that, through integration and the often frighteningly
large cross-border financial exposures, a crisis that started in emerging markets could rapidly engulf the rest of the world.

The rest of this essay is organized as follows. The first part reviews some
of the financial crises that have afflicted many emerging market countries in
recent years.[4] The second part speculates on how a terrorist group could engi-
neer financial crises as a way of drawing world attention to their cause. For
further reading, visit www.nineteenthstreetnw.com or www.imfo.org.

Financial Crises

Indonesia's financial crisis, alluded to in Chapter 2, was part of a wider array
of financial crises afflicting East Asia. The trouble started when the Bank
of Thailand was forced to devalue the Thai baht on July 2, 1997. The crisis
spread quickly to Indonesia, Malaysia, Korea, and the Philippines. It even
threatened to engulf Hong Kong and Singapore. But these East Asian emerging market countries were by no means alone in suffering major financial
crises; others have included Mexico (1994), Russia (1998), Brazil (1999),
Turkey (2001), Argentina (2002), and Uruguay (2003). What made the East
Asian crisis unusual was its origins in the private sector (banks and corporations over-borrowing), rather than the public sector (the government living

above its means). It was also rare for an entire region to be engulfed in crisis at the same time—a region that had previously been known for its stellar economic performance.

While each financial crisis is unique, its effects are usually much the same: a devastating impact on the economy and on the lives of ordinary citizens caught up in the chaos. In Indonesia, for example, gross domestic product (GDP)—the most common measure of economic well-being—fell by 13 percent in a single year. (By comparison, during the first year of the Great Depression, US GDP fell by about 10 percent.[5]) The economic collapse had widespread repercussions, with the proportion of the population living below the poverty line increasing by 20 percentage points as jobs were lost and the price of food, clothing, and other basic necessities more than doubled.[6]

But economic dislocation is just part of the story in a financial crisis: the social and political upheaval is often worse. Thus, in Indonesia, "rhetoric against Chinese Indonesians heated up in January and February [1998], and strong pressure was placed on large Chinese Indonesian companies to buy rupiah, as they became scapegoats for the economic crisis. There was a spate of riots in small towns across the country, apparently sparked by higher food prices, with ethnic Chinese shopkeepers often the targets."[7] Social unrest continued until a second series of riots broke out in May 1998, following the shooting by police of four student demonstrators. The riots are estimated to have resulted in at least 500 deaths; 4,940 buildings and 1,026 homes being damaged or looted; and 1,120 cars and 821 motorbikes being set ablaze.[8] These riots resulted in the eventual ouster of President Suharto, who stepped down on May 21, 1998, handing power to Vice President Habibe.

Similarly, when Argentina's currency collapsed and the government defaulted on its bonds in December 2001, riots broke out in more than 20 cities across the country, with thousands of Argentines sacking supermarkets and looting shops. The riots killed 27 people and brought down the government of President Eduardo Duhalde (Argentina's fifth president in the space of a few weeks). Violence erupted again in early January 2002 when the government imposed a freeze on the withdrawal of almost all bank deposits, and the Argentine people realized that, once again, they had been robbed of their life's savings.[9] A fifty-nine-year-old woman who could not get her dollars out of her account walked into the bank, doused herself with alcohol, and set herself ablaze.[10]

So what causes these crises? In essence, they occur when investors lose confidence in a country's currency and no longer want to hold it. For a foreign (e.g., an American) investor to want to put his money in a country like Thailand or Turkey or Indonesia, he must expect it to be worth his while. His expected return, taking account of the risk that the currency will depreciate, must be greater than what he could get by keeping his money at home. For instance, suppose that the investor can get an interest rate of 5 percent per year by holding US treasury bills but 15 percent per year by investing in Thailand. Is it worth investing in Thailand? At first glance, sure—he makes an extra 10 percent per year by putting his money in Thailand. But if he expects the Thai baht to depreciate by more than 10 percent over the course of the year, it is not a good deal. Taking account of the fact that the baht he earns will be worth 10 percent less in US dollar terms, it would be less than what he could earn by simply keeping his money in the United States.[11]

The key here is the *expected* depreciation of the currency. If the Thai baht is expected to remain fixed against the US dollar (as it should under a fixed exchange rate regime[12]), then the money starts rolling in. And that is precisely what happens in the run-up to most financial crises.[13] Private capital flows to emerging markets increased almost tenfold between 1990 and 1996, reaching more than US$ 300 billion by the eve of the Asian crisis.

The trouble is, if there is the slightest whiff of a devaluation, there will be a mad scramble to get out of the currency before it collapses.[14] The reason is obvious: continuing the example, the investor's 10 percent profit turns into a 20 percent *loss* if the Thai baht devalues by 30 percent before he is able to get his money out.

Thus while capital flows are generally beneficial—allowing emerging market countries to finance productive investments while earning investors a good return on their money—they can also be fickle, suddenly fleeing the country in a self-fulfilling "run" on the central bank's reserves. If confidence in the currency is lost and investors believe that it will depreciate or be devalued, then they will want to pull out their money to avoid the capital loss before that happens. But the very act of pulling out their money puts downward pressure on the exchange rate, and—if the central bank runs out of reserves—could lead to the depreciation that had been feared.[15] The extreme sensitivity of capital flows to changes in investor perception, together with the risk of triggering a self-fulfilling run, is why they can easily undermine exchange rate stability and cause financial crises.

This is what happened in East Asia. While these economies had been among the fastest growing for many years, their banks and corporations had also been borrowing heavily in foreign currency, often short-term, and with high leveraging (meaning their debt was high in relation to their equity). At the same time, the central banks did not hold sufficient foreign exchange reserves (especially relative to the massive foreign borrowing by banks and corporations). In this setting, currencies became extremely vulnerable to shifts in investor sentiment for three reasons. First, there could be self-fulfilling runs on the central bank's reserves since, if other creditors are pulling their money out, each creditor has an incentive to join the queue before the foreign exchange reserves are exhausted. Second, as the central bank runs out of reserves, the exchange rate depreciates, making it more difficult for firms that have borrowed in foreign currency to repay their loans, ultimately driving them into bankruptcy. Third, the heavy indebtedness of banks and corporations poses a dilemma for the central bank, since raising interest rates to try to lure back foreign creditors also risks precipitating more bankruptcies and undermining confidence further. (Episodes like this, including most recently in eastern Europe, have re-opened the question of whether emerging market countries should consider imposing controls on capital inflows when these threaten to overwhelm prudential regulation and risk fuelling asset bubbles, for instance in house prices.[16])

Given these vulnerabilities, it was perhaps only a matter of time before a crisis struck. In the event, the crisis was first triggered in Thailand on July 2, 1997, when the central bank ran out of foreign exchange reserves and was forced to let the Thai baht depreciate by 25 percent. Thereafter, the crisis spread rapidly through the region; by year's end, the currencies of the afflicted countries had lost between one-half and two-thirds of their value against the US dollar. The local currency value of foreign debt had more than doubled, bankrupting many corporations and causing massive unemployment and economic collapse. While other emerging market financial crises differ in their specifics—for example, in Turkey and in most Latin American crises, it was the government rather than banks and corporations, that had over-borrowed; in eastern Europe in 2009 it was households that had taken on foreign-currency denominated home mortgages—the mechanics and basic economics are generally the same.

═══

So what should a country facing such a crisis do?[17] Governments often delay taking preventive and corrective measures, including going to the International Monetary Fund (IMF), which was set up to help countries facing financial crises.[18] The delay is natural: politically, few governments want to admit that the country is in an economic mess, and IMF loans come with "conditionality"—measures that the government is required to adopt before IMF funds are disbursed.[19] Once the government does turn to the IMF, however, a program of economic measures is quickly cobbled together, along with emergency financing.[20]

The first decision in designing a program is whether to try to defend the exchange rate at its current level or let it depreciate and make a stand at a lower level. While there are theories to help determine the "correct" level of the exchange rate—including Purchasing Power Parity or Fundamental Equilibrium Exchange Rate models (see Appendix A)—what matters most in a crisis is investors' confidence. If confidence can be restored, there can be a virtuous cycle: investors come back, buying the currency, leading to an appreciation of the exchange rate, and therefore the prospect of higher returns in US dollar terms—inducing further capital inflows.

But restoring confidence is easier said than done. Typically, in a currency crisis, the central bank will raise interest rates. This reduces the supply of domestic currency, putting upward pressure on the exchange rate. It can also raise demand for the currency by offering investors a higher rate of return, inducing capital inflows which put further upward pressure on the exchange rate.

While interest rates rose sharply during the East Asian crisis, they fell shy of the very high nominal interest rates seen in some other currency defenses.[21] Thus interest rates in Indonesia peaked at about 80 percent per year, compared to about 10–15 percent per year prior to the crisis. But inflation was also very high, so that in real terms, interest rates were quite low and even negative during the early part of the crisis.

Nevertheless, the high-interest rate defense was extremely controversial during the Asian crisis, especially in Korea where, in early 1998, interest rates rose to 30 percent per year in nominal terms and 20 to 25 percent per year in real terms. In theory, higher interest rates should induce capital to return to the country. But interest rates also raise the debt burden on corporations, increasing the likelihood that they will go bankrupt, which naturally deters investors from lending to them. If fears about such bankruptcies dominate, raising interest rates can have the perverse effect of inducing greater capital outflows and further weakening the exchange rate.[22]

Beyond raising interest rates, the other way to help restore confidence in the currency is to provide the afflicted central bank with foreign exchange reserves. This is the purpose of loans from the International Monetary Fund and bilateral creditors (such as the US and Japanese governments). In the Asian crisis, such loans were exceptionally large by historical standards but arguably too small in relation to these countries' financing needs. To help boost confidence, therefore, the official community tried to fool the markets with phantom financing packages. During the Korean crisis, bilateral creditors announced a "second line of defense," amounting to some $23 billion (on top of IMF, World Bank, and other multilateral funds of $34 billion). Ironically, if the announcement of a large financing package is successful, it obviates the need for the money, since private capital inflows resume spontaneously. This is what makes it tempting for the official community to announce a larger financing package than is actually available. While this can be a successful strategy, it is also a risky one, since the market may call the bluff. If it transpires that the financing does not really exist, confidence is likely to collapse further.[23]

Indeed, trying to bluff the markets is great if it works—but disastrous if it does not. One of the factors that deepened the Thai crisis was that the market learned that the Bank of Thailand did not even have the reserves it claimed on its books. Over the previous few months, it had sold them in the forward market in a desperate bid to prop up its currency. (Under a forward contract, the seller promises to deliver the foreign exchange in the future—usually 30 or 90 days later, according to the contract—and therefore does not have to cough up the foreign exchange immediately.[24]) In Korea, markets learned that the Bank of Korea (BoK) no longer had the reserves it claimed, having lent them to the country's ailing banks, which were not in a position to repay them when the exchange rate was under attack and the BoK needed them back—with equally disastrous consequences for confidence.

Finally, neither raising interest rates nor providing the country with foreign exchange reserves will restore confidence unless the underlying problems are tackled. In some cases—such as Argentina and Turkey—this meant cutting the government's deficit. In East Asia, it meant clamping down on the lax financial sector and corporate governance, increasing prudential regulation, and closing down problem banks. But closing banks is always a tricky business, especially in the midst of a crisis. In November 1997, for example, Indonesia closed sixteen banks, including several owned by the president's family. The closure of such politically well-connected banks contributed to a sense of panic, with depositors inferring that if banks belonging to the president's family were being closed, then there had to be others that were weak and would be closed as well. Confusion about deposit insurance and uncertainty about which banks were vulnerable led to a full-scale run on the country's banking system as depositors panicked that their bank would be the next to close—and without a government guarantee, their life's savings would disappear.[25]

Thus once a crisis breaks, the government must act decisively. But the policy options are few—and none are palatable. Even with best efforts, and unstinting support of the international community, the economic, social, and political costs are likely to be enormous.

Could Financial Crises Be Exploited by Terrorists?

The first years of the twenty-first century were extraordinarily benign in terms of global growth, low interest rates, and strong demand for the commodities and other exports that emerging market countries produce. But this proved to be the lull before the storm. While many emerging market countries used the breathing space of those years to improve their resilience—reducing their external debt, gradually accumulating foreign exchange reserves, enhancing regulation and supervision of their banks and financial sectors—others did not. Indeed, in eastern Europe, many countries had very large current account deficits, and housing booms fuelled by borrowing in foreign currency. When the 2008–09 global financial crisis broke, all emerging market countries were hit by a collapse in demand for their products and—those that had been relying on foreign borrowing—also a sudden reversal of capital flows when major banks in the United States and Europe scrambled to plug holes in their balance sheets as the losses on sub-prime mortgages and other toxic assets racked up rapidly. Many emerging market and developing countries had to turn to the IMF for financial support.

The effects of the 2008–09 crisis will be felt for many years (among others, the sharp increase in public debt due to financial sector losses and stimulus packages in most advanced economies will leave them vulnerable to crisis for decades to come).

But what about future crises? Some commentators argue that the very efforts to reduce vulnerabilities is helping to sow the seeds for the next crisis.[26] In particular, many emerging market central banks—having learned the lessons of previous crises—are rapidly stockpiling reserves and trying to keep their exchange rates from appreciating or becoming overvalued. But in the process of doing so, they have been buying foreign reserves by selling domestic currency. This increases the money supply, and risks inflating stock prices and housing prices, leading to bubbles that, if they burst, could precipitate another crisis. There is also the danger that as central banks stockpile trillions of dollars in reserves—mainly in the form of US treasury bills—they will lose confidence in the US government's ability to honor its obligations, ultimately undermining the "reserve currency status" of the dollar and leading to its collapse. A sudden dumping of dollars is much more than a remote theoretical possibility—already, the People's Bank of China, the largest single holder of US treasuries, has hinted its concerns about the future value of the dollar, and while it would not be easy for the Chinese to get out of holding dollars, it could be disastrous if they tried (see Ghosh, Ostry, and Tsangarides, 2010).

Even if this does not happen, there is always the danger that policy makers will be fighting the last crisis, not the next. Just as the East Asian crisis taught the world that major financial crises could originate in the private sector, it is hard to tell when and how the next crisis will occur. Indeed, prior to the 2008–09 crisis, there was a widespread assumption that major financial crises simply could not happen in advanced economies, and the bank runs by panicked depositors queuing up to get their money was unimaginable. To help guard against the possibility that policy makers will be preparing for the last crisis and not the next one, the International Monetary Fund and the

Financial Stability Board have launched their "early warning exercise," which seeks to identify risks that threaten the stability of the global financial system.[27] As always, however, imagining the unimaginable, and then guarding against it, is no mean task. (As part of its crisis prevention efforts, the IMF has also increased its emergency lending with its new Flexible Credit Line— the real-life counterpart to the Systemic Intervention Facility that was rather presciently foreseen in *Nineteenth Street, NW*; see IMF 2009b.)

Crisis prevention efforts can help guard against known risks, but how to inoculate against new threats is less clear. What is clear is that global financial markets are in constant development, and financial innovations—exotic instruments involving swaps, derivatives, structured finance products—are always one step ahead of the regulators. Many of these instruments are so sophisticated, with risk characteristics so complex, that no one really knows what would happen in a major financial crisis. As in East Asia, crises can spread rapidly from one country to another—and possibly from one region to another. When Paul Blustein was writing about the Asian crisis, he noted "Most chilling of all was how perilously close the US economy came to joining the global meltdown in September and October 1998 . . . the convulsions on Wall Street might well have engendered a worldwide slump."[28] And in the 2008–09 crisis, not just the United States but the whole global economic and financial system came to the very brink of an absolute collapse, with not just trillions of dollars lost, but the livelihoods of hundreds of millions destroyed.

How could such vulnerabilities be exploited by some group intent on making mischief? Because speculative attacks—if large enough—can be self-fulfilling, the trick would be to convince the market to jump on the same bandwagon and take positions against the currency being attacked. Markets are driven by the hope of making profits (or avoiding losses). Because successful speculation is profitable, what matters for getting other speculators to join an attack is convincing them that it will succeed. And if enough speculators can be convinced, the attack will indeed succeed—as George Soros showed when he successfully attacked the British pound, forcing its devaluation and ejection from the European Exchange Rate Mechanism in 1992.

To get other speculators to jump on the bandwagon requires two things: information and money. On the exchange market, profits can be made either by knowing in which direction the exchange rate is headed or—using derivatives—by knowing whether the *volatility* of the exchange rate is going to increase or decrease (see Appendix B). Both of these depend very heavily on the reaction of the country's central bank: will it let the exchange rate be buffeted by market forces? Or will it intervene to stabilize the exchange rate?

Traditionally, central banks have been secretive about their operations, and while they are becoming more open and transparent in their dealings, their foreign exchange interventions remain shrouded in secrecy.[29] Nevertheless, some of this information is required to be provided to international financial institutions; for instance, the International Monetary Fund's Articles of Agreement mandate that all member countries report their foreign exchange reserves, including forward transactions—although not necessarily on a real-time basis.[30]

Even with real-time data, however, predicting exchange rate movements is enormously difficult. Research shows that exchange rates follow a "random walk" (sometimes called a "drunk man's walk")—that is, successive movements are random, so that to predict the future exchange rate, one can do no better than simply assume that it will be the same as the current exchange rate.[31]

Of course, speculators will occasionally bet the right way on an exchange rate movement—sometimes making spectacular profits. But at least standard models of exchange rate dynamics are incapable of systematically forecasting short-term movements with the accuracy that would be necessary to persuade the rest of the market that the attack is a winning proposition—and thus create self-fulfilling pressures on the currency.

One relatively new and unexplored class of models is so-called "neural networks." A neural network is a non-traditional form of computing that is loosely based on, or at least inspired by, the functioning of the human brain. Unlike a traditional computer program, which processes information sequentially, a neural net solves problems non-algorithmically—that is, without following a pre-set sequence of rules. To see the power of non-algorithmic methods, consider the following pieces of text:[32]

_ st_tch _n t_m_ s_v_s n_n_.	_ p_nny s_v_d _s _ p_nny __rn_d.	D_n't thr_w _w_y th_ _ld b_ck_t _nt_l y__ kn_w wh_th_r the_ n_w _n_ h_lds w_t_r.

Trying to decipher these pieces of text sequentially—that is one letter at a time—is virtually impossible. (Try it: using a piece of card to cover up the other letters as you read each one.) Yet looking at the text as a whole, the pattern soon emerges—proverbs with the vowels missing. Even the third proverb, less familiar than the others, is easily grasped. In fact, a particular strength of neural networks is their ability to recognize patterns, and they are often used in such applications.

In the financial field, for instance, neural networks have been used for assessing credit risk, identifying forgeries, interpreting handwritten forms, rating investments and analyzing portfolios. Using neural networks for exchange rate forecasting is still relatively new, but preliminary work is promising. In one review of studies, neural networks outperformed traditional forecasting methods 86 percent of the time.[33]

The other key ingredient that terrorists would need to launch speculative attacks is money—and plenty of it. Without sufficiently large amounts of money, no one is even going to notice a speculative attack, let alone join it. How would terrorists finance such a speculative attack? Probably through a hedge fund (see Appendix C).[34]

Given their often high profitability and general secretiveness, hedge funds have always had a certain mystique. Hedge fund managers have a reputation for astuteness, so that a rumor that hedge funds are taking a position may encourage other investors to follow. It is all the more likely that hedge funds may act as "lead steers" for investor herding behavior, since they can themselves undertake a volume of sales that drive interest rates to levels that the central bank regards as unacceptably high until it abandons the defense of the exchange rate. To the extent that other large investors follow, the hedge fund would not even have to undertake all the transactions—it would merely need to signal its intention to do so.

In addition to the highly successful speculative attack against the British pound in 1992, hedge funds have also been implicated in the East Asian currency crisis. As fears of an impending devaluation of the Thai baht intensified during early 1997, investors—not only hedge funds, but also mutual funds, banks, and others—began to sell the baht forward.[35] Estimates suggest that of the Bank of Thailand's US$ 28 billion forward sales of foreign exchange at the end of July 1997, around US$ 7 billion represented transactions with hedge funds (though total amounts are likely to have been larger, since hedge funds may have acted through offshore intermediaries). In a celebrated article in the *Wall Street Journal*, Malaysian Prime Minister Mohamad Mahathir accused hedge funds of being "highwaymen of the global economy," noting that "with these self-serving systems [short-selling and leverage] the big players can wreak havoc in the markets."[36] Over the past few years, hedge funds have grown enormously in importance. Whereas in the early 1990s, there were a few dozen hedge funds with perhaps a couple hundred billion dollars, today there are thousands of hedge funds with assets running to the trillions of dollars under their management.

Hedge funds' other attractive feature—from the perspective of a potential terrorist—is that they are subject to very little regulation and supervision.[37] Because participation in hedge funds is restricted to "high net worth individuals"—meaning people rich enough that they are expected to be able to look after themselves—there is virtually no regulatory limit on how risky their investments can be. From time to time, usually after a crisis, there is interest in greater supervision and regulation of hedge funds—though as the crisis passes, so normally does the political will to do anything about them.[38] Thus, while major Western governments spend a fortune on combating money laundering and the financing of terrorism, it apparently has not occurred to them that hedge funds could provide the perfect financing instrument for terrorists.

So, can it really happen? Of course it can. Will it happen? We can only hope not.

Rex Ghosh
Washington, DC

APPENDIX A

PURCHASING POWER PARITY AND FEER

AS DISCUSSED IN THE TEXT, a key question for speculators intending to attack a currency, and for central banks trying to ward off such an attack, is whether the exchange rate is at its "correct" level. This appendix describes two simple models that are often used to help answer that question.

Purchasing Power Parity

Purchasing power parity (PPP) states that, converted into a common currency, national price levels should be equal. To understand why, consider first the price of a single good. Suppose that the price of a personal computer in the United States is $1,500, and that the exchange rate is 30 baht per US dollar, then the price of the same computer in Thailand should be 45,000 baht. If it were higher, then it would be worth shipping computers from the US to Thailand; if it were lower, then it would be worth shipping them from Thailand to the US. Of course this "law of one price" does not hold exactly because of trade barriers and transportation costs. But if these costs are fairly constant, then the law of one price should hold in terms of changes—that is, if the exchange rate depreciates by 10 percent, then the price of computers in baht should go up by a corresponding amount.

Purchasing power parity extends this "law of one price" to the entire price level of the country. Why is this useful? Because in terms of rates of change, this translates into the rate of depreciation of the exchange rate equalling the inflation differential between the "home" and "foreign" country. For instance, if inflation in the US is 5 percent per year, and if inflation in Thailand is 30 percent per year, then the baht should depreciate by 25 percent. Therefore, PPP can be used to help decide whether an exchange rate has depreciated "enough"—and whether the parity is now worth defending.

One of the first applications of PPP was in the interwar period. At the outbreak of World War I, most countries had left the gold standard, and at its conclusion, the question arose of what were the appropriate exchange rates at which to re-establish the parities, especially since the various belligerents had suffered very different degrees of economic dislocation. In a series of influential articles, the Swedish economist Gustav Cassel suggested that purchasing power parity theory could be used to establish appropriate exchange rates between countries—in particular, according to how much inflation they had suffered since the beginning of the war.

Classic texts on PPP are Cassel (1921, 1922); Officer (1976) provides the historical background, while Rogoff (1996) is a good survey.

Fundamental Equilibrium Exchange Rates
A more sophisticated variant of the PPP methodology is the fundamental equilibrium exchange rate (FEER) approach. This approach assumes that countries' exports are not identical and are imperfect substitutes for each other (a Ford is not the same as a Mercedes). As a country's exchange rate appreciates, its exports become less competitive while foreign imports increase (since they are cheaper). Both these effects tend to widen the country's trade deficit, which, in turn, must be financed by a capital inflow—that is, by borrowing from foreigners.

The FEER methodology turns this relationship between exchange rates and capital inflows on its head by asking how large a deficit a country might expect to be able to finance through capital inflows in "normal" times, and what the corresponding level of the exchange rate might be. This is known as the fundamental equilibrium exchange rate. A variant of this approach is to determine what the current account "should be"—based on such factors as the country's demographics, external debt, and its growth prospects.

If the actual exchange rate is higher than the FEER, then it is overvalued and should be allowed to depreciate, thereby gaining competitiveness and reducing the deficit to a level that can be financed. But if the actual exchange rate is already below the FEER, it is worth defending against excessive depreciation. While FEER is more sophisticated than using simple PPP calculations, it also requires fine judgments about how much capital is likely to flow to the country, which may be particularly difficult to gauge in the midst of a currency crisis. See Isard and Faruqee (1998), IMF (1998), Lee et al. (2008) on the FEER methodology as actually applied at the IMF; IEO (2007) presents a useful survey.

APPENDIX B

TRADING VOLATILITY—PUTS, CALLS, AND DERIVATIVES

A DERIVATIVE INSTRUMENT IS a contract whose value depends on—or derives from—the value of an underlying asset. For instance, the value of an option on IBM stock depends on the price of IBM shares. While derivative instruments can be highly complex, their fundamental building block— the option—is relatively straightforward and is key to understanding how derivatives can be used to place bets, not only on which direction a currency is headed, but also on whether the volatility of the exchange rate (which depends heavily on whether the central bank intervenes and whether there is a speculative attack) will change.

A call option gives the buyer of the option the right, but not the obligation, to buy a financial asset at a specific price on or before a particular date in the future; the specific price is called the "exercise" or "strike" price. A put option gives the buyer of the option the right, but not the obligation, to sell a financial asset at a specific price on or before a particular date.

An example from everyday life makes it easier to understand how options work.[39] Suppose a house-buyer finds one she likes whose asking price is US$

1 million. The potential buyer can: (a) buy the house immediately; (b) wait for one month in the hope that the price will go down, while recognizing that the price may increase in the meantime; (c) ask the seller to provide her with an option such that the seller would hold the property for her at the same asking price for one month. If the seller agrees, he is selling a call option (on the house)—for which he will charge a fee (what determines that fee is discussed next).

What happens after one month? If the market price increases, the buyer will exercise her option to purchase the house at US$ 1 million (even if she does not want the house, she can sell it at a profit because the market price is above her purchase price).

To understand why trading options allows taking positions on the volatility of the underling asset's price, consider what determines the option fee. In the house example, suppose that house prices are very stable—so the likelihood that the price of the house will go up (or down) significantly in a one-month period is small.

Therefore, the likelihood that the seller is going to lose (or the option buyer is going to gain) from the option is also small, so the option fee he will charge (or that she would be willing to pay) will be low. On the other hand, suppose that house prices are very volatile. Then there is a high risk that the price of the house will have increased above US$ 1 million. (There is also a high probability that the price will have decreased, but this is irrelevant since the option seller only loses, and the option buyer only gains, when the price rises.) But if there is a high risk that the option seller will lose money because the house price rose, he will charge a large option fee. Likewise, since there is a good chance that the option buyer will gain, she will be willing to pay a large option fee.

Hence, the value of an option (i.e., the fee) is intrinsically linked to the volatility of the price of the underlying asset, and trading options (i.e., buying and selling them) means taking bets on whether that volatility will change. (So much so, options are usually quoted in terms of the implied volatility of the underlying asset). This also explains why it is so important for speculators to know the central bank's intervention strategy, since such interventions can fundamentally alter the volatility of the exchange rate.

APPENDIX C

HEDGE FUNDS

HEDGE FUNDS OFTEN FIGURE prominently in the press, especially when there are crises. But what is a hedge fund? And how does it work?

The term was coined by Carol Loomis in a 1966 *Fortune* magazine article to describe investment partnerships that combine two investment tools: short selling and leveraging. Short selling means borrowing a security (a stock or a currency) and selling it in anticipation that its price will fall before the time that it must be repaid to the lender. Leveraging means using borrowed funds, so the hedge fund's total market exposure may be several or many times its own capital base. While each of these investment tools is considered highly risky in isolation, the sociologist and financial journalist Alfred Winslow Jones showed how they could be combined to reduced market risk while earning high returns.

To understand Jones's insight, consider a single stock, say, IBM. The price of IBM's stock reflects two factors: the performance of IBM relative to other computer manufacturers, and the fortunes of the computer industry generally. To eliminate the latter risk, a hedged portfolio would consist of a long position in IBM stock and a short position in the stocks of other computer manufacturers. In other words, the hedge fund would buy IBM stock, and would borrow and sell stocks of the other computer manufacturers. If there is a boom in the computer industry, the portfolio gains from holding the IBM stock, but loses on its short sales since it must repurchase, at the new, higher market price, the borrowed securities that it has sold. Similarly, if there is a slump in the computer industry, the portfolio loses on its holding of IBM stock, but gains because it has sold at a high price the stocks of IBM's competitors, and their market price has fallen at the time that the hedge fund must repurchase them in order to repay the lender from whom it had borrowed the securities.

The vicissitudes of the computer industry are thus canceled out by the combination of the long and the short positions, and the portfolio is perfectly "hedged" against them, leaving only the risk associated with IBM's performance relative to its competitors.

By leveraging, this difference in performance is magnified. Jones also made the manager's incentive fee a function of the hedge fund's profits (in his case, 20 percent of realized profits).

Hedge funds proliferated in the late 1960s, but because they had come to rely more on leveraging than on short sales, they lost heavily during the extended market downturn that started at the end of 1968. By 1970, the 28 largest hedge funds had lost 70 percent of their assets. Hedge funds became popular again in the mid-1980s, especially with the success of the Tiger Fund (and its offshore counterpart, the Jaguar Fund) which had purchased a large number of foreign currency call options in the expectation that the US dollar, having risen sharply since 1982, was going to decline against the Japanese yen and the European currencies. (The call option gave the hedge fund the right, but not the obligation, to buy these non-dollar currencies at a predetermined price. As these currencies appreciated, the fund was able to exercise its options to buy these currencies at their previous, low price and immediately resell them for a handsome profit.)

Currently, there are more than one thousand hedge funds in existence, with more than one and a half trillion dollars under management. With leveraging, their total market power could be three or four times that amount. While some funds go bankrupt, others return spectacular returns—in one case, earning a return of 1,000 percent in one year. Finally, hedge funds are usually structured so that they are subject to minimal regulatory and disclosure requirements.

For a general description of hedge funds, see Eichengreen et al. (1998), on which this note draws heavily, and Lavinio (2000); for a history of Jones's fund, see Caldwell (1995).

NOTES

1. Harry's anagram: "Nature Lane" = "A Neural Net."
2. The term "emerging market" was coined by Antoine Van Agtmael, a former World Bank official, who wanted a sexier name for a "Third World" equity fund that he was trying to start. Today, the term refers to countries that are neither advanced economies (such as the United States or Germany) nor very poor, developing countries (such as Chad or Malawi)—but somewhere in between, such as Argentina, Brazil, China, India, Russia, and Turkey.
3. No doubt reams will be written on the causes and consequences of the 2008–09 global financial crisis; various editions of the IMF's *World Economic Outlook* and *Global Financial Stability Reports* provide a real-time view of how the crisis evolved; see also IMF (2009) and Blanchard et al. (2010).
4. Two books by Paul Blustein (2001, 2006) are excellent journalistic accounts that provide fascinating backdrop to the drama of these crises. More academic treatments may be found in Lane et al. (1999), Corsetti, Pesenti, and Roubini (1999), Ghosh et al. (2002), Collyns and Kincaid (2003), Daseking et al. (2005), Roubini and Setser (2004), Ghosh et al. (2008) and Ito (2007). Useful websites where materials on emerging market financial crises may be found include the International Monetary Fund (www.imf.org); the National Bureau of Economic Research (www.nber.org); and Roubini Global Economics (www.rgemonitor.com). An online tour of the Palais des Nations is available at: http://www.unog.ch/virtual_tour/palais_des_nations.html.
5. The Great Depression lasted longer, and the cumulative decline over a four-year period was around 25 percent; data are from Temin (1994).
6. See Booth (1998) and Lee (1998).
7. Johnson (1998).
8. Johnson (1998), quoting the *Jakarta Post*, May 18, 1998.
9. The previous occasion had been during the hyperinflation in 1989–90. Blustein (2006) describes a woman on Argentine national television screaming at the presidential

spokesman: "How can I get my money? It's my savings. I'm furious." The crisis left nearly a quarter of the workforce unemployed and a majority of the population below the poverty line. Average annual income per capita sank from US$ 8,500 in the late-1990s to US$ 2,800 in 2002.

10. Blustein (2006), p.2.

11. In fact, strict parity is unlikely to be enough: investors will demand an additional "risk premium" to compensate for the greater risk of investing in an emerging market country.

12. On the merits of fixed versus floating exchange rates, see Ghosh et al. (2003); on currency crises, see Kaminsky et al. (1998), Kaminsky and Reinhart (1999), Dornbusch (2001) and Ghosh and Ghosh (2003).

13. Indeed, even when investors start getting nervous that the country is borrowing too much— like Argentina in the 1990s—managers of big mutual (and other investment) funds have the incentive to keep pouring in money because their performance is judged against an index of emerging market bonds, where the index has greatest weight on the country that is borrowing the most. As Blustein (2006) explains "the habit of cleaving to the index virtually forced these investors to lend vast sums to Argentina even if they feared the country was likely to default . . . Money managers who shunned Argentine bonds completely, or held only small amounts, were taking a huge risk, because in the event that Argentine bonds rallied for some unforeseen reason, their portfolios would almost certainly underperform the index for a period of time, a potential disastrous blow to their careers."

14. For the analytics of how a speculative attack happens, see Krugman (1979) and Flood and Garber (1984).

15. This is known as a "multiple equilibria" problem because, equally, if there is no fear of devaluation, then no devaluation occurs. On multiple equilibria and speculative attacks, see Obstfeld (1986, 1994) and Masson (1999).

16. See Ostry, Ghosh, Habermeier, Chamon, Qureshi, and Reinhardt (2010).

17. See Ghosh et al. (2009) on policies for emerging market countries to cope with the 2008–09 global financial crisis.

18. The International Monetary Fund (together with the World Bank) was established at the Bretton Woods Conference in July 1944 and opened its doors in December 1947. At the time, most balance of payments problems were "current account" rather than "capital account" crises—that is, caused by countries running out of foreign exchange reserves due to trade deficits rather than because of large and sudden capital outflows. Indeed, John Maynard Keynes, one of the key architects of the IMF at Bretton Woods, favored using capital controls to prevent crises.

19. This is known as IMF "conditionality"—which serves two purposes: first, it provides safeguards to the IMF that the borrowing government will be in a position to repay the loan when it matures; second, it provides assurances to the borrowing government that IMF financing will be available—and cannot be withheld for political reasons—as long as it fulfills the conditions. Nevertheless, IMF conditionality remains controversial. In terms of the economics, conditionality can also play a crucial role of providing the government with a pre-commitment device, giving credibility to its reform programs, and allowing it easier and cheaper access to international loans.

20. There is a vast literature on IMF-supported programs. For an overview of such programs, their design, and their success and failures, see Ghosh et al. (2005).

21. The most famous example is Sweden during the speculative attacks against the European Monetary System in September 1992, when interest rates were raised to an unprecedented 500 percent per year. Although the defense was successful in staving off the crisis, Sweden

eventually devalued and exited the European Exchange Rate Mechanism. For a detailed description of the events surrounding the ERM crises, see IMF (1993).

22. Furman and Stiglitz (1998) claim that this is may have happened during the East Asian crisis, particularly in Korea. Empirical studies of the East Asian crisis countries, however, have found little evidence to support this contention, perhaps because interest rates did not rise sufficiently high; see Goldfajn and Gupta (1999) and Basurto and Ghosh (2001); for a theoretical model of balance sheet effects, see Aghion et al. (2001).

23. As Ghosh et al. (2002) note, "But reliance on bilateral support was not without its risks. In Indonesia and Korea, funds pledged by bilateral creditors formed a second line of defense but were not subject to well-defined terms and conditions and were never disbursed, contributing to market anxieties that may have influenced the decisions of private creditors to continue to exit."

24. Forward transactions are used either for hedging or for speculation. Suppose a Japanese company is exporting to the US and expects to be paid in US dollars three months from now. The Japanese company is interested in locking-in the value in terms of yen. Therefore, it can sell forward (at an agreed exchange rate) the dollars it expects to receive in three months' time, and not face the exchange rate risk that dollar might depreciate in the meantime. But forward sales can also be used for speculation. For instance, if a bank does not have the dollars, it can still sell them in the forward market—which commits the bank to providing the dollars in three months' time. When the contract matures, if the dollar has depreciated, the bank simply buys the (now cheap) dollars in the market and sells them at the agreed (higher) exchange rate, making a profit. But if the dollar has depreciated in the meantime, the bank suffers the corresponding loss.

25. Some commentators such as Radelet and Sachs (1998a,b) have argued that the middle of a crisis is not the time to start closing banks, but others (Ghosh et. al. (2002)) contend that problems in the financial sector were at the root of the crisis and restoring confidence would have been impossible without decisive action on bank closures. Lindgren et al. (1999), Enoch et al. (2001), and Pangestu and Habir (2002) provide thorough discussions of the restructuring of the Indonesian banking system; for a description of the events surrounding the closure of the sixteen banks, see Soesastro and Basri (1998) and Blustein (2001). Ultimately, the mistakes made in the closure of the Indonesian banks reflected a complex confluence of unfortunate decisions and events. In the text, for purposes of fiction, these are brought together in the actions of a single character, Xavier Adanpur; in reality, they cannot be blamed on any one person or institution, and no similarity to any individual, living or dead, or to any actual institution is intended or implied.

26. Nouriel Roubini, a professor at New York University, and well-known authority on emerging market crises argues that Asia (and other emerging market countries) is vulnerable to a new and different kind of financial crisis, caused in part by efforts to build up huge foreign exchange reserves. (Roubini's website is an excellent resource for understanding current economic news.) Terry Checki, an official of the New York Federal Reserve, likewise claims that "the recent long period of stability may contain the seeds of its own undoing." On crisis prevention efforts, see Ghosh et al. (2008).

27. See IMF Fact Sheet on IMF-FSB Early Warning Exercise http://www.imf.org/external/np/exr/facts/ewe.htm; and Ghosh, Ostry, and Tamirisa (2009).

28. Blustein (2001, p.13).

29. Since foreign exchange intervention results in a change in the central bank's holdings of foreign exchange reserves, researchers often use data on reserves to infer central bank intervention. In practice, however, the relationship between changes in reserves and

intervention is weak (Neely (2000)), because the central bank can reverse the intervention before it shows up in the monthly reserves figures (other strategies include selling reserves in the forward market—as the Bank of Thailand did on the eve of its 1997 devaluation—in which case the intervention does not show up in the reserves figures until the time the contract matures and the central bank actually has to deliver the foreign exchange). On reasons why the central bank may prefer secret intervention, see Ghosh (2001); on intervention practices, see Ishi et al. (2006). Information on central banks' foreign exchange reserves is available at the IMF's Dissemination Standards Bulletin Board: http://dsbb.imf.org/Applications/web/sddshome/

30. Specifically, under a decision known as "Strengthening the Effectiveness of Article VIII, Section 5," member countries are required to inform the IMF of "the international reserve assets and reserve liabilities of the monetary authorities, specifying separately any reserve assets which are pledged or otherwise encumbered as well as any net derivative positions."

31. See Meese and Rogoff (1983), Frankel and Rose (1995), MacDonald and Taylor (1992); Dornbusch (1976) gives a theoretical explanation for why exchange rates often "overshoot" in response to news about the economy or policies.

32. The example is taken from Nelson and Illingworth (1991).

33. Adya and Collopy (1998); see also Refnes (1995), McNeils (2004), and Medeiros (2000) on neural networks and genetic algorithms.

34. Another possibility would be a "sovereign wealth fund." These are funds that are established by governments to invest foreign assets—typically oil revenues of oil-rich countries. While these are perfectly respectable, government-run investment funds, their secrecy and sheer size—often running into the hundreds of billions of dollars—has attracted attention and some concern. Moreover, in the hands of a rogue government intent on state-sponsored terrorism, a sovereign wealth fund could be used to wreak havoc on the international financial markets.

35. *Wall Street Journal*, September 23, 1997. Forward selling the baht meant that these investors promised to deliver Thai baht at an agreed exchange rate in a few months' time. If the Thai baht was devalued in the meantime, they would make a profit. In order to stabilize the exchange rate, the Bank of Thailand had to take the counter position—buying baht in the forward market and promising to deliver US dollars, incurring a loss if the baht was devalued in the meantime (as happened).

36. In fact, available evidence does not suggest that hedge funds were especially active against the Malaysian ringit. Correlations between currency movements and returns to hedge funds suggest that hedge funds speculated actively against only the Thai baht and, to a lesser degree, the Indonesian rupiah and the pound sterling during the European ERM crisis; see Chadha and Jansen (1998) and Brown et al. (2000).

37. There are some disclosure requirements, but in practice hedge funds have considerable latitude not to disclose their operations. See Cullen (2001) for a detailed discussion of the legal and regulatory requirements on hedge funds, including those established "off-shore," (e.g., in the Cayman Islands).

38. In the wake of the collapse of Long Term Capital Management, a number of bodies issued reports and studies, including the Basle Committee on Banking Supervision (Sound Practices for Banks' Interactions with Highly Leveraged Institutions, January 1999), the International Organization of Securities Commissions (Hedge Funds and Other Highly Leveraged Institutions), The President's Working Group on Financial Markets (Hedge Funds, Leverage, and the Lessons of LTCM, April 1999), The General Accounting Office (Long Term Capital Management: Regulators Need to Focus Greater Attention

on Systemic Risk, October 1999) and Financial Stability Forum (Working Group on Highly Leveraged Institutions, April 2000). Enhanced regulation could, in principle, affect a number of aspects of hedge funds' activities, such as their ability to raise capital from investors or their putative ability to manipulate market prices. But direct regulation would run into a number of practical difficulties, not least because hedge funds are often established offshore, and without the cooperation of the authorities in these offshore centers it is not clear there could be effective jurisdiction of hedge funds located there.

39. The house-buyer example is taken from a superb booklet *Derivatives in Plain Words* by Frederic Lau (1997); see also Luca (2000), Hull (2002), and Neftci (2004).

REFERENCES

Adya, Monica, and Fred Collopy (1998), "How Effective Are Neural Networks at Forecasting and Prediction? A Review and Evaluation." *Journal of Forecasting*, 17, No. 5/6, pp. 481–495.

Aghion, Philippe, Philippe Bacchetta and Abhijit Banerjee (2001), "Currency Crises and Monetary Policy in an Economy with Credit Constraints." *European Economic Review*, 45, No. 7, pp. 1121–1150.

Basurto, Gabriela, and Atish Ghosh (2001), "The Interest Rate–Exchange Rate Nexus in Currency Crises." *IMF Staff Papers*, Special Issue, 47, pp. 99–120.

Blanchard, Olivier, Giovanni Dell' Ariccia, and Paulo Mauro, "Rethinking Macroeconomic Policy," SPN/10/03 (Washington DC: IMF).

Blustein, Paul (2001), *The Chastening: Inside the Crisis That Rocked the Global Financial System and Humbled the IMF.* New York: Public Affairs.

Blustein, Paul (2006), *And the Money Kept Rolling In (And Out): Wall Street, The IMF, and the Bankrupting of Argentina.* New York: Public Affairs.

Booth, Anne (1998), "The Impact of the Crisis on Poverty and Equity." *ASEAN Economic Bulletin*, 15, No. 3, pp. 353–361.

Brown, Stephen J., William N. Goetzmann, and James M. Park (2000), "Hedge Funds and the Asian Currency Crisis." *The Journal of Portfolio Management*, 26, No. 4, pp. 95–101.

Caldwell, Ted (1995), "Introduction: The Model for Superior Performance." In eds. Jess Lederman and Robert A. Klein *Hedge Funds: Investment and Portfolio Strategies for the Institutional Investor.* (New York: McGraw-Hill).

Cassel, Gustav (1921), *The World's Money Problems.* (New York: E. P. Dutton & Co).

Cassel, Gustav (1922), *Money and Foreign Exchange After 1914.* (New York: MacMillan).

Chadha, Bankim, and Anne Jansen (1998), "The Hedge Fund Industry: Structure, Size, and Performance." In eds. Barry Eichengreen and Donald Mathieson *Hedge Funds and Financial Market Dynamics.* IMF Occasional Paper No. 166 (Washington DC: International Monetary Fund).

Collyns, Charles, and G. Russell Kincaid (2003), *Managing Financial Crises: Recent Experience and Lessons for Latin America.* IMF Occasional Paper No. 217 (Washington DC: International Monetary Fund).

Corsetti, Giancarlo, Paulo Pesenti, and Nouriel Roubini (1999), "The Asian Crises: An Overview of the Empirical Evidence and Policy Debate." In eds. Agénor et al., *The Asian Financial Crisis: Causes, Contagion and Consequences.* (Cambridge: Cambridge University Press).

Cullen, Iain, and Helen Parry (2001), *Hedge Funds: Law and Regulation.* (London: Sweet & Maxwell).

Daseking, Christina, Atish Ghosh, Alun Thomas, and Timothy Lane (2005), *Lessons from the Crisis in Argentina.* IMF Occasional Paper No. 236 (Washington DC: International Monetary Fund).

Dornbusch, Rudiger (1976), "Expectations and Exchange Rate Dynamics." *Journal of Political Economy,* 84, pp. 1161–76.

Dornbusch, Rudiger (2001), "A Primer on Emerging Market Crises." NBER Working Paper No. 8326 (Cambridge MA: National Bureau of Economic Research).

Eichengreen, Barry, Donald Mathieson, Bankim Chadha, Anne Jansen, Laura Kodres, and Sunil Sharma (1998), *Hedge Funds and Financial Market Dynamics.* IMF Occasional Paper No. 166 (Washington DC: International Monetary Fund).

Enoch, Charles, Barbara Baldwin, Olivier Frécaut, and Arto Kovanen (2001), "Indonesia: Anatomy of a Banking Crisis: Two Years of Living

Dangerously—1997–99." International Monetary Fund Working Paper WP/01/52 (Washington DC: International Monetary Fund).

Flood, Robert P., and Peter Garber (1984), "Collapsing Exchange Rate Regimes: Some Linear Examples." *Journal of International Economics*, 17, pp. 1–13.

Frankel, Jeffrey, A., and Andrew K. Rose (1995), "Empirical Research on Nominal Exchange Rates." Chapter 5 in eds. Gene Grossman and Kenneth Rogoff, *Handbook of International Economics, Volume III*. (Netherlands: Elsevier Science).

Furman, Jason, and Joseph Stiglitz (1998), "Economic Crises: Evidence and Insights from East Asia." *Brookings Papers on Economic Activity* No. 2, pp. 1–114.

Ghosh, Atish R. (2001), "Central Bank Secrecy in the Foreign Exchange Markets." *European Economic Review*, 46, 2, pp. 253–272.

Ghosh, Atish R., Marcos Chamon, Christopher Crowe, Jun Kim, and Jonathan Ostry, (2009), "Coping with the Crisis: Policy Options for Emerging Market Economies," Staff Position Paper 09/08 (Washington DC: International Monetary Fund).

Ghosh, Atish R., Charis Christofides, Jun Kim, Laura Papi, Uma Ramakrishnan, Alun Thomas, and Juan Zalduendo (2005), *The Design of IMF-Supported Programs*. IMF Occasional Paper No. 241 (Washington DC: International Monetary Fund).

Ghosh, Atish R., and Swati Ghosh (2003), "Structural Vulnerabilities and Currency Crises." *IMF Staff Papers*, 50, 3, pp. 481–506.

Ghosh, Atish R., Anne-Marie Gulde, and Holger C. Wolf (2003), *Exchange Rate Regimes: Choices and Consequences*. (Cambridge MA: The MIT Press).

Ghosh, Atish R., Bikas Joshi, Jun Kim, Uma Ramakrishnan, Alun Thomas, and Juan Zalduendo (2008), *IMF Support and Crisis Prevention*, IMF Occasional Paper No. 262 (Washington DC: International Monetary Fund).

Ghosh, Atish R., Timothy Lane, Marianne Schulze-Ghattas, Aleš Bulíř, Javier Hamann, and Alex Mourmouras (2002), *IMF-Supported Programs in Capital Account Crises*. IMF Occasional Paper No. 210 (Washington DC: International Monetary Fund).

Ghosh, Atish R., Jonathan D. Ostry, and Natalia Tamirisa (2009), "Anticipating the Next Crisis," *Finance and Development*, September 2009.

Ghosh, Atish R., Jonathan D. Ostry, and Charalambos Tsangarides (2010), "Exchange Rate Regimes and the Stability of the International Monetary System," IMF Occasional Paper 270 (Washington DC: International Monetary Fund).

Goldfajn, Ilan, and Poonam Gupta (1999), "Does Monetary Policy Stabilize the Exchange Rate Following a Currency Crisis?" IMF Working Paper No. 99/42 (Washington DC: International Monetary Fund).

Hull (2002), *Options, Futures and Other Derivatives.* (New Jersey: Prentice Hall).

Independent Evaluation Office (2007), "An IEO Evaluation of IMF Exchange Rate Policy Advice, 1999–2005—Background Document III, The Equilibrium Exchange Rate: Alternative Concepts and Their Application in IMF Surveillance." (Washington DC: International Monetary Fund).

International Monetary Fund (2001), *The Methodology for Current Account and Exchange Rate Assessments.* IMF Occasional Paper No. 209 (Washington DC: International Monetary Fund).

International Monetary Fund (2009), "Initial Lessons of the Crisis," available at www.imf.org.

International Monetary Fund (2009b), "Review of Fund Facilities—Analytical Basis for Fund Lending and Reform Options" available at www.imf. org.

Isard, Peter, and Hamid Faruqee (1998), *Exchange Rate Assessment: Extensions of the Macroeconomic Balance Approach.* IMF Occasional Paper No. 167 (Washington DC: International Monetary Fund).

Ishi, Shogo, Jorge Canales-Krilijenko, Roberto Guimaraes, and Cem Karacadag (2006), *Official Foreign Exchange Intervention.* IMF Occasional Paper No. 249 (Washington DC: International Monetary Fund).

Ito, Takatoshi (2007), "Asian Currency Crisis and the International Monetary Fund, 10 Years Later." *Asian Economic Policy Review*, 2, pp. 16–49.

Johnson, Colin (1998), "Survey of Recent Developments." *Bulletin of Indonesian Economic Statistics*, 34, No. 2, pp. 3–60.

Kaminsky, Graciela, Saul Lizondo, and Carmen Reinhart (1998), "Leading Indicators of Currency Crises." *IMF Staff Papers* 45, pp. 1–48.

Kaminsky, Graciela, and Carmen Reinhart (1999), "The Twin Crises: The Causes of Banking and Balance-of-Payments Problems." *American Economic Review*, 89, No. 3, pp. 473–500.

Krugman, Paul (1979), "A Model of Balance of Payments Crises." *Journal of Money, Credit, and Banking.* 11: 311–325.

Lane, Timothy, Atish Ghosh, Javier Hamann, Steven Phillips, Marianne Schulze-Ghattas, and Tsidi Tsikata (1999), *IMF-Supported Programs in Indonesia, Korea and Thailand: A Preliminary Assessment.* IMF Occasional Paper No. 178 (Washington DC: International Monetary Fund).

Lau, Frederic (1997), *Derivatives in Plain Words.* (Hong Kong, China: Hong Kong Monetary Authority).

Lavinio, Stefano (2000), *The Hedge Fund Handbook: A Definitive Guide for Analyzing and Evaluating Alternative Investments.* (New York: McGraw-Hill).

Lee, Eddy (1998), *The Asian Financial Crisis: The Challenge for Social Policy.* Geneva, Switzerland: International Labour Office.

Lee, Jaewoo, Gian Maria Milesi-Ferretti, Jonathan D. Ostry, Alessandro Prati, and Luca Ricci (2008), "Exchange Rate Assessments: CGER Methodologies." IMF Occasional Paper No. 261 (Washington DC: International Monetary Fund).

Lindgren, Carl-Johan, Tomás Baliño, Charles Enoch, Anne Marie Gulde, Marc Quintyn, and Leslie Teo (1999), *Financial Sector Crisis and Restructuring: Lessons from Asia.* IMF Occasional Paper No. 188 (Washington DC: International Monetary Fund).

Luca, Cornelius (2000), *Trading in the Global Currency Markets.* New York: New York Institute of Finance.

MacDonald, Ronald, and Mark P. Taylor (1992), "Exchange Rate Economics: A Survey." *IMF Staff Papers*, 39, No. 1, pp. 1–57.

Masson, Paul (1999), "Contagion: Macroeconomic Models with Multiple Equilibria." *Journal of International Money and Finance*, 18, No. 4, pp. 587–602.

McNelis, Paul (2004), *Neural Networks in Finance: Gaining Predictive Edge in the Market.* (Burlington, MA: Academic Press Advanced Finance Series).

Medeiros, Marcelo C., Alvaro Veiga, and Carlos E. Pedreira (2000), "Modeling Exchange Rates: Smooth Transitions, Neural Networks, and Linear Models." Discussion Paper 432, Pontifical Catholic University of Rio de Janeiro.

Meese, Richard A., and Kenneth Rogoff (1983), "Empirical Exchange Rate Models of the Seventies: Do They Fit Out-of-Sample?" *Journal of International Economics*, 12, pp. 3–24.

Neely, Christopher J. (2000), "Are Changes in Foreign Exchange Reserves Well Correlated with Official Intervention?" *Federal Reserve Bank of St. Louis Review*, 82, No. 5, pp. 17–31.

Neftci, Salih (2004), *Principles of Financial Engineering.* London: Elsevier Academic Press.

Nelson, M.C., and Illingworth, W.T. (1991), *A Practical Guide to Neural Nets.* (Reading, MA: Addison-Wesley).

Obstfeld, Maurice (1986), "Rational and Self-fulfilling Balance of Payments Crises." *American Economic Review*, 76, pp. 72–81.

Obstfeld, M. (1994), "The Logic of Currency Crises." *Cahiers Economiques et Monetaires.* 43:189–213.

Officer, Lawrence H. (1976), "The Purchasing Power Parity Theory of Exchange Rates: A Review Article." *IMF Staff Papers*, 23, No. 1, pp. 545–79.

Ostry, Jonathan D., Atish R. Ghosh, Karl Habermeier, Marcos Chamon, Mahvash Qureshi, and Dennis Reinhardt, (2010), "Capital Inflows: The Role of Controls" Staff Position Paper 10/04 (Washington DC: International Monetary Fund).

Pangestu, Mari, and Manggi Habir (2002), "The Boom, Bust, and Restructuring of Indonesian Banks." International Monetary Fund Working Paper WP/02/66 (Washington DC: International Monetary Fund).

Radelet, Steven, and Jeffrey Sachs (1998a), "The East Asian Financial Crisis: Diagnosis, Remedies, Prospects." *Brookings Papers on Economic Activity* No. 1, pp. 1–74.

Radelet, Steven, and Jeffrey Sachs (1998b), "The Onset of the East Asian Financial Crisis." NBER Working Paper No. 6680 (Cambridge, MA: National Bureau of Economic Research).

Refnes, A. N. (1995), *Neural Networks in the Capital Market.* (New York: Wiley).

Rogoff, Kenneth (1996), "The Purchasing Power Parity Puzzle." *Journal of Economic Literature*, XXXIV, pp. 647–668.

Roubini, Nouriel, and Brad Setser (2004), *Bailouts or Bail-ins? Responding to Financial Crises in Emerging Economies.* (Washington DC: Peterson Institute).

Soesastro, Hadi, and M. Chatib Basri (1998), "Survey of Recent Developments." *Bulletin of Indonesian Economic Studies*, 34, No. 1, pp. 3–54.

Temin, Peter (1994), "The Great Depression." NBER Working Paper on Historical Factors in Long Run Growth, No. 62 (Cambridge, MA: National Bureau of Economic Research).